THIS BREAD

THIS BREAD

Rosemary Buchanan

THE BRUCE PUBLISHING COMPANY
MILWAUKEE

Copyright, 1945
The Bruce Publishing Company
Printed in the United States of America

PROLOGUE

WORSE than a love affair?" Uncle Thomas Blakney lifted his fine eyebrows. "Impossible, my dear. There is nothing so devastating. Or have young people changed so much since my day?"

"At least that would be understandable." Mrs. Maddox was on the edge of tears. "Some people might not care, but I feel as if it were the end of the world! I can't imagine how it happened, and to Valerie! Why, Uncle Thomas, you know we've been good Methodists for generations."

Uncle Thomas gave his cynical little smile which barely stirred his thin lips and only deepened the vertical lines about his mouth.

"Religious upset," he murmured. "I might have known it. Rome, of course? Well, I think we can fix that, if it hasn't gone too far, though Romanism isn't as easy to cure as some ailments. Just how did it happen, or do you know?" He shifted a little on his hospital pillows and looked at his niece expectantly.

"It was the day we got the wire about your being ill," she began. "It caught me at a bridge party, and I was just going home when I got another phone call from Val asking me to come by and pick her up after school. She wasn't at school then, though — oh, dear! I wish she had been! It seems she was just on her way home when she remembered she had to ask one of her schoolmates something; and the girl, who is a Roman Catholic, was just going into her church for some reason."

"And Valerie followed her into the church," prompted Uncle Thomas as Mrs. Maddox paused, overcome by the recollection of what came next, "and got interested in what she saw there."

"How did you guess?" She looked startled.

"Elementary, my dear." He waved a thin hand. "Go on."

"Well, at the time I didn't think much of it. She told me it was pure accident, and seemed to regret it, so I didn't think she needed a scolding for just an impulse like that. I was so worried about you, and George and I were busy getting reservations on the plane and packing, so I didn't pay much attention. We made arrangements to leave her with Susan—you remember her, don't you? She married George's cousin, Charlie Maddox. I don't care much for her, but she's a good woman, and I thought would take care of my poor child—" her voice broke, and Uncle Thomas stirred uneasily.

"What made you bring the child along then?" he asked. "Didn't that Susan woman want to take her?"

"Oh, yes, Susan was perfectly willing. Incidentally, she and her little boy Jasper had seen Val coming out of the church— I'm so glad Val told me about it herself and didn't wait until Susan and Jasper came in with their story, which they did just a few minutes after we got home. I believed Val, of course. I never knew her to tell me a lie before, and it never occurred to me that she was telling one then."

"And was she lying?" Uncle Thomas began to look really interested.

"I can't bear to think of it, but she must have been!" wailed Mrs. Maddox. "She looked me straight in the eye and told me that was the only time she had set foot in a Romish church, and that it had been only the accident of her having to tell that Mary Anderson about something. And, of course, I took her word for it. But the next morning, on her way to school, she stopped in there again with Mary. Jasper saw her go in, and he followed her to the door and saw her bowing to some image. Then he ran back to tell me."

"Sounds like a nasty little brute," observed Uncle Thomas. "I suppose he followed her on purpose?"

"Probably—I don't know," she replied absently. "And so of course George and I took her out of school and brought her along with us so that we could keep an eye on her. She insists that she hasn't actually joined the Romanists, and I have seen

[2]

nothing out of the way since we came here. Still, I'm not comfortable about her. As you say, these Romanists are so *tricky!*"

"Well," comforted Uncle Thomas, "let's not worry. Most futile exercise in the world, worrying. Either we can do something about it, or we can't. I doubt, though, if we need consider the latter alternative. This sort of thing isn't unusual, you know, among the very young. If you like, I'll try my hand on Valerie and see what I can make of her."

"Oh, Uncle, if you only would!" she responded gratefully. "If anybody can do anything with her, you can. And it is taking her a long time to get back from the post office!"

But just then Valerie came hurrying into the room, with postage stamps in her hand, and her golden head apparently full of interesting things about the little town of Los Pericos and its inhabitants, also the exciting news that Clark Gable was to appear tomorrow night at the picture theater. So natural was her manner that her mother hoped her recent fears were unfounded.

Uncle Thomas eyed the tall fifteen-year-old, wondering if this gush of high spirits were quite home-grown, or if those clear gray eyes concealed anything. They looked innocent enough, but Uncle Thomas had seen a good deal of life in his seventy-five years.

Had he really been a mind reader, though, he would have seen that his grandniece had done a little plotting of her own on the way back from the post office to the hospital. There were only a dozen short blocks between the two points, yet Chance had traveled a long way with Val as she walked lightly down the King's Highway, as somebody had explained the meaning of *Camino Real*.

There had been another Roman Catholic church there, too, and Val had yielded to her curiosity and entered. She had salved her conscience by telling herself that she really wasn't disobeying her parents who had been so wild over that St. Columban's affair. They hadn't exactly made her promise never to go into a Romish church again, though it had been taken for granted she would not. At the time it had been considered such a disgrace to the family that Val herself thought she had gone pretty far (though it had worked out to her advantage about being taken along to Los Pericos, which they had at first refused to do); and since she had gained her point about this trip there was no need for again doing anything extreme like that. In a way she was rather ashamed of the whole business, though it had started so accidentally.

However, this church she was now passing looked like one of the early mission churches that people had told her about; and as a visitor to New Mexico it was more or less her duty to see all the sights. There seemed to be something going on in the church, too — people coming and going through the heavy doors, and it might be frightfully interesting to see what it was. It wouldn't do any harm just to take a peek, particularly as Jasper wasn't there to tell on her.

The instant Val had entered the church and caught a whiff of the mingled odor of incense and the half sad fragrance of heavy-headed chrysanthemums, she had the sensation of time turning backward, and she was just where she had been that afternoon three weeks ago, though nothing could be less like the dark majesty of St. Columban's than this whitewashed adobe church, with floods of New Mexico sunshine pouring in through the windows, and the great white angel with flaming sword poised high above the altar. And yet she felt she was doing something quite familiar and dear — something warming to the heart and full of peace. For there, gleaming in the candle flames, was that wonderful golden sun which Mary Anderson had called by some peculiar name, and told her that it contained the Real Presence of God Himself. It was the Forty Hours again. Val dropped to her knees.

She did not stay in the church very long, remembering in time that she had been sent out only to mail a letter and buy some stamps. If she delayed getting back, one of those trying explanations would have to be made to Mother, and just now the family relations were fairly comfortable.

A woman just leaving the church gave her a friendly smile, and in answer to Val's impulsive inquiry as to how long the

Forty Hours lasted, told her that it would be over tomorrow night at eight "with the procession of men, you know." Guiltily thrilled to the core, Val could hardly stammer out her thanks. The woman apparently mistook her for another Romanist!

As she hurried back to the hospital Val boldly decided to go to that closing exercise tomorrow night, come what would. If Mother could be brought to understand that it was just one of the interesting things to be seen, like that Indian dance that Uncle Thomas' foreman had taken them to, there wouldn't be any trouble at all. But, of course, Mother would get all excited and forbid her to go. Why couldn't she be more broad-minded and liberal!

She hastily sketched out a plan of what must be done in order to get her own way. She didn't want to lie, of course, but she might compose a little.

Luckily the motion picture theater was also on the *Camino Real,* just opposite the church, and what was more natural than that Val should go to see the play on Sunday night? She knew, in the way young girls do, that Miss Bacon, one of the floor nurses, had her day off this coming Monday. If the present plan carried and Uncle Thomas went back to the ranch Monday morning, there was not a chance in a thousand that anybody would check up on whether or not Miss Bacon had actually taken Val to the show Sunday night. So it was no wonder that Val's eyes were bright and her talk animated when she got back to the hospital that Saturday morning.

Everything went along smoothly with her little plot. True, Mother was inclined to be fussy after supper on Sunday, wanting to know why Val hadn't gone to the matinee if she had to see Mr. Gable; but fortunately some callers, friends of Uncle Thomas, came in just then, and her mother hadn't time to probe too deeply. Val's conscience did prick her rather sharply as she sped along through the early darkness. Not only was she going once more to the forbidden church, but she had been forced to tell a deliberate lie about it. Well, after tonight she would be good!

The Litany was in full swing as she timidly edged her way

through the crowd at the rear of the church, and the strange chant with its rolling syllables in a foreign tongue, tossed back and forth between the clergy in the sanctuary and the congregation in the pews, both thrilled and frightened the girl.

This, then, was one of the occult, awful services of Rome; and she was present to witness it! How it would end she could not make a guess. Even human sacrifice would not have surprised her, after all the revolting tales she had heard about this dark, mysterious sect; but somehow Val did not look for any such bloody excesses. Not in front of that beautiful gold sun, the very center of everything because it contained the Real Body of Christ, if Mary was to be believed. If Roman Catholics were just worshiping God with all this burst of ceremony, then they weren't idolators at all, she concluded, startled at her own logic.

After the Benediction was over, and the Blessed Sacrament put away, Val still lingered. It seemed very flat to walk out of the church — Val's little soul had been greatly shaken during the past hour, and the thought of going back to the ordinary routine of life after this tremendous experience was unthinkable. She simply must do something about it! She'd have to belong to the Church so that she could know about these things and be able to sing the chants. She would go right away to the parsonage and tell them she was joining, and then trust to luck afterward about squaring it with her family.

"Are you the — what do you call it, high priest or something?" she demanded in her clear young voice to the priest who opened the door at her imperious ring. "The one in charge here?"

"Yes," he replied, "I'm Father Carey, the pastor."

"I'd like to talk to you a minute if you have time." Val was fundamentally a direct soul, if sometimes forced off her course by circumstances. "I've come to see about joining your Church."

It has been said that no Catholic priest can be shocked, which is probably why Father Carey, without a quiver, courteously invited her to come in and tell her story.

"I've been awfully interested in your Forty Hours," the girl came straight to the point. She rather liked the priest's look, with his studious face and mop of graying hair. He seemed kind and pleasant, and might be very nice once she got used to that black gown. "It's just like what they had back home, though I didn't see the finish there. It really was slick this evening. I don't like going to church very much, though Mother expects it. We're Methodists, you know. Anyhow, your church is so different and interesting, and I think it would be a lot more fun — I mean, I'd get more — well, you know!" She abruptly ran down here.

Very gently Father Carey questioned her. How old was she? How long since she took a leaning toward Catholicity? She knew nothing of Catholic doctrine, of course? How did her parents feel about it?

Val answered candidly, explaining all the steps leading from her dodging into St. Columban's in pursuit of Mary.

"I wanted to ask her about the club's dinner party the next night, but after I got in and saw how wonderful everything was in the church, I simply forgot. I knew my family would be wild, of course, so I only stayed a minute; but I had the strangest feeling when I saw that gold thing, what's its name? Ostensorium? How funny! Anyhow, I was fascinated, but I didn't stay. And I explained to my mother and everything, and I think she understood, though Cousin Susan and Jasper — he's a frightful little boy — came right over afterward and tattled!"

Father Carey listened with fixed attention. The gaps in this story sounded as interesting as the sequence.

"When I got home I found that Uncle Thomas was awfully ill and they had wired for Mother (do you know Mr. Thomas Blakney?) and she and Dad were taking the plane to leave right away — or the next day, anyhow — so, of course, I thought they were taking me. But they said no, as I had to go to school, and that terrible Cousin Susan and Jasper would come and stay with me, and snoop and tattle on me. (They didn't say they would, but I knew it!) I wanted frightfully to come, though I couldn't think of any way to make them. You know how I felt, don't you?"

He nodded, and she thought delightedly what an understanding person he was.

"Well, the next morning Mary and I were going to school, and when she got to that church she said she was going in to make a visit, and I started to go on to school. I really did. But just then I saw Jasper trying to hide behind a lamp post and spying on me, and it just came over me like that!" she snapped her fingers sharply. "I knew he thought I'd go in, and then he'd run home and tell Mother, and Mother would telephone Dad, and then they'd come and take me out of school because they'd think I was going to join St. Columban's. So, of course, I asked Mary if I could go in with her, and she said yes. I know Jasper followed to peek in and see me, so when Mary got down on both knees I did, too. And then Dad and Mother brought me along, and here I am. They think I'm a lost soul!"

Val giggled at the thought of Jasper's white-eyed espionage having done her a service, which was the last thing the dreadful boy would have wanted. Then she sobered and looked a little ashamed.

"It was kind of mean to do that to Mother and Dad, but I did want to come so badly. It has been very educational, too, so it won't be time wasted," she added primly, and waited for a word of praise from her listener about her cleverness. Instead, he asked:

"And how did you happen to come tonight? Do your father and mother know about it?"

Val colored and moved restlessly in her chair. Of course, he would ask that!

"I'm sorry—I know you think I'm awful," she confessed. "I told Mother (Dad's gone out to the ranch) that I was going to the movies. I don't like to tell lies, and I very seldom do. But I knew she'd have a fit if I told her I was coming here." Hoping to distract him from this point of view, she went on to explain how she had found out about this evening's service.

"And I was awfully surprised when I found you were having exactly the same thing here as we did at home; but that made it seem more like—what do you call it?" She waved her hands with a circular motion.

"The Universal Church," he summed up.

"Yes, that's it. And I just loved it tonight, that procession and chanting and everything. The most gorgeous thing I ever saw in my life. I want to join as soon as I can." She paused hopefully again, but as he did not reply at once she added generously, "I don't believe the things they told me about the Romanists, at least not now. All that Dark Ages stuff is terribly out of date, don't you think?"

Father Carey remained silent for a long moment after this large minded speech. Then he said the last thing she expected to hear.

"My dear child, you go home tonight and talk this over with your parents before we go into it any further."

"But I can't talk it over with my parents," she replied indignantly. "That's just it. Don't you remember I told you how they were simply raving because I only went into that St. Columban's for a minute? I think it would be lots better just to go ahead and join. Then they can't do anything about it."

Father Carey was firm.

"Valerie," he said, rising to his feet and seeming to expect her to do likewise, "it's after nine o'clock. I'll send somebody to take you home." She opened her mouth to protest, but he went suavely on. "I would be very glad to instruct you in the doctrines of the Church, but unless I have your parents' full consent I can do nothing. You understand that, I'm sure. Now, you go home like a good girl, and tomorrow if you still feel the same way, ask your father and mother to come with you, and we'll see what can be done."

"But still you don't understand!" Val's eyes were flashing with angry tears. "I couldn't make them consent. I told you I had to say I was going to the movies tonight—"

"Little girl," the priest interrupted quietly, "in the spread of His Kingdom, God does not require deceit."

The Maddox family had been staying with some of Uncle Thomas' friends living near the hospital, and the drive from the church was short. Val was deposited on Mrs. Smith's doorway by the elderly couple whom Father Carey had asked to escort the girl, and she slipped in quietly. Luck was with her in that the visitors were still in the sitting room, with refreshments being passed around, and it was easy for Val in this convenient hubbub to go to her own room carrying her plate with her.

For the first time in her life she found that ice cream and cocoanut cake had no charm for her. Without giving them so much as a glance she dropped them on the bureau, and casting herself on her bed began angrily to consider the treatment she had received from that *priest!* She had been just as nice and honest as she could be, and told him again and again it was no use to drag her parents into the affair — but he was simply dumb!

She had wanted to join the Church, too, she thought miserably, burrowing her head into the pillow. It had all been very real, that sensation of being one of a huge crowd all intent upon a single purpose — that overpowering desire to stay there forever in front of the glowing altar — that bewildering consciousness of the presence of Something beyond her ken, and the longing to pour out her heart to It. It was vague and formless, that feeling, but it had been more poignant than anything she had ever dreamed about.

Then indignation lashed her again. Was or was not this a free country? People were allowed to join any political party or any church they wanted. If she wanted to be a Republican or a Democrat, what business would it be of this country priest? All right, then, was he going to dictate to her what church she could belong to? She'd like to see him try! And with this resolve she suddenly remembered the ice cream melting on the bureau.

Next morning Uncle Thomas was wrapped up and tenderly conveyed back to the ranch. He seemed in good spirits and glad to be alive, at which Val privately wondered. Anybody so old as that ought to be ready to die, she thought, though it was nice he was better, of course. She was glad, too, that he was the object of everybody's attention just now, and hoped that nobody would remember to ask her about the show last night.

In this hope she reckoned without her Uncle Thomas. Though perhaps one of the world's most self-centered men, the old gentleman had a mild sense of obligation to his favorite niece who had come so far to take care of him in his illness; also he was never averse to having a fling at the papists. Therefore when Alice Maddox, with tears in her blue eyes, begged him to do something toward saving her child from popery, Uncle Thomas was not the slacker to say he would and then welsh afterward. Consequently that afternoon when Alice was taking a much-needed nap, and her husband was out in the corrals with the foreman, Uncle Thomas felt the time had come. He was rested and fresh after his siesta, and pleasantly stimulated at the prospect of theologically putting his grandniece straight.

"Was the show good last night, my dear?" he asked, settling more comfortably in his wing chair and giving a sweet smile to the girl who had just dutifully brought him his orange juice.

Val flushed at the memory of just how the show had ended, but replied with what she felt was adroitness, that the show was well enough acted but not convincing as to plot.

"That, I should say, is the trouble with nine out of any ten plays you might mention." Uncle Thomas was surprised at this erudition in one so young, though he recognized and applauded good work wherever he found it. Evidently the girl was not to be caught napping in so elementary a matter as not knowing all about the picture beforehand. His respect increased for her ability to fence. Then he decided to take the button off his own foil.

"And how was the affair at St. Michael's?" he asked.

Val's gray eyes flew open at this direct attack. "St. M——, what?" she demanded.

"Interesting bit of pageantry, isn't it? Though one is likely to find rather too many of the unwashed at the more important services." Uncle Thomas sipped his juice. "I've been there a time or two, but found it rather overpowering — the papistical smell, I mean."

"How did you know?" Val abandoned the impulse to flat denial, shrewdly suspecting that Uncle Thomas was not just guessing. She must have slipped up somewhere.

"Your mother said you'd gone with Miss Bacon to see Clark Gable," replied her great uncle languidly, his tone implying that this sort of explanation should be unnecessary. "I happen to know that Miss Bacon had a birthday party at her home last night. I suppose you didn't think to congratulate her? Too bad. People are sensitive to little things like that. But, of course, you didn't know about it. I forgot."

Val gazed at him dumbly. Why was it that Uncle Thomas could always make her feel like a fool? And why, oh why, had she picked on Miss Bacon!

Uncle Thomas was speaking again.

"When I was very young, nearly as young as you are now, I used to drop in on some of the Roman churches now and then, if the music was good. I rather enjoyed a little spiritual shaking up, something like one of your dear mother's revival meetings. In small doses that kind of emotionalism is stimulating, like a glass of champagne. And it wears off in about the same way — leaves a slight headache the morning after, but does no permanent harm."

"I don't know that it's just emotionalism," contradicted Val, beginning to see how little chance she had in an argument with so experienced a person as Uncle Thomas. He wasn't like Dad.

"Well, we'll not quarrel about terminology." Uncle Thomas smiled indulgently. "Perhaps you're right. It is less like champagne than, say, a dose of hasheesh with its dreams and delusions. But call it whatever we like, we always wake up just the same." He shook his silvery head reminiscently. "And like all dope runners, it's the business of the management to keep the market going. Rome has a lot of active salesmen in her priesthood."

Again Val opened her mouth to protest. That priest last night had acted as if he hadn't wanted her to buy —. But as if he had read her mind, Uncle Thomas went on smoothly.

"There are different ways of doing the job, my dear. A good salesman knows when to make it easy for a customer, and when to offer opposition." It had not escaped the old gentleman's eye that the child had been smoldering all day about something, and he made a bold guess. "The popish priests are hand-picked, and they know all the answers. If they see you mean business, they don't want to seem too eager. Just a little hanging back on their part made you that much more determined, didn't it? I've no doubt they saw into your mind as if it were a pane of glass. You were all ready to go back and demand to be taken in, weren't you?"

Val's cheeks were scarlet, remembering her vow last night in almost the same words as Uncle Thomas was saying with that silky disdain in his voice.

"Yes, my girl," Uncle Thomas finished his discourse and his orange juice simultaneously, "just about this very minute they're waiting for you to come a-begging."

He handed her the empty glass, thanked her courteously, and asked for the late copy of the *Saturday Review*. The interview was over, and Val left the room, bewildered, resentful, and very unhappy. Uncle Thomas had at least one thing in common with the popish clergy—his insight into the girl's mind had been crystal clear.

The invalid continued to improve, so by the end of that week it was considered safe to leave him, Mr. Maddox being anxious to get back to his business. The question of what to do with Val then came up with renewed force, both parents wondering if it were advisable to take her back to those dangerous influences.

"There's something queer about her, George," said Mrs. Maddox as they lingered over the breakfast table on Friday morning. Mrs. Winter, the housekeeper, had carried Val off to see a new family of kittens which had arrived during the night, and husband and wife were alone. "No, she's not sick, but she's just lifeless these past few days. I think she tries to act as if everything were all right—I wish she'd confide in me more. You know how she keeps things to herself sometimes."

"Maybe it's just because she hasn't enough to do," ventured George hopefully. "She's been taken away from her normal life, and that's upsetting. Do you suppose we could leave her here for the time being, and let her go to school in town? I can inquire into the standing of the high school. Old lady Winter could look after her, couldn't she?"

His wife looked doubtful, but suggested they talk it over with Uncle Thomas before they made too many plans.

This proposition made no hit with Uncle Thomas when he heard it. Now that his health was mending so well he wanted only to have his bachelor solitude undisturbed by callow youth, but, of course, he had more tact than to put it that way.

"I wouldn't do that, Alice," he said, and proceeded to relate the talk he had with Val on Monday afternoon. "That snake isn't even scotched yet. Rome's agents are everywhere. If I were you I'd think a long time before I went off a couple of thousand miles and left that kid where they could get at her."

"Oh, Uncle Thomas!" wailed Alice. "What have they done to my baby! I thought her so safe out here!"

"You did say that priest turned her down, though, didn't you?" asked Mr. Maddox. "Do you suppose that was just a stall?"

Uncle Thomas shrugged his thin old shoulders.

"Your guess is as good as mine, George. I wouldn't trust that outfit too far. If they find an enthusiastic youngster like Valerie who would pitch in and work like the devil for them after they got her hooked—I'm sorry, my dear!" He broke off compassionately as Mrs. Maddox sobbed. "So I think you'd be wise to get her out of harm's way."

Mr. Maddox nodded in reply, and laid a comforting hand on his wife's shoulder.

"Don't worry, dear," he said gently. "Nothing's going to happen to our kid."

So it was settled that they would all take the train that night, and Mr. Maddox went to notify his daughter. He found her alone in the back yard, languidly tossing handfuls of corn to the squabbling chickens. She looked very downcast, but as soon as she noticed his approach she straightened her shoulders and smiled up at him.

"How would you like to go home tonight, honey?" he asked,

noting with a pang how she was trying to seem her usual self. A girl of that age oughtn't have things like this to bother her, he thought, his anger rising against the rascals who had dared to make an assault on one so young and innocent.

She said she would be delighted, and at once ran off to help her mother pack, while her father looked after her broodingly. He wanted to say something more, to tell her it was all right and that her daddy wouldn't let anything hurt her ever again; but something about the child made him wary of offering sympathy when she had so definitely not asked for it. She had confided in no one but Uncle Thomas, who admitted that he had surprised it out of her. This reticence was a bad sign. She must have been hurt pretty badly. He only hoped the wound had gone deep enough to kill the crazy idea completely.

Then his wrath boiled over, and acting upon an impulse he decided to go to town and have it out with that priest who might even now be waiting for the kid to come back. By jingo! he'd settle with him — make him understand what it meant to a man to have his child all but stolen from him!

He borrowed Uncle Thomas' car, and with a word to his wife about going into town now to make their reservations, he drove the twenty miles into Los Pericos in record time.

"I'm very glad to meet you, Mr. Maddox." Father Carey greeted the irate father courteously when admitting him into the rectory office. "I asked your daughter to bring you in, and your wife, too, of course."

"You're under a misapprehension, sir," broke in Mr. Maddox curtly. "I'm not here to talk about letting my daughter join your Church. I'm here to tell you to let her alone!"

The priest raised his eyebrows, but went on quietly.

"That's just what I was thinking. The child so evidently didn't know what it was all about. The only thing she was sure of was that you would object strongly. I rather expected you early next morning, to tell me where to head in." He smiled, and Mr. Maddox blinked suddenly as if he had been hit in the face.

"I don't get you," he said, scowling fiercely.

[15]

The priest explained patiently. The little girl, he said, had come in with her preposterous demand, and realizing at once that she had no idea what she was asking he had promptly sent her home, telling her to bring in her parents to talk it over.

"We don't take people in just on the spur of the moment," he went on, "and certainly not children without their parents' consent. A convert to Catholicism takes on a huge moral responsibility, and we're very cautious about letting people in for something like that without an intensive study of the doctrines and duties of the Church. You get the idea, I'm sure."

Mr. Maddox felt he saw through this. In their discussion this morning Uncle Thomas had repeated his theory about popish salesmanship.

"Is this your usual pep talk?" he inquired with a rudeness that surprised himself. The man deserved it, however. "You think that making it harder for that kid will get her so anxious that she won't rest until she can join your outfit. I'd heard that was your system, but I never really believed I'd see it in action. Now I'm telling you, and you can tell the rest of your gang: it doesn't work in this case. You lay off!"

In the silence which followed Mr. Maddox sat glowering at the black-robed figure opposite. By habit kindly, and by nature tolerant, George Maddox had never expected to walk into a man's house and insult him; nor would he have done so now had anything less been at stake than the safety and happiness of his beloved young daughter.

Father Carey remained motionless for a moment after this outburst, his eyes fixed on the hands loosely clasped on the desk before him, while the harsh voice seemed to echo through the stillness. Then the priest drew a long breath and looked up.

"I appreciate how you feel, Mr. Maddox," he said mildly. "I probably would react the same way under the same circumstances, if I knew as little as you do about the Catholic Church. No, I'm not going to start explaining anything about the inner mysteries," he smiled faintly, and Mr. Maddox found himself feeling unaccountably abashed for the moment, "but may I point out just one thing? I don't know what you expected us to do to the child if we took her into the Church; but if I, or any of my assistants, had any designs on her, what was there to prevent us from baptizing her on the spot? Once we had her here, and neither you nor your wife had any idea that she was not at the theater, we could have done anything we pleased, and you would never have known."

The other gave an embarrassed cough.

"Yes," he muttered, "that's true."

"Evidently," went on Father Carey, "somebody has been giving you the old line — crafty priest making it seem harder and therefore more desirable — poor little victim wiggling on the hook — I do get so fed up!" He threw himself back in his chair and clasped his hands behind his head, while Mr. Maddox also shifted his position, looking very uncomfortable.

"There would have been no sense in playing her along," pursued Father Carey. "The youngster was all ready to be landed, though she hadn't the faintest idea what would happen next. In her then state of mind she'd have thought it great sport to have the water poured on her head, and let me welcome her in with bell and book." He laughed suddenly. "Don't let it worry you, Mr. Maddox. Not a thing happened except that I sent her home, mad as a wet hen, with a couple of irreproachable middle-aged people who reported to me the next day that they had delivered her safely."

The other man regarded him soberly.

"That was all, was it? If that's so — I beg your pardon, but — well, anyhow, if you're on the level with me I apologize for blowing off like that. But you know that kid is all we have, and my wife and I are trying to be careful of her. She scared us once before, did she tell you? And we brought her out with us to get her away from those da——, I mean, before she joined the St. Columban outfit. I hardly credited it at the time, though my wife was all upset. It seemed such an unlikely thing to do; but when we got here, and she pulled the same thing again, I'll admit it scared me. Sorry."

They shook hands on it.

"I wish I could be sure those St. Columban people are out

of it. I don't know how far it went." Poor Mr. Maddox sighed and wiped his overheated brow.

Father Carey considered a moment; then in fairness to St. Columban's clergy he decided to explain. Val had spoken confidentially, but he felt that this was no time for scruples.

"I don't know that it makes much difference from your viewpoint," he said, "but I'd like to set you straight on that. From what I gathered, she was in no danger of joining St. Columban's, and in fact had never considered it. She told me she had been inside the church only twice, the first accidentally, and the next—" His voice took an apologetic drop. "She has a boy cousin whom she dislikes? Well, she caught him spying, and decided to make it worth his while. Also, being an opportunist, and this trip with you hanging in the balance—well, you remember how we got around *our* parents at that age. It's humiliating when we find ourselves being worked on by the next generation, but that is youth for you. You promptly decided you'd better bring her along."

Mr. Maddox looked at him in astonishment for a moment, then burst into a shout of laughter in which Father Carey joined him.

"To think that kid played me for a sucker!" said Maddox ruefully after he had his laugh out. "I wish she'd use her talents to some better purpose. You don't suppose she had any reason like that for coming to your church, do you? She's a little young to be starting serious blackmail."

"Might be," replied Father Carey thoughtfully. "If so, she can think faster than both of us. I imagine, though, that her visit on Saturday was just from curiosity. For the rest—well, there *is* something very inspiring about the public devotion to the Blessed Sacrament, and probably it got hold of her to some extent. The pageantry is very fine, good music and all; and the child appreciated it and thought that her enthusiasm was a real conversion. Those things do sometimes happen; but in general a conversion that came so fast would wear off the same way. I wouldn't trust it."

Some ten minutes later Mr. Maddox took his leave with a

revised opinion of the priest, and perhaps some slight removal of old prejudices against the Catholic clergy in general. This man might be playing some deep game, of course, but he had talked and acted like a sensible man and a sincere one. Being about to shake the dust of Los Pericos from his feet, Mr. Maddox felt he could afford to give Father Carey the benefit of the doubt and concede that he was a pretty good scout.

As to Val, he hoped she would soon feel better. Luckily she was young and resilient. Time is a good friend to people who get their bumps early in life, though it seems hard to the kids, and it was particularly regrettable that this hard knock had come to his child. In the long run, though, it would probably be good for her — make her a little more cautious about the people she went with. He and Alice would have to find a place to send her right away, some good, solid, Methodist boarding school with a firm discipline in all things. They'd get all this popery out of her system in short order!

So taken up was he with these reflections that he forgot his excuse for coming to town, and was several miles out on the road to the ranch before he remembered that he was supposed to get tickets for tonight's train.

CHAPTER I

THE handsome new curate of St. Giles's was about to make his first appearance at the eleven o'clock service that Sunday morning, and the choir, being composed almost entirely of maidens in the romantic teens, was a seething mass of curiosity.

"Can you see him, Betty? Is he good looking?"

"Don't block up the way — let somebody else see!"

"Does anybody know what his name is?"

In this buzz of speculation the thirty young ladies, forgetting the time, the place, and the robes they were supposed to put on, stood on tiptoe to look over each other's heads at the young clergyman who was in a last-minute conference with his gray-haired superior just outside the vesting room.

"Somebody told me his name is Anthony Drew," one better-informed chorister answered proudly. "My father says he's just been ordained—"

"Isn't he good looking!" gurgled another. "Do you suppose he's married?"

"Girls!" Miss Maddox, organist and choir director, herself already in cap, gown, and cotta, turned from the music cabinet. "For goodness' sake, get into your things! It's almost eleven. And don't talk so loud — they'll hear you all over the church. I'd be ashamed!" with a frown as severe as she could make it. They really were funny!

"Not to say that Mr. Anthony Drew may hear them, though I don't suppose he'd mind too much." Mrs. Stone, the plump soprano, with her matrimonial worries off her mind could afford to laugh.

"Most men take kindly to admiration," Mrs. Coffey, the tall

rangy alto, was likewise amused. "Why not let the girls go on?"

"Let's not pamper him too soon, though," answered Val, urging the girls toward their lockers.

The choir reluctantly obeyed, though certain hissing whispers showed that excitement was still at the boiling point. They were fair enough to admit, however, that if they didn't get into their vestments before the clock struck, they'd be late for the service. Not such a good way to impress Mr. Drew.

Having got the choir into this mood, Valerie disappeared into the chancel and took her perch on the organ bench, where she fiddled with stops and made soft devotional music while the congregation rustled into place. Exactly as eleven solemn strokes boomed from St. Giles's tower the organ pealed a louder note, and the choir took it up as the procession started.

"Rejoice, ye pure in heart!
Rejoice, give thanks, and sing!"

caroled the fresh young voices joyously as the two black and white lines filed through the door into the chancel. Without giving it too much thought, the girls were vaguely glad that Miss Maddox usually picked cheerful processionals—certainly she had done so today. This, they felt, was really an occasion for rejoicing.

"Bright youth and snow crowned age"

they went on happily, stealing a glance at the two clergymen who had followed them in and were now taking their own stations. The girls marveled at the appropriateness of the words they sang. Dr. Havern wasn't exactly snow-crowned, though what hair he did have on his smooth pink scalp was pretty gray; but there was no doubt about Mr. Drew's being a very splendid youth.

Though Val had suppressed her choristers with stern words, she was more than a little interested herself as to what sort of person the new curate might be, and took advantage of his reading the First Lesson to observe him closely, as did every man, woman, and child in the church. What they saw was a tall young man of perhaps twenty-five or six; a little on the thin side, but well set up; dark enough to be interesting, clear-cut features, and a very pleasant voice. Altogether most satisfactory. It remained to be seen what kind of a preacher he was and how he worked out socially, but it was nice to have him a well-looking person at any rate. A man may be a little runt and still have the soul of a great divine, but it didn't hurt for the curate of St. Giles's to make a good appearance and start off right. She hoped, as did everybody else in the church, that he might turn out to be a better preacher than the rector. Dr. Havern was a good man, if something of a bore, and his flock held him in high esteem; but everybody likes a change.

But those who were pleasantly stirred at the prospect of hearing somebody new and different were fated to disappointment. When the time came for the sermon, Dr. Havern mounted the pulpit as usual, while Mr. Drew sat down quietly to listen.

Val sighed inaudibly. It was too bad the old dear thought he had to preach this morning, but perhaps they had decided it would be easier for the new man to break in on a simpler service when not so many people were there to look him over, with their ears open for every slip in voice, manner, or doctrine. She remembered her own stage fright that morning, two years ago, when she had taken over this job as organist, her first job since leaving college. She hadn't belonged to the church long enough to know just where all the responses and things fitted into the service, and she had been very nervous. Dad was very encouraging, though, and assured her afterward that she had acted like an old hand. This was decent of him, because neither he nor Mother had liked her taking on the new religion.

Mother, stanch Methodist that she was, had taken it pretty hard when Val announced her intention of being baptized by Dr. Havern. In fact, she had been almost crushed. Fortunately she was soon reconciled, and she and Dad now came to St. Giles's quite regularly. Their daughter knew this was purely on her account, as they had never given any sign of wanting baptism themselves. They liked being where they could see her and hear her play — they were so proud of her, the dears!

[23]

Affection and remorse swelled in Val's breast as she thought of their never-failing devotion to her, and the trouble she had been to them in return.

"I always was a little brute," she thought, watching her mother's intent face as she listened to Dr. Havern expounding the story of the loaves and fishes.

"This incident is not to be taken literally," the rector was saying. "No one in this day and age believes in miracles. Jesus simply called upon those who had the foresight to bring a lunch with them to divide their bread and meat among the less fortunate. He, with His well-known charity and consideration for the poor and needy, set the example by distributing among those nearest Him, as they sat upon the stony ground of the desert, the few loaves and fishes which He had (as we now say) commandeered from the more prosperous. To Jesus it was just a matter of encouragement, yea, even censure, to the thoughtless, the indifferent, the *selfish*, who made up that vast congregation." The orotund voice increased in volume with each point in the indictment of that multitude of long ago. "I say to you: people are like sheep! This example set them by Jesus touched their hearts and reminded them of their obligation to their brother!"

Dr. Havern, who had been gesticulating vigorously, here paused to wipe his ruddy brow; then resumed his discourse on a deeper note.

"But to say, as the fundamentalists would have us believe, that a miracle was wrought in that desert place, and that baskets upon baskets of broken fragments remained after that frugal banquet — all coming from five pitiful little loaves and two *fishes!*" great stress here as if to say the rector could have borne with anything but those fish, "I tell you, my friends, reason revolts against it. *It is not to be taken literally!*"

During this impassioned period Val's glance had wandered again to the new assistant, and she was interested to note the sudden jerk of his head as if he were startled by the rector's liberal interpretation of the gospel. Then apparently recollecting himself, the young man lengthened his involuntary start

into a complete shifting of his long limbs, and resumed his attitude of respectful attention to his superior.

Val wondered what really had upset the curate's calm. Was he less advanced than Dr. Havern had suddenly shown himself to be, or was he just surprised to hear the rector give open expression to what so many people believed in their souls, whatever they said in public. Some people, like dear Mother, actually believed in the Bible implicitly; and if it said that the loaves and fishes multiplied themselves like that, Mother would have died rather than question the statement.

"Common sense must govern in our devotion to the Scriptures," Dr. Havern went on. "Didn't Jesus Himself always speak in parables? Then why should He not have acted them out, somewhat in the manner of our modern charades?"

From nowhere at all a memory flashed into Val's head just then of a plump, rosy faced, earnest little girl glaring at her with flashing blue eyes, and crying indignantly: "Do you mean to say He lied?"

Val imitated the new curate and stirred uneasily. Of course, that hadn't been exactly the same sort of argument on that morning eight years ago. She and Mary Anderson hadn't brought up the question of that miraculous banquet. What they had been quarreling about was the Last Supper and whether or not it was to be taken literally. Mary had been so positive, and Val had to admit that she had somehow got the idea over.

She remembered the thing so well. It was the morning when she had blackmailed the family into taking her to Los Pericos by letting Jasper see her walking into what, in their circle, was considered the Gates of Hell; though as a matter of fact, by the time she and Mary had finished their short visit to the Blessed Sacrament and had left the church, Val was almost too deeply interested in what she had seen to give so much as a passing thought to Jasper.

Bursting with curiosity, she had bombarded Mary with questions. Why did everybody get down on two knees before they went into the pew? What was that gold thing on the altar? Well, if they bowed to *that*, wasn't it the same as idolatry?

Mary had tried to explain. Nobody bowed to the gold thing, she said; they bowed or knelt to our Lord Himself in the Blessed Sacrament. That, she said, was what Val had seen in the middle of the gold thing. And Mary had stoutly denied anything even remotely resembling idolatry.

"We kneel to our Lord," she had said, "because He is really there on the altar."

Startled almost beyond words, Val had then demanded what made Mary say any such outrageous thing.

"How could He be there?" she had said in horror.

Mary had made an attempt to explain the Sacrament — the Real Presence, she called it. Much to Val's surprise (considering that papists were not allowed to read the Bible), Mary seemed to know enough Scripture to recite the text from St. Luke: "This is My Body . . . Do this in commemoration of Me."

Val had thought she had the answer to that.

"Why," she had said loftily, "they say that was just meant symbolically. I thought everybody knew that!"

"Then why did He say 'This is My Body' if He meant 'This is a *symbol*'?" Mary had countered.

"Because He supposed people would have sense enough to understand what He meant." Val had become scornful. "He didn't have to be literal on a thing like that!"

"He had to be literal!" Mary stuck to her guns. "He knew just how much sense the Apostles had, and He knew how much sense everybody would have to the end of time. So that's why He made it definite. Anybody would know that in such a serious thing it wouldn't be safe to take chances."

"He was always talking in parables," Val had insisted. "You know — the Prodigal Son and the Good Samaritan, and all that."

"Well, wasn't there ever a prodigal son?" Mary was certainly a stubborn person. "Wasn't there ever anybody like the Good Samaritan? Our Lord was just telling them what was so, the same as He always did. It was just like when He said, 'This is My Body.'"

"But it wasn't His Body!" Val had begun to get angry then. "Anybody could see that!"

[26]

And then it was that Mary had bristled up in her turn, demanding to know if Val implied that Jesus had been lying.

"No, of course not!" Val was shocked. "I never said anything like that. I just said He meant it as a memorial — 'do this in memory of Me.' He *did* say that."

"Can't you remember anybody better when he's really there than if you only have a piece of bread to remember him by?" Mary had persisted. Once give her an idea, and she never knew when to let go. "A picture would have been a better memorial, if that was all He wanted. And the Jews had a good symbol in the Paschal Lamb. Why didn't He stick to that, if He only wanted a symbol for people to remember Him by?"

Val had felt she was getting beyond her depth there, and was greatly relieved to hear the school bell break in then.

"I'll talk to you about this later," she had said hurriedly as they had started to run down the street.

Well, there had never been any subsequent talk after all. Not a half hour after this conversation Mother had come in excitedly, and taken Val out of school in time to catch the two o'clock plane, and she had never come back to the North Side high school. On their return from New Mexico Dad and Mother had bundled her off immediately to Miss Swither's Seminary, and after that it had been Wesleyan U. These two solid Methodist institutions had taken all the nonsense out of her!

The Andersons had moved to Washington, she believed, and she had never seen Mary again. She had heard something about Mary's being at Trinity College, but beyond that she knew nothing of her one-time friend's whereabouts. One of those ships that pass in the night in the Longfellow poem that Miss Swither was always so fond of quoting. If Mary was one of those ships, she certainly had left a long trail of something in her wake, and Val found it impossible to escape from it.

She had been happy enough before she had run into that church after Mary — it was in October, wasn't it? Just about this time of the year. And she had been so frightened by the stillness, she remembered. It had been more than a mere ab-

sence of sound. It was as if weighted by something from an unseen world — something that radiated from the altar — And Mary had told her afterward that she had been in the actual presence of God!

What was she thinking of, anyway? Mary was just an extremist, even at that early age, and had got Val all stirred up and crazy to the extent that she had actually tried to join the Roman Church, like a fool! Val winced as she always did at the recollection of her abortive attempt to become a Catholic. Well, it was all over now, thank goodness (poor, dear, disagreeable, old Uncle Thomas had at least that one good deed to his credit, peace to his ashes!), though there was a scar on Val's soul somewhere that nothing seemed to heal. She could thank Mary for that!

The sermon seemed endless, and what was it all about? Why did a person have to go to church just to sit through a long dissertation on what *not* to believe about the Bible? What did Dr. Havern really know about it, when it came to that? How could he say for sure what had been in the mind of Jesus so long ago?

Now that she came to think of it, it *would* have been peculiar if Jesus had gone in for charades and things, just as Dr. Havern had said; and then all of a sudden had become deadly serious and thrown a bombshell about the Real Presence, as Mary had said He did, and expected people to take it literally. Had people taken it literally then, and how many did now, outside of Romanists like Mary? It would be such a wonderful thing if a person could believe in it — to get down on your knees before the Lord on the altar, and pray!

There were so many times when you wanted to do that — when things went wrong and worried you. That would be something you knew you simply had — it was yours. It was something to hold on to, something to fill this aching emptiness in your heart that nothing seemed to cure. It was just there all the time, no matter how much you tried to put it away from you, or how busy you were with your studies and your choir. You did think you had forgotten sometimes, but

any little thing was sure to bring it up again, like this sermon today, or maybe it might only be a whiff of chrysanthemums as you passed a florist's shop. Why should it be so hard to get over this particular disappointment, when there had been a lot of other plans that went wrong, and you didn't fuss about them too much — "why should this have to happen to me?" she almost cried aloud.

Thank goodness, Dr. Havern seemed to be coming down the homestretch at last. "And now —" he was intoning solemnly. Val slid back onto the organ bench.

After the service Dr. Havern got out of his surplice with practiced ease and was down at the church door to shake hands with his congregation and introduce young Mr. Drew to its more important members. The young ladies of the choir, hurt that no introductions had been made in the choir room, copied their rector's speed in tearing off their own vestments. While the organ was still roaring out a musical dismissal of the congregation, the choir in their smart fall hats and dresses were swarming around the two clergymen at the door.

"Ah," said Dr. Havern gaily, as the bevy presented itself before him, "and here is our choir. Mr. Drew, you must meet all of our little St. Cecilias." The rector decided it wasn't necessary to be too fussy about individual names. Let Drew find that out for himself, if he felt it worth his while. "And here is our Mrs. Stone, the lovely soprano," he relented as he saw the soloists coming at a more moderate gait, "and Mrs. Coffey, with her luscious alto."

Mr. Drew seemed to have good manners even under these trying conditions, and smiled delightfully at the little Cecilias, saying he would make it his business to learn in no time just which was which. He also expressed deep admiration of the music, both as to solos and chorus.

Presently the choir, all giggles and gratification, got out with the rest of the flock, leaving only a vestryman who had the collection on his mind, and Mr. and Mrs. Maddox who were waiting for their daughter.

Dr. Havern shook hands with these aliens, infusing into his

greeting an extra cordiality as though to indicate that in the sight of God even a Methodist had a soul, and presented his curate.

"These good people," he said with heart-warming affability, "have the honor to be the parents of our charming organist. Beautiful hand on the instrument, hasn't she? What a touch! Ah, here she is now. My dear Miss Maddox, I hope you didn't hear that last—are your ears burning? Do come and meet our new shepherd—that is to say, our assistant shepherd, Mr. Anthony Drew."

Anthony Drew took the hand whose artistry had brought such praise from the rector, and said that he was happy to meet her. As the words left his mouth he realized that out of the many times he had used that polite phrase this morning, this was the time he really meant it. She was tall and straight and fair, and she looked right into his eyes with her own as if there was nothing in their clear gray depths that might not be published to the whole world. He liked the firm grip of her slim, strong fingers—the way her tawny gold hair lay in soft waves against her head. And when she said, "How do you do?" it was practically a poem. He wanted everybody to go away at once—his smiling superior, her parents, the vestryman with the collection basket—and leave them to talk over the important things of life, such as where she had been all this time, and how soon she would marry him.

But Dr. Havern was talking again.

"We think that St. Giles's is fortunate to have captured our St. Cecilia," he shamelessly plagiarized himself. "Mustn't tell tales, but a little bird said something about the Brick Church wanting to get our sweet musician away from us. I hope the little bird wasn't quite telling the truth, eh?" He shook a playful forefinger at the current St. Cecilia, while the waiting vestryman scowled.

"What's he putting ideas in her head for?" thought the vestryman. "Does that mean we have to raise her salary?"

Val lifted her eyebrows slightly.

"I don't know the name of the little bird," she said, laughing

[30]

politely, "but I wouldn't trust it too far." With which cryptic answer she slid a hand through her mother's arm, and the Maddox family departed.

"Charming girl," commented Dr. Havern, free at last to pay some attention to the patient vestryman. "Too bad her parents didn't see their way clear to join the church when she did. Worthy people. Yes, Davison? You wanted to see me?"

"That seems like a nice young man," remarked Mr. Maddox as he and his ladies walked the short distance between St. Giles's and home. "I hope he turns out as well as he looks now."

Mrs. Maddox assented, but in so preoccupied a manner that her daughter stole a sidelong glance at her. The gentle little lady's soft cheek was flushed, and her mouth compressed as if she had set it firmly over indiscreet words. Val smiled.

"Go ahead, darling," she said. "You want to find fault with the sermon, don't you? — without hurting my feelings. I thought myself it was pretty poor, if that's any help."

"Val, dear, if you're sure you don't mind?" Mrs. Maddox's voice trembled. "I was surprised at Dr. Havern. What could he be thinking of! And all those nice young people there, and at so impressionable an age. I was brought up to believe that when the Bible said something, it meant it."

"Seemed to me he was a little off the track," observed her husband. "I've heard other people talk that way, but this is the first time I've caught him at it. What was the matter with him, Val? Trying to show off before the new man how liberal minded and modern he is?"

Val considered this a moment as she passed through the gate and went up the walk. "I shouldn't wonder you're right, Dad. And from the look on Mr. Drew's face, I judge he was just as surprised as anybody."

Mr. Maddox's guess at the rector's purpose that morning was a shrewd one, and fairly accurate. Dr. Havern had resented what he called the officiousness of his vestrymen in insisting upon a curate at St. Giles's, though they had been very tactful about it. They had laid great stress on the growth of the congregation and the corresponding strain on the rector's time and strength, and had said nothing about any slipping on his part.

"We'll get a good, strapping young fellow in here to take some of the load off your shoulders," they said with a heartiness which the rector sourly dubbed spurious, "and you'll have more time to do the really important things. No use working a good man to death. You can't drive yourself beyond your strength," and so on and on, until the badgered rector had to give way.

Yes, he'd been obliged to submit, he told himself bitterly, but he didn't have to like it. They squeezed a man's brains for fifteen years or more, and then tried to get rid of him. They couldn't go quite that far, of course, since he had arranged matters so that he was their permanent rector, and furthermore, he had quietly bought up the mortgage on the church property some years back. He doubted if many people knew this. However, if they thought they wanted a change — some young squirt with a lot of modern ideas — then everybody would flock around and say how wonderful the new man was, and they'd forget all about the older, wiser man who had guided them all this time.

Well, he'd show 'em. His ideas were just as modern as anybody's. He had known for a long time that it was the thing to disregard some of the old beliefs about the Bible and its parables — fables, most of them. He had never tried it out on his congregation, because they were a prize lot of reactionaries who would faint if you told them to use a little judgment in religion. However, if that was what they thought they wanted now, he'd give it to them!

It was in this frame of mind that he had faced his flock this morning, perfectly aware that their hope had been for a sermon from Mr. Drew, but determined to show the vestrymen that he understood their little game. He was still boss. And if Drew thought he could air his advanced theories in the pulpit of St. Giles's and thrill everybody with his brilliance, he'd find his fireworks a bit damp. Dr. Havern would have beaten him to it.

Glowing with gratified and holy spite, Dr. Havern disposed of his vestryman Davison; then taking the curate by the arm, he bore him off to Sunday dinner at the rectory.

"And what do you think of our little church, Drew?" he lilted gaily. "Some of the decorations are not bad, though it's far from perfect. I do a little now and then, but it's slow work. The vestrymen are well-meaning souls, but limited. You saw —" a providential cough stopped him, and Drew hastily cut in.

"I think it's a beautiful little church, sir. Everything in good taste, and very devotional. And an extremely nice choir. Who trains them?"

"That girl I introduced, Valerie Maddox." Dr. Havern had his second wind. "Her people are Methodists, but I baptized her a couple of years ago. Plays nicely, though just a beginner. My dream is to get some really good organist, like this man Pietro Yon; but, of course, with our poor little five thousand dollar organ, and the pinchpenny ideas of the vestrymen, what could you expect? Now, next year —"

By this time they had reached the house, and the rector's wife came to the rescue. She was a faded little woman with a faint, tired voice and a limp manner, as if any vitality she ever had was now completely sapped by her thirty years with such an exuberant husband.

"You're late, Wilbur," she murmured, giving a chilly hand and a wan smile to the guest. "I'm afraid the dinner won't be so good. Savannah gets out of patience if she has to stay late on Sunday."

"Oh, it'll be all right." Dr. Havern waved away all annoyances with his usual smiling aplomb. "Just a plain little meal, Drew. We never break the Lord's day any more than we can help, and it's good to curb the appetite occasionally. My dear, does Savannah know we're ready?"

Dr. Havern justified himself as a prophet. Savannah's temper may have gone off somewhat — the expression on her round black face was distinctly lowering — but the clear soup, crown roast, candied yams, green salad, lemon meringue pie, and superb coffee made the rector's plain little meal rank as a magnificent understatement.

The rector frankly enjoyed his dinner after the labors of the morning. Soothed and expanded with good food and the consciousness of having put one over on his natural enemies, the vestrymen, he became even more talkative and waggish; laughed merrily over many a playful little story which he told about the various parishioners who had been introduced this morning; and in general kept his good humor at a high level.

"A great many odd people, my dear Drew," he summed up these little histories. "It certainly takes a sense of humor to get along with them, and sometimes even that is a bit strained by the pressure put on me; but I think I'm equal to it."

Having finished her coffee, Mrs. Havern here said plaintively that she believed she'd go and lie down, leaving the gentlemen to their cigars and conversation.

"I'm sure you and Wilbur have a lot of business to talk over, Mr. Drew, and you won't mind my — Such a pleasure having — Good-bye," and she gently melted out of sight.

Anthony remained on his feet and consulted his watch.

"I'm afraid it's time for me to go, sir," he said. "It's been so very pleasant, but I don't want to be in the way."

"Sit down, sit down!" urged Dr. Havern. "Or perhaps we'll find it more comfortable in the study," catching a gleam of Savannah's baleful eye through a crack in the kitchen door. "Much nicer in the study."

The study was indeed nice, as was all of the house that had come under Anthony's eye; and he couldn't help thinking that Dr. Havern either had some private means, or else the deliciously funny congregation did pretty well by him. Drew envied him, and said so.

"Not a bad little place," replied his beaming host, rubbing his hands together in gratification. "I rather like this room, though my wife calls it the star chamber; and indeed history has been made here. Yes, indeed!" He settled himself cosily in his chair, lit an excellent cigar, and then shot out the question he had been burning to ask all during the meal. "And how did the service go this morning? Fairly smooth, didn't you think? And what did you think of my talk?" It seemed to him it was about time this fledgling said something one way or the other about that sermon.

Anthony wished he hadn't asked that. All during dinner he had been hoping Dr. Havern might be so occupied with the pleasures of the table and his funny stories that he would forget to ask embarrassing questions. It would have been only decent of him to allow his curate to get away just this once and have a day or two to think it over so that he might decide whether to answer diplomatically, or to give his real opinion and throw up the job.

For all his inexperience Anthony was no fool. There must have been some strong reason for a sermon like that by a man whose reputation heretofore had been anything but iconoclastic, and at present Anthony didn't want to commit himself. He regretted that he had been persuaded into the study after dinner. Regrets were of no use now, though. Here was Dr. Havern in his sleek, well-cut blacks, his bald head and chubby face pink and shining with good living, his prominent eyes gleaming with curiosity as they bored into the curate's mind. Anthony took a long breath.

"I don't know, sir," he said, trying to sound casual though his face was burning. "I haven't quite got my bearings here yet. You're of the modern school, aren't you? I had thought this parish was more — more — conservative — Very eloquent sermon, and clearly expressed," he added hastily, noting an extra glitter in the rectoral eye.

Dr. Havern's hand scraped his chin reflectively, and he regarded his subordinate with a thoughtful stare. So all the fireworks had been unnecessary — this boy belonged in the fundamentalist camp. He was plainly ill at ease because he couldn't come out openly and either agree with or denounce the rector's ideas. Dr. Havern decided he had made a slight tactical error — should have waited a bit and sounded the lad out before taking such a decided step. The vestrymen wouldn't like it, either — not that that would matter unduly. Well, after all, perhaps there was no real harm done; and it had been pleasant to see how the drooping congregation had come alive after he got started. No smothered yawns or closed eyelids this morning!

"Oh, we try to keep up with the times," he replied, willing

[35]

to meet his subordinate half way and drop the subject. "Glad you liked it. Now," he went on briskly, again rubbing his plump hands, "one of these days we'll have to work out a program for you. No hurry, of course — take your time; but I suppose the vestrymen will expect you to earn your salary, as they put it." Quotation marks here were plainly indicated, and Dr. Havern laughed heartily as if somebody had just said something rather good. "They certainly do want their pound of flesh, though. You don't know anybody who would be willing to donate pretty handsomely toward a new organ, do you? I wish we could afford a really good choir!"

"I thought it was very sweet this morning," protested Anthony, remembering Miss Maddox with a shaft of sunlight falling on her hair, her slim fingers lying warmly in his.

"Oh, for a lot of little school girls!" Dr. Havern shrugged. "And those two soloists are quite second rate, quite," turning thumbs down on all of his St. Cecilias. "What I should like is a good male quartette, with a men's chorus to sustain them, and an organist who wouldn't be afraid to get a little sound out of the instrument. A good choir, like they have at St. Udolph's. And I could get it, too, if I weren't blocked by this set of mossbacks I have to contend with." Harassed lines disturbed the sunny calm of the rector's brow. "Twenty thousand dollars would do it."

Annoyed at this slur on Miss Maddox and her work, Anthony was on the point of suggesting that little St. Giles's wouldn't know how to handle the volume of sound to be produced by this magnificent setup, but stopped himself just in time. No use to start a row right at the beginning of his job which even now seemed beset with pitfalls if one could judge from the rector's hints about parsimonious vestrymen, to say nothing of the rector's own strange interpretation of the gospel. Anthony began to feel a little sorry for himself.

"Ah, well," Dr. Havern dismissed his troubles, and thought it about time to dismiss his guest as well, "the afternoon is wearing on, and I mustn't keep you. Do you think you can get along with the evening service, my dear Drew? I have an appointment at the University Club tonight — I *could* break it, of course — But you won't have a bit of trouble, I know. You might get Davison to read one of the lessons; he does it sometimes."

That seemed to be all. Drew rose hastily, glad to be allowed his freedom for the time being. The rector shook hands cordially, received his thanks for the good dinner, assured him that Evensong was simplicity itself, and closed the door after the departing guest.

"Hum!" the rector remarked thoughtfully to himself as he went back to his study for a delayed Sabbath nap.

CHAPTER II

WITH the help of Mr. Davison and Miss Maddox, Anthony pulled through Evensong very creditably. There never was more than a handful present on Sunday evenings; but they, being the tried and true, looked with kindly eyes at the young neophyte, and spoke up heartily in the responses. His sermon was brief; and with the memory before him of Dr. Havern's criticisms of his flock in general and the choir in particular, Anthony limited his fifteen-minute talk to strictly orthodox, if platitudinous, comments on the words of St. Paul:

Wherefore be ye not unwise, but understanding what the will of God is . . . speaking to yourselves in psalms, and hymns, and spiritual songs, singing and making melody in your heart to the Lord.

The choir quite thrilled over this text which seemed to have direct reference to themselves. And as Mr. Drew included them all in a friendly smile after the service, and thanked them for being so lenient with his mistakes, the young ladies decided that St. Giles's was frightfully lucky to get such a grand curate.

Mr. Drew genuinely appreciated the kindly interest he was getting on all hands; but after the St. Cecilias had twittered themselves away in company with the more staid members of the flock, he waited a little anxiously for Miss Maddox, who had stayed behind to be sure that the choir's lockers were in order before closing up for the night. She came out at last, and Drew's heart told him she was lovelier than ever.

"I liked your sermon," said Val, smiling up at him with her usual directness. "I never could see why religion shouldn't be cheerful — unless it be a funeral, of course."

Anthony agreed with her on the general principle, though modestly deprecating his own abilities as a speaker; and he managed to walk with her as far as her own gate. He needed a brisk turn after a quiet day, he said, which was not in the least true. Anthony had walked miles that afternoon, partly to think out his sermon for the evening, and partly to wear off the excitements of the morning.

All too soon they reached the Maddox house, and as Val seemed to think it unnecessary to invite him in, he swiftly decided it would be only decent to ask after her parents. Anything to prolong this precious moment.

"They weren't at church tonight," he said.

"No, they rarely come in the evening." The girl's voice was all warm affection. "They don't really belong to St. Giles's, you know; and they only come on Sunday mornings because they want to see their darling child in action."

"I remember Dr. Havern said something about their not being of the faith." Anthony spoke from a divided mind, the clergyman in him wanting to know the reason for this disparity of religion in one family, while the lover held it to be of no importance.

"Dr. Havern baptized me a couple of years ago, but naturally Dad and Mother didn't change just because I did. We've always been Methodists, but I felt the need of something more — more solid, in a way." Anthony nodded sympathetically, and she went on. "The lambs were a little shocked when I told them I was going to St. Giles's, but they said all they wanted was to see me happy, and they've been wonderful about it ever since."

"And it wasn't as if you had gone over to Rome," added Anthony, by way of confirmation.

"What made you say that?" The girl looked so startled that he hastened to explain himself.

"I only meant it wasn't as if you had done something really radical — Romanism or atheism — any of those extreme things. Of course, we're a long way ahead of the Methodists in our way of thinking — though I have many good friends among that faith," he appended hastily, finishing in somewhat stately manner. "I hope it may not be long before we welcome your father and mother into the Church. They'll find so much more happiness with us."

Val replied a little absently that she supposed so. Recovering herself, she smiled brightly and dismissed him with a word of thanks, both for his escort and his good wishes.

Not being able to think of anything to say that would detain her further, Anthony had to let her go. A moment later the door closed behind her, leaving him to continue his restless walk of the afternoon, or to go home and finish his meditations there. After a brief hesitation Anthony decided upon the second course, and went home to the furnished flat which he had taken so conveniently near the church.

It was an extremely small apartment, but Anthony had been very excited yesterday afternoon as he unpacked his books and pictures and clothes. Some day, of course, when he was pastor of a large city church, he would have a beautiful study lined with bookcases, a large living room with a grand piano, also a bedroom big enough for Grandmother's old four-poster which he supposed his mother might be talked into giving him. In the meantime everything here seemed adequate for the present needs of a young cleric. The place was his own. He was launched on his career of saving souls. In all of his twenty-five years Anthony Drew had probably never ended a day with a happier heart than that Saturday night when he had closed his door on the outside world with a prayer that God would bless him and his new home.

Now, just twenty-four hours later, as he let himself in at that door and turned on the light, Anthony felt that eons had passed. He was now an experienced man, immeasurably older than that untried youth who had lightheartedly moved in here and whose plans were about nothing more vital than rugs and furniture. Somewhere in that fateful span he had met and recognized the love of his life, and now all things were changed. Just who or what this perfect being, this Valerie Maddox, might turn out to be, or how she might react to his own ambitions and beliefs, mattered little right now. It was enough that she was fair and young and lovely, with eyes like pools of clear water in the morning light; and never, if he had anything to do with it, should those eyes cloud over with the pain of loss, of disappointment even, such as he'd had this very day. . . .

Just as Macbeth overdid it with his injudicious harping on Banquo's absence from the party, so did Anthony now call up his own ghost. No sooner had his mind reverted to happenings earlier in the day than the vision rose before him of Dr. Havern's shining bald head, his plump, rosy face with its self-indulgent mouth, preaching heresy and retailing ill-natured gossip. Instantly the young man's exhilaration faded.

Instead of leaping like a young hart upon the mountains of spices, Anthony found himself back in his dingy little sitting room, conscious that someone farther down the hall had a passion for fried onions. He was tired and disillusioned, balked in his hopes of beginning a life of service under the guidance of a man grown old and wise in godly ways; and his feet hurt. Drearily he began to get ready for bed.

His all too brief moment with the girl of his dreams was the one bright spot in the whole miserable day, he thought, trying to find his other slipper. At the start it hadn't seemed too bad, though he had naturally been a bit edgy before making his first appearance before a congregation, even though he had nothing more to do than read the lesson from the printed page of the Bible. However, after the sermon started the real trouble began.

By upbringing, as well as his own inclination, Anthony was definitely orthodox. His family tradition had all been for safety, sanity, and respectability in everything. The best people, so his ancestors had held, obeyed their country's laws, kept out of the scandal sheets, voted the Republican ticket, and belonged to the Episcopal Church. They lived in the right part of town, wore the right clothes, and read the right books. They paid their just debts, contributed to charity as generously as possible, believed in the Bible without any pretense of trying to understand it, and in general kept a nice balance between God and Mammon.

His great-aunt Maude, the family terror, had shown disapproval, not to say disgust, when Anthony decided to take Orders, holding that ministers weren't men; but his mother had backed him up sympathetically. It wasn't at all an unheard of thing for a Drew to enter the clergy, she insisted. Every once in a while you ran across somebody in the family history who had filled his pulpit admirably — remember the dear bishop who was a friend of Phillips Brooks? And she thought Anthony would look sweet in one of those long-sleeved surplices. Later on, when Anthony was finally ordained and Aunt Maude was so indignant at his proposed burial in the obscurities of St. Giles's, his mother offered herself as a sacrifice and played cribbage with the old vampire for practically two whole days without stopping.

Anthony himself sincerely believed in the sanctity of his calling, and hoped to do as much credit to God as to his family. He had never questioned the morals of his family any more than he had their manners; and in the same way did he believe in the tenets of his faith. If a faint disquiet had ever assailed him that some odds and ends of religious practices in that faith were at variance — that the High and Low divisions held exactly opposite views on the Real Presence, for example — he took refuge in the comforting text, "In My Father's house there are many mansions," and decided that his own journey to that house would be along a middle course on which he would bring as many souls with him as he could turn from the paths of real error.

Consequently it was a shock when he heard Dr. Havern's heretical opinions about the miraculous banquet of the loaves and fishes. The bald statement that the beautiful story of our Lord's compassion on the multitude was merely a charade to jog His audience's attention to the hungry people among them, not only startled but annoyed him. To a lot of the congregation no doubt that sacred story was as dear as it was to Anthony. It was bad taste as well as poor religion to try to take people's faith away from them. What good could come from belittling the mystic side of the incident, especially when Dr. Havern plainly had nothing to offer in its stead? The young man had a sudden inpulse to rise then and there and protest; but on reflection had controlled it. The sanctuary was no place for a brawl, he reluctantly decided; and though burning internally, he had sat quietly until the end.

Anthony went to sleep that night firmly resolved to hand in his resignation the next morning; before doing which, however, he would deliver a short discourse of his own which he hoped would burn the rector's ears to a crisp. Charades indeed!

With the morning came a cooling thought, to wit: there was nothing he could do about it. If Dr. Havern really had those sacrilegious ideas, and had spoken from a genuine disbelief of the divine power of Jesus, he had plenty of company among some very distinguished clergy. Furthermore, he was twice Anthony's age, also the permanent rector of the church where Anthony was having his first tryout, and his word would carry at least some weight with the bishop. The younger man had no particular standing in the clergy as yet, and in all probability a row with his first superior would militate against his getting in somewhere else more to his taste. So, little though he liked it, Anthony realized there was nothing to do but swallow his private opinions and try to make the best of a bad bargain for the time being.

Also there was Valerie Maddox. In her official capacity as organist she would surely be in and out of St. Giles's a lot, a circumstance not to be overlooked. So, taking it for all in all, the new curate decided to stay where he was.

He would have been less pleasantly resigned had he known how far he was from Val's thoughts after they had parted at her gate last night. His chance remark had upset Val pretty thoroughly, when he said it was fortunate, when changing her religion, that she had not fixed upon either Romanism or atheism. Unflattering though it would have been to Anthony had he known it, the speech made far more impression on her than the speaker did. The latter she had forgotten at once, but the words lingered tormentingly, to be mulled over long after she should have been asleep.

If he had merely congratulated her on having escaped a complete lack of faith, the girl would have forgotten it easily. Val believed in God sincerely, if vaguely. The other alternative, however, had come too near the truth to be agreeable; and she shifted her pillow restlessly as she remembered once again how narrowly she had missed being caught in that trap. That, indeed, was cause for thankfulness. Still, the linking together of the two schools of thought furnished much unquiet reflection.

Romanism or atheism. Were these two extreme cults to be considered as the opposite ends of some gigantic seesaw poised over an abyss into which the unwary might drop if he got too far from the safe Protestant middle? And what happened when he landed in the pit? Was it the same at either end, or were there two abysses? Were they equally bad, though different in character? And if one was worse, which one?

Val answered herself promptly: Atheism. That barren credo of disbelief began in nothingness and ended in the same place. A complete waste of time, she thought, dismissing it.

Roman Catholics, for all their errors, at least believed in *something*. Mr. Drew's implication was that denial of any God at all was no worse than worship of false gods. However, even so slight a contact as Val had had with Rome inclined her to the opinion that whether or not papistry included the worship of false gods, at least it admitted the existence of the same Supreme Being as was known to any good Protestant. If that was the case, then how did it work out in the divine plan? Did God really want the homage of idol worshipers? — assuming that Romanists did worship idols. Mary had said they didn't —

God was hard to find sometimes, and hard to understand.

She did believe that He was around somewhere, keeping an eye on the people of His pasture, as the psalm said; but she wished He would give her some inkling of His purpose in all this confusion of dogma and controversy. And she switched back to the sermon of the morning.

It undoubtedly said in the Scriptures: *"He blessed and broke and gave the loaves to His disciples, and the disciples to the multitude. . . ."* What had started Dr. Havern off on a line that was so different from his usual Sunday sermon? She believed she didn't like it. His sudden appearance as a scoffer wasn't in the best of taste, whatever his private opinions might be.

Suddenly she sat bolt upright in bed. Why should his real opinion be different from the words he spoke in public? If Jesus had the power to multiply the loaves and fishes, then He had it. If the Bible was to be believed when it made a definite statement (the Thirty-nine Articles said flatly, *"Holy Scripture containeth all things necessary to salvation."*), then there should be no private opinion that was any different. And in exchange for the joy and comfort that Mother, say, had taken all her life from the belief that the Son of God took pity on the hungry people, and had manifested a little of His unlimited power that they might eat—all that Dr. Havern had to offer was to say that the Light of the World was just acting a charade! The word for that was: Cheap! she summed up. And on that she fell asleep.

The next morning brought its own troubles. Val was scarcely away from the breakfast table when Dr. Havern telephoned her to say that the Men's Club had asked for music at their monthly luncheon meeting today, and Dr. Havern trusted that Miss Maddox would be prompt. To her dismayed exclamations, the rector admitted that he should have told her about this before, only it had slipped his mind in the press of business during the past fortnight, but he knew Miss Maddox always had something up her sleeve so it really didn't make any difference. He expressed the cheerful belief that everything would turn out beautifully, said it was a lovely morning, and hung up.

"He knows more than I do, then, if he thinks it's going to be beautiful!" muttered the girl, reaching for her address book.

For the next half hour her telephone was busy, and her spirits fell lower and lower, while her temper waxed higher. She called up singer after singer, urging them, if they loved her, to come to the rescue; but while practically all of them said they were willing to die for her personally, singing for the Men's Club was out for today. Everybody was sorry, but each had a date.

Having to take a music lesson of her own right then, Val put the matter by temporarily, and hurried to the studio, discouraged, angry, and on the verge of panic. It was now ten o'clock and the Men's Club always met in the parish hall at twelve fifteen sharp. Take a half hour out for her piano lesson, and she would have precious little time left to provide entertainment for the gentlemen who paid her salary. There was nothing flattering in Dr. Havern's bright faith in her ability to do the impossible. Perhaps it was that he did believe in miracles, after all!

These luncheon meetings were of regular order, being prepared and served by the Ladies' Guild, after which parish business was discussed and a speaker brought in from the outside to give a short talk on some timely topic. Sometimes they had music, which Val more than suspected was only when no speaker was available. Probably today was one of those times. Ordinarily this would not have meant so much; but today, due to her hurry and worry and all those telephone calls, Val found it particularly hard to bear. Music should not be just something to fall back on when all else failed, to be turned on and off like the kitchen spigot, she told herself passionately.

Sizzling rage and a sense of injury do nothing for a dainty Mozart concerto, as Val found out very soon. Bursting with the kind of emotion not transferrable to the keyboard, Val proceeded to give such a wretched exhibition of what not to do on a piano that her teacher was moved to protest.

"What's the matter with you?" scolded Madame after the first five minutes of this performance. "I never heard anything like this in my life. What have you been up to? Are you in love?"

"Good gracious, no!" Val took her hands off the keyboard. "I just want to kill somebody, that's all." She poured out her woes to a sympathetic ear.

"These men!" cried Madame, lifting her hands toward heaven. "No consideration for anybody!" Having been married and divorced four times, Madame might be said to be an authority on the subject, which perhaps was why she ordered Val to leave the studio instantly and get the business settled at once. "We'll make up the lesson some other time when your mind is all Peace," she concluded reverently.

The girl gratefully submitted, and presently was out on the street again, wondering how to begin the biblical prescription of dredging the highways and byways for somebody to haul in to the banquet. She appreciated Madame's kindness immensely, though she felt there might be something more than pure altruism behind it. Perhaps Madame, too, needed some extra time for personal affairs. There had been a vague reference before the lesson began of the need for another permanent wave. Val only wished she had anything as definite as a beauty shop to bring into the present crisis.

Then, not a dozen paces from Madame's door, she met Mr. Drew coming along with some books under his arm. When he saw her his face lighted up to an extent any girl would notice.

"You look worried," he said "— headache or something?"

"No, I'm fine." Val was touched. Perhaps there were some nice people in the world after all. "I wish, though, it were anything that an aspirin could cure."

Pressed for her reason in saying this, Val explained once more. This time, out of deference for the cloth, she touched lightly on Dr. Havern's part of the affair, and laid stress on the unworthy singers. "I've played their accompaniments so many times when they were in a jam, just at the last minute!"

"Must it be a singer?" Anthony wanted to know. "I think they'd consider it a real treat if you played for them."

"Oh, I could go and bang out Handel's *Largo* for them," she shrugged, "but they'd just have to talk a little louder, that's all. Nobody ever listens to a piano at things like this."

"Well, then," he went on diffidently, forced to admit the truth of this, "if it has to be singing maybe I could help you. I'm not sure if I can get them, but I'll try. You see, we had a quartette when we were in college, and as it happens we're all living right here in town. It probably won't be very good—"

This was no time for quibbling. What Val needed right now was singers, good or bad; and she rapturously thanked him.

They set off at once in search of a telephone, so busy with their own affairs that they did not see a young man on the opposite side of the street who had been watching them. He was a small, spare young man, with sharply pointed features, and hair so blonde as to be almost white. It was Val's cousin, Jasper Maddox, now come to man's years, but keeping his childhood interest in Val's actions.

Jasper still had the white eyelashes which had been Val's bane in past years, through which his pale eyes seldom missed anything of interest; and while his taste in current history was broad enough to take in almost anything about anybody, Jasper's favorite subject for research was Val's private and public life. When he saw her so engrossed with the handsome new curate, his easily roused curiosity was stirred.

"I thought her joining that church meant something," nodding to himself with solemn satisfaction; and on their hurrying away, as if with a purpose, Jasper dropped into his best sleuthing glide and followed after.

The unconscious couple descended upon the first drug store they met, and began telephoning. From his post at the window the watcher gathered that his cousin and the curate were delighted with their phone conversations, Drew having called up several people, while Val stood at his elbow and handed him nickels when his own supply gave out.

The telephoning over, Val and Drew frittered away some more time over a soda at the counter, then walked off briskly in the direction of St. Giles's, pursued by their unseen guardian. They disappeared in the parish hall adjoining the church, and presently three lively young fellows drove up in a large and expensive car. They also went into the hall.

Nobody came out after that, though sounds of music arose on the clear October air as of gentlemen practising for some public appearance. Jasper's musical ear was undeveloped, and the men's voices were muffled by distance; but even with these handicaps a logical mind could easily explain the mystery of all those telephone calls, especially as other gentlemen began drifting toward the parish hall shortly after twelve o'clock with a look about them suggesting that lunch was their object. Satisfied on all these points, and being stirred by pangs of hunger on his own account, Jasper went away. He promised himself, however, that he would lose no time in making the acquaintance of this Mr. Drew who seemed to be getting so chummy with Val.

CHAPTER III

THE program delivered at the luncheon was a great success for everybody. The club members, who had expected nothing more exciting than some nervous young soprano doing the best she could with *The Indian Love Call*, were delighted by the lusty male voices roaring out *The Song of the Vagabonds*, and growing sweetly sentimental over *She Sleeps, My Lady Sleeps*. The visiting singers, glowing with the consciousness of having helped a classmate out of a hole, ate largely of homemade chicken pie and chocolate cake, and absorbed the ringing applause with equal zest. The accompanist was passionately grateful to the quartette's first baritone who had made all this possible; and the baritone was even more happy in being allowed to serve her. The meeting therefore closed with much hand clapping and thanks and compliments for everybody.

"I'll never get over being thankful to you," declared Val, after the guests had gone and she and Anthony lingered to gather up the music.

"Don't worry about that," he responded. "If you knew how much we enjoyed it, you'd realize the obligation is the other way. We used to sing all over the place when we were at college. I shouldn't wonder but we might take it up again and make a permanent thing of it." Then he added in a lower tone, noting the solid phalanx of the Ladies' Guild bearing down upon the wreckage after a long and patient wait in the serving pantry, "Come into the office where we can talk. It looks as though there might be too much woman's work going on around here pretty soon to be comfortable for the bystander."

"Oh, I'm sorry!" The girl's regret was flattering and entirely genuine. She had just begun to wonder why she had not noticed before this that Mr. Drew seemed made of something finer than ordinary clay. "I'm playing again this afternoon at an affair at St. Udolph's, and I've got to go home and dress."

"Must be St. Philomina's tea," he observed, as they turned their steps toward the outer door. "It's usually about this time. That's my family's parish. Mother used to be pretty active in the Guild," hopefully trying to make conversation to detain her. "Maybe you'll run into her this afternoon."

"I'd love to!" Val's tone was enthusiastic, but inwardly she had a sudden pang. Maybe Mrs. Drew wouldn't like her! She wished she had thought of getting a new dress for the tea, and wondered if she had time to get her hair done. If she hurried she might, with a glance at her watch.

Anthony's well-meant effort to prolong the golden moment therefore failed in its purpose, though had he realized what her haste meant he would have been encouraged. When girls begin to get panicky over what their men friends' mothers think of them, it is a hopeful sign for the young men. However, not being psychic, Anthony was denied this consolation, and with dejected eyes he saw her hurry away. Everything he touched lately immediately missed fire, he thought gloomily, watching the slender figure in the smart tweed suit disappear around the corner.

The bright afternoon called loudly to him, suggesting a walk through the gaily-colored woods. Anthony was tempted, but conscience triumphed, and he turned into the parish office. He also had work to do.

It was a small office and not too comfortable, but Dr. Havern had been quite definite this morning, in his jovial way, as to where he expected to find his curate during working hours. The curate didn't mind that particularly. It was a novelty, exciting in its way, to have any kind of an office in which to be found working, and the old-fashioned roll-top desk with its tipsy-looking swivel chair seemed of small moment. Sometime and somewhere Anthony would find the perfect job in the right kind of parish, neither at grand old St. Udolph's on the West Side, wealthy and slightly stuffy, where the best people had worshiped for over half a century, nor yet in this dubious little St. Giles's. Just now he had studying to do and a sermon to write — he doubted if Dr. Havern would ask him to preach at the eleven o'clock services next Sunday, but if he could show results with the Evensong and build up the attendance to something a little better than that pitiful gathering of last night, that would be worth while. It ought not be too hard — the people seemed friendly.

Full of good resolutions, he sat down at the desk with a large pad of paper and a fountain pen, and plunged into *The Preacher's Friend,* one of the books which he had been bringing over this morning when he so miraculously ran into Miss Maddox with the worried frown between her beautiful brows. Surely Providence was taking care of him after all!

Having been drilled in a school which held that sermon writing was the really important work of ministerial life, Anthony seriously bent to his task. Nothing, so one of his professors had said, took precedence over preparation of the Lord's word. So with this dictum in his ears he became so engrossed in his work that it was startling to hear his name pronounced in Dr. Havern's cheerful tones some two hours later.

"Ah, Drew!" Fresh from his postluncheon nap, Dr. Havern was rosy and smiling and more or less at peace with the world. "Working on your sermon, I see. Very good, *very* good indeed! I haven't had a chance to ask you how you got along last night — but I'm sure it was charming," adroitly sidestepping the answer Drew had just opened his mouth to give. "It's good for a young fellow to try his wings a little at these lesser services, just to get in practice for some time when the real emergency comes." He smiled benevolently, and let himself down into the sagging chair.

"Yes, sir," replied Anthony respectfully, with a sidelong glance at the closely written page before him. It had been coming along so nicely after he once got started.

"But it's right to keep on working," went on the rector encouragingly, crossing his legs and making himself as comfortable as the visitors' chair permitted, while he considered what to do with this young man who had been foisted upon him.

Now that he was here, Drew would have to be made to work. The vestrymen had put a fast one over on him while his back was turned, attending that conference week before last. It just went to show why you couldn't trust 'em. The three-day conference had closed on Friday in order that the visiting clergymen might get back to their parishes in good time; but Dr. Havern hadn't been able to make it. The golfing had been so good down there, and some of his friends had been so insistent that he stay over and fill the local pulpit on Sunday (it was nice to give a congregation a chance to get some new ideas), and what with one thing and another it was Wednesday before the rector finally got back to town, to be met with the news that the officious vestrymen had got a callow youth just out of the seminary for the new curate. And when the rector made a reasonable protest, as he had every right to do, Davison, the chairman of that venal body, had the nerve to tell him to his face that he, Dr. Havern, had agreed to it before he went to the conference. Well, a man might agree to a lot of things if he was in a hurry and had his mind full of important matters like that paper he had to read on modern trends, but that was no reason why he should be held to anything as bad as this had turned out to be!

In his resentment, the rector had at first declined even to see the new man, leaving it up to Davison and the rest of them to handle the matter as best they might; but after a while curiosity got the better of dignity, and he relented. Drew was brought in for a brief interview, and though just the look of the fellow had caused some misgivings as to his modern ideas, Dr. Havern had then decided to accept his fate. After all, it did sound rather well to be able to refer to "my assistant." He had really needed some help, as a matter of fact, so long as the curate could be made to understand that he *was* a curate and nothing more. There was plenty of work to be done in the parish which Dr. Havern had never quite got around to doing.

However, it was evident that there would have to be a strict watch kept. It had not escaped the rector at luncheon today that Drew was being lionized just a little. Having turned the program over to Miss Maddox at the eleventh hour, the rector had promptly dismissed it from his mind; and it was with a distinct sense of shock that he saw his new assistant lining up on the stage with the three other young men, and heard them announced as the entertainers for the meeting. Davison, the chairman, had laid special stress on the fact that one of these splendid young singers was "our own Mr. Drew," and the round of applause which followed seemed directed principally at young Drew. Dr. Havern believed that Davison and the hand clappers were only being polite; but for the life of him he could not but feel the noise had an ominous sound.

After that very mediocre singing was over, a few well-chosen sarcasms might have helped a little — something jocular and stinging about the quartette needing only a trifle more polish to do themselves justice, or perhaps a faint shudder when anybody got off key would have had the desired effect. Under the circumstances, however, even that was denied him. Drew might be a reptile, but he certainly picked his friends in high places. Sons of rich bankers and other magnates, who drop their business and pleasure to come and entertain a second-rate club in an obscure uptown parish simply to oblige the curate, are not to be treated to irony and wincing. Dr. Havern's hands were tied.

But in general parish matters, thank goodness, Drew could be kept in his place. All those Mothers' Meetings and Girls' Friendly rummage sales were to be his portion from now on.

Slum visiting, too, and sick calls, with a few notable exceptions. Distribution of the Christmas baskets, of course, Dr. Havern would attend to himself. That was the pastor's work, and it kept before the people the fact that he really was their spiritual father. The poor always appreciated a little attention, and it looked well. Nice feeling all around.

It was high time, then, that a definite schedule of work was mapped out for young Drew, which Dr. Havern now proceeded to do. As they were recited in Dr. Havern's unctuous voice, Anthony jotted them down on his sermon paper, noting ruefully that his high calling as a preacher seemed to be a dead letter in this scheme.

"Oh, of course, a few words on Sunday evenings," Dr. Havern conceded. "Anything you feel like saying, though nobody comes Sunday night who amounts to anything, so you won't have to do a lot of preparation. It won't take up too much of your time from other things." He glanced at his watch, then began hoisting himself from the cavernous chair. "Another thing: you'd better take the early morning Communion service, too. Eight o'clock, as you know, except on the First Sunday of the month. You'll get along splendidly."

He smiled again, begged his assistant not to stay too late on his first day, and then went to get ready for an hour's practice in putting. The Golf Club hadn't yet fixed a date for the fall tournament, but Dr. Havern meant to be ready whenever the call came.

Let to himself, Anthony quietly read through his manuscript, referred to his Testament to be sure his quotations were right, put in a couple of commas, and then laid the sheets carefully in his brief case. "Another hour's work ought to make it a pretty good sermon," he said half aloud, and suddenly found that his voice was shaking. He got up and began to pace the little office while he reviewed the high lights in the interview just past in which the rector had outlined a pretty comprehensive program for an unusually active parish.

At the time of his appointment to St. Giles's, Anthony had a distinct impression that in clerical circles Dr. Havern was regarded as one of the tame variety. Indeed he had noticed faint grins accompanying the good wishes of some of the older hands whom he had told of his new job, and one of them had said flatly that if Anthony was looking for work, St. Giles's wasn't the place to find it. "Not but that it needs some," this outspoken one had added grimly.

With the enthusiasm of youth and a certain loyalty to his appointment, Anthony had rather discounted these belittling smiles and hints. Not that there could be any jealousy among the clergy, of course, but perhaps the men attached to the wealthier and more important churches, or even the ones in the slums, might not understand the system which applied to what was practically a suburban district made up of people of moderate means for the most part.

Yesterday, however, had been illuminating in more ways than one. St. Giles's was, as a building, very much on the small order and with a limited seating capacity; but even with that the pews were far from being overfilled at the morning service, while in the evening the crowd was practically nonexistent. Furthermore, in reading off the announcements before beginning his sermon, Dr. Havern had very little to bring up in the way of parish activities. The most outstanding of these had been the Men's Club luncheon of today and an outing for indigent children sponsored by one of the downtown churches which had sent an invitation to the poor of St. Giles's. Beyond these and a few passionate words about the overdue coal bill, the rector seemed to have very little to bring up before touching off the fireworks which composed his main discourse on the text: "I have compassion on the multitude."

So when Dr. Havern had come in this afternoon and started chanting this litany of chores for his assistant to fit the needs of every variety of parishioner from the Old Ladies' Home to the Tiny Tots' Bible School, benevolent societies and rescue societies, church suppers and sewing classes ("you can work up something there" was the refrain after each verse), it sounded odd from the lips of a man whose motto hitherto had appeared to be "anything for a quiet life."

In fact, as he remembered certain inflections in the rich voice, and certain glints in the prominent eyes, as if the rector were taking this means of working off a little quiet spite, Anthony began to sense a hostility in that quarter not explainable by anything of which he could accuse himself. Yesterday after dinner, under direct questioning he had expressed surprise at Dr. Havern's brand of theology, though he had no recollection of saying anything critical. In their meetings since then nothing had come up between rector and curate which was in any way out of the common, though (here a light began dimly to dawn) maybe Dr. Havern had thought it undignified for his assistant to appear as one of the entertainers at the luncheon. Well, if that was it, and he had come in afterward to lay out a staggering work program as a punishment, Anthony thought it a pretty poor business.

It wasn't that he minded the work, the young man insisted, glaring at an outdated map of Europe on the wall. God knew that was why he was here — why he had been ordained. He knew that as a beginner he was supposed to do all the odd jobs and take the bumps. He wasn't even sore because the rector had prohibited his preaching at the Morning Prayer —

"But he might at least have asked me decently!" he muttered, halting at the window to scowl blackly at two children and a dog who were playing in the yard next door. "Nobody at Evensong who matters! How would he know whether I'm a rotten preacher or not? He's never heard me. Oh, well," he sat down at the desk again, "what's the use? I'm not going to be here forever. Wonder how they got on at St. Philomina's this afternoon."

This proved a cheering speculation, and under its influence he was able to put in another hour in the office working out a schedule which would take in as much of Dr. Havern's program as was humanly possible. It might be interesting at that.

The clock in the steeple overhead boomed out the hour of five, and he took a survey of the neat tabulation he had drawn up on the sermon paper. A most conservative schedule, he thought, as he gathered up his books and papers and decided to call it a day. Dr. Havern had said not to stay too long; and while Anthony was speedily learning that the rector was given to figures of speech, and might object to too liberal an interpretation of the word "early," he believed that five o'clock was a conservative hour.

With the pleasant consciousness of having been tried by fire and coming out none the worse, Anthony swung up the street with his bulging brief case where he had laid the embryo of his little sermon which the rector had rejected and cast out this afternoon. Well, so far as that went, he might get along and finish it according to plan, and deliver it next Sunday night. The rector had given him enough scope there with his "anything you feel like saying." All right, then, the faithful few would have Anthony's best.

"I beg your pardon," said a voice in his ear. "Is this the Reverend Mr. Drew, the new minister at St. Giles's?"

Anthony turned to face a smallish young man with pale hair and eyes, and a sharply inquisitive nose, who had slipped up beside him noiselessly, and now addressed him in a high-pitched voice.

"Why — yes," replied Drew. "At least I'm the curate."

"I thought so." The stranger nodded with satisfaction. "I don't belong to your outfit myself, but I'm kind of interested in what goes on there. My cousin's the organist, you know — my name's Maddox, same as hers. Jasper Maddox," he added to clear up any mysteries, and held out a small bony hand which Anthony found clammy to the touch.

"I'll walk on with you," continued Jasper, beginning to move in the direction which Anthony had taken. "I saw you talking to Val this morning, and thought I might as well introduce myself. I don't hold with all of her ideas about religion; but she's my cousin, and all that concerns her concerns me, you understand."

"Er — naturally," replied Anthony vaguely, as the other paused, seeming to expect some praise for this display of clannish spirit. "I enjoyed hearing Miss Maddox play at the services yesterday," with a warm feeling about his heart as he remembered that wasn't the only time he had heard her play.

"Oh, she's all right, I guess." Apparently Jasper's interest in his cousin did not extend to her musicianship. "I read about your ordination in the papers," he went on. "Made quite a time of it, didn't you? Your mother fainting all over the place —she all right now?"

"You've got the wrong Drew," replied Anthony, with an amused recollection of his mother's happy complaisance on that wonderful day. No fainting fits for Mother! "There was another Drew in my class, and I believe his mother was knocked out during the ceremonies. They're long, you know, and it was a hot day. But they said she was all right afterward."

"Oh!" Jasper was disappointed. "Well, what became of him, then?" he demanded truculently, seeming to hold it against Anthony for not being able to make the newspaper headlines.

"Lives down the valley somewhere," Anthony found himself answering apologetically. "I was out of town some weeks last summer, and I sort of lost track of him. But I can find out, if you like."

"Doesn't make any difference," returned Jasper in a nettled tone, irritated to be caught in a mistake, however slight. "I just asked." Then after a short pause he asked inquisitively, "Just where do you come from, then? St. Timothy's?" with a disdainful glance at the other's clerical collar.

"St. Udolph's," replied Anthony a little stiffly, annoyed in his turn though he had no love for St. Timothy's. "Why? Do you know St. Timothy's?"

"Who, me? No, indeed!" Jasper firmly repudiated that little gem of ecclesiastical architecture and its ritualistic congregation. "I wouldn't go near that place, not if you paid me! In fact, I don't like your St. Giles's or —" His tone changed, and he went on thoughtfully, "Did you say St. Udolph's? Then you must live on Cyrus Avenue or some of those joints."

For a moment he wavered uncertainly, wanting to get up on any occasion and denounce any religion not his own, and at the same time slightly overcome by this contact with a scion of a family from the exclusive West Side. Young Mr. Drew of the valley Drews, was to have got a rousing blast for his own good about the mummeries of his religious ritual; but a Cyrus Avenue Drew was a different matter. Snobbery would probably have won, except that Anthony unconsciously helped turned the scale.

"Well, I suppose we'll have to stand it, even if you don't like us." For Val's sake he had tried to be civil, though puzzled to account for any kinship between her lovely self and this queer young man; but by this time he was willing to dispense with the society that had been wished on him. He glanced up the street for help, and saw a bus just entering the block above. He eyed it earnestly as he went on, "Maybe it's just as well that we don't all think the same way.

"No, it isn't a good thing!" Jasper was himself again. "And your outfit had better take warning before you get any worse. You're getting too much popery into your Church. The time will come when we Protestants will have to rise up against the Great Harlot, and if you people haven't got back to the old-time religion, you'll wish you had! Did Val ever tell you how she nearly—"

"Sorry, Mr. Maddox." Driven to desperation by this reference to Val, Anthony raised his own voice to drown Jasper's thinner pipe. "I have to leave you. Some other time." He waved a compelling hand to the bus.

"But I wanted to tell you—" began Jasper, just missing as he clutched at the other's arm.

"Sorry," Anthony repeated firmly, swinging on to the bus which had stopped at his signal. Before Jasper had time to realize he could follow and continue this interesting talk on the bus as well as anywhere, it had rumbled away leaving him standing on the sidewalk.

As they rolled along, Anthony tried to shake off his irritation over the late interview, and found solace in thinking that at least their paths need never cross again, if *he* had anything to do with it. Just how Valerie Maddox happened to be related to this boy remained a mystery, but, of course, she couldn't help it. Practically every family had some odd characters in it somewhere — there was Aunt Maude in his own, for instance. And at least this Jasper had been shut up before he started gossiping about his cousin, Anthony congratulated himself, in happy ignorance that in stopping these confidences he had cut himself off from a bit of history about Val which would have interested him keenly.

The bus had gone several blocks before it occurred to Anthony to find out its destination, and he was pleased to note that it took him within easy walking distance of his home on the famous Cyrus Avenue. He had every intention, when he left the office, of going back to his flat and spending the evening on some research work on the subject of recreation centers and juvenile delinquency, two points which Dr. Havern had spoken of this afternoon as needing attention; but this happy accident of the right bus coming along made it seem like a leading. Perhaps it was right that he should look in on his parents this evening. Also he wanted to know what his mother thought of Miss Maddox, in case they had met at St. Philomina's Guild tea.

His mother, large and calm and handsome, received him as lovingly as if he had been away for many months.

"But you look tired, dear," she said, searching his face with her mild hazel eyes. "Don't let Dr. Havern work you too hard. There's no necessity for your killing yourself."

Having no mind to carry tales home this early, Anthony disclaimed this at once. He had only just come from the parish office where he had spent some time in going through old and dusty records, and so was looking less fresh than was proper. Then, giving her an additional hug, he changed the subject.

"How was St. Philomina's tea?" he asked. "Or did you go this afternoon?"

"Of course, she went!" Great-aunt Maude snapped at him in her sharp voice which was not unlike a parrot's. She looked something like a parrot, too, with her small, hooked nose and beady eyes, as she huddled in her armchair near the tiny wood fire in the grate. She was a widow and had made her home with the family as far back as Anthony could remember.

[59]

"Never could see why Caroline thinks she has to spend her time on silly things like that. All that gabble and chatter about nothing. People you don't care if you never see again. They've got nothing to say to you that hasn't been said a million times already. Wouldn't hurt if it had never been said at all!" She emphasized this speech with a rap of her ebony cane on the floor. "Come over here, young man, and let me look at you."

Murmuring that he was afraid his make-up wasn't on right, Anthony obediently came and dropped on the hassock at her feet. The sharp old eyes twinkled as they looked him over, whether with mirth or malice no one could say.

"Yes," she said after a long moment of scrutiny which her nephew found hard to endure. "This week end's done something to you, and I don't believe it's just a dirty face, either. (It is dirty, too.) You've grown up. What happened?"

He took time to consider this, smiling up at her and wondering if the terrible little old woman really had second sight, and if there would be any way of keeping information from her when she had made up her mind to have it. He was not surprised that the two women had noted a change in him since their parting last Saturday noon, since he had packed enough new emotions and experiences in that period to make the Anthony Drew of forty-eight hours ago seem a mere child just out of the nursery. Still he was uneasy that his face was giving him away like that.

"I suppose a wage slave does show his age pretty soon," he said as lightly as he could make it without annoying the old lady too much. "I had stage fright last evening before I started my sermon, Mother. Do you ever feel like that when you have to talk to your clubs? I thought I was used to talking on my feet, but the minute I got into that pulpit and realized I was actually there, an ordained priest — funny!" he ended musingly, living again that sensation.

"No," replied his mother, who hadn't a nerve in her body. "Women's clubs, you know, are just — women. It doesn't bother me to talk to them. I'd rather do that than stand in the receiving line for three hours — my poor feet! I was so glad today that I wasn't doing anything at all. I just had tea and then came home."

"And yet you keep on going," muttered Aunt Maude. "You'll never learn sense any younger. But I'm not through with Anthony yet," raising her voice and returning to the topic which he had hoped was gone by. "How do you like being a wage slave, and what do you do? I hope they make you work, though I don't see what work ministers do."

"Never mind, Aunt Maude," interposed Mrs. Drew. "Anthony will do nicely, I know. He always does, don't you, dear?"

He laughed a little at this and, unfolding himself from the hassock, went over to sit on the arm of her chair.

"Still think your little boy's all right, don't you?" putting his arm across her plump shoulders. "I certainly will have to do nicely, not to let you down." Then noting that the old lady was still waiting impatiently, he gave them a detailed account of his two days in office, from the settling into his apartment to the preaching of his maiden sermon.

"Then today I had a talk with Dr. Havern and we figured out a program of work for me. He's been needing some help, I think. By the way, you should have heard your child sing at the luncheon!" He gave them what he hoped was a humorous description of the quartette's work, and the relief it had been to the accompanist. He flattered himself that he had brought in Val's name casually and cleverly during this recital. Not that he would mind telling his mother about her, but it did seem a little premature to have his tender young affections subjected to Aunt Maude's comments.

"I think I met that young lady this afternoon. Such a sweet girl, too," said his mother in her comfortable voice. "She was playing at the tea, very nicely, too; but everybody was talking, the way they always do through a piano number. I was sitting where I could see her face, and she looked up and smiled to herself as if — well, I don't know what she was thinking about except that she wasn't amused. And so I went over to speak to her afterward and tell her how much I liked it. I asked her name and where she had studied, and then she said she was the organist at St. Giles's, so, of course, I asked her about you.

[61]

She said they were all so pleased to have you there." Mrs. Drew's smile was the happy one of a mother who has learned that outsiders confirm her own judgment about having the most wonderful son in the world.

"You wouldn't fool me, would you, Mother?" Anthony hoped they would think his burning face was the result of personal modesty.

Aunt Maude cackled at this.

"Caroline can fool anybody," she said, hitching her chin by way of emphasis, "even herself. Don't get to feeling too cocky about yourself, young man. It's dangerous. Those people up there may start out all right, but they can turn on you if you aren't careful."

"He won't do anything he shouldn't," Mrs. Drew said serenely. "You musn't worry about him. You can stay here tonight, can't you, dear?" turning her attention to her baby and privately wondering how it happened that she had such handsome children. Anthony was every bit as good looking as Howard, though in a different way, of course. Mrs. Drew had no favorites among her three children; she just idolized them all. "Are you comfortable in your little apartment?"

Anthony said he was very comfortable indeed. He regretted he could stay only for dinner, as he had a lot of notes to go over tonight — "but I'm not working myself to death," he added hastily, seeing the alarm in her eyes. "Just some references that Dr. Havern gave me this afternoon."

"I must meet Dr. Havern some day soon." Mrs. Drew's anxiety was soothed. "That is, I did know him slightly, years ago before I was married. He used to be one of the curates at St. Udolph's, but I doubt if he'd remember me, and I don't remember too much about him except that he seemed an agreeable young man, and very conscientious, I'm sure."

"I remember him, too," said Aunt Maude. "I never thought him especially conscientious, but I agree with you that he was out to please."

"Oh, Aunt Maude!" Mrs. Drew was gently reproachful. "You shouldn't say things like that about a clergyman!"

"Clergyman or not," sniffed Aunt Maude, "he was able to look out after number one. I'm surprised that he didn't get himself made bishop or something, instead of buying his way into that stupid little parish out in the rural district. How does it look out there, Anthony? Shabby, genteel — or what?"

"Oh, no! It's suburban, if you like, but very pretty and green. Nice houses and nice people, and the church is good looking. You and Mother will have to come out and see me after I get settled. Bring Muriel, if she can take time off from the baby, and I'll give you tea." Then reverting to his rector's past history, in which he was burningly interested, "What did Dr. Havern do when you knew him?"

"He was just there at St. Udolph's," replied his mother. "He used to come to our teas and things. It was about the time we started St. Philomina's Guild, I remember. He really was very nice, Aunt Maude."

"I still say he knew on which side his bread was buttered." Aunt Maude gave another smart rap on the floor with her cane. "He knew it was good policy to be friendly with that crowd of young women — got himself invited out to dinners. Doing the same thing now, I shouldn't wonder, with those nice respectable people Anthony likes so much. Havern wasn't like that young scamp Ranley. You remember him, Caroline? Always getting into hot water, but somehow I liked him."

"Yes," replied Caroline thoughtfully. "I remember Mr. Ranley. He was a little extreme about some things. I never felt comfortable with him for some reason. I wonder what became of him."

Aunt Maude cackled again.

"The funny part of that," she said ghoulishly, "is that Ranley was made bishop of some place, Chicago or California or somewhere. It began with a C, I think, unless it was Seattle. Anyhow, he got himself promoted, while Havern is still just a country parson. I know you don't like me to call him that, Anthony, and it's just as well you've decided to make the best of things."

The entrance of Mr. Drew, accompanied by his older son

Howard, saved Anthony from any further going over by the inquisition; and though immensely intrigued by the women's reminiscences about Dr. Havern, he gladly rose to meet the newcomers.

"Well! And how is the Bishop of St. Giles's?" Howard made a deep reverence to his brother, then smote him on the back affectionately.

"How are you, my boy?" was his father's less spectacular greeting, holding out his hand.

Caroline Drew gazed fondly at the three men as they stood chatting. Anthony was more like his father, she decided, both in looks and build, while Howard took after her side of the house. She was glad they were all tall, and it was wonderful to have two sons like that. Also it was lovely to have a daughter like Muriel, so beautiful and charming, and such a good mother to little Jeff. Caroline thought she had enough blessings for twenty women.

The Drews made quite an occasion of this casual little visit of Anthony. Howard telephoned his wife that he would not be home for dinner, as he was feasting with the prodigal son; and though Muriel had to decline her mother's invitation because of little Jeff's teething problems, she sent her love and promised to pour tea for him at his apartment whenever he said the word. And when he left, early enough to get in a couple of hours' work before going to bed, Anthony felt he was turning his back on all the old peace and security of his boyhood. As Aunt Maude had astutely put it, he was grown up.

CHAPTER IV

DR. HAVERN had never seriously looked upon himself as an agent of Cupid, even in the springtime when weddings were so delightfully frequent. Furthermore, the last thing he would have planned was the doing of a gratuitously good turn for his curate. But the fact remains that the rector's cavalier dumping of the Men's Club program in his organist's lap at the last minute had consequences far beyond anything he could have hoped for had he been the curate's dearest friend and well wisher.

Left to itself it is a question if Anthony's romance could have gone along so rapidly and smoothly as the final results showed. He, of course, had gone down before Val's loveliness within the first ten seconds of their meeting; but on the other hand Val had her mind occupied with a different matter just then, and for a brief space she had thought little about him. While no one would be rash enough to say that in time she would not have succumbed to the young man's undeniable charm, he might easily have languished much longer if Fate, cleverly disguised as the rector, had not stepped in.

In her distress that morning, with less than two hours to produce something for the club which would not disgrace her — in fact, to produce anything at all — Anthony's prompt help had stirred Val's gratitude to its depths. She had instantly thought him the most understanding person she knew, and now that she looked at him closely, probably the handsomest. Also a man's ability to deliver never hurts his chances with a lady. The rest was simple. Gratitude is only a step away from a warmer sentiment, and Val had practically gone the distance by the time she had rushed to the hairdresser's to be put in shape to meet Anthony's mother.

Even as he had predicted, their respective jobs brought them together quite naturally and often, and to very good purpose. While October flamed its royal way through the countryside, many a happy hour was spent by these two in the parish office, planning a treat for the choir, a benefit concert for the Girls' Friendly Society, or even just going over the hymns for Sunday. Any topic will do when one is young and twenty, and in love.

There was also opportunity for the exchange of confidences about their own hopes, ideals, and aversions, in most of which they happily found great likeness of opinion. It might be noted,

[65]

though, in these talks, that no active criticism was ever made about the rector and his ways. In their public appearances together Dr. Havern might sometimes be said to take his curate up a little shortly if the junior made any suggestions; but as Anthony soon learned to keep his mouth shut, on the whole their relations seemed normal. Being behind the scenes, however, Val had a good many chances to discover the real state of affairs, and her indignation burned high when she saw the slights and belittlings and criticisms to which the rector treated his assistant.

Anthony took it all very quietly, making no comment or complaint even when he and Val were most confidential, and Val hesitated to express herself too freely on a subject which he seemed to avoid. Val had her own reticences. She often wondered what he would say if she ever told him about her excursion into the forbidden paths of popery, but decided it was not necessary to put him to the test.

Anthony gave his tea party one sunny afternoon at the end of October, inviting his mother and sister and great-aunt to meet some of the ladies of St. Giles's, so he said, and his family obligingly came. Due to the smallness of his quarters the young man wisely decided to keep the company of a size to fit his little sitting room, arguing that it would be impossible to ask certain of his parish without giving offense to the great majority who would be left out. Therefore his guest list was limited severely to Val and her mother and Mrs. Havern.

In asking permission for taking the afternoon off he used great tact by inviting Mrs. Havern, and the rector was so gracious as to say: "Quite all right, Drew. Take the afternoon by all means. You can make it up some other time," and added that he might look in later himself to meet Drew's good mother.

From this it can be seen that Dr. Havern did not yet grasp the social implications of this modest little tea. Mrs. Drew was unquestionably a good mother, but heretofore nobody had ever thought of patronizing Mrs. Livingston Drew of Cyrus Avenue.

In his outraged state of mind at the time of his curate's appointment, the rector had declined even to talk about the interloper's antecedents, even to the extent of looking at his credentials. Since it had been the vestry-men's idea to get a curate in the first place, then let them take the full responsibility! So far as he was concerned, Anthony Drew was only a name, not too pretty, for a most obnoxious young squirt just out of the seminary, and the rector didn't care which side of the tracks he hailed from; but later, when he had cooled off to the extent of allowing the squirt to be presented, Dr. Havern had softened still further and invited Drew to dinner that first Sunday. When notifying his wife to expect a guest, the rector had confessed, with perhaps a little pride, that he hadn't the faintest idea who the fellow was, but that he had decided to do the handsome thing by him just this once. *"Noblesse oblige,* and all that," he said with a shrug.

To his surprise, Mrs. Havern, who read the newspapers, seemed to know all about young Mr. Drew. She, like Jasper Maddox, had devoured the item about that Mrs. Drew from down the valley, who had fainted so spectacularly at her son's ordination; and (again like Jasper) Mrs. Havern had leaped to the conclusion that her husband's new curate was the same ambitious young fellow who had worked his way through college by stoking furnaces and washing dishes. This being fully explained to him, Dr. Havern was more than ever convinced that the invitation to Sunday dinner would have worked off all the obligations imposed upon his rank; hence his superior manner some weeks later in speaking of Mrs. Livingston Drew as "your good mother."

Fortunately for the success of the tea party Mrs. Havern found she had another engagement. Hoping that something would come up to prevent the rector also from carrying out his threat to drop in, Anthony lunched on a cup of coffee and rushed away to get ready. By means of much persuasion and a large tip he induced a woman to come in to clean the apartment while he stowed away his books and shoes and pipes, then ran out to buy some roses.

It was a very nice party, too. Muriel brought in some delicate sandwiches and little cakes for him, and poured the tea with as much grace as if the whole of the fashionable West Side were present. Val played Debussy and Scarlatti on the tiny piano to a sympathetic audience, and Mrs. Drew and Mrs. Maddox found many points of common interest in their federation meetings and housekeeping concerns. Even Aunt Maude forbore to contradict anybody, and in general behaved like the sweet gentle old lady which she emphatically was not. To make it all quite perfect Dr. Havern either changed his mind about looking in or else forgot it entirely. After waiting for him a decent time, the party then went over to see the church and Anthony's office in the parish house, pausing dutifully at the rectory, and learned from Savannah that "bofe Misto an' Miz Hav'n had done gone out earlier in the afternoon, she didn't know where." The time of their return was therefore a sealed mystery, and she flashed a smile at the curate as if she could read in his mind that he thought this all very satisfactory. In general, Savannah and Anthony understood each other.

Val and her mother went home then, while the Drew ladies insisted upon going back to the apartment to clear away the tea things. This was done over Anthony's protest, though he grew reconciled when he heard the gratifying things they had to say about the other two guests, as Muriel washed and her mother dried the thick cups provided by the landlord.

"We must ask Mrs. Maddox and her daughter over to dinner some time soon," continued Mrs. Drew, inspecting the shelves critically before she decided they were clean enough to have the dishes put back on them. "And Mr. Maddox, of course. I'd like to meet him."

Muriel warmly seconded the motion, and even Aunt Maude remarked quite seriously that the Maddox child was the first girl she had met in countless years who could talk to an old woman without acting as if she thought her a congenital idiot.

"I know I'm in my dotage," said the old lady, "but I don't like to be reminded of it all the time."

Anthony felt he had a wonderful family.

"Well, Mother," said Muriel as they drove away some fifteen minutes later, leaving a much gratified host waving to them from the curb, "I suppose you know that's your new daughter-in-law?"

"Oh, yes," replied Mother tranquilly. "The dear boy looks so happy, too, doesn't he? I'm sure everything will turn out all right, bless him! But I do think we should have seen Dr. Havern. He said he was coming. Perhaps something important turned up."

Aunt Maude sniffed, but for once made no comment; and as Muriel began talking about little Jeff's new tooth, the subject passed.

Having thus pleasantly settled the matter among themselves, the Drew family were in nowise upset when Anthony came in a few days later with the news that he and Val were engaged. He was soundly kissed and congratulated, and Val was promptly brought over to the house to receive her share of kindness and cordiality. It was noticed by both young people, with some embarrassment, that no surprise was shown in either the Drew or the Maddox families; but as the welcome was genuinely warm on both sides, naturally there was no complaint made by "the children," as they were called.

For reasons which seemed good it had been thought best by the engaged pair that no public announcement be made as yet until Anthony's prospects were in a better condition. In his secret opinion the St. Giles's job was an almost complete failure, and he had settled it with himself to start looking for something else right after the first of the year. For the present he was saying nothing, and without a word being exchanged between them Val understood and agreed. So beyond a quiet little family dinner at the Drews' as an engagement party, nothing else was to be done for the time being.

When giving his mother a convenient date for the party, Anthony had picked an evening which seemed free from meetings, social or religious, and on Sunday morning he had notified his superior that he would be dining at home Thursday. There was no reason whatever why he should not go, but in the spirit of maintaining discipline Dr. Havern had taken it very much amiss.

"We can't have too much running around this way, Drew," he said severely, closing the wardrobe door with a bang after putting away his surplice and stole. "Your duties here ought to keep you well enough occupied that you needn't find the time hanging too heavily on your hands."

Anthony counted ten, then said mildly that he was arranging the schedule so that nothing would suffer. "The coal committee said they wanted to postpone their meeting until the following Thursday. Everything is shot to pieces this week on account of the election, you know."

The rector threw his overcoat across his shoulders and prepared to go to the house. "All right," he said finally, assuming an injured air. "I suppose I can carry on alone again. Take your evening!" He stalked out, and Anthony telephoned his mother that Thursday would be free.

It very nearly wasn't, though. As the weeks had gone by and Dr. Havern found time to brood over his wrongs, he had become more and more convinced that this curate business was all nonsense. The parish had been getting along very well as it was. However, granting for the sake of argument that the rector did need help (and after all, a man shouldn't be asked to kill himself for the good of others), at least the vestrymen should have got somebody who knew something instead of this inexperienced schoolboy.

On top of that, young Drew was beginning to take a good deal on himself, getting people to call up and ask for him by name, and acting as if he thought himself indispensable. The vestrymen, too, seemed to think they'd found a paragon. Only last evening Davison had been so tactless as to talk about how zealous and capable the fellow was, and said they were all to be congratulated on having found him. Fortunately Drew wasn't present to hear this sickening puff, so there was no real harm done, but it just went to show!

The question was, therefore: could or could he not fire Drew before things got any worse? He really could dismiss his curate for cause — the fellow made enough mistakes for that. On the other hand, if Davison and the rest of them were making a pet of him there might be some awkwardness. The best course, probably, was the old tried and true method of having things so uncomfortable around the place that Drew would decide he couldn't stand it any longer, and would voluntarily quit. He could then hand in his resignation and nobody would be the wiser. That sort of thing was being done every day in any business office in the land, and in the long run it was really kinder.

Acting upon this principle, Dr. Havern suddenly appeared on Thursday morning with a list of things calculated to take up the curate's whole day, leaving not a minute to spare. The rector had gone to a good deal of trouble to root through his desk and hunt out letters needing answers these many weeks. He also required lists and statements of every kind of statistics known to a parish, which the curate had to write out on the broken-down old typewriter. He devised errands to be run and people to be telephoned, and in general had outlined a day's work that would take considerable gimp out of this fresh young nobody and teach him to go to dinners!

However, nothing of this was evident in the young man's demeanor that evening as he sat at his father's hospitable board and received the congratulations of the company assembled. These, of course, were only the immediate families of the contracting parties, including Muriel's husband and Howard's wife, with Uncle Billy Maddox, Val's bachelor uncle, to balance Aunt Maude numerically.

"Is there any reason why we can't drink a toast to these youngsters?" The senior Mr. Drew lifted his glass filled with the best from his cellar. "Anthony, my son, if you have any scruples—"

"Then keep them to myself," finished the young man, flushing as all eyes were turned upon him. "I assure you, Dad, I haven't any, and we'll both be much obliged, won't we, Val?"

The girl nodded shyly.

"Very well, then." Mr. Drew made a courtly bow to the young people, then looked at Mr. Maddox. "To our children. May they never be anything but happy."

The toast was drunk joyfully by everybody.

"I don't see why they should not be happy." Mrs. Drew beamed affectionately upon them both. "They have so much in common — the church, you know, and all that. You think alike about so many things, don't you, Valerie dear?"

"Yes, I — I think we do." Val surprised herself by stammering. "At least we hate the same people," coloring brightly at the laughter which followed this naïve statement.

"Oh, Val!" Her mother laughed with the rest, but was mildly shocked. She had been faintly upset at Anthony's acquiescence in the use of champagne when the toast was drunk, though, of course, it was at his father's table. Mrs. Maddox herself had only touched the glass to her lips, without so much as tasting its contents. "He doesn't seem as much like a minister as I thought he did," she confided to her husband.

"I'd say that is a bond between them," observed Aunt Maude loudly. "Any two people can agree to like something obvious, but it takes a real meeting of minds to find a discriminating hate in common. I drink to your health, Valerie, all by yourself." Which she proceeded to do on the "bottoms up" principle.

After dinner the company kindly gave the young couple a chance to slip away for a few minutes to themselves. Anthony found a comfortable chair for Val in front of the library fire, but was himself too happy to sit. He paced up and down the room as he always did under stress of emotion, and told her over and over how wonderful she was and how much his family liked her.

"Even Aunt Maude is strong for you, and that, young woman, means you're good!" pausing in front of her to give her an approving look on his own account before he moved on again.

Feeling foolishly happy and excited, Val laughed as she thanked him, and gazed up at his goodly proportions with adoring eyes. Under cover of her handkerchief she gave herself a quiet pinch to see if she was dreaming. It couldn't be true that she was really sitting here in this beautiful room, actually engaged to Anthony! A month ago she had never even seen him. How *could* she have lived all this time without knowing that such a wonderful person existed!

[72]

And how sweet everybody had been, drinking toasts in her honor and giving her such a generous welcome into the family. The Livingston Drews were well known as shining social lights; and while not so overpoweringly conscious of social layers as Dr. Havern or even her distant cousin Jasper, Val knew she was an extremely lucky girl to have had such a cordial reception into the fold. Then she thought pridefully that her own family was nice, too, with a few minor exceptions. Dad and Mother were all that anybody would want in parents, and Uncle Billy was swell, and some of the Fortunes — well, in fact almost all of them except that awful Jasper. Val's spirits took quite a drop when she remembered that youth who had been her bane from childhood.

Jasper Maddox was the sort of person who is born to make trouble as surely as the sparks fly upward. Sometimes it happened merely through his curiosity and desire to know everything and have a finger in every pie, in which case it might not get beyond simple confusion and bewilderment on the part of the people whose affairs he investigated; but one couldn't count on it. If he took offense at anything (and he was very touchy) he was likely to turn malicious, and nobody knew what he would do or where it would end.

Val had earnestly begged her parents not to tell the family of her engagement until it was ready to be published to the world, not that she had anything against her kinfolk but just that she dreaded having Jasper get hold of the news. She had made a concession in favor of Uncle Billy Maddox, Dad's younger brother, who, being a bachelor and a trustworthy person, would be able to keep the secret; but, for the rest, they'd have to wait until such time as her fiancé decided to make it public. Jasper simply must not be allowed to find out about it and start his usual procedure.

Still, Anthony was entitled to know what kind of a family he was getting into, and now was perhaps the best opportunity she would ever have to break the news to him. She was not responsible for Jasper in any degree, but he was somebody who simply had to be reckoned with. All his life he had stuck to her like a leech, and there was no reason to suppose he would change his system now. And if Anthony wanted to back out of the engagement when he learned what he could expect, she thought with grim humor, she couldn't blame him.

"I love to hear you say that." She gave a little gulp, but went on bravely. Her voice had lost much of its usual gay lilt, and he glanced at her in surprise. "I'm afraid, though, I've got to tell you something that may make a difference."

Anthony stopped dead in his tracks, looking startled as well he might.

"For heaven's sake, Val, you haven't anything you've got to tell me! What are you talking about?"

"Oh, yes, I have," she persisted gamely. Then she colored up and laughed a little. "Well, perhaps not so bad as that, but at least it's something I should have told you before now. It's this: I'm afraid you'll find some of my relatives aren't as nice as yours are. I never told you about Cousin Susan and—and—"

"And Jasper," he interrupted, manfully suppressing a desire to laugh wildly as he came to sit on the arm of her chair. "I know the worst, darling. I met Jasper weeks ago, and I've been dodging him ever since. Of course, if I ever have to kill him, you can start worrying; but aside from that I can't see what difference he makes to us."

"I know it sounds crazy." Val was feeling more and more ridiculous, but she stuck to it. "You don't know that Jasper. He isn't just an inconvenient relative like his mother. Cousin Susan was a nut and a gossip and a frightful bore (poor soul, she died a couple of months ago), but Jasper is an active menace. He's always rooting around to find out something on everybody. I feel awful in wishing him on you!"

"He can't do anything," repeated Anthony, allowing an amused grin to appear. "Anything that counts, I mean. If you've managed to live through it, I imagine I can. What does he do, anyway?"

"Not much of anything—in the way of work, I mean. His father—Cousin Charlie was a second cousin of my father— left them pretty well off when he died, and Jasper is the only child, so he gets all of his mother's share, and he's not in any kind of business. He spends most of his time (when he's not pestering people) in working with some religious sect — the High and Holy Somethings, I forget the name. He wants to be one of their ministers, and he keeps talking about getting back to pure religion, whatever that is. He says he's a Protestant, but I never heard him say anything about loving God or doing good to anybody. It's all about 'rising in their might and beating the unrighteous flat to the ground' — rabid things like that."

"He said something like that to me, and I'll admit I resented his 'we Protestants.' I didn't like being put in the same category as he is; though for that matter, our Church seems to be in his black books. He told me there was too much popery about it." Anthony laughed at the recollection, expecting her to do likewise; but she only regarded him thoughtfully.

"'Too much popery,'" she repeated slowly. "I wonder how he got that idea."

"How does he get any of his ideas?" Anthony was growing a bit fed up on Jasper. "By the way, Miss Maddox, did we come in here just to talk about the hope of the High-and-Holies, or what?"

She roused herself then and laughed with him; but by that time it was too late to go back to the pleasanter subject which had held them in the first part of the conference. A discreet knock sounded just then, and Muriel hurried in immediately after.

"Sorry, kids," she said, closing the door carefully behind her. "I hate to tell you to break it up, but Mother thinks you ought to know that Dr. Llewellyn is out there, and that you'd better come out and see him. I don't agree, myself," as Anthony looked pained, "but that's just Mother's idea. She sent me to tell you."

"I suppose we'll have to go out and talk to him," Anthony got up reluctantly, "though I don't see why he couldn't pick out some other evening to land. You know him, don't you, Val?"

"I never met him, though I've seen him lots of times." Val obediently followed him to the door. "He seems very nice —"

"Yes, he's all right," grumbled Anthony, "but I still think he might have stayed at home tonight, anyway."

"It won't hurt you," said his sister. "He was always nice enough to you. Who knows, he might even find you a better parish if you ever got tired of St. Giles's."

Anthony's reply was a low inarticulate sound in his throat which might mean anything.

"You don't have to moo at me like that!" protested Muriel in a whisper as they arrived at the drawing room door. "He just might!"

Val decided she liked the newcomer on sight. He was tall and well set up, probably somewhere in the vigorous fifties, with a frank, unlined, handsome face, and a manner that dominated without being overpowering. He was just then standing in the midst of the family group who gave every sign of pleasure at seeing him, while he apologized for breaking in on what was plainly a party.

"I couldn't pass your house, Mrs. Drew, without coming in for just a moment," he was saying with that rare smile of his which was largely responsible for keeping St. Udolph's the leading church in town. "But it will be only a moment."

"It's not a party at all — just the family and a few friends, you see. Oh, here are Anthony and Valerie — Miss Maddox. Would it matter, Valerie, if we told Dr. Llewellyn?" beaming on the girl with such affectionate pleasure that the rector would have been very dense indeed not to know what it was all about.

Val's cheeks flamed at the suddenness of it, but she said "No-o —" hesitatingly.

"Of course not!" her fiancé asserted himself. "Valerie and I are engaged, though she's ashamed to admit it."

"It's not being announced yet," explained his mother. "The children thought they'd better wait until Anthony's thoroughly settled. You did say something, though, to Dr. Havern, didn't you, dear?"

"No." Anthony gave his head a determined shake. Then realizing that they would all get the idea that he was holding out on Dr. Havern for cause (which was quite true), he went on with less emphasis. "No, we haven't told a soul outside the family — families," with a smile at Mrs. Maddox, who smiled back, thinking what a lovely boy he was, though different from her idea of a clergyman. "You're getting a scoop, Dr. Llewellyn."

The rector was full of congratulations, and promised to be silent as the grave about the secret into which he had stumbled.

"I think you're quite right to take your own time about publicizing the news, and I appreciate the honor of getting the beat before Dr. Havern," he added genially. "I might even bespeak the job of tying the knot when the time comes, if agreeable to everybody."

Val joined Anthony in thanking him, and was honestly thrilled. She had been wondering more than once if it would be possible to sidestep Dr. Havern's ministrations when the time came for the wedding; but for the famous Dr. Llewellyn to have volunteered to marry them was beyond her wildest hopes. She gazed at him reverently.

By and by Mrs. Drew got the rector in a quiet corner where she could tell him all about Anthony and how hard he was working and how much his new parish liked him, and other items of maternal interest to which Dr. Llewellyn listened with gratifying attention, though he privately discounted her talk of hard work. Not with Havern in charge, he thought.

"He's a very fine young man," agreed the rector when Mrs. Drew began to show signs of repeating herself. "I know we'll all be proud of him. In fact we are now!"

"And how do you like my new daughter?" asked Mrs. Drew a little tremulously as she wiped the happy tears from her eyes. "Isn't she a pretty thing?"

He directed a long look at the girl who was now sitting at the piano, joining the other young people in trying to coax Anthony to sing. He, unaccountably turned modest, was protesting that he didn't know a thing, and couldn't sing anyhow. Some good-natured bullying was going on in which Valerie was doing her full share.

She was a lovely creature, he thought, watching her as she sat at the big black piano with her dress of creamy white flowing about her, her fair hair shining in the lamplight, and her eyes raised to Anthony's face, laughing yet adoring.

" 'Behold thou art fair, thou hast doves' eyes,' " murmured the rector, half to himself. Then he chuckled shamefacedly. "I was just finding the right quotation to give Anthony, in case he needs it—which he probably doesn't. A married man doesn't go around quoting the *Song of Songs* on his own account, you understand." Then he went on with a seriousness that made her slightly uneasy. "Anthony is a very fortunate youngster to get a girl like your Valerie. There's more to her than just a pretty face and a nice disposition. Underneath all that she'll surprise him some day." He paused and then added thoughtfully, "I hope he may be ready for it."

"Oh, Dr. Llewellyn! What in the world do you mean?" The mother was perturbed in a moment. "You scare me!"

He laughed again, this time so cheerfully he almost persuaded her that he had been joking.

"My dear lady, I was just running on—you know how we preachers have to moralize or we don't think we've said anything. I just meant that the girl has character under all that prettiness. But Anthony has, too, for that matter, so I can't imagine a better combination to start with, can you?"

"Well—" Mrs. Drew's flutters subsided, though she still looked disquieted. "I hope nothing's going to happen. We all like the child so much, and dear Anthony is so happy. But still, if anything is likely to go wrong—"

"Not in a thousand years," he declared comfortably. "I personally wouldn't give a dime for a girl who didn't have a pinch of salt in her composition. My dear Mrs. Drew, you've nothing to worry about. Listen—they've persuaded him after all," as the piano began to sound in the sudden quiet.

Anthony began Schumann's exquisite song, *Du bist wie eine Blume,* as if his heart was in it.

CHAPTER V

THE golf tournament, after being twice postponed on account of bad weather, took place on Monday, Tuesday, and Wednesday of that week, and was fought to a hard finish. To the disappointment of Dr. Havern and his well-wishers, the honors went elsewhere than to the rector of St. Giles's, a fact which nobody regretted more than the curate of St. Giles's, unless it were the handmaid of the same. Defeat had soured the rector's disposition to an extent that both Savannah and Anthony had seriously considered throwing up their respective jobs and going out into the wide world; while even Mrs. Havern languidly protested she didn't see what there was about losing that little tin cup to make a man forget he was a Christian. To this her husband had angrily retorted he had never heard that Leonidas at Thermopolyae was considered anything to laugh at, and furthermore the cup wasn't tin!

Fortunately some good friends, Mr. and Mrs. Butterfield of Ferndale, came to the rescue with an invitation to spend the coming week end at the Butterfields' charming country home some forty miles distant; and while Dr. Havern protested that he couldn't do that, Sunday being a day he had to see through personally, he might be induced to visit from Thursday to Saturday evening.

"Nothing is ever done around here on Sunday unless I do it," the rector turned a severe eye on Anthony, who had the ill luck to be present, "so I'll be back either late Saturday night or early Sunday morning, in time for the Morning Prayer."

The latter part of the week, therefore, was singularly tranquil around St. Giles's, and on Saturday night Anthony went to bed happier about his work than he had been at any time since the first morning of his curacy. Nobody had criticized him for three mortal days, nor had anybody interfered with his routine or upset his plans by giving him a lot of contradictory orders. Also he had several good visits with Val, which was more than he could have done with the rector in town, and that in itself was enough to make him whistle himself to bed in a very good humor.

Val had been looking a little pale and tired this week, but as she had declared she never felt better, and was only making the most of a cut finger to get some attention, he was reassured. They discussed, as they often did, the advisability of announcing their engagement — whether to be discreet and wait, or to go ahead and let the consequences take care of themselves; and as usual they decided to let it stand. After Christmas, they hoped, matters might have adjusted themselves to everybody's satisfaction, and the news would be more in harmony with the general gladness.

Sunday morning broke wet and chill, but it took more than a rainy morning to dampen Anthony's good humor. For one thing he genuinely enjoyed the early Communion service, the quiet, intimate ceremony with a few devout souls who, like himself, preferred the early hours of Sunday before the distractions of the day set in. While he regretted (as what zealous minister would not?) that only a handful of his flock availed themselves of this privilege, he looked forward with a beginner's optimism to the time when he should have huge crowds coming to this great spiritual banquet. Meanwhile he happily ministered to the faithful few who had turned out in the driving rain this dreary November morning. With extra fervor he prayed over them and gave them the symbols of the Lord's Supper; and from a heart full of genuine kindliness he invoked a blessing on their bedraggled heads before they went out into the deluge again.

The only worry he had this morning was that Val seemed not so well during the service; but as she smiled cheerfully at him afterward, he hoped it was nothing serious. He tried to get a word with her before she left the church, but was prevented by having to listen to the complaints of an old lady who thought the service had been too long, and of a younger lady who gushingly thought it too short. By the time he had finished with them Val was gone.

Whistling a cheery stave, he dashed across to the rectory for a cup of coffee which Savannah said she would have ready for him, and he hoped she would also have a telegram for him from the rector in case anything had happened to upset the plan agreed upon. Dr. Havern had not come in last night, perhaps due to the rain which had started up late in the evening, but he still might be in time for the eleven o'clock service if he came this morning. On the other hand, if the weather had proved too bad for traveling, no doubt he would have got a wire through to that effect. The curate hoped it would come in time for him to think up a few ideas for a brief sermon.

Sure enough, as he came into the hall Anthony was pleased and a little excited to see the yellow envelope lying on the table. The old man had some good points after all. Without so much as looking at the address Anthony tore it open, only to find it was for Dr. Havern, and contained a half dozen words to the effect that Bishop Ranley was to arrive this morning on the ten o'clock train.

"Savannah!" shouted Anthony. "When did this get here? Have you heard anything from Dr. Havern yet?"

"He ain' said nothin'." Savannah padded in from the dining room. "Dishyer telegram done come ten minutes ago."

Anthony leaped to the telephone. If the roads had proved too bad for the rector's car, perhaps he might come by train, in which case Anthony would have to devise some means of getting word to him to stay at the station and meet the bishop's train. He called Information to find out how many trains ran from Ferndale on Sunday mornings, and learned to his dismay that there were only two, one coming at the early hour of five, and the other shortly before twelve. Nothing else would be in until late afternoon. Railroad transportation, therefore, was out, since the rector would be here already had he done the impossible and come in with the milk.

He then tried to put in a long distance call to Ferndale, but that was even more barren of results, since last night's storm had interfered with the wires so that nothing was going through just now.

"Looks as if it's up to me to meet that bishop," said Anthony,

[81]

taking the coffee from Savannah. Between scalding gulps he directed the maid to get a room ready for the guest; then he rushed over to get his own car from the garage, and thence on to the railroad station as fast as the wet pavements allowed.

His early morning mood had been completely blasted. Not unnaturally he blamed his superior for not being there and on the job to meet his own guests; also he wondered angrily how he was supposed to pick out the bishop in a crowded station, considering that he had never laid eyes on the man. Clergymen were constantly traveling on trains, and lots of them dressed alike. It was practically impossible to tell which was which these days, and Anthony was in no humor to get mixed up with a lot of Roman Catholic clergy, even if it was afterward clearly proved to be a mistake.

"I wonder if he'll wear a rose in his hair," growled Anthony as he parked his car and tore into the waiting room just three minutes before ten o'clock. A hurried look at the bulletin board showed that No. 86 was some twenty minutes late, which both relieved and exasperated him. At least he was there in time, but if he had known about the delay he could have had some breakfast.

He wiped the raindrops and perspiration from his brow and telephoned Savannah. No, the rector hadn't come, the maid told him, and he then began to get anxious in real earnest. Just what would happen if Dr. Havern failed to come at all, and this train was any later? Twenty minutes was only a figure of speech when a train really began to lose time. There was no question but that the bishop must be met, but what about Morning Prayer?

Sure enough, twenty minutes lengthened into forty. Distracted, Anthony again telephoned, and was greatly cheered to learn that Dr. Havern had arrived some five minutes ago and was at that moment taking a bath. "An' he sho' is hystic!" breathed Savannah into the transmitter, giving an effect of rolling white eyeballs as she diagnosed the state of the rector's temper.

"Did you tell him the bishop is coming?" asked Anthony.

[82]

"Yas'uh, ah did; an' ah'd hate fo' you to know what he done replahed," responded Savannah darkly.

"Well, tell him we'll get there as soon as that train comes in." Anthony suppressed a laugh. At least the rector could begin the service, no matter how hysterical he might be.

Quite calm now, Anthony went back to the gate and whiled away the time trying to remember what he had lately heard about Bishop Ranley. He must be the sometime curate at St. Udolph's whom his mother and Aunt Maude had discussed some weeks ago — "that young scamp" Aunt Maude had called him. Anthony had wondered at the time what that meant, but his interest then had been much greater in regard to Ranley's contemporary, Dr. Havern, whom the ladies had also talked over very freely. He seemed to recall that Mother said young Ranley had made her feel uncomfortable. On the other hand, Aunt Maude had said she liked him. It would be interesting to see what time and episcopal honors had made of the young "scamp," in case Anthony didn't miss him altogether.

As it fell out, the young man had no difficulty in identifying the tall, stooping figure in rusty black when, just at eleven o'clock, Bishop Ranley came through the gate. This was partly because of the pectoral cross he was wearing, and partly because Anthony instantly knew that he looked exactly as he should. Aunt Maude had said Ranley wasn't at all like Havern in the old days, and this ascetic, with his thin, lined face and deep-set, tired eyes, was the antithesis of Dr. Havern's ruddy sleekness. The eyes lighted up pleasantly when Anthony accosted him; and the bishop willingly accepted the apologies Anthony took upon himself to make on behalf of the rector.

"Thank you very much, Mr. Drew," said the bishop in the mellow, preachers' voice which Anthony had not yet acquired. "My telegram was a little unceremonious, I fear. Something important came up, and I packed my bag and caught the first train. I hope my old friend, Dr. Havern, will forgive my barging in on him this way, but I felt I just had to see him."

"I have my car just outside, your Grace. I suppose you've had your breakfast?" Anthony wondered how far it would be

[83]

safe to go with Savannah in the matter of feeding itinerant clergy at odd hours, even if they were among the hierarchy.

The bishop shook his head.

"I'm hoping to say Mass," he said. "It can be arranged for after we get to the church?"

Anthony was conscious of a shock, but answered as cordially as possible that he was sure Dr. Havern would be glad to accommodate the bishop with an altar. Probably this was one of the things about the Ranley of long ago which both Aunt Maude and Mother had thought extreme. No wonder Mother said he made her uncomfortable, if he believed in the Mass and all the other rites which skirt Rome so perilously. However, that was none of Anthony's business.

"It's too bad your train was so late, then," he said. "You might have — er — given your Mass before the Morning Prayer, and you wouldn't have had to wait so long for your breakfast. Couldn't you have just a cup of coffee or some orange juice or something?"

The bishop smiled, but said it made no difference at all, that he had to continue an absolute fast until after Mass. Mr. Drew was not to worry about him in the least.

"And how is Havern?" he asked, as they drove away from the station. "It's many years since we were together at St. Udolph's. He was the senior assistant there, and I was a few years his junior. He was always so matter of fact, I remember — took life in such a safe and sane way. I was the one who always went off half-cocked, as he used to tell me." He looked wistfully back over the length of years to those days filled with hope and youthful courage. Then he repeated, half under his breath, "I felt I had to see him!"

Feeling a little awed, though he had no idea why, Anthony replied that Dr. Havern was in excellent health at the last count, and explained about the visit to Ferndale.

The distance between the station and St. Giles's was not great, but it was close upon eleven-thirty when the two clergymen arrived at the church. Anthony hoped the rector wouldn't take occasion to preach a long sermon, with the bishop starving.

"You would like to go into the house and rest a while, wouldn't you?" he asked.

"I'd rather slide quietly into the rear of the church if it can be managed," replied his Lordship. "I'd love to hear Havern's sermon. He used to preach very well in the days at St. Udolph's. Wonderful old church — wonderful old days!" he finished with a sigh.

Meanwhile at the rectory Dr. Havern had indeed been in a frame of mind bordering on the hysterical. No friend to early rising at any time, Dr. Havern made mental reservations when he had allowed himself to be persuaded by his hosts to stay over Saturday night and drive down in the quiet of Sunday morning. When the first dash of rain fell on Saturday evening, he had welcomed it as a sign that he ought to stay where he was — if the rain would be so obliging as to keep going. Certainly nobody could criticize him for not hazarding his life on those wet roads into the city.

A moment of wakefulness during the night confirmed him in this opinion, as he heard the lashing of the wind and rain against his windows; and he had burrowed still deeper into the snugness of his bed. At times like this, he thought, there really did seem some excuse for that bunch of vestrymen after all. They had provided somebody to take over when their rector was enjoying a much-needed holiday. Bless them! And if Drew tried to put anything over in his absence, that could easily be settled. Sighing luxuriously, he had rolled over and drifted back to sleep.

But sorrow came with the morning, this time. The Butterfields were perfectly willing to let Dr. Havern take his ease in his bed until such time as his own inclinations lifted him out of it; but unfortunately for the rector Mrs. Butterfield had a sister visiting her, and the sister had a conscience. She also had a great reverence for the cloth, and could never have been brought to believe that anything short of death would prevent a minister of the gospel from being with his flock on the Sabbath.

This zealous lady had insisted upon rousing the good doctor

[85]

in the gray wetness of Sunday morning. Indeed she had exchanged some heated words with her sister when Mrs. Butterfield, roused from her own slumbers, had urged Amelia to mind
her own business. To this Amelia had replied that *she* was not
going to be a party to the devil's work; whereupon she had
rustled down the corridor and rapped smartly on the ministerial
door.

With her own hands she had served his breakfast when,
yawning, unshaved, and indignant, he had stumbled down-
stairs, leaving his wife warmly tucked up in her bed. To do
him justice, the rector had used every argument against the
journey, even to the extent of saying that his tires were unsafe;
but Amelia, ever resourceful, easily countered this by remembering that young George somebody was driving a truckload of
something down to the city, and she knew he would be only
too happy to take the rector.

"My heart just bleeds for those poor people, without your
hand to guide them," she had added prayerfully. When the
rector, driven to the wall, had tried to explain that his curate's
hand, while less experienced than his own, might do a little
guiding in the present emergency, Amelia had swept this puerile
suggestion aside.

"It would not be the same," she said. "They need *you!*"

Forty odd miles on a slippery road in a heavy-going truck
did nothing to improve Dr. Havern's temper. In fact, the temper would have reached the exploding point except for the
thought that though the meddlesome Miss Amelia had managed to rout him out and send him to the city in this weather,
she had no way of making him work after he got there. He'd
like to see her try! The first thing he would do after getting to
his own house would be to take a hot bath and crawl into his
own bed, while Drew conducted services as best he could for
that infernal congregation — "and serve 'em right!" he thought
viciously.

It was considerably after ten o'clock when young George
dropped him at the rectory gate and drove away. Dr. Havern
tramped angrily into the house to be greeted with the news

that "Misto' Drew had done gone to the train to meet a Misto' Bishop, and was bringing dishyea Misto' Bishop back to stay in the guest room." Whereupon Dr. Havern blew up and uttered the words which Savannah had remarked upon, after which he plunged into his own room.

A leisurely hot bath and a shave refreshed him somewhat; and attired in the dressing gown in which he purposed to meet this uninvited guest who was so mysteriously arriving, the rector shouted to Savannah to bring him a fresh cup of coffee and to send Mr. Drew up the minute he arrived.

"I'm going to bed—think I took cold in that truck," he explained, coughing as an afterthought. "If that man Bishop wants to see me, he'll have to come up, too."

"Misto' Drew ain' comin'," responded Savannah, regarding him unwinkingly from the foot of the stairs. "He done telephone me fo' times, an' he done say dishyea train ain' in yit, an' ax ef youall kin'ly tek dem suvices."

Barely saving himself from a repetition of the speech which had so shocked his handmaid, the rector went back to his room and dressed hastily. Drew should hear from him on this subject —chasing all over the country Sunday morning to meet utter strangers. Probably just one of Drew's classmates—somebody else from down the valley! He thought he'd fire Drew out of hand, and right now! Maybe that would teach the fellow to stick to business.

It was a good eight minutes after eleven when Dr. Havern strode into the vestry, his brow so black that nobody ventured to address him. With hands that trembled with strong emotion he jerked his surplice over his head, forgetting his usual ritual of vesting, and getting his arms in the wrong places. Again muttering strange words under his breath, the rector dragged the surplice off with a yank which ripped the garment jaggedly down the front. A strand of the torn fabric caught in his glasses as the garment went violently over his head, and with the final heave his expensive bifocals leaped onto the stone floor where they shattered. The rector turned livid, while the St. Cecilias in the next room looked on with bated breath.

[87]

It says much for the value of a definite habit that in spite of this catastrophe, and only a few moments later, the choir filed into the chancel chirping excitedly:

> "Sing, ye faithful, sing with gladness!
> Wake your noblest, sweetest strain!"

followed by Dr. Havern in a fresh surplice and stole, his ruddy face slightly purple, and wearing a pair of old reading glasses which some kind hand had found for him in the cupboard. The congregation, who had been wondering what on earth was the matter in there, rose thankfully to their feet and joined in the hymn which the rector considered far too light and frivolous under the circumstances.

"The Lord is in His holy temple —" began the rector.

Hoping against hope that Drew would arrive, with or without the perfidious Mr. Bishop, in time to take over at least some of the service, Dr. Havern began the prayers. Every drop of falling rain, every tap of the ivy against the windows, fell upon ears preternaturally sharpened, bringing the hope that help was near; and with each disappointment the rector's sense of outrage waxed greater. Certain phrases of the General Confession struck him as fitting the truant remarkably well: *"left undone the things which he ought to have done . . . miserable offender . . . !"*

As his fury mounted the rector unconsciously quickened his speech, and by the time he reached the words *"turn from his wickedness and live,"* his practiced tongue was rattling off the syllables like a machine gun. The congregation, after the first surprise, interpreted this burst of speed as an effort to make up for lost time; and falling into step they assisted the good work by responding as fast as possible. Catching the infection, the choir also darted through the hymns and canticles in double time; and without the slightest idea of being less devout, the whole churchful of people rushed pell mell through the prayers and hymns and readings, much to the astonishment of two gentlemen who, arriving late, had stayed modestly in the rear pew.

Morning Prayer was in the midst of its wild way when the two clergymen entered the church, and for a moment they stood utterly unregarded. The ushers, usually a model of courteous attention to even late arrivers, paid no heed whatever to their respected curate and his companion; but with eyes glued to their books, their lips babbling feverishly, made their responses to the Psalm. Anthony shrugged apologetically, and at his companion's nod led the way to a vacant seat at the back of the church, where they listened in amaze to what Anthony privately likened to a relay race, with the pastor, the congregation, and the choir catching the baton from each other without a break.

Sooner than anyone could have believed possible, Dr. Havern was leaping into the pulpit, while the excited congregation, hot and moist after their exertions, sank exhaustedly into their seats with a feeling of a job well done. Dr. Havern, still at the top of his stride, shot through the announcements for the coming week; then for the first time paused to wipe his steaming brow and wonder what in the world he was going to preach about.

During his all too short stay in the country Dr. Havern had naturally postponed any work on his sermon on the principle that a man deserved *some* rest. The weather had been perfect for golf, and the sermon could be thought up on his way back to town Saturday evening — anything would do for that congregation. Then when the rain came Saturday evening, there was no earthly reason for bothering with it at all. Mrs. Butterfield's sister, having interfered with what looked to the rector like a direct work of Providence, had really given him a second chance at the congregation's souls; but unfortunately during that long homeward drive in the truck Dr. Havern's meditations had not been sermon material.

He glanced about the church, seeing only an indistinct blur to show there were actually people sitting in the pews, all due, of course, to the accident to his bifocals, and for which Drew was obscurely but entirely responsible. The old reading glasses retrieved from the cupboard were no help, and he plucked them off and cast them from him with a dramatic gesture as though he had just discovered in them the property of Satan. The congregation gazed at him round-eyed, and the two late comers in the back pew held their breath.

"My friends," began the rector in deep, hurt tones, "on this dark morning we are gathered together, gathered in this place of worship for just one purpose!" His voice sank even lower as he ended this preface; and though he could not see their faces he knew that he had electrified his flock. A wave of tense expectation flowed through the stillness — surely something sublime must follow this! Not a creak or a rustle from the pews disturbed the absolute silence. If only he knew what ought to come next!

Hastily he cast about for a text that would come up to anticipations. The Psalms? The Collects? The Lessons? The Second Lesson, now, had vaguely annoyed him when he had read it a moment since. Just why he hadn't liked it had not occurred to him in that inexplicable hurly-burly (*why* had they been rushing along like that, anyway?). Last Sunday before Advent — John 6 — the loaves and fishes, wasn't it? He recalled having scored that story pretty smartly a few weeks ago when Drew had upset his routine that way. Probably the loaves and fishes could stand another going over. Furthermore, as everyone knew, the Romanists were pretty keen about John 6, and — Here the answer came like a ray of sunshine: *All paths lead to Rome.* You couldn't go wrong.

Taking a fresh grip on the edge of the pulpit desk, he closed his eyes that he might not be infuriated anew with the sight of those indistinguishable spots of pinky blur against a dark background, which was all he could see of his audience. Then he solemnly intoned:

"Whence shall we buy bread that these may eat?"

The sermon, now that he had got into it, was not greatly different in matter from what he had preached before; but having generated a surprising head of steam in the past twenty minutes, he rather surpassed himself in invective.

"I have spoken to you before about this so-called miracle of the loaves and fishes," he began severely, "and I think it is time to settle, once and for all, the claims of Rome that this trifling incident deserves to be classed among the great events of history. Have these claims anything to support them? Or is it actually worth bothering about at all? Let us see, then, what really happened."

He groped for the despised spectacles with which to read the offending gospel; but they eluding him, he had to depend upon his memory for what came next. Another black mark against Drew and that Bishop friend of his. Drew should certainly be fired for this day's work!

"After eating their fill — trust them for *that* — the disciples came to Jesus and asked for a sign — a sign, mind you! saying: *'Our fathers did eat manna in the desert, as it is written, He gaveth them bread from heaven to eat. Give us a sign that we may see and believe Thee,'* said they. Then Jesus said to them: *'My Father giveth you the true bread from heaven.'* And then they said — mark you, they were a greedy lot, always wanting more and more — *'Lord, evermore give us this bread.'* You see, *'evermore give us this bread!'* And Jesus said — wasn't He patient with their stupidity and greed? — *'I am the bread of life: he that cometh to me shall never hunger; and he that believeth on me shall never thirst.'* You see," Dr. Havern spread his hands wide and his voice took on a pleading note, "that was all there was to it. 'He that believeth on Me shall never thirst,' or hunger, or whatever it was at the moment."

He paused and gazed beseechingly into the dimness before him. Confound those bifocals! A man can't get anywhere when he can't see! The angry flush on his brow deepened perceptibly, and he burst forth on his loudest note. "And the Romanists would have you believe that this — *this!*" he smote the desk, "justifies their superstitious, idolatrous practice of the Mass!"

Anthony felt the quiet figure beside him tense suddenly, and remembering that Bishop Ranley had just asked for an altar on which to say his Mass, Anthony turned as red as the rector had done. What a horrible thing to say in front of a man who, doubtless sincerely, thought he was about to offer a true

[91]

Sacrifice of the Body and Blood of Christ! The young man marveled again that anyone within the safe and sane confines of Protestantism should have gone so far from the truth as to believe in what Dr. Havern had uncompromisingly denounced as idolatrous; but even so, how dared Havern fling an insult like that into the very teeth of his old friend?

Wisely for his own safety Dr. Havern abandoned St. John at this point, not trusting his memory to quote any farther into that strange gospel. Having thus dramatically introduced Rome to the congregation, he plunged at once into a sea of accusations against that hated sect, its history and operation from Peter on down to Pius, smiting the pulpit desk from time to time for the proper emphasis, and in general working off a lot of spleen against his oppressors of the morning, from Miss Amelia who had snatched him from the arms of sleep, young George who had rattled his bones in that terrible truck, and ending with that lost soul Drew who was trying to thrust one of his low friends upon the rector's hospitality.

He paid his usual tribute to Alexander VI, whom he styled "a typical pope of the first water," and took time out to explain how Mary of England had earned the title of "Bloody." For some reason the rector always confused Mary Tudor, the Queen, with Mary Tudor, the sister of Henry VIII, and when he preached about her (which was often), never failed to speak his mind as to her marriage with the French King Louis XII. Today he was especially bitter about it, ending with the remarkable complaint, "and as if *that* wasn't enough, she hadn't even the decency to stay a widow after his death, but must immediately marry her paramour, Charles Brandon!" striking the desk with his open palm.

These words had no sooner left his lips than he remembered an announcement he had made last Sunday that today he would talk about religions of modern times, a very simple subject. Too bad he hadn't thought about this before — it would have saved him a world of trouble! However, being in full flight just now with Alexander VI on one wing, and Bloody Mary on the other, he decided that the recent religions would fit in just as well some other time. He *could* touch up Henry VIII, though, while he was about it.

"Henry VIII," he cried, raising his arms on high, "was a Roman Catholic. He was called the Defender of the Faith — the Roman faith. Very well, then, let them have him. *We don't want him!*" and down came both hands on the pulpit in his favorite slap.

At the close of the service Dr. Havern again departed from custom, and instead of hurrying to the front door to shake hands with his congregation, he ran hastily over to the house with one thought in mind — he must find another pair of glasses! With the help of Savannah, angrily summoned from her kitchen, a pair of spectacles of the "far" order was found; and with these astride his nose, Dr. Havern felt himself again.

"And I hope dinner is ready, Savannah," he said by way of thanks. "If Mr. Drew and his friend are not here when the time comes, I shan't wait for them. Call me when you're ready. Infernal imposition!" he added to himself, striding into the library.

Mr. Drew and his friend made no effort to see the rector. Noting that the bishop's face looked a little gray at the close of the sermon, Anthony was moved to suggest in a whisper that they get out before the offertory. The bishop silently assenting, they slipped through a side door, where the cold dampness somewhat revived the prelate, though he still looked pinched and wan.

They waited through what remained of the service, and presently a burst of excited chatter was heard as the congregation streamed out, demanding of each other what had happened! Dr. Havern had come in so late, and had seemed so upset — *Hadn't* he given the Roman Church a blast! Was the Pope really coming over, just as they used to think he would when Mr. Al Smith — He *might come,* too, with all this war going on in Europe, and the Axis and Mussolini and everything! Fortunately the rain did not lend itself easily to outdoor conversations, and before very long the people went home, leaving the church to silence.

The two clergymen then quietly went back. Under the bishop's direction Anthony prepared the altar for the rite which Dr. Havern had just called idolatrous, while the bishop vested in the robes he took from his satchel. When everything was ready the bishop looked at Anthony inquiringly.

"Are you familiar with the Mass?" he asked; then as the young man said no, he went on deprecatingly, "Would you mind making the responses for me? You haven't any scruples — ?"

"Oh, no, no!" Anthony had plenty of scruples just then, but even stronger was his sense of the insult just given the bishop by his one-time friend. He took the manual which the bishop held out to him, and with some prompting from the celebrant served on the altar as well as answered the prayers, doing it awkwardly enough but making out better than he had expected. Out of curiosity he had once assisted at this sort of service during his seminary days, but had not enjoyed it and never went again. So far as he could see there was no use in this aping of Rome, though a good many excellent clergymen went in for it. To Anthony it was unnecessary and dangerous.

He remembered hearing, when he was a very little boy, a serious discussion between his grandmother and Aunt Maude about somebody around St. Udolph's — was his name Burnham? — who had gone in for the ritualistic practices. Something quite awful had happened to Burnham, if that was his name. What it was he couldn't remember — he must ask Aunt Maude. Meanwhile, if Bishop Ranley really believed that way —

Midway of the rite he noticed that the bishop paused a long time over the prayers of the consecration, and at one point he thought the celebrant was going to quit altogether. He turned white and held on to the edge of the altar, much as if he were about to faint, so that Anthony sprang to catch him. Recovering with an obvious effort, the bishop waved him back, and proceeded to the end.

Just as he was finishing the last prayers, Dr. Havern suddenly burst in through the side door and into the chancel with a loud, indignant: "Drew! What in the world are you doing over here?

Oh!" His voice dropped to a faint squeak, and he stood rooted to the spot, with staring eyes beholding the close of the ceremony which he had scored so bitterly a half hour ago. His mouth opened in astonishment as he recognized the celebrant; but after that first wrathful outburst he kept silent, even going to the length of kneeling in one of the choir stalls until the bishop left the altar. Afterward, when he had shaken hands with his sometime fellow curate and assisted him to disrobe, the rector's voice was sweet and low.

"I can't believe it, Ranley!" he said over and over. "How did you happen to come? Why didn't you *tell* me? I'd have had everything ready! Do come over to the rectory, my dear fellow," propeling his friend by an elbow, "and have a glass of wine or a cup of coffee — don't tell me you were fasting all this time? You must be exhausted. Drew, I'm surprised at you. Why didn't —"

"Don't worry, Havern," interposed the bishop, his gentle voice cutting through the other's busy speech. "I don't mind fasting. And Mr. Drew has been very kind," his thin face lighting up with a smile that somehow hurt Anthony. "I apologize for bursting in so unceremoniously —"

Dr. Havern interrupted in his turn, insisting that no apology was ever necessary for so old and dear a friend; and Savannah, abandoning her principles about people coming in late to meals, set a most delectable breakfast on the table before the tardy ones. She liked Drew, anyhow, and that puny looking bishop appealed to her strongly as being in need of a little "fatting up."

The rector sat at the head of the table while his guests ate, recounting such of the morning's adventures as seemed pertinent, breaking off every now and then to urge another cup of coffee on his old friend. Anthony was relieved when he heard of the accident to the bifocals. At least the insult had not been deliberate, though even at that it must have been painful enough to the bishop to sit there and listen.

"You know I'm as blind as a bat without them," went on the rector, laughing as though it had all been a grand joke to a good sport like himself. "I give you my word, when I got up in that pulpit I was almost dizzy. Gave me an awful headache —but no matter," bravely. "Here I've been running on about myself all this time, and I want to know everything about you. How are things out in your part of the country?" Then without waiting for an answer he burst out again, "Just how long have you been here—I mean, when did you get in this morning?"

The bishop considered, crumbling a bit of bread between his thin nervous fingers, while Savannah shook her head sorrowfully to see all that good breakfast unnoticed by him. "Let me see—it's just about two hours since that train got in. It was around eleven-thirty when we came to the church." The apprehension in Dr. Havern's face deepened, as did his ruddy color; but the quiet voice went on mildly.

"I wanted to hear your sermon, Wilbur. I remember I always liked to hear you at St. Udolph's. Envied you, too, sometimes. You always seemed so definite. It was quite wonderful to me to listen to a man who always knew so exactly what his convictions were."

"Well, of course—" murmured the rector, glad that his friend was taking it that way. "I always try to keep my feet on the ground, as the saying goes."

Bishop Ranley arranged his crumbs in a row in front of him, seeming intent on their exact alignment; while Dr. Havern and his curate watched him anxiously. Apparently the subject was finished, as presently the bishop looked up with that odd little smile which Anthony was beginning to recognize, and spoke of other matters. He admired the church, spoke of the good people in the congregation, seeming to take their merit for granted; asked about old friends at St. Udolph's. All very commonplace.

Remembering the bishop's urgent wish to talk with his friend, Anthony soon decided it was time for him to go.

"Will you excuse me, your Grace?" he said. "I'm sure you and Dr. Havern have a lot of things to talk over. In case you need me, sir, I'll be at my house," he added to the rector.

"Might I impose on your good nature, Mr. Drew, to drive me to the station?" The bishop also got to his feet. "Your car is still out there? It's been very nice to see you, Wilbur, even for this little while."

"No!" The rector was aghast. "You're not going. Why, John, we haven't *begun* to talk about things, old times, your work, and everything. Why, what's this all about?"

But the bishop was firm. He had to go to New York this evening on some business that could not wait, and he put an end to the conversation in a way that only a bishop can.

"You must be worn out after that drive in from the country. I know you need a good sleep."

"Your train doesn't leave until around four o'clock," protested the rector, uncomfortably torn between the demands of hospitality and a desire for his regular Sunday nap of which he was in sore need today. "I thought you were going to spend at least a night with me."

"Thank you, old friend," said the bishop with a sadness in his voice which the occasion did not seem to warrant. "I'm sorry—but I'll have to go." He held out both hands to Dr. Havern, who grasped them warmly.

"Good-by, John," said the rector, genuinely affected by this parting with his one-time inseparable companion. "Write to me, won't you? It's been a long time since we've met."

"A long time!" echoed the bishop with a little sigh.

Over Dr. Havern's shoulder he smiled at the maid who had just now come in with another plate of hot waffles, and stood transfixed with dismay to see that the guest was about to leave.

"Thank you for a very nice breakfast, Savannah," he said. "May God reward you."

"Thanky, suh. Dumenshunit," responded the awed handmaid.

They drove away through the rain, leaving a worried looking rector on the porch, waving his handkerchief. Dr. Havern was not particularly sensitive to impressions, but it had suddenly come over him that there was something queer about this unheralded visit of John Ranley. It was many years since he had seen John, but as time had gone on and neither had made any special effort to revive the friendship it was odd, to say the least, that John should now have suddenly decided to come all this way to see him. He had come very much out of his way, in fact, the city being off his direct route to New York. Then he had sat and talked commonplaces for perhaps thirty minutes, and with more than two hours to kill before train time, had taken his leave. The parting had seemed a final one — Dr. Havern couldn't say exactly why it had struck him that way, but it had.

"John always did go off half-cocked," he consoled himself as he went back into the house. "What a day this has been!"

After they had driven a block or two Anthony inquired if the bishop had some other errand he wanted to do, pending train time. He couldn't really want to go and sit in the station for a couple of hours.

"No, no, just set me down there, and I'll get along very well," replied the prelate. "I have something to read, and I'm used to making myself reasonably comfortable even in a railroad waiting room. I've taken up your whole morning, as it is, and I hope you know how I appreciate it."

"I've got a better idea," ventured Anthony. With a conviction growing on him that the older man was in deep trouble of some kind, it seemed unwise and un-Christian to let him brood alone all the dreary afternoon. Like Dr. Havern, Anthony had come to the belief that something had gone wrong about this brief visit. "Let me take you over to my club, and we can sit there. Or we could ride around for a couple of hours. I think the roads aren't especially slippery, and it may clear before long," hopefully.

"Well," replied the bishop gratefully; and though the rain was falling as fast as ever, which made the sight-seeing expedition a trifle ridiculous, Anthony turned the car in the direction of the country. Even in its leafless state the country was a better bet for aimless driving than watching traffic in town.

The bishop was a courteous guest and made conversation as they sloshed along. He asked about Anthony's work and plans, a topic which was sweet to an ambitious youth. After a while, however, Anthony bethought him that he was monopolizing the talk, and stopped with a jerk.

"I'm wearing you out, your Grace," he said, abashed. "This can't be very interesting to you. You knew all about this years ago," with a flash of insight which was painful to his ego, but no doubt good for his soul. When a youth first realizes that before his own advent the world got along somehow, he may be said to have reached man's estate.

The bishop insisted he had been much interested. It did remind him of his own early experiences, he said, but it was none the less agreeable for all of that.

"Havern and I used to talk things over this way, in the days of St. Udolph's — oh, it must be nearly thirty years ago," he said musingly. "We were together there immediately after I was ordained. He was a little older, and I liked him very much. Such a forthright, matter-of-fact person. I used to go off on flights of fancy, and he would always pull me down to solid ground again. I was eager to make the world over, and do it *now* — not wanting to wait even the seven days that it took the Lord Almighty. Havern said it couldn't be done, and he was so right. Ah, well, I've learned that, too, but it's been a hard lesson."

"Where did you go after you left St. Udolph's?" Anthony was eager to know.

"I took a notion to go to Oxford in the summer of 1912, to do some work. Havern didn't want me to go, I remember. He said I would gain less than I lost by it. I never saw him again after I left him at the station." He sighed again, and for a moment was lost in thought. Then recovering himself he went on.

"Then the war broke out in '14, you know, and I joined up there. They needed chaplains; but when our men came in, in '17, I managed to get a transfer to the American forces. Fearful business. . . . Well," he went on more lightly, "after I got back to the States I had a call to Philadelphia, then I was sent west; and by and by some misguided person got the idea of making me bishop. So here I am."

They just barely caught the train. Anthony watched the tall, bent figure striding through the gate in the wake of the redcap, and had a smile ready for the bishop as he turned for a last look at his companion of the day. The bishop raised his hand. To the uninitiate it might appear to be only a friendly good-by wave, but Anthony knew the thin fingers were lifted in benediction, and he bared his head.

~~~~~~~~~~~~~~~~

CHAPTER VI

IN SPITE of the assurance she had given Anthony, Val had been anything but happy during the past week. All her old restlessness of spirit had come back. Recently she had hoped that was gone forever — since Anthony had come into her life she had known peace for the first time in eight years. For nearly two blissful months she had been mercifully free from that haunting sense of regret and pain. He had filled her whole horizon; no longer was she troubled by a vague memory of starry heights glimpsed once, then lost. She believed in him, and that was enough — until a trifling happening came and again upset everything.

As in the first instance, this was the result of a most ordinary little accident. A cut finger had interfered with her music studies and left a good deal of idle time on her hands, which she had thought to fill by catching up on some neglected reading. Among the books she had laid aside for just such an emergency was a volume of poetry; and one snowy afternoon she settled herself comfortably on the *chaise longue* in her room, prepared to read English verse as long as she could keep awake. It was as simple as that.

Opening the book at random, the first thing that met her eye was *The Hound of Heaven*, which she had read at school as part of her literary course. For some unexplained reason she had immediately and thoroughly disliked it, without even going to the trouble of trying to understand it, and had thereupon deliberately forgotten it. Now she idly began to skim through it again, wondering why it had annoyed her in the first place, and what it was all about anyway. It seemed very good poetry, as she remembered it, if a bit intense. She read:

> *"I fled Him, down the labryrinthine ways*
> *Of my own mind; and in the mist of tears*
> *I hid from Him, and under running laughter."*

The capitalizing of "Him" startled while it enlightened her. The poet had meant God, then, from whom he was trying to escape. Why had he done that? she puzzled, all thoughts of an afternoon nap forgotten. Why would anybody want to run away from God?

With quickened interest she read on, half of her mind enjoying the beauty of the rushing words, while the other half fretted against their meaning. Did God (if it was God) ever pursue anybody like that, and for what reason? The fugitive called Him "this tremendous Lover," but to Val it was confusing. If he knew it was through love that God was following him — chasing him even, the poem said — why should the man run away?

Of course, there were plenty of people who didn't believe in God at all, and it wouldn't be surprising if *they* tried to dodge Him. This opened up another line of thought as to why God would bother with somebody who persistently denied His existence; but Val sternly recalled herself from this side issue, because the present fugitive undoubtedly believed in the Deity. Well, then, if he knew who was after him, and that he was being followed only through love, why did he run? Did people ever do that? Would she — had she ever tried it?

Suddenly Val sat bolt upright, shivering from head to foot. Sometime, somewhere, that Voice *had* spoken to her! It was in a crowded church — people on their knees — a hush broken only by a silver bell tinkling — a priest in golden robes holding up the sacred vessel containing the Real Presence of God. In that great silence the Voice had said something to her which her ignorant little mind had caught and clung to confusedly and unavailingly. Then afterward had come the heavy roll of voices in unison, like waves beating against the altar:

> *"Blessed be God!*
> *Blessed be His Holy Name!"*

The girl sprang to her feet, while the book slid to the floor, where it lay crumpled. Frantically she put both hands over her ears to shut out the sound.

"Oh, dear God!" she prayed wildly. "Don't let me hear that any more! That wasn't meant for me — it's all over and done now. I can't go there, I won't! You know it's wrong, and that I mustn't!"

Still the chant seemed to go on and on:

> *"Blessed be Jesus in the most Holy Sacrament*
> *of the altar!"*

Hearing it only that once, so many years ago, it had burned itself into her brain.

Terrified, she ran to the window and pushed open the casement, letting a great draft of cold air rush in upon her. She drew it into her lungs in long gasps while she tried to steady herself with the sights and sounds of the street below. It was all so blessedly normal, with people in galoshes clumping by, cheerfully demanding of each other how they liked the snow, and children building a snow man with much high-pitched chatter. Not a problem among them! Here she was, growing morbid reading all that neurotic stuff, and it would be lots better for her to go down and help the children with that snow man and get her blood circulating. She could do something, even with one hand, that would do her more good than brooding over all that superstitious nonsense!

Hurriedly she donned slacks and leather jacket, exchanged her slippers for stout boots; and dropping the volume of *Collected English Verse* back of the desk where a too lax housemaid would probably never explore, she ran down to help the children in their work. She hoped also to find peace.

To some extent she did. The spasm passed, and she resolutely took herself in hand to keep her mind from wandering too close to the forbidden subject. She wrote letters to all of her correspondents until she hadn't an idea left. She dutifully went calling with her mother, drinking innumerable cups of tea and exchanging platitudes by the hour about the weather and the war in Europe. She went to the movies with her father on the evenings that Anthony was unable to come in, and in general managed to get through the days pretty well.

The nights were bad, though, and she had to put up a fight with that specter that came and tried to sit on her pillow as soon as her light was out. A thousand times did she push him away. A thousand times did she build up her defensive wall with bricks made of all the legends of superstition and depravity she had ever heard about the ancient Church, cementing it with her own prejudices and aversion. She built it high. But always did he manage to slip in through some tiny chink, and there he was.

He said he was her conscience. He told her she was deliberately running away from her duty — was ignoring a direct call from God Himself. And when she tried to argue with him that God wasn't so unjust as to demand that she sink her intelligence and embrace a creed of idolatry and ignorance, his retort was:

"What do *you* know about it?"

Whereupon she was driven to turn on her lamp again and read mystery stories into the small hours, when she dropped asleep from sheer exhaustion.

In this state of strain it was no wonder that she had not been at her brightest and best, even when she was with Anthony. She longed passionately to tell him and ask his help in her struggle with the powers of darkness (though in a curious way she knew it wasn't that, even when she feared it most), but she resolutely kept silent. For one thing, she knew Anthony had his own troubles; and for another, this was something she had brought on herself, accidentally or not, and therefore it was up to her to battle it out alone.

It was a long week to Val, with practically only one bright spot in it. Her cut finger was well enough for her to take the Friday night rehearsal, and that was a comfort. At least she'd have something to do.

"You're sure your hand is well enough?" Anthony wanted

to know that Friday evening, coming into the choir room as she was getting out the music before the arrival of the Cecilias. This was always a treasured moment for them whenever they could manage to be alone, which was never certain. The rector all too frequently came bustling in, wanting Val to try a new *Te Deum* or an anthem, and the curate had to give way.

Tonight, however, the rector did not appear, and on Val's inquiry Anthony told her that Dr. Havern had not been feeling quite up to the mark this past week, and had gone to Ferndale for a few days. Then dismissing the rector he again begged to know if the injured finger was well enough for business.

"It's fine," she insisted. "Anyhow, I'm pampering it by getting out the easiest stuff we do," reflecting cynically that the congregation wouldn't know the difference anyway, what there were of them. After that burst of oratory early last month, the congregation had seemed to prick up its ears — Val thought they were not only startled by the rector's ideas, but interested, and in some cases pleased. Certainly there had been a decided increase in the crowd the following Sunday, and everybody looked either eager or apprehensive.

However, after that one departure from custom, the rector had fallen back into his usual gait, and instead of giving the fundamentalists another blast, he had merely talked some forty minutes about his trip to the Holy Land several years ago. After that interest had waned, and the disappointed congregation promptly fell off to its usual size.

"I'm afraid you've been in worse pain than you admit, though," went on Anthony, regarding her anxiously. "You look as if you hadn't felt well at all these past several days. Can't you just quit everything and take a rest? I do wish you'd let me look after you. I'd make you stand around!"

The intent was humorous, and she laughed dutifully even while she shook her head in response to the eloquent tenderness in his dark eyes. It wasn't time for matrimony just yet, she said, and he submitted, though only partly convinced this time.

In spite of the bad weather Sunday morning Val rose early

and as usual attended the Communion service at eight. She prayed fervently that she'd forget all that silly nonsense, and as the service proceeded she almost did forget, until at the moment of kneeling at the small communion railing. She looked at the bread which Anthony had just placed in her hands. Then she had the same old tormenting vision of the Sacrament high up on an altar with adoring crowds kneeling before It. Could she imagine herself ever making a genuflection before these bits of bread lying in her palm? And yet she had been on her knees before the Blessed Sacrament of the Romanists —

"Take and eat this in remembrance that Christ died for thee —" Anthony was saying reverently as he passed on to the woman beside her.

The minutes ticked by, and still Val knelt motionless with the bread in her cold hand. Presently the deep voice of the young minister was heard, coming nearer and nearer, as he gave the cup to the kneeling communicants: *"Drink this in remembrance that Christ's Blood was shed for thee, and be thankful."* Then Val hurriedly put the bread in her mouth. She took the most minute sip of the wine; and without pausing, as etiquette demanded, for the kneeling row to finish and depart in order, she almost ran back to her place.

Anthony's startled eyes followed her. For an instant he was tempted to put the cup back on the altar and go to her, but controlled himself and finished the line waiting before him. He glanced at her again as he brought down the bread for the next row of communicants, and was relieved to see that the girl was kneeling quietly with her head up and her eyes fixed on the altar, much as she usually did after communion. Thank God, she was all right now, he thought gratefully. It must have been just a sudden faintness, but he hoped to see her after the service and make sure.

In this, of course, he was disappointed, being buttonholed by the two complaining ladies, and Val was gone before he could get rid of them. She did manage to flash a reassuring smile at him behind their backs, and he was content. Anyhow, he could have a talk with her after the Morning Prayer. But as it fell out, after the late service his hands were full by reason of his attentions to Bishop Ranley.

Had he but known it, this was far better for him than if he had tried to talk to her at the close of that historic rite, for Val was in no mood to chat with any clergyman for a while. Dr. Havern had been more convincing than he ever dreamed of.

The moment she was free Val, like the rector, left the church in haste. For the first time in weeks she forgot that such a person as Anthony Drew ever existed. In the beginning she had been worried about his unexplained absence from the service, but now she didn't care what had happened to him. All she could hear was Dr. Havern's voice ringing in her ears in a sort of chant, like the Litany:

" 'I am the Bread of Life' — *superstitious and idolatrous!*

" 'Lord, evermore give us this Bread' — *superstitious and idolatrous!*

" 'I am the Bread of Life' —"

Val walked on and on through the rain with no idea of where she was going, wanting only to get away from St. Giles's and all that it contained. Who was Dr. Havern to tell the Lord that He was superstitious and idolatrous! Was it for this she had prayed only this morning, when she begged God to give her peace and comfort once more in her faith? Apparently God had not thought well of her plea, then or now. Even at the moment of taking the communion she had the sensation that it didn't really matter; and now along had come Dr. Havern to say that this Living Bread was nothing at all. *"He that cometh to Me shall never hunger."* Surely the promise of the Lord had meant more than *this!*

She wished she could find somebody who would tell her the truth. Dr. Havern didn't know, that was plain. Anthony could, of course — she had a twinge of remorse as she remembered to wonder if he had been suddenly taken ill. Perhaps he had just been called away for something, a sick call, perhaps. Anyhow, this wasn't anything she could take to him. She must fight it out for herself.

Finding that in her abstraction she had walked a long way

past her home, that she was soaked to the skin, and that the family dinner hour was past, she retraced her steps with all speed, deliberately running the last two blocks in order to arrive panting as well as dripping. Then if the family noticed anything queer in her manner, they would naturally put it down to the violent exercise. No need to worry the darlings.

As she expected, they greeted her with affectionate scoldings and inquiries as to wet feet and what on earth had kept her so late, but made no trouble in accepting her explanation about the delay in starting the service. Being fifteen minutes behind time at the beginning, and with a longer sermon than usual, naturally the schedule was upset somewhat.

"And how did everything go at church, after they once got started?" inquired Mr. Maddox as they sat down to the delayed dinner. Mrs. Maddox had been kept home by a slight cold, and her husband had stayed with her for company, offering as an excuse that he believed his religion was now strong enough to hold over by itself for one Sunday. "Anything new in the sermon line?"

His daughter replied with admirable calm that she had not cared for the sermon, but that they had missed something by not attending the service. Warmed and dried and fed, she was recovering her poise by this time, and was able to go on with a laughing account of the strange scampering and rushing of the worshipers through the Morning Prayer.

"But couldn't Anthony have begun, if Dr. Havern was so late coming in?" asked her mother.

"That was the odd part of it," answered Val thoughtfully. "He wasn't there, and I didn't see him afterward. Maybe he was out on some sick call — unless they had a row afterward," she added to herself. That would have been an explanation, both as to the rector's lateness and the state of his temper when he did appear.

Considerably to her surprise, this same idea occurred to her father, who also gave as his opinion that if the two men hadn't had a scrap that morning, it would come some time.

"Anthony will blow the lid off one of these days if Doc

Havern doesn't let up on him," said he, helping himself to more spoonbread.

His wife took him to task for saying anything so dreadful about two clergymen, but his daughter looked at him with new respect. After all, it wasn't so very easy to fool Dad.

In the hush of that afternoon, dinner being done and both parents placidly drowsing over the Sunday paper, Val went to her own room for a little quiet reflection. Some of the turmoil in her soul had been calmed by the normal family routine, but deep within her she knew that the time had come for her to make some sort of decision one way or the other. Her first duty was to find out, if humanly possible, what Jesus had meant by His promise of the Living Bread, and after that she would have to go where the Bread could be found.

As she stood at her window, turning this dreamily over in her mind, she caught sight of the graceful spire of St. Giles's across the dripping trees. Well, why not go there and pray awhile? Maybe the Lord would answer her in His own way, there in the dim silence of the empty church. Then a second thought struck her — what if she ran into Dr. Havern prowling about? It wouldn't do any good to talk to him, though she used to plan that she would when these doubts assailed her. What use would he be in this crisis, with his babblings about the compound Mary Tudor? Or worse still, suppose he started talking about charades again to explain the miracles of Jesus? She felt physically ill at the prospect.

Of course, she might run into Anthony instead, she thought, her heart warming as she remembered his quick understanding and love, his steady, sane outlook. Then she forced the thought away. Anthony was never to know about this insanity until she had cured it herself. So perhaps it would be a mistake to go to St. Gile's at all.

Still, she'd have to go somewhere — there was the Brick Church, for instance. Maybe that would serve. Val had been happy enough there at one time, and stranger things had happened than that she might find peace in the first church she had ever known.

Without giving herself any more time to think, Val slipped on her coat and a snug little hat, and tiptoed softly down the stairs to get out the car.

Any stranger in this part of town would be impressed by the godliness of the neighborhood, she mused as she drove along. There was a church in almost every block of Tenth Street. St. Giles's in lovely red sandstone with ivy growing over it; the austere white Presbyterian Church, cool and aloof; the North Side Baptist in yellow brick, sprawling a bit as to design but cheerful in effect; the Christian Science in reinforced concrete, solid and dignified, though its architecture suggested anything from a public library to a railroad station, rather than a church. The Methodist was, as its name implied, of sturdy red brick with a neat white painted trim and a firm little steeple pointing the way heavenward. There were a lot of small chapels, too, looking rather hurriedly run up and transient in character, each giving a hint as to the stability of the sect which assembled there.

Farther down Tenth Street, and much older than any of these other houses of worship, stood the dark gray stone St. Columban's, with its square tower dimly outlined against the leaden sky, built to withstand the storms of time, grim and implacable. Val shuddered and averted her eyes. If it hadn't been for that ill-fated dash after Mary Anderson, maybe she would never have left the fold of the Methodists. But she *had* gone into St. Columban's, and life had never been quite the same again.

With a sense of deep relief she saw that she had come to the Brick Church, and she darted up its steps as fast as she could in order to shut out the sight of that reminder of misfortune. She pushed open the smooth, neat door, and came back to the church of her childhood.

It looked very much as it had when she left it two years ago, yet seemed strangely alien to eyes grown accustomed to the rich colors and soft carpetings of St. Giles's. There was none of that in this businesslike, efficient room with its sloping floor and pews built semicircularly in the modern way, so that everybody might have an uninterrupted view of the minister. The windows were of an amber glass which let in a soft subdued light entirely adequate for the daytime, while the lamps for night use were the result of scientific planning. The organ and choir stalls were behind and well above the minister's desk, so that the music had no obstruction when the choir held forth, and made it easy for congregational singing. And that was all.

The day being Sunday, the church had been left open for prayer and meditation; but as she sat in a pew near the door and looked around at the once familiar scene, Val thought that prayer didn't come very easily here. It was warm and quiet, you could say that much for it, but that could be said of any well-conducted auditorium. An empty theater would have had more character, she said to herself, and then was sorry. That was no way to think about any place where good people met to pray and sing hymns to the Lord and hear a sermon on right living. But still, when the people were gone away, leaving the building to itself, what was left? Some empty pews, a desk, and an organ.

"Oh!" cried the girl's distressed heart, "how can anybody come to a place like this and call it a church? There's nothing here!"

The quiet, blank room held nothing to contradict this, though she waited a moment as if in the hope that a still small voice would tell her she was wrong. In the empty silence she got to her feet somehow, and stumbled blindly out of the church. The doors closed behind her with a final sound, seeming to echo and emphasize her own words, "There's nothing here for you!"

Out on the street again she paused uncertainly. What was to happen to her now? If the Lord wanted her to do anything about it, couldn't He tell her in some way, give her a sign as He used to do in the Old Testament?

"Ask thee a sign of the Lord thy God; ask it either in the depth, or in the height above."

She remembered hearing that read some time in the Lessons, and had wondered how it would seem to have a direct answer from God. It would be presumptuous to ask it — certainly it would be nerve for her to expect it. Probably only the old prophets and saintly people like that were worthy to get a miraculous answer. Still, she wanted to do the Lord's will if she could, but how was she to know what it was unless He told her somehow?

Maybe after all she ought to go to St. Giles's. The chances were very much against her seeing either Dr. Havern (who was probably taking a nap) or Anthony, who usually took dinner with his family on Sundays. So she might have a quiet half hour there in the church to pray and study this out. Surely God would let her find something! So back she went to St. Giles's.

The first thing to do, she reflected, remembering her impressions of the Brick Church after her long absence, would be to act as if she were a perfect stranger, a far more sensible idea than to use the viewpoint of somebody who was in and out of the church a half dozen times a week. So with this firmly in mind she pulled open the heavy door with its wrought iron hinges.

"It must be a well-to-do parish," she said, in the character of the visiting lady.

This impression was deepened as she walked up the middle aisle over its beautifully laid tiles and found a seat near the chancel. The pew was comfortable with its long red velvet cushion, and the red plush hassock under her feet was consoling. In spite of the dull day it was plain that when there was any light it would fall mellowly through the rich stained glass of the windows, bringing out the carving in the oak of pulpit and choir stalls, the soft colors of tapestries and banners hanging on the walls and from the rafters, the shining brass of lecterns and railing, with a special shaft to touch the white marble altar with its gilded candlesticks and cross.

"A very pretty, artistic church," thought the visiting lady, considerably diverted by this little act she was putting on. "They probably have lovely services here. I wonder what kind of an organist they've got."

As she gave a little smile at this bit of whimsey, recollection hit her abruptly. This wasn't what she had come for! She wasn't a child playing at going to church — she'd started out this afternoon seeking the Lord —

> "I will rise now, and go about the city in the streets,
> and in the broad way I will seek him whom my soul
> loveth: I sought him, but I found him not."

Strangely enough, she didn't seem to care so much now. Somewhere in that short journey between here and the Brick Church her mood had changed. She had lost that sense of urgent need. The whole thing had melted away, and now she was able to peer around the church like any sightseeing tourist, making silly jokes about the organist. What she needed was to get down on her knees and pray!

She dropped on the comfortable hassock, her hands clasped so tightly they ached, and looked up at the altar for help. It was such a pretty altar, too. The rector was so proud of it, and he said he had paid a lot for the fittings, the communion set, and everything. That was a nice window, too, above the altar — worked into the pattern of the stained glass was St. Giles in a purple cloak. It wasn't too obvious. You had to look at it several times before you got all the outlines of the good saint, so there was no question of images or anything. The altar was easy to decorate, with flowers banked on it, and weddings always looked lovely there. It was a pity, in a way, that she and Anthony couldn't be married here. That nice Dr. Llewellyn had implied, if not actually promised, that they could have the wedding at St. Udolph's, which was much more distinguished —

"My God!" Val cried half aloud in her distress, "let me pray!" And she began to repeat the first thing she could remember: "Our Father, Who art in heaven —"

Why did she have to come here to say that prayer? ran a parallel current of thought as she whispered the sacred words. Couldn't she have done it just as well at home? Did it mean anything to her to have come all this distance to kneel on a cushion in front of a beautiful empty altar and say "Thy Kingdom come —?" God was everywhere. He could hear her just as well if she knelt on the floor of her own room and looked out of the window at His sky. *"Thy Will be done—"* It would be different if He had taken on some kind of tangible form and had appeared on the altar here, as He had done at St. Michael's when the people all burst out with *"Blessed be God!"*

Val jumped to her feet, leaving the Lord's Prayer hanging unfinished. Was there no way to silence that wave of sound that seemed to be beating against her ears, hundreds of voices crying out to the Holy Sacrament of the altar? This place was no help. She must go somewhere else—anywhere, just so she could shake off this horrible feeling of pursuit.

Maybe if she went directly to one of the actual Romish churches (not St. Columban's!) and disgusted herself thoroughly with what she found, she might finally get rid of this unhappy ghost. There ought to be the right sort of church for this, in the foreign part of the town south of the railroad, where it was dirty and smelly, and where people did such queer things. That ought to do it!

The trip was long—through the pleasant, comfortable neighborhoods of the North Side where the houses were modern and attractive, set in well-kept grounds; then through the prosperous business section of midtown, now deserted.

By and by the buildings grew less imposing, the shops smaller and dingier, and presently, still farther on, she came to what was unquestionably her goal.

It was in the low-lying section between the railroad and the river, squalid and unlovely at any time, and inexpressibly forlorn now in the rain. The houses were rickety, unpainted, weather beaten, and frankly dirty. Paper, old cans, and other rubbish lay in the unkempt little yards enclosed behind broken pickets. It was the very spot of spots for the papists to choose when building a parish. It only remained now to find where they had put up their church.

Turning into a narrow street, Val found herself immediately blocked by a group of ragged children who, despite the rain, were screaming and quarreling over some game they were playing in the middle of the thoroughfare in utter disregard for any traffic that might be trying to get by.

Val sounded her horn to no purpose, ably seconded by a large, rough-looking man in a ramshackle car who was trying to worm his way through the children from the opposite direction and who, in addition to the loud squawks from his horn, shouted fierce commands to the youngsters to get out of the way before they were all killed. This he said he would do personally unless they moved at once. The children paid not the slightest attention to these threats, and perforce the two cars stopped dead.

With slow, deliberate movements the man got out of his car, and taking two of the ringleaders by their ragged coat collars, he lifted them bodily onto the sidewalk with a warning not to do that again; then turned to scowl blackly at the remaining little urchins, who suspended their game and looked on with mild surprise.

"You kids better beat it into church and say your prayers!" finished the man sternly.

Much to her surprise, Val saw the whole flock immediately wheel like so many pigeons, and without a word of protest go scampering off around the corner. The man bestowed a friendly grin on his fellow sufferer, who returned it brightly; then he climbed into the old car and rattled away.

Left to herself at the close of this dramatic scene, Val started her engine again and carefully picked her way over the broken pavement in the direction taken by the children, where a steeple with a cross on it began to show above the buildings around it. Her instinct had been right.

She wondered what nationality these people had been originally. The children had all spoken English, so far as she could gather between their screams; and the man's speech, while slightly accented, had been fluent enough. Apparently they were all Americans now, though still under the domination of dreaded Rome. She shivered at the thought, but went doggedly on.

The church was a large brick building of no particular style of architecture, and dingy enough to be in harmony with the rest of the neighborhood. A good many feet had apparently passed over that threshold since it was last cleaned, to judge by the generous deposit of mud on the steps. There was plenty of activity here, she thought resentfully, remembering the deserted Brick Church uptown.

Her hand on the latch, she glanced about with belated caution to see if by any chance her cousin Jasper had followed, but he was nowhere in sight. She went into the church.

A gush of warm, stale air met her, heavy with the scent of dying flowers and hot candle wax, also the odor of many unwashed bodies which had been in the church that day. She halted a moment, then thinking grimly, "If this doesn't cure me, nothing will!" she pushed against the vestibule door.

Of the scene which greeted her Val saw little for the moment, neither battered pews, grimy walls, nor cheap, gaudily-colored statues. She was only dimly aware that here again were many people kneeling—in the pews and even on the bare floors in the aisles. That was nothing, because there in the sanctuary, on the altar of painted wood, with fading flowers heaped around it and candles burning hotly—looking strangely familiar, stood the Blessed Sacrament.

"Is this Forty Hours everywhere?" cried out her dismayed soul as she dropped to her knees on the muddy floor in the midst of the flock of little ragamuffins who just now had been shrieking and fighting in the street without. "Can't I ever miss it?"

All the old terror came back to her of that first time she had stumbled upon this devotion at St. Columban's, only this time it was a thousandfold worse. She knew now!

Val never remembered how long she knelt there. The children rose up after a few minutes and tiptoed out, recommencing their shrill cries the minute they reached the outer air. Other people came and went, stepping over and around and sometimes on her, occasionally whispering a word of apology but never expressing any surprise as to her being there. Everybody went to the Forty Hours, they seemed to think.

By and by the spasm passed, leaving her quiet and a bit numb. She was even able to drag herself into the nearest pew, left vacant by the departure of a couple of young girls in imitation fur coats much the worse for being out in the rain, and she crouched there, half kneeling, half sitting, while she tried to call up enough strength to leave the church. She wordlessly prayed to the Being there on the altar to release her from this spell and let her go back to the things that made up her normal world. Without any consciousness that it had happened, Val was believing in the Real Presence as firmly as any born Catholic. The struggle now was not to surrender to It. That was something she could not, would not do!

"Let me go home!" she begged. "I don't fit in here — You can see that I don't. It's all emotionalism and superstition and ignorance. It's all right for them because they don't know any better. I'm different. I couldn't accept what they do!"

They were a rough-looking lot, some in rags, others better clad, but all coming from the poorest class socially, financially, intellectually. Unkempt men and women in unlovely old age; young girls of the cheap-finery type; rowdy young men in the back of the church allowing but a single knee to their devotions. What could they know of rational doctrine?

Perhaps some of them were a bit touching. That man in the threadbare army overcoat left over from the last war, with a string of rosary beads in his gnarled, work-worn hand, mumbling prayers in gruff undertones. A sturdy, red-faced woman, some years his junior, in a faded green cloth coat and knitted hood, answered him expertly, leading a gabbling chorus from their brood of children gathered about them. Val could not but wonder how the rest of the congregation liked this interference with their own private devotions; but so far as she could see nobody was paying any attention to them.

The priest, a frail, tired old man in an extremely shabby cassock, came out of a door near the sanctuary, and after the usual deep genuflection walked slowly down the aisle. Pausing a moment near the family group, he looked them over and smiled, then whispered something in the man's ear. From the expression, gratified and embarrassed, on the faces of the parents, and the self-conscious, smothered giggles of the children, Val made an easy guess at what the priest had said. In spite of herself her heart warmed toward the old cleric, though she wondered why he hadn't seen fit to put on a decent robe on an occasion such as this. It was clean enough, perhaps, but so shiny and frayed and worn that it seemed barely to hold together. If the priest didn't lead in things like this, what could one expect of his ignorant flock? Of course, he might be very poor —

He walked on toward the back of the church, and obeying a sudden impulse Val hastily followed him, forgetting all her fright of a few moments ago. They met in the vestibule.

"Could you — might I give you this — toward getting a new cassock," she was about to say, but something in his face made her swiftly change it to, "for the altar," as she thrust a crumpled bill into his hand.

He thanked her. "God bless you," he added, with a smile so sweet and so kind that the girl felt her heart turn over. What difference did it make if his cassock was a mess? she decided to her own surprise.

"You are a stranger down here," he went on, more as a statement than a question.

Val admitted this was her first visit, and they exchanged a few commonplaces about the weather, interrupted every half minute by "Good afternoon, Father," as his parishioners came and went through the vestibule. The priest answered every salutation cheerily, seeming to remember everybody's name without trouble, frequently adding a query as to how the baby or the grandmother felt today. Val marveled at him.

"It's not so easy for people to come out to church on a day like this," she observed just for something to say, meanwhile wondering how she could get away from here without anything happening more damaging to her morals than a five-dollar contribution toward that ghastly altar. "Your people are making the effort, though."

"Yes. They're doing very well," he replied, giving her a sudden keen glance. "You are not a Catholic, then?"

"How did you know?" Val was alarmed.

"I don't know," he replied, looking surprised himself. "I just felt it, perhaps. You're employed down here at the Settlement House, I suppose."

She shook her head. Probably she ought to make some explanation of why she had come. He must think it strange.

"I can't really tell you how I happened to come — just an impulse of some kind. I do queer things every now and then." She laughed without reason. "I would like to know something, though, about your Forty Hours. That's what it is, isn't it? I've run into it several times, but I don't know one thing about it, or about your Church, for that matter."

"Would you like to come into the rectory for a few minutes and ask me some questions?" he said, adding with a smile as he saw the look of consternation that crossed her face, "I'm not going to insist upon it, but you can see for yourself this is no place for much conversation."

She pulled herself together. After all, even though she had brought it on herself out in Los Pericos, she had got away from a Roman priest then. She was lots more experienced now. And she would like to know what this was all about.

"If you're not too busy, I'd be awfully glad," she said, hoping she didn't look as excited as she was beginning to feel.

They went into the shabbiest, dreariest reception room Val had ever seen. Even the office at St. Giles's was nothing to it; but the priest did the honors as easily as any trained courtier in a royal palace.

"You wanted to know about the Forty Hours' Devotion," he began as they were seated in a pair of hard wooden chairs; and upon her eager assent he told how the devotion had started some four hundred years ago, as a counteract of reparation for the sins committed during the Milan Carnival.

"Those were pretty wild times, and though the authorities stopped some of the excesses after the better element made a protest, the real reformation came in this form. Politicians don't always worry about the morals of a community, at least not officially; but the devout people who got down on their knees in front of the Blessed Sacrament really meant business. You know what the Blessed Sacrament is, I'm sure."

"A friend of mine explained it to me years ago," she replied absently. "But if that business, the original devotion, I mean, was started in Milan, how do you happen to have it over here? And at such odd times — or is it all the time? There's no carnival going on here, is there?"

"It spread, just as the Church does spread. No, there isn't any particular carnival going on right now, but I regret to say we have a good many sins being committed in other ways that get no other atonement than what is made vicariously by decent people in this way. Did you happen to notice that family in the church just now, saying the rosary? The children don't know what the intention is, except that it's to make bad people good; but I happen to know that the parents are very anxious to have some evil influences removed from this district. Some things are going on around here that make it very undesirable to bring up children in the neighborhood, and yet the man's livelihood depends upon his job here. The civil authorities won't do anything about it, so the parents are applying to Headquarters." He smiled faintly at his own mild joke, but Val did not notice it.

"Maybe my father could do something about that," she said thoughtfully, forgetting her own problem for the moment. "He isn't exactly in politics, but he knows some of the influential politicians. And he's crazy about children. Shall I ask him to come down and see you about it?"

"That would be most kind of you both." There was awe in the priest's grave eyes as he looked at the beautiful, eager face opposite, luminous in its self-forgetfulness. The ways of God were strange indeed! he thought reverently.

Remembering then what had brought her here, the brightness began to fade from Val's eyes.

"This is all very interesting," she said, wondering if it were now time to go, "and I'm glad to find out about the Forty Hours. It's haunted me for years."

"Do you mind telling me how you happened to run on to it in the first place?" he asked.

"Just a silly accident. I was trying to get a message to a

friend, and followed her into the church where they were having Forty Hours. I got frightfully interested without any idea of what it meant. In fact, I was so wrought up I wanted to join the Church, but the priest wouldn't let me."

"Wouldn't let you?" He looked interested. "Why?"

She replied, briefly and dryly, and asking no sympathy.

"He was right," nodded the priest, leaning back in his chair. "You hadn't the remotest idea of what you were asking. He'd have been criminally liable if he'd taken you into the Church on a foundation like that."

Val gave him a suspicious look. Was this more of the priestly sales talk of which Uncle Thomas had warned her?

"It doesn't really matter," she tried to speak lightly. "My feelings were very much hurt at the time, but one outgrows that—" She caught her breath suddenly. She couldn't lie to this old man who looked at her with his kindly, experienced eyes.

"I never got over it!" she burst out suddenly. "I think of it all the time, and I don't know why. I don't like your religion —I don't know anything about it, but I don't like it. It's all emotionalism and sentimentality, and keeps people stirred up. That's why I came down here this afternoon, just to— I don't want to hurt your feelings, but I did think if I disgusted myself— I really beg your pardon, but that's what I thought!" She stopped, embarrassed, frightened, and miserably unhappy.

The priest smiled again, with such understanding and pity that she took it for permission to go on.

"So I came, and the minute I got into the church it was the same thing over again. Something was dragging me, hypnotizing me! You don't know what that means!" She was very near tears.

He got to his feet, slowly and painfully, then walked to the window and looked out. She knew it was to give her time to get hold of herself, and was grateful. After a moment he spoke without looking around.

"I think I do know, my child," he said gently. "I'm a convert to Catholicism myself, and I had my own troubles before I got straightened out. It took me a long time to get even as far as you are now. I couldn't believe in the Real Presence at first, but you do already, without knowing anything about It. You've had a most unusual experience. Right now you don't appreciate it —it's unsettling and irritating and you wonder why it had to happen to you!" He glanced around at her quizzically, and she nodded.

"It's terrible!" she replied, feeling rather comforted to know she had met a fellow sufferer. "I really don't want to be a Romanist. I don't have to be one, do I?" appealingly.

He shrugged.

"The answer is strictly up to you," he said with a direct look she found hard to bear. "You want peace of mind, don't you?"

"But can't I have it in my own Church?" she insisted a little wildly. "I've changed my religion already. My people have always been Methodists, but a couple of years ago I felt it wasn't enough, so I was baptized in St. Giles's. I don't see why I have to change again, or what I'd get in your Church that I can't have in my own. They're my sort of people, yours aren't. Why do you Romanists think you have *everything*?" She was now on the verge of hysterics.

He replied mildly and, it seemed, irrelevantly.

"The first thing you can do is to quit calling us Romanists. You wouldn't like it if I said you were a St. Gileser, would you?"

The reproof had the desired effect. Blinking as if he had dashed some cold water in her face, Val gasped and began to think she was making a fool of herself. She didn't usually go to pieces like this. Something was very wrong with her today.

"I'm sorry," she apologized, though her voice still shook. "I didn't mean to be rude, but that's what people say, and I suppose I just have the habit. You Catholics, then. Though," she went on quickly, "we call ourselves Catholic, too."

"I know." He looked amused. "I used to be in the choir at St. Udolph's myself, years ago—many years ago—and some of us were very ritualistic. There isn't anything you can tell me about that. I even started to study for the ministry. Then I became a complete atheist, or thought I was; and by and by I got my feet under me again, and here I am at St. Stanislaus'."

Val regarded him dumbly at the close of this brief auto-biography. What did one say to him — offer congratulations or condolences? Hardly congratulations, though. If he came from St. Udolph's, he must certainly have had a respectable position in society, even wealth. His voice was cultured, his speech that of an educated man. He might have gone on to a brilliantly successful life, either in or out of the ministry, if his destiny lay that way. Instead, here he was in impoverished age, working among a lot of low, ignorant people in this dreadful neighbor-hood, in this miserable house, with apparently nothing to look forward to but the same thing over again till he died.

He seemed to read her thoughts, for he laughed a little and begged her not to feel sorry for him, as there was nothing to be sorry about; and he added a sentence that puzzled her.

"I hope God would give me the grace to do it again," he said in a half undertone, with such genuine humility that she had a sensation of awe.

Why must he have given up everything on account of reli-gion? Wasn't it possible to love God and do good to your neigh-bor, and all that, and still have a decent standard of living? Hadn't Anthony left his beautiful home to go out and do the Lord's work, and wasn't he just as good and conscientious as this shabby old priest, even though he did maintain his respecta-bility? St. Giles's was far from being in the slums. What had Romanism — no, Catholicism, since he wanted it that way — to offer this old man, making it worth while to exchange the security and gracious living of the West Side for this spot in the lower depths of town where the dregs gathered? Of course —"sell all thou hast and distribute to the poor," but surely that could be carried too far!

She tried to stammer something, she didn't know what, but again he seemed to understand.

"My dear little girl," he said, and with wonder she saw that his intention was to console her, "don't think you have to be tactful, because I've nothing to regret. I've been immeasurably the gainer all along the line. Could you imagine what it means to be able to walk into that church at any hour of the day or night and find the Lord Himself waiting for you? As a building it isn't much to look at, since the congregation is poor both as to pocket and artistic sense; but if He doesn't mind, why should I? It could be cleaner, you'll say; and as a matter of fact it generally is cleaner. However, since God sent the rain for His own reasons—maybe to see if His poor little ignorant children were willing to slop through it in order to visit Him—He probably looks only at their loving faces. The mud on their feet (some of 'em hardly have shoes, you know) doesn't interest Him. 'I am the Good Shepherd,' He said, 'and I know mine—*and mine know Me.*'"

The quiet, beautifully-modulated voice ceased, and for a long moment the silence was undisturbed save for the drumming of the rain and muffled noises from the street without. Motionless Val sat and pondered the priest's words. God was in that church over there, he had said, waiting to see her at any time she chose to take the trouble to visit Him. He was always there. This, then, was the fulfillment of the Lord's great promise to be with His people. All she had to do was to walk perhaps twenty yards, and there she would find Jesus in the Holy Sacrament of the altar, as the people had said out at St. Michael's, waiting for her!

"What do I have to do?" she asked finally, almost in a whisper; but her eyes said that she had found peace.

It was very simple after that. Val promised to come tomorrow afternoon to begin a course of instruction in the doctrines of the Church, and the priest gave her a copy of the Little Catechism to glance through meanwhile. Then he held out a fine, thin hand.

"Good-by," he said with a kindly smile. "Do a little praying this evening that God will give you the light you need. Prayer is everything. Make a visit to the Blessed Sacrament here if you like. He's there, you know, and I think He must love you very much, my child."

"Thank you, Father," she said meekly, using the name for the first time in her life.

CHAPTER VII

I T WAS growing pretty dark by this time, the dull November afternoon having closed in, though the rain had finally stopped. As she drove along in the early dusk Val was conscious of a great content. By some magic her recent terror was gone, and all the old unrest, leaving only a sense of peace. With the realization that our Lord had actually left this great tangible evidence of His love, everything had been miraculously clarified. Dimly she knew that there was much to be learned and unlearned before she could be initiated into the Great Mysteries, but that could come when it would. She would be ready.

Breaking the news to the family was the hard part, requiring all the fortitude she had. Having actually changed her religion once before, she wished that the shock would not be too severe now, though she had no real hope. The first change had been to a faith that, while foreign to her family's belief, was at least a respectable form of worship practiced by people of standing. Romanism (she called it by that name for the last time) was something very different. Without thinking of them as being snobs in any degree, Val felt it was asking a good deal of her parents to give their approval of a faith whose tenets were peculiar, and whose followers were a conglomerate lot, according to general belief, mostly among the poor and dirty. However, those dear parents must be put to the test. Val quaked as she thought of opening the subject tonight at the supper table.

She'd have to tell Anthony, too, and he would have the same jolt as her father and mother, and would be terribly hurt. On the whole, though, she thought that after the first shock he would be able to see it her way. With his own unsullied honesty and his burning desire to let people follow the dictates of their own consciences, his deep sympathy and understanding of spiritual matters, and beyond all, his love for her, she felt that once he saw what it meant to her he would not put a straw in her way.

As it happened, the disclosure at home had to be postponed,

owing to the presence of guests who stayed for the evening; and owing further to the demands of hospitality she was almost late for Evensong. She came tearing in at the last minute, but managed to whisper to Anthony as she flashed past him, that she had something frightfully important to tell him.

He thought she looked very pale and excited, and seemed in the grip of some emotion that was probably pleasant, since her eyes were so strangely bright and happy. On the other hand she acted as if extremely nervous, and she worried him very much by making a surprising hash out of a simple little hymn which any beginner could have played at sight. This, added to her strange conduct in the morning, made it seem as if something very much out of the ordinary was in the wind.

In his anxiety to find out what had happened he rushed through Evensong somewhat in the manner of the rector at the Morning Prayer, and dismissed his small congregation with speed. The night was so bad, he said in explanation, that the best place for everybody was by his own fireside, a piece of reasoning which his flock appeared to find very sound.

Val redeemed her professional reputation by sending the congregation out with the Crusaders' March from *The Siege of Acre* ringing in their ears, though her hands were icy on the keys and she had an all-gone feeling inside her. What would Anthony think when she got through this roaring piece and went in to tell him that she was about to start negotiations for joining the Roman Catholic Church!

The congregation faded very quickly, and the minute the door had closed behind the last worshiper Anthony came striding up the aisle, looking very tall in his long black gown and very much concerned about whatever was bothering his girl.

"Do shut that thing off," he said, crossing the chancel in a step and a half and coming to a halt beside the organ, "and tell me what's the matter. I was worried about you this morning, but I've been so busy all day I haven't had a chance even to telephone you. Are you all right?"

She cut off the power and began closing her instrument.

"I wasn't at home most of the afternoon, so you couldn't

have got me anyway," she said, growing more and more scared at what she was about to tell this dear boy who looked at her with anxious dark eyes. He believed in her so — he trusted her! "It's rather a long story. Have you time to walk home with me so that we can talk? I think the rain is over for awhile."

"By all means," he answered. "Just wait till I —"

But the confidence was not made that evening. A gust of cold air blew in from an opening door, and a stern voice sounded in the entry.

"Drew! What happened? Didn't you have any Evensong?" The rector appeared before them with an accusing eye.

"Yes, sir." Anthony's voice was as calm as a mountain lake just before a volcano erupts through its middle. "But there were only eight people (I counted 'em), and it didn't seem worth while to preach much of a sermon on a bad night like this."

"Eight souls are just as well worth saving as eight hundred," said the rector severely. "Well, so long as you're through, come over to the house — good evening, Miss Maddox. Hand all right again? That's fine — and help me with these lists."

"Wouldn't tomorrow do?" Anthony rebelled for the first time. "I've something rather important on hand —"

"Tomorrow will not do!" Dr. Havern's face grew a little redder. "Is your business any more important than getting food to starving little children?" He paused impressively, but as the curate's mouth was opening for another protest, the rector cut him off neatly. "I shall expect you in five minutes, Drew. Good night, Miss Maddox. Take care of that hand." And he vanished as swiftly as he had come.

"I know it's only the Christmas baskets!" Anthony turned a harassed face to the girl. "They could wait a few hours longer, I think."

"Maybe tomorrow would be better for us, after all." Val was eager to unburden her soul, but at the same time was conscious of an ignoble relief at the delay. Telling him wasn't going to be a pleasant job, no matter how it turned out. She dropped her keys into her pocketbook and slid off the organ bench.

"Call me up early tomorrow, and we'll make a date," she said.

[126]

But tomorrow fared no better. Promptly after breakfast the rector appeared in the parish office with the Christmas list which he and Anthony had checked and rechecked last night until a late hour.

"Ah, good morning, Drew." He smiled sunnily as he saw Drew's hand pause in the act of reaching for the telephone. A personal call, no doubt, had been stopped by his coming, and that was all right, too, as part of the plan for making his curate good and sick of his job. He might even get rid of the fellow before Christmas at this rate.

"I'm not quite satisfied with this, and I think it would be well for you to make a personal checkup on these people. Some of them are getting help from the Salvation Army right now, and I've no doubt they'll levy on a half dozen charitable organizations before they get through, and come whining around here for more." He sighed over the rapacity of the people whom only last night he had tenderly called starving little children. "You'd better start in on this the first thing this morning, so that in the afternoon you can go with me to that Red Cross meeting. I don't think St. Giles's is getting the representation it ought in these national societies."

"Yes, sir." Anthony took the list and glanced at the clock. "But I'm sure I can't finish these all in one morning."

"No, no, of course not!" Dr. Havern laughed cheerily. "No sense in trying to do the impossible. Take a couple of days to do it, but get as many in today as you can, because I want to put a stop to this chiseling."

It had not escaped his sharp eye that Drew was spending considerable time in the company of pretty Miss Maddox — probably that was the reason he had dismissed the congregation so early last night and had kicked about working. Wanted to take the girl to the movies, no doubt. Dr. Havern could put a stop to that, too, for the fellow's own good. He continued briskly:

"The Red Cross meeting is at two-thirty, so don't be late getting back here. Then there's that North Side Chamber of Commerce meeting at four. Davison was telling me last night they want to do something different about this neighborhood

Christmas celebration this year, and if we don't get in on that right away the Brick Church will try to run it. They always do. You better attend that, too. And tonight you have your Boys' Club. Plenty of work, my dear boy, plenty to be done. Let's not waste any time."

After getting rid of the rector, Anthony managed to make a brief telephone call to Val, explaining that their conference would have to be off for the day. He was hopeful of making it by tomorrow, he said.

Val spoke sympathetic words, then went back to her present job of trying to explain herself to her parents, grateful for the reprieve though the reckoning would have to come sometime. But at least it would not be today, thank goodness! Her hands were quite full enough as it was, without Anthony's reproaches. At that moment Mother was weeping on the library sofa, while Dad stood scowling at the fireplace. One more disconsolate person would be just too much.

After a nearly sleepless night in which her fears had hourly grown stronger, Val got up in the cowardly hope of being able to sidestep, at least for today, her duty to ruin the peace of the three people she loved most in the world. At the breakfast table she made a really heroic attempt to be bright and lively — too much of an effort, in fact. The contrast between her sparkling conversation and her heavy eyes struck Mrs. Maddox at once. Questions were asked about headaches and temperatures, a visit to the doctor strongly urged, and so much sympathy was poured on her by both parents that in sheer honesty she had to tell them.

"Come into the library," she said, getting up from the table, "and let's give Sweet Magnolia a chance at these dishes. Anyhow, I've got something to tell you."

This wasn't much preparation to give them for the shock of their lives, but as soon as the door was closed behind them she spoke her piece. They took it as hard as she had feared.

"Oh, please don't feel that way about it!" she begged, coming to kneel by the sofa on which her mother had collapsed in a passion of grief. "You don't know how I hate to hurt you so, but I just had to!"

"Have you committed yourself to anything?" asked her father, finding his voice at last.

"Yes," she said, steadily if fearfully. "I'm going down this afternoon for some instruction."

"Where?" he demanded.

Sitting on the floor beside the couch, the girl very quietly told about yesterday's adventures, from the early communion service at St. Giles's down to her visit to St. Stanislaus'. She had not quite finished the recital when she was interrupted by Anthony's telephoned excuses, which at the moment seemed a direct interposition of Providence. A girl could stand only so much!

On her return she found her mother had struggled to a sitting position, and she held out loving arms to this incomprehensible but adored daughter.

"Val, my baby," she begged through her tears, "don't go down there! You know what those Romanists are — you can't be serious about wanting to join them. I had so hoped you'd forget, but I see that Uncle Thomas was right. Once they get hold of you, there's no hope."

"But, Mother, I don't know what they are," protested Val. "We've been told a lot of things, but we haven't checked on any of them. The people can't be as bad as we've been told, because — Mother, do try to understand! — because they have the Blessed Sacrament with them."

Again they looked at her in silence.

"Child, what do you mean?" asked her mother at last.

Val tried to explain, but without much success. Mrs. Maddox shook her head, while her tears began to flow again.

"Darling," she said piteously, "if you feel you must have the Sacrament that way, why don't you go over to St. Timothy's? That's very high, you know. I'm pretty sure it's a great deal like the Roman Church — but at least it's *Protestant!*" The poor lady gave a great sob.

"Yes, I know it's like the Roman Church." Val was almost ready to give up in despair. "But if that's the case, why couldn't I just go to the original Church instead of the imitation?"

To her surprise, her father suddenly became an ally.

"The girl's right, Mother," he said. "She can't be both Catholic and Protestant at the same time. She's either got to go the limit or drop the whole business."

"Why, George!" His wife's tears dried in a blaze of indignation. "Do you realize what you're saying? Do you want Val to be an *atheist* if she doesn't go with the Romans?"

"I didn't mean that," he replied impatiently, while Val gazed at her mother, marveling at the similarity of her reasoning with Anthony's. "Of course, I want her to have some religion. What I meant was: I don't blame her for taking another thought about a Church that can't make up its own mind. God knows I don't want her to join the Romanists, but at least they can stick to their line, whatever it is. They know what they believe." Then he turned to his daughter, still seated on the floor. "You're sure you haven't got yourself too far involved in this business — baptized, or anything?"

She assured him she had done nothing but have a talk with the old priest at St. Stanislaus', and had arranged to go for a course of instruction, but that it was all very indefinite as yet.

"Well, then," he said with a glance at his watch, "I've got to get down to the office now, but what do you say we take the afternoon off and go around to see some of these churches and look them over? Or are they open on a weekday?"

"I think they are — I've seen people going in and out at odd times." Then Val added a diplomatic word. "I told Father Burnham that maybe you could help him with some funny things that are going on down there. He said it was bad to bring up children in the same neighborhood with them, and that the politicians aren't doing anything about it. He didn't go into any details, of course."

Mr. Maddox grunted noncommittally, but when Val got up to come and kiss him gratefully, he patted her on the back and gruffly told her to be a good girl while he was gone. Then he went through much the same rite with his wife, adding the suggestion that she take something and lie down. He promised to be home for lunch.

He then went down to his office, where he put in a morning calculated to strike terror into the heart of any employee who crossed his path. Whatever had gone wrong with the chief nobody could guess, but not a man, woman, or office boy on the pay roll of Maddox & Maddox felt secure in his job for more than a few hours longer. Many were the relieved sighs that went up when, at a quarter to one, a flushed and jittery secretary announced to the force that he had gone for the day!

As he drove home Mr. Maddox thought grimly that he had a score to settle with that officious little Mary Anderson who had started all the trouble in the first place. There was no question but that when once Rome stuck in its fangs, a person was a gone goose. Now that he came to think of it, he believed in his heart he had always known they hadn't seen the last of this popery business, at least since Val had joined St. Giles's. Well, maybe some day the kid would come to her senses and be satisfied with sound Methodism, but in the meantime Alice and he must let her have her head and just hope for the best. If you fought them it only made kids more determined to go their own way, after they got too old to spank. They did it when they wanted to marry, and it looked as if this notion of Val's was just some more of the same.

The head of the House of Maddox rarely came home to lunch, and today Sweet Magnolia celebrated the event by dishing up a meal that soothed his temper to some extent. Feeling almost normal at its close, and ready to cooperate with his daughter so far as a reasonable man could go, he announced that he was ready to start their inspection tour whenever they wished.

"It still looks pretty cloudy," he said, glancing at the window, "but at least it isn't raining. You girls get into your things, and I'll get the car serviced."

Mrs. Maddox looked at him piteously, but like a good wife and self-sacrificing mother she obediently went to get her coat and hat. The morning had been hard on her. For one thing, she had been alone most of the time, Val having to take a music lesson, the first she had had since the accident to her finger; following which she had been summoned by Dr. Havern to talk over plans for some music program. Mrs. Maddox hadn't spirits to inquire what it was, when the girl came in just a few minutes before her father's arrival, and therefore she had nothing to do all morning but worry.

She had been concerned about Val all this past week. The girl had seemed so tired and depressed, though not gloomy — thank God, Val was never that — but she just wasn't quite herself in spite of her obvious effort to act as usual. The mother's heart had ached to comfort her, but as Val had said nothing, her mother couldn't force a confidence. Mrs. Maddox suspected a quarrel with Anthony, which would be natural enough, though distressing. However, now that Val had confided in her parents, it was found to be worse than anybody could have suspected.

Mrs. Maddox sighed heavily. Why did this have to happen? Val had been such sunshine all her life — a little self-willed sometimes, but always loving and sweet and reasonable. And life had been opening out for her so promisingly, too, with the prospect of marrying a most excellent young man of high character as well as great charm and exceptional family connections. What would happen there if Val persisted in this fantastic idea of joining the Romish Church?

She was just leaving her room as the thought crossed her mind; and meeting Val in the corridor, the mother spoke impulsively.

"What does Anthony say about this?" she asked abruptly.

"Oh, Mother, I don't know! I haven't said anything — He'll be terribly hurt, I know. I hate to think about it."

Her mother put tender arms about her, and the girl clung to her tightly.

"Let's not worry about it now, darling," soothed the older woman. "He may take it in the right spirit. You're entitled to think for yourself (God forgive me for saying that! she added under her breath). I hear the car now. Let's not keep Daddy waiting."

It was a strange pilgrimage they made that afternoon. The first stop was at the nearest of those dread churches, old St. Columban's, dark and forbidding as ever from the exterior.

Mrs. Maddox shivered and clung to her husband's arm as she entered a Catholic church for the first time in her life; and Val, for all her resolution, was disposed to abandon the whole project and go home. Could anything be more crazy than taking her family into this temple of strange worship, introducing them to some unknown religion that she couldn't explain to them? It was too ridiculous, and she couldn't go through with it! Then she put out a steady hand and opened the door.

Immediately everything became all right again. The church was dim and empty and still. There was no blaze of light from the great altar, no sound of music from the choir loft, no kneeling worshipers. Yet in some strange way a great Presence filled the silent aisles with light and life and color, for this was indeed the House of the Lord.

As one led, Val quietly and steadily walked toward the altar, her parents following uncertainly, and dropped on her knees at the communion rail. After a brief hesitation the other two did likewise, but their daughter was not conscious of them for the moment.

This was a real church. People came here to worship and to petition, to weep and to rejoice. They laid their griefs and joys before the altar; they begged help in affliction, for strength to fight their sins, for comfort in sorrow. The feeling was everywhere — the very walls were impregnated with prayer, the stones of the floor were rich in devotion. And there was the lamp before the altar, indicating that our Lord was truly present — Jesus who had compassion on the multitude out in that desert place, and miraculously fed them — Jesus who had said, *"I am the Living Bread . . . if any man eat of this Bread he shall live forever."*

She started when her mother touched her gently on the arm.

"Val, dear, are those the idols that they worship?" whispered Mrs. Maddox. Whatever her daughter's new beliefs, she must speak respectfully of them.

"Where?" asked Val, looking around.

With a forefinger her father silently indicated a pair of handsome marble statues above the side altars, one a sweet-faced woman in flowing robes with her hands stretched out as if in welcome, the other a young man who strangely carried his heart in his hand.

"Oh no," Val spoke confidently. "Catholics don't worship any idols. They just worship the Blessed Sacrament there in that little house on the altar. Mary Anderson told me that when you see the red lamp burning, you know the Blessed Sacrament is there."

"Then what are those images for?" rumbled Mr. Maddox. "There are some more over there, and on that side, too. What do they do with them?"

Val shook her head. It really had been rather silly to bring them here before she knew how to explain things. Then she looked back at the first two statues, and light broke.

"Oh, those! Of course! The woman is the Virgin Mary, and that one must be intended for Jesus, though I don't understand about the heart. It might be to show that He loved people, don't you think?"

Her father shrugged, and Mrs. Maddox gave a little gasp. Of course, it was the Virgin Mary, and everybody knew that the Romanists worshiped her! Val was being terribly hoodwinked.

They went to many other churches for a brief visit in each. Val had taken the telephone book along to get addresses, and they were surprised to see how well established the papists seemed to be in the town. It was frightening, too — a church in practically every neighborhood. Some of them were small, cheap, and garish. Some were large and handsome, or large and ugly; in some there was evidence of wealth and good taste, others made no secret of their poverty.

There was the Blessed Sacrament Church over on the West Side which, for the honor of its name, Val was glad to see was a lovely austere Gothic, with exquisite windows and statuary, and the plainest sort of a liturgical altar which looked priceless. There was shabby old St. Joseph's, down near the railroad station where it was convenient for travelers, grimy with smoke from ten thousand engines, its floor worn thin by the tramp of many hundred thousands of feet.

After they once got accustomed to it, the pilgrims always knew what to look for. The statues of the Virgin Mary and Jesus with His Sacred Heart never failed to be present. Then there was an older man with a branch of lilies over one shoulder and a Child on his arm who, by some burst of intuition, Val decided was Joseph. The really old man with the keys in his hand, appearing sometimes but not always, was probably Peter; and while it was only by an association of ideas, they assumed the corresponding statue with the sword must be Paul. There were other images of saints quite unknown, though Val did recognize Francis with the birds around him; and, of course, there were plenty of angels everywhere. But always they found that red lamp burning before the tabernacle where the Blessed Sacrament was hidden, no matter how poor the church was— or even how rich. Mr. Maddox finally admitted it was beginning to get him.

In most of the churches they found anywhere from one to a dozen people in the pews, absorbed in their own private devotions and paying no attention to the visitors. Occasionally a church would be entirely empty, and then the family tiptoed about, frankly snooping.

In one of these inspection tours they discovered the confessionals. Mrs. Maddox recoiled in horror as from the plague, but Val's blood was up by that time, and she boldly pushed one of the curtains aside. The sight that met their curious gaze was disappointing—just a tiny cubicle only big enough for a man to stand upright, a little grille set into the inner wall with a crucifix hanging over it and a narrow kneeling bench below.

"This isn't anything," said Val in a letdown voice. "I wonder what's in here. Probably where the priest stays," and she put out a hand to open the little half door in the center.

In an agitated whisper Mrs. Maddox begged her to let it alone, but Val persisted and found the priest's section no more exciting than the penitent's. A bench to sit upon, and tiny white curtains on the wall at either side. Val pried into this and found the little sliding doors under these curtains. She peered through the grille.

"Why, you can't see a thing!" she exclaimed.

"Are you sure?" her father wanted to know. "Let's try."

So while Mother nervously did sentry duty to warn them if anybody was coming, Mr. Maddox and Val took the time-honored positions of priest and penitent, and found that yet another cherished myth was in danger of being exploded. In the darkness of the confessional all that they were to each other was a voice going through that little grating from one unseen person to another.

"I wonder what they do in here," muttered Dad. "They certainly can't enjoy it very much unless they wear pads on their knees." He rose stiffly to his feet and began rubbing his own injured kneecaps.

"We'll have to find out," replied Val. "I can ask —"

At this point an excited whisper from the sentry interrupted this guessing with the announcement that somebody was just outside, and the explorers were soon busy admiring a window representing the Good Shepherd, so that the newcomers were in no way scandalized.

Mother hurried them away from that church, declaring she had almost died of fright, and anyhow she thought they were going too far in this business. In fact, she felt the whole expedition was flying in the face of Providence, and that no good could come of it.

"I think we'd better go home!" she said emphatically.

"Couldn't you come with me to this last one?" coaxed Val. "We'll just have time before my lesson with Father Burnham, and I would like you to meet him. He wants to see Dad, too. You remember I told you. But you won't have to stay long. I do wish you'd look at the church and see if you understand what I mean."

Mother sighed resignedly.

"All right, dear. If you two want to risk your souls this way, I'll risk mine. We'll all be lost or saved together."

"You didn't think it was a particularly nice church, you said?" observed Mr. Maddox as he started his engine.

"No, not at all nice. But the way Father explained it, I could see where it really didn't make too much difference—" Val hesitated, at a loss to convey her meaning. "Wait till you see it, and then maybe you'll have the background. I'll ask Father to repeat what he told me."

Bridge Street was pretty much as it had been yesterday, except that there were more people in evidence, especially as to the children, who whooped and rioted in the middle of the street with even more abandon than before. The houses and yards looked worse, and Mrs. Maddox's tidy instincts revolted from the disorder and dilapidation; but she only set her lips and silently prayed for strength to go through with it. Her husband was more vocal.

"My Lord, Val! How did you come to find a place like this? What brought you here, anyway?"

Val replied truthfully that she didn't know. "Must have been trying to run away—from my conscience, that is," she added, noting her mother's startled face. "But I'm afraid it caught up with me after all."

The visit, as it turned out, was disappointing in one sense. The neighborhood had prepared the visitors for something pretty awful; but as the short, dark afternoon was far gone by that time, they found the inside of the church full of softening shadows. The grotesque statues, the battered pews, were now but the merest outline. All the grime and discoloration had melted into the kindly dusk, leaving but an impression of silence and mystery. There was only that familiar lamp burning clear, glowing like a ruby in the dimness, lighting the way to the Lord in the tabernacle.

"Nothing very bad about this," commented Mr. Maddox in his strident whisper.

"It's dark," supplemented Mrs. Maddox tremulously. "If we didn't have that lamp—" Then after a pause, during which her daughter stood silent, she added, "Do we just kneel and pray?"

CHAPTER VIII

THE young couple had hoped that tomorrow's sun would not go down before they had the good long talk they had promised themselves — at least Anthony hoped it, and Val prayed for courage to go through with it. But neither hopes nor fears mattered in the least in the final analysis, because nothing happened. In their plan they had not reckoned with Dr. Havern.

The district canvass to find out who were worthy to receive the Christmas baskets, and who were to be cast out and ejected as chiselers, took many days and much running around from one welfare office to another. The neighborhood Christmas celebration, sponsored by the North Side Chamber of Commerce, also required time and an eagle eye kept on the subversive Brick Church, added to which the rector let out another link and went in seriously for a great many other civic and religious enterprises, such as the Red Cross, Bundles for Britain, Books for Soldiers, Christmas trees for the Sunday School and the Boy Scouts, personal gifts for everybody in the Old Ladies' and Old Men's Homes, and a dozen more worthy objects, all of which he performed vicariously through his curate.

Dr. Havern also paid some attention to his organist. He knew she had a good many other interests besides her work in the church; so for good measure he inaugurated a joint carol service for several churches in the neighborhood to be held on the Sunday before Christmas in the Scottish Rite Temple as on neutral ground, and entailing endless rehearsals at strange hours. This, together with a most elaborate Christmas program for St. Giles's itself, took pretty good care of Miss Maddox. Personally the rector had nothing against her, but everything had to be utilized in his plan for the chastening of Anthony Drew.

This scheme worked with a smooth perfection that stamped Dr. Havern a strategist of the first order. Not only was Drew kept busy day and night, with barely time out for food and sleep, but his young soul was annoyed almost to the exploding point. A little more, and the curate would hand in his resignation of his own accord, the rector could have his parish to himself, and the conditions before would be resumed to everybody's satisfaction. Dr. Havern might get himself another helper — as a matter of fact, he saw where it was a delightful thing to have somebody to order around, as well as to be active on civic and national society boards with a subordinate to do the work — but at least he would do the picking next time and get somebody he liked.

The only mistake the rector made in his campaign was underestimating Anthony's endurance. Time after time the curate was all but going over to the rectory to explain just what he thought of his superior and the job generally, and each time he fought down the impulse. The first of the year had been the date agreed upon between him and Val, both as to a possible change in his work and the setting of the wedding day, and he grimly held on. He would show the rector and Val that he was no quitter. It would be only a few weeks more, and in the meantime he could and would take it!

His mother complained that she never saw him any more, even on Sundays, and his long confidential talk with Val was postponed to an indefinite date. It was simply ridiculous that he shouldn't get at least an hour to himself, and he more than suspected the rector's hand in this sudden burst of activity on Val's part. That was another point to be gone over when he and Dr. Havern had their final reckoning.

In all of this activity not the least of Anthony's troubles was the sudden intrusion of Jasper Maddox into the rushing current of his life. After that one encounter on the first day of his tenancy Anthony had very little contact with Jasper, partly through his own skill in sidestepping and partly because Jasper himself had not really given the matter too much attention, being occupied with more important matters. In due course, however, Jasper got around to bringing his mind to bear on the problem of what connection there might be between Drew and his cousin Val.

Late one afternoon about the middle of that last week in November, being the day before Thanksgiving, in fact, Anthony was working busily in the parish office. Diligence had been rewarded with some measure of success, and by now he had made fair progress in the work of sorting out the chiselers and the nonchiselers from among the poor of the parish, his present task being to decipher the almost illegible notes he had hurriedly jotted down that day on his rounds, and was about half through the job when he heard his name pronounced in a voice vastly different from Dr. Havern's rich tones.

"Afternoon, Drew," said the voice, and looking up with a start the curate saw standing in the doorway none other than Jasper Maddox who had dropped in to pay a call.

"Oh, it's you, is it?" was Drew's not overly cordial greeting to the intruder. Since the night Val had confessed to being a third cousin of Jasper, as one introducing the family skeleton, Anthony had no scruples about being a little short with the young gentleman. "What's the matter with the bell — won't it ring?"

"I didn't bother," replied Jasper easily. "Door wasn't locked." He dropped into the visitors' chair unbidden and looked about him curiously. "How do you like it around here by this time?" he demanded.

"All right." To himself, Anthony excused this deviation from the truth on the grounds that it was none of Jasper's business.

Jasper made an inarticulate sound in his nasal passages to express something — whether gratification or incredulity it would be hard to say.

"I don't see much of old man Havern these days," he went on, shifting about in his chair in an effort to find out if the cushion was all lumps. "He all right? I've been so busy myself lately that I haven't got around very much."

"Really?" Anthony raised his eyebrows politely, though he went on with his work. "Dr. Havern seems in pretty good shape so far as I can judge."

Jasper waited briefly for Anthony to inquire what it was that had been taking up his time during the past few weeks, but as the curate merely went on writing as if nobody else were present, the visitor was obliged to volunteer the information.

"Yes, sir," he said, crossing his knees as best he could from an angle of about sixty degrees, "I've been busy. I tell you there's a lot of work about building a chapel, and if I hadn't been right there all the time I don't know what would have happened."

In spite of himself Anthony's attention was caught.

"What chapel was that?" he asked, lifting his gaze from the mass of scribbled papers on the desk.

"Ours," returned Jasper, gratified at this interest. "We just finished building it out in Rixton Gardens. Had our first service there last Sunday. I was the one who got it done, too. If it hadn't been for me, they never could have made it."

"Good for you," Anthony congratulated him, meanwhile wondering if the Church of High Holiness was increasing as fast as all that, and at the same time thinking, with a little pang of envy, that St. Giles's was in no danger of overflowing for some time to come. "Has your membership outgrown the place on Ninth Street?"

Jasper hesitated a moment.

"Well, no," he said finally, feeling a little reluctant to give out figures. "It wasn't that exactly — it was a matter of conscience. You see, we had to do what you'll be doing one of these days if you don't want to go down into the pit. I tell you, Drew," warming to the subject, "your Church is tottering on the verge of Romanism, and if you don't look out—"

"You don't mean to say," broke in Drew, regarding him with astonishment, "that your church over here has got in communion with Rome? How did that happen?"

"No!" denied Jasper explosively, his tow-colored head with its pale eyes and outstanding ears rearing up indignantly behind the knees which formed a sort of breastwork in front of him. "What are you talking about? What put that into your head?"

"Sorry," apologized Anthony, stifling a laugh. "It was just an association of ideas I suppose. Skip it, anyway, and let's start all over again. What did happen?"

The outraged Jasper was of two minds, whether to go on with it or not, and replied stiffly that he hadn't come in there to be insulted; but on Anthony's repeating that it was just a misunderstanding, he cooled down and condescended to explain. After all, that had been one of his main reasons for coming to call in the first place — letting Drew know what an important figure he was in the Church.

During the previous summer, so his story ran, a schism had sprung up in the fold of the Church of High Holiness. The tenets of faith were clear cut and definite — Rum, Romanism, and Roistering must be put down, nor were the religious ceremonies in any degree complex. The Sunday and midweek services were conducted by a group of earnest souls for the purpose of singing some rousing hymns, reading such texts from the Old Testament as called down vengeance upon the unrighteous, and delivering a fiery sermon on the evils of drinking, dancing, card playing, theaters, and other forms of "carrying on," taking up these subjects in regular rotation; also no discourse was complete without a special denunciation of Rome, the Scarlet Woman.

At first blush it might seem difficult, if not entirely impossible, to work up a heresy on such a simple creed, but it had happened; and the dissenters, led by Jasper, thereupon were moved to build their own chapel in the new district of Rixton Gardens, just being developed on the outskirts of the fast-growing city, and far enough away from the parent church that they might conduct their affairs as they pleased without interference.

"They were fallen upon evil ways," said Jasper with reference to the original congregation. "The sons and daughters of Belial were serving other gods."

Pressed to explain what this meant, Jasper answered vaguely that their eyes were held and their tongues were as the adder's. Not being gifted with powers of divination, Anthony was at a loss to know what this meant until he remembered Val's remark that she thought Jasper wanted to belong to the Holiness clergy. Perhaps the sons and daughters of Belial had not been able to see eye to eye with him in this respect, which might account for his bitterness in the matter. Anthony followed his hunch.

"Do you mean to say they wouldn't let you preach at all?" he asked in a sympathetic voice which robbed the question of any impertinence.

"They certainly didn't!" replied Jasper solemnly, his guard entirely down. "That fellow Hofer thinks he can run the church to suit himself, and he won't let anybody else have a show. He doesn't know the first thing about preaching, and everybody is getting sick of him. Well, we showed him, all right! Maybe next time he won't try to hog the whole business." He smiled smugly as he thought of the baffled Hofer. "I got a good half of the congregation to go with me, and I bet that burned him up."

"That was a pretty good following," commented Anthony. Maybe the white-eyed youth had something to him after all, if he could split a congregation wide open in retaliation for being slighted. Anthony wondered briefly if his Evensong flock would rally around him that way, in case matters ever came to a showdown between himself and the rector; but after a moment's consideration he decided there was nothing to it. With something like respect he gazed upon his visitor, partially submerged in the visitors' chair. "And you had enough to build a new chapel out of hand! What do you call it?"

"The Church of the New Sanctity," replied Jasper, purring with satisfaction. "Yes, we built it, all right. One of the men had a lot out in Rixton Garden — or his wife owned part of it anyhow, and she made him donate that, and three or four of them contributed their work, and the others gave their notes for one hundred dollars each. That made a thousand dollars, so I took their notes and made up the rest. I didn't begrudge the fifteen hundred, not for a minute, so long as I'm running things out there!"

"That makes about fifteen families all told," ventured Anthony after a swift mental calculation, and thinking how small the chapel must be, also that Jasper wasn't doing so badly in a financial way.

"What if it does?" Jasper suddenly realized that as the leader of the new sect he had been perhaps a little too outspoken to this underling in an old line, orthodox (he called it reactionary and outdated) denomination, even if the underling had come from Cyrus Avenue. "Anyhow, we've got the good, old-time Bible religion out there, which is more than you have here with all your aping of Rome!" he finished vindictively.

As a firm believer in the extremely Low branch of his Church, Anthony was less affected by this fling than his caller hoped he would be.

"It's nice to know you are taking the Bible with you," he replied with an amiable grin. "I suppose you preached at the service last Sunday, then?"

"In a way." A slight shade crossed Jasper's brow. "You see, the women were all so busy gabbling around and looking at everything that we didn't have much time for anything else. I gave out the hymns, though."

"Well, that was something," returned Anthony encouragingly.

Jasper glared at him with suspicion, but the other looked quite grave as he continued to riffle through his notes, so Jasper let it pass. After all, he had a second reason for coming in here today.

"Speaking of hymns, where's Val this afternoon?" he asked with a sly look at Drew's handsome profile.

"I wouldn't know." Anthony's recent exercises in self-control stood him in good stead right here, and neither by voice nor expression did he betray any emotion at the sound of the well-beloved name.

"Doesn't she hang around here a lot?" pursued Jasper, craning his neck forward as far as his knees permitted, the better to scrutinize the curate's face.

"Hang?" echoed Anthony, reaching for a baptismal register on the roll top of his desk and checking a date against his notes. "People don't hang around here, as a general thing. They usually have some business when they come — with a few exceptions." Over his shoulder he cast a cold look at his caller, who wriggled uncomfortably.

"Well, no harm in asking, is there?" mumbled Jasper, willing to leave the subject for the time being since Drew was acting

[144]

so touchy. Important though his own mission in life might be, there was no blinking the fact that young Drew stood a full head taller than he, and had a lean, hard, muscular look about him which held possibilities.

"I just thought," he continued brightly, "that you might be interested to hear about my new chapel. Drop around some time and see us. You might get some ideas about pure religion that would do you some good. I don't want to make you sore, Drew, but I don't mind telling you I think your outfit had better think what you're doing. Before you know it you'll be swallowed up in the maw of Rome. Popery is stealing silently but swiftly into the heart of their — I mean, your ecclesiastical institutions, and total submersion — no, that's the Baptists — what's the word again?" Jasper snapped his fingers in an effort to catch the elusive term.

"What's all this line of talk?" demanded Anthony in surprise at the outburst. "Is this the sermon you didn't get to preach last Sunday?" But Jasper wasn't listening.

"Wait a minute — I've got it now." He pointed a bony fore-finger at Anthony as he continued in his reediest head tones. "Subversion! That's it. Total subversion will ultimately ensue. What I mean to say is that if your Church doesn't look out you'll be groaning under the iron sway of Papal power. Take Italy, for instance, once the acknowledged mistress of the seven hills — I mean, once the acknowledged mistress of the world as she sat enthroned on the seven hills — uh, hills —" Once more he paused as memory appeared to fail him, while the astounded Anthony regarded him open mouthed.

"That must have been a powerful sermon," he observed. "Too bad you didn't manage to get it out while it was hot. Did you think it all up yourself?"

Jasper drew a long breath and plunged in again.

"Well, anyway, she is now a miserable waste, divided between petty sovereigns, and a byword for guilt and degradation. The glorious image lies a ruin at our feet, devoured by the monster Hydra!"

"Hey, back up!" interrupted Anthony, puzzled to account

for the familiar sound of what was evidently a quotation from something, though imperfectly memorized by the leader of the Church of the New Sanctity. "Italy's only got one king right now, unless you count Mussolini. Don't you think you'd better get your references a little more up to date before you spring them?"

Taken aback, Jasper looked at him in silence for a moment, then began to struggle to his feet.

"Well, I just meant to say," he replied at last, deflated and at a loss, "I wasn't thinking about anything political, exactly, but it does go to show that you can't hook up Church and State and get away with it, doesn't it?"

There was a hint of appeal in his voice — apparently his speech hadn't gone over quite as well as it should.

"All right, have it your own way," agreed Drew, again picking up his pen. "Congratulations on the new meeting house, and I hope you have a nice holiday tomorrow. Good-by."

"Good-by," echoed Jasper pensively, and slowly withdrew.

Thereafter, every few days Jasper made it his business to drop into the parish office at odd hours, in the hope of getting a line on his cousin and finding out how much time she spent with the curate. In this he had no better luck than the curate himself who, if he saw Val at all, which was rarely, met her only in the presence of the St. Cecilias, or with the even heavier chaperonage of the massed choirs of the neighborhood, all of whom were rehearsing Christmas music for dear life. Jasper grew almost as discouraged as Anthony.

Neither of the gentlemen felt any worse about the situation than Val did, though she was equally powerless to do anything about it under all the circumstances.

One of her many engagements was something that neither Anthony nor Dr. Havern dreamed of in their wildest moments, though the more wily Jasper might have given them a tip. Regularly, two evenings a week, the Maddox family drove down to the rectory of St. Stanislaus', and took instructions in Catholic doctrine; but on all seven nights a week Val spent many hours worrying. Not only was she obliged in common courtesy

to tell her fiancé about her change of faith, but it was impera-
tive that he be allowed to say what he wanted to do in the
matter, before any hint of their engagement got out. Val was
beginning to realize what might happen if a Protestant clergyman found himself with a Roman Catholic wife on his hands.

In the first flush of her ardor that Sunday night Val was
simply bursting to tell Anthony all about it. Being the most
high-minded, reasonable, sympathetic man in the world, with
ideals so like her own in practically everything, she felt sure
he would understand and approve after he got over the first
shock. It would take considerable explaining, of course, but
since Catholicism was the true faith, and she could never be
really happy outside of it, Anthony was sure to see the matter
through her eyes when it was properly presented to him.

Perhaps if she had talked with him that night, with the
momentum generated by her own enthusiasm to carry her
through, she might have been able to bear down some of his
preconceived ideas and prejudices; but the Christmas baskets
had interfered. After that, with each day's delay, it was harder.
It was plain that this was not a subject for hurried discussion —
in fact, it would probably need several talks to thresh it out
properly. Anthony had all the Protestant objections to the Catholic Church which she had ever entertained, but without the
queer bias toward Rome which had so suddenly appeared in
the fabric of her own life. He would have far greater difficulty
in adjusting himself to accept the truth than she had, once she
met it face to face.

Then there was the matter of his standing as a clergyman. In
this instance it wasn't just a question of agreeing to disagree in
religious matters, as in the case of an ordinary mixed marriage.
She had never known an instance of a minister with a wife
of even some different Protestant faith, but it was unthinkable
that he should marry a Roman Catholic. Any minister doing
that would instantly have to resign his pulpit and try to find
some other profession where such things didn't matter; and
knowing how dear his ministry was to Anthony, the girl saw
where this would be a very painful choice for him. She knew

[147]

he loved her, deeply and sincerely; but in all humility she wondered if she or any woman was worth such a sacrifice.

Still, lack of courage was never one of Val's failings, and she had honestly tried to arrange a time when they could get together and have it out. In this, though, she was foiled by Dr. Havern. Failing a personal interview, she had repeatedly tried to write a letter which would get her ideas over to Anthony, but this also had been without avail. The explanations were too many and too long and complicated, and she knew she could never make the thing clear without hurting him to the soul.

One Friday morning when December was nearly half gone, Val hurried from her house to a rehearsal of the carol service, the inconvenient hour of nine-thirty being a rare time when the Scottish Rite auditorium could be had for outside purposes. As usual, one half of her mind was on her own personal problems which haunted her waking and sleeping, while the other half wrestled with the job coming up. Had Mrs. Coffey got well of her cold? Would the organist from the Baptist Church remember to bring in the violinist who was supposed to do the obbligato to the Lullaby? Would any power on earth make that man from the music store get the orchestra parts done in time for the closing number? What would she do —

"What are you looking so sour about?" said a voice in her ear at this point.

"Gracious!" Val shied violently to the curb, then turned indignantly on her cousin Jasper who had quietly slipped up on her from behind. "What do you mean by sneaking up on me like that!" She grabbed at the armload of music which at her start had all but slid to the ground.

"You could have heard me if you hadn't been thinking about something you didn't want known." Jasper's look was hideously coy.

"I'm perfectly willing to tell you." Val was beginning to recover. "I thought my arm was about broken. So now that you're here, you might carry some of these books for me."

Jasper accepted the load gloomily.

"You're wasting your time if you think you're going to get anything out of this fool concert," he told her, scuffling his feet irritatingly on the pavement as he walked along. "Nobody'll come anyhow."

"Maybe," she replied, and wondered why he seemed so low spirited this morning. Jasper's attitude toward life being one of burning eagerness, though most of his enthusiasms had disastrous results for other people, it was strange to see him so wilted and cast down as he appeared this morning.

In truth the whole edifice of Jasper's dreams had fallen in ruins last night at the prayer meeting (held on Thursday night just to show their independence of the mother church, whose midweek service was on Wednesday) when matters had come to a crisis between himself and Mr. Larkin, the donor of the land on which the new chapel was built. Or rather, it was Mrs. Larkin who really made the trouble.

Jasper had felt, with some reason, that he had every right to dictate the policy of the New Sanctity, since the migration had been largely on his account; also his contribution to the new building was far and away greater than all the rest of them put together. Therefore it seemed to follow as the night the day that he was to be the guiding star in all things connected with the church, not the least of which was the preaching.

As he had told Anthony, the first Sunday of the congregation's settling into the new meetinghouse had been just one of those things; but he naturally expected by midweek that the novelty would have worn off, the ladies' curiosity satisfied, and that a regular routine could be established without further delay. To his surprise and annoyance, however, midweek was practically a counterpart of Sunday's doings, some of the High Holiness crowd having come out to inspect the new chapel and see what was going on, and instead of a religious service the affair rapidly degenerated into a species of pink tea which Jasper was powerless to stop.

The next Sunday fate took a hand, laying Jasper low with a severe cold involving an attack of laryngitis which kept him in bed and speechless the greater part of the week. And by the time he arrived in Rixton Gardens on the Sunday after that (a little late, perhaps, but who could suppose the outfit would keep hours like a railroad timetable!), to his shocked amazement he found Mr. Larkin firmly established in the pulpit of the New Sanctity. Whereupon all the old trouble broke out again.

After the service Jasper made what he believed to be a just complaint, saying that his absence last week, both on Sunday and Thursday, had been something beyond his control, and didn't mean that he had forfeited his right to the pulpit; but to this Mr. Larkin had only replied evasively that they were glad to see Brother Maddox was so much better, and that things seemed to be going along their appointed way. Jasper took what comfort he could out of this; but he promised himself to be on the spot bright and early for the midweek.

At a quarter to eight on Thursday evening, therefore, he presented himself at the chapel, only to find that the hour of prayer had been abruptly advanced to seven-thirty, and Mr. Larkin again in the saddle. This, Jasper felt, called for a show-down, then and there.

Mr. Larkin stoutly resisted the demand that he "come down from there!" and Mrs. Larkin backed him up with wifely zeal. In fact, she took over the proceedings from then on, pointing out to the hotly protesting Jasper that in addition to being actually in possession, Mr. Larkin had the further advantage of owning a magnificent, rolling bass voice that did far greater justice to the words "Woe unto them" (the backbone of all New Sanctity sermons) than Jasper's reedy pipe. And when Jasper threatened to collect on the congregation's notes which he held, and to shut up the church, Mrs. Larkin not only dared him to try it, but urged him to do it at once.

"You get this building off our land!" she shrilled, a menacing forefinger within an inch of his nose. "Take it down right this minute. There's plenty of people here that would be glad to help!"

A murmur, approaching a roar, rose from the throng. At the High Holiness meeting the evening before a rumor had gone around that there were likely to be high doings out at New Sanctity, and tonight practically the entire congregation had arrived in a body. These, added to the local worshipers, now packed the little meetinghouse to suffocation, and having nothing to lose in any regard, also disliking Jasper intensely as one who had started trouble in the city church, said that they would be only too willing to lend a hand.

One visitor gave confirmation to this generous response by instantly breaking a window, and the session thereupon took on the aspect of a Donnybrook Fair. The New Sanctity-ites, while solidly in favor of Mr. Larkin, considered that pulling down the chapel over Jasper's ears was really going a little too far, at least while those hundred dollar notes were out; and resenting this piece of highhandedness, they turned upon their former associates. The visitors were not slow to answer in kind, and the original dispute was very soon forgotten in the general uproar.

It took a good while to restore order, but it was done at last. The visitors, feeling that they had had a pleasant and satisfactory evening, put on their coats, tidied their hair, shook hands heartily all around, and withdrew with many good wishes for the success of the chapel under the able direction of Mr. and Mrs. Larkin. The new pastorate having been thus confirmed through blood and fire, as it were, the defeated Jasper stole sadly away into the night. His one consolation was that those notes drew a good, healthy interest, and that, come what might, they weren't going to be renewed when the ninety days were up.

All of this explains why his looks were so pale and wan that Friday morning just twelve days before Christmas, and why he dragged his feet so heavily as he walked down the street with his fair cousin Val. It also explained something that was not immediately apparent, that is, why he was all ready and waiting to take out some of his ill temper on the first person who crossed him.

"What's the matter with you, when it comes down to it?" asked Val, somewhat in the manner of his greeting to her when they met. "And for goodness' sake, don't drag your feet."

Her cousin sighed.

"Oh," he responded glumly, "I just don't feel so good."

"That's too bad," she responded with a touch of sympathy. After all, Jasper was at least half a human being, and he'd had flu recently. "How's your cold?"

"Rotten." He coughed hollowly. "It was going out to that church last night that did it."

"Too bad you had to go so far," murmured the girl vaguely, as a new difficulty presented itself to her already overladen mind. If Jasper had a cold, why shouldn't the various choirs come down with flu also, either simultaneously or in relays? What would she do then? Mrs. Coffey was only just recovering from hers, the tenor from the Brick Church had the sniffles last night, and who knew how many more would have succumbed by this morning!

So busy was she with this distressing picture that she was only dimly conscious of her cousin's voice as he painstakingly described his aches and pains and temperatures, lack of appetite, and the number of hours he stayed awake at night. Even when he started to tell about the gross injustice he, a sick man, had suffered at the hands of the Larkin family, she had only half an ear to give him.

"I tell you, they're no better than that monster hydra down the street!" he finished viciously, jerking his head in the direction of St. Columban's square tower which stood out starkly against the bright winter sky.

"What hydrant?" asked Val absently, her eye fixed on the auditorium door which they were now approaching, and thinking it would just be her luck to find it locked and have to hunt up the key from somewhere.

"I didn't say hydrant—I said hydra. Your old friend St. Columban's down there. Everybody knows that's one of the monster hydras—"

Val interrupted with a hoot of laughter. She not only found the quotation familiar, as Anthony had, but she recognized whence it had come.

"Jasper, for goodness' sake!" she exclaimed, testing the door to see if it was open. It was, thank haven! "Why don't you look up a word in the dictionary before you use it? Some day somebody's going to think you're pretty funny. Thanks for the lift. Good-by — I'll send you a dictionary for Christmas if you want it. And don't drag your feet!"

Jasper followed her with malevolent eyes as she disappeared, still laughing. After a short, reflective pause he turned away.

"All right for you, old girl!" he thought, all the bitterness of last night's defeat rushing into this pin prick. "Think I'm funny, do you? You'll be laughing out of the other side of your mouth before I get through with you!"

Anthony was busy as usual at his desk that morning, and so deep in the mass of notes before him that he paid no attention to the sound of the front door opening.

"Well," piped a familiar voice from the doorway, "how's the pride of St. Giles's this morning?"

Anthony looked up stonily. He was getting very fed up with Jasper, whom he had long ago put in the class of undesirables.

"Good morning," he returned shortly, and went on with his work. Jasper was not shaken off so easily.

"Making notes for your sermon, are you?" He boldly craned his neck to see how far the work had got. Forgetting the object of his visit for the moment, he opened out on a subject of perennial interest to him. "I heard part of one of your talks a couple of weeks back when I was passing the church here one evening. I didn't have anything special to do and I thought I'd drop in for a few minutes. I don't mind telling you, Drew, I didn't think much of it. Too soft, too milk-and-watery. Now, when I'm preaching I always tell 'em: 'Woe unto you, ye —'" Remembering Mrs. Larkin's strictures, he dropped his voice an octave and a half into his lowest register and tried again: " 'Woe unto you, ye hypocrites —'" Again he stopped. The effort was too much for his vocal chords, and he choked on the last word.

"You ought to do something about that cough," observed Anthony, ignoring the good advice. "And if you haven't anything important to talk about I'll have to tell you I'm busy."

"Oh, I think you have time to listen." Jasper lowered himself into the only available chair, then cleared his throat again. "But I just thought I'd mention this for your own good. You're missing your opportunities in your preaching. You've got to admit that your Church isn't following the old-time religion that was handed down by our forefathers. It's getting too much like popery — all those bowings and scrapings and candles and stuff. The next thing you know you'll all be worshiping idols and kissing the Pope's toe, like the Romanists. It isn't Protestant, Drew."

"Well, Jeremiah," returned Anthony, looking up a citation in the encyclopedia, "what do you think you have to do with it?"

"I just don't like it," asserted Jasper with a solemn shake of the head. "The Romanists are getting too strong over here right now, with their degrading superstitions and confessionals and Jesuits and all that, without your joining —"

"If that's a sample of what you have to say," broke in Anthony, "I'm still busy."

But Jasper held up a hand for silence, and drawing a long breath he began to intone impressively:

"The fat Romish priests grind down the workingman and then make 'em pay for indulgences. Unscrupulously employing every method, the fagot, the wheel, and all the secret horrors of the Inquisition, they were — I mean, they will be — brought to bear upon all who dare to assume the privilege of worshiping God according to the dictates of an unfettered conscience. If the bloody tragedies of the Middle Ages are no longer acted on the theater of a more enlightened world, it's because the power so awfully abused has been wrested —"

Genuinely interested, Anthony had lifted his head from his work and was regarding his caller with a bright-eyed, intent stare. Confused by this sudden attention, Jasper, whose voice had been almost sonorous, here stumbled in his speech.

"The power so lawfully abused — at least, I mean awfully abused has been wrestl — wrested from the scarlet-robed tenants of the Vatican." He paused uncertainly. "The — the Vatican — uh — Vatican. They are scarlet, you know!" defensively. "The

[154]

Scarlet Woman on the Seven Hills. Anyhow — what are you doing?"

Silently Anthony left his chair and walked over to the bookcase where he found a brightly-bound volume of ordinary lending library appearance, and began looking through its pages.

"Go on," he said. "I'm listening."

"Well, I was just saying that the Popish Church is the Scarlet Woman of the Vatican." Jasper was beginning to perspire and to wish he hadn't commenced this flight of oratory. Once started, it seemed impossible to stop, so he struggled on bravely. "The bloody tragedies of the Middle Ages — I said that before, didn't I? Anyway —"

Anthony leaned against the corner of the bookcase, facing his visitor.

"Here you are, page 178." He read aloud:

'. . . scarlet-robed tenants of the Vatican. The same fierce, intolerable tyranny is still exercised where their jurisdiction is unquestioned.'

And so on. You'd better work on that speech a little more before you spring it again. Any time you want me to hear your lesson for you, I'll be delighted."

"Give me that book!" As scarlet of face as the robe of any tenant of the Vatican, Jasper grabbed for the volume which Anthony's longer arm held out of his reach.

"Get your own copy," replied Anthony. "This is probably contaminated by association with us anyway."

Scowling angrily, Jasper sat down again and wiped his overheated forehead. "Think you're smart!" was the best he could do in the way of repartee.

Anthony reopened the book and reminiscently read a paragraph or two.

"Good old Augusta!" he said. "It's a long time since I've even thought of her, much less quoted her; but she's something a man can't really forget! How did you happen to hit on her for the backbone of your talks, Maddox?"

"Well, I thought it was pretty good stuff," said the other sulkily. "It's all true, every word of it. And you'll find it out one of these days." Recovering himself somewhat, he leered up at the taller young man lounging against the bookcase. This was as good a way as any for letting this smart-alec know what he had come to tell him in the first place.

"Yes?" Anthony responded dreamily, still absorbed in Augusta.

"Yes. What does it say there about the hand of bigotry snatching a girl from her mother and sticking her in a convent?"

Anthony raised his eyebrows at this, but obligingly read the passage:

'Ah! how many fair young members of the household band have been decoyed from the hearthstone and immured in gloomy cells. Ah! how many a widowed parent has mourned over the wreck of all that was beautiful in a cherished daughter, snatched by the hand of bigotry from her warm embrace and forever incarcerated in monastic gloom.'

"Thinking of taking the veil, Maddox?" he said politely.

Jasper muttered something under his breath.

"No, I'm not," he growled, "but somebody else probably is. Somebody you know."

Anthony returned the book to its place and suppressed a yawn.

"Give her my love," he said, again seating himself at the desk. "Good-by. You have to slam that door or it doesn't shut."

Jasper obediently stood up and edged toward the door. It would be just as well to have his way clear to the outer air when he opened his big guns.

"Don't say I didn't warn you," he tittered. "She may not have done anything final as yet, but I'll bet it won't be long now, the way she's running around to these Romish churches. Got her father and mother going, too, like they always do. You don't mean to say she hasn't told you? All these long talks you have when you think nobody's around — just for nothing?"

His implication was but too plain, and Anthony's change of expression told him the shot had gone home. He darted toward the door as soon as the words were out of his mouth, but Anthony reached him in one stride, and catching him by the collar shook him until his ears flapped.

"You—vermin!" Anthony's face was white with a passion that surprised himself. "Say anything like that again, and I'll break you in two. Get out of here, and don't you ever come back!"

"All right, all right!" squeaked the other in terror. This young cleric certainly acted as if he meant what he said. "I was only fooling—leggo!"

"I'm not!" responded Anthony between his teeth, as he deposited his caller on the front steps with a parting shake that surpassed all former efforts. "Here, take your hat!"

He tossed it after Jasper, who made a brilliant running catch as he fled down the walk.

"Little rat!" The militant clergyman slammed the door himself with an emphasis that rocked the parish house.

Whatever Jasper had thought he was going to gain by starting a story about Val, he had picked the sure way of infuriating Anthony. That, of course, might have been his object, thought Drew, striding up and down the office in an effort to cool his temper. Perhaps in spite of all their caution the white-eyed little weasel had discovered the engagement somehow, eavesdropping probably. He had implied as much. And resenting not being told about it sooner, or from natural meanness, he had made up this lie by way of getting even, just to start trouble between them. Anthony thought with alarm that the story might be all over town by now, unless by some freak of mind Jasper had wanted to start his broadcasting here.

He reached for the telephone in the hope of warning Val before she should hear the foul rumor from someone who would be less gentle about it. Here again he met with disappointment, the bad luck which had followed him lately seeming to hold. Val was out, the maid didn't know where, nor was her mother in.

Anthony kicked over the wastebasket in futile rage. Were he and Val ever going to get together again? He wondered how Jasper had managed to discover anything about them; certainly there had been none of the long talks the little snipe had mentioned, at least not recently. But since the secret had leaked out, by whatever means, Jasper was now spreading the most injurious lie he could think of about Val and her parents; and apparently being short of the right kind of language, had memorized some of Augusta's cutting remarks about popery to introduce it.

In spite of himself, Anthony smiled at the memory of how Jasper had got himself lost in the mazes of the Vatican. It would serve the little brute right if the Inquisition did revive long enough to toast him over a slow fire for a few minutes!

Anthony went back to work, keeping a watchful eye on the clock meanwhile. He hoped there would be no more interruptions, and that he'd get the notes finished before the rector remembered to come in and demand them. They had to be right, Dr. Havern had impressed upon him.

"This is one time when Mary Tudor, in any of her guises, won't do!" the curate muttered as he bent to the task of getting up data for a paper which Dr. Havern was to read before some conference of the local ministry. Anthony suspected that the paper would not be actually written until the final minute before the meeting assembled, but he had no doubt that his superior would keep right after him until the notes were finished.

Fortunately, in the interests of peace, for the next couple of hours nobody bothered him, and by noon he had finished his research and had begun to transcribe his notes on the typewriter. He was thankful for this when Dr. Havern suddenly appeared at his elbow to inquire if anything had been done about the matter.

"I don't suppose you've even thought about that address I have to make right after the first of the year," he began pathetically. "I don't know why we can't have some cooperation around here — oh!" as his probing eye came to rest on the page now assuming proportions under the industrious pecking of Anthony's forefingers. "I see you have started. How much longer will it take?"

Mentally laying the rector beside Jasper on the gridiron, and setting an able and willing demon to work on him, Anthony pledged himself to have the manuscript done by two o'clock.

"Very well, then," replied the rector with an air of conceding

afternoon Anthony was ringing the Maddox doorbell, feeling radiantly happy though the weather was dreary and wet and he had had no lunch. At least he was going to see Val!

Her greeting dampened his high spirits, however.

"Anthony," she said, looking at him with tragic eyes as she eluded his embrace, "if you hadn't come today I think I'd have died. No, don't kiss me. Just come in, and we'll talk, first."

"What in the world—!" he began in amazement, but she waved him off, and led the way in silence to the pretty living room where they had spent so many happy hours until the rector had interfered to part them.

"Now, you sit over there, and I'll sit here," she said, appearing to have trouble with her breathing, "and then I'll tell you."

"I've something to tell you, too." Anthony thought he'd better give her a little time to get hold of herself, since she was obviously so troubled. "Maybe I'd better start first."

"No," she declared, sitting very stiff and straight, with her hands clasping the arms of her chair. "I might as well say it first as last, because you won't like it any better when I do tell you." She looked him straight in the eyes. "Anthony, I'm going to join the Roman Catholic Church."

His pitying look changed to one of astonishment. This being exactly what he was about to touch upon in his warning about Jasper, for the moment he did not take in her meaning.

"How did you guess that?" he asked.

"How did I guess what?" It was Val's turn to be mystified. "There's no guesswork about it. I am!"

"It's all right if you can make a joke of it." He had expected her to take the news angrily, or possibly with derisive laughter, but this was a queer way to act. "I didn't know the little snipe had got to you yet, but if you really don't care, then I'm not going to worry about it."

"I wish I knew what you mean!" Val's forehead was knotted in bewilderment. "I don't know where the joke comes in—it certainly isn't one to me. And as to a little snipe—oh! you mean Jasper? Good gracious! I might have known he'd be in it!"

Anthony nodded.

"Yes, that was what I was trying to tell you yesterday. He came and told me you and your family were joining, or had joined, the Roman Church, and, of course, I threw him out. Little rat! I thought if he told me, it was probably all over town by now, but I did hope you hadn't heard it. I must say, dear," noting her stricken face, "you're taking it awfully well to make light of it, but maybe you'd better not be too airy about it, or some people may believe you really have joined."

Val swallowed hard. This was worse than anything. Now she'd have to begin all over again.

"Anthony," she said distinctly, holding her voice steady by a great effort. "Listen to me carefully. I'm not taking it lightly at all, and I don't want you to think it's a joke. It isn't. I don't know how Jasper got hold of it, but for once he was telling the truth. I am going to join the Roman Church! About Dad and Mother — well, I think not. They'll probably go along with me as they did when I joined St. Giles's. We're all taking instructions two nights a week, and I want to be baptized as soon as the priest will let me. I'm horribly ignorant about it all, but I'm studying hard."

It was out now, and she saw that comprehension had dawned in the dark eyes regarding her so steadily. He believed at last that she was really in earnest, though incredulity plainly battled with enlightenment. The silence was heavy between them.

"I can't believe it," he said after a moment, passing a hand over his eyes. "Val, if you mean what you say, you simply don't know what you're talking about. You, joining that superstitious rabble! Why, it's impossible!"

"They're not all superstitious rabble," she argued. "You know a lot of people who are Catholics, like Mrs. Hungerford, and Dr. Murphy, and Judge Crozier—"

He stopped her with a weary gesture. Just like a woman to go off on particular instances, regardless of the main issue!

"I know," he said patiently, "they're very worthy people. But that isn't the point. The whole system of the Roman Church is in error, and while Mrs. Hungerford and all of them may get by on their natural goodness, it doesn't make popery a decent religion because they happen to belong to it, any more than it would hurt our faith if somebody like — well, like Jasper, belonged. You say you haven't joined yet? Val, darling, don't go into it headlong! You admit you're ignorant — you don't know what you're bringing on yourself!" Anthony was scared by this time. She seemed terribly in earnest, and yet she couldn't know what she was about to do.

"I think I do know," she replied with a pitiful little quiver in her voice as she saw her fears being realized. Her hold on him was slipping fast — the break would be complete if she couldn't make him understand and see what she was seeing, and what would she do then? "I've worried about it for years, and I've tried to stop myself from thinking. Finally it came to me that it was inevitable. I've just got to!"

Again he regarded her, astounded. He had thought he knew every turn of her mind, every desire of her heart; and yet all the time she had been hiding this!

"How did you happen to get started on this fool idea?" he asked roughly.

She told him, quite simply and briefly.

"I thought I was cured," she went on. "I was so mad at that priest out West I thought I'd never put foot into a Catholic Church again; but something kept haunting me. I suppose it was the Blessed Sacrament calling me — I don't know — but I never felt comfortable again. I couldn't find any peace in the Methodist Church, because there's no pretense of anything like the Blessed Sacrament there, and that's really why I joined St. Giles's. At the time I wouldn't have admitted it, but it is something like the Catholic Church in a good many ways. I suppose it was the ritual that attracted me, as if God had more to do — more action in the service, and I thought it would fill up that emptiness! The Communion was more real, too, than the bread and grape juice at the Brick Church. It seemed closer to what our Lord intended."

Here Anthony made an unintelligible sound.

"Well, it did seem like it," she argued, misinterpreting him. "I was pretty well satisfied for awhile."

"Seemed like it!" Anthony could bear no more. He jumped up and began pacing the room. "It is like it! I can't understand you. Is that why you didn't take Communion these last two Sundays? I wondered if you were ill."

"No." She gave a great sigh. "I was just through, that's all. The last time I did take it was that Sunday when Dr. Havern acted so peculiarly, you remember. For a long time after you had put the bread in my hand I couldn't make up my mind to swallow it. It was just bread, and I could have had that at home. What I wanted, and what I'm going to have some day," her eyes lit up as with an inward fire, "is the real Body and Blood of Christ."

"My God!" Anthony stopped dead. "Do you mean to say you actually believe in *that*?"

"Yes," she said quietly.

Another thick silence fell between them which the girl was the first to break.

"Dear," she pleaded, "I haven't gone into this blindly. I told you how I fought it for a good many years. But in the back of my mind, after I once started to think about it, I kept wondering why Jesus had made such an elaborate ceremony of something that stopped right there. He said It was His Body and Blood, and that if anybody wanted eternal life he'd have to eat It; but apparently nobody could take It but just those few men right then. I supposed it was all right, but still I thought: Why did He say that if He didn't mean it?" Val was getting a little tearful.

His heart wrung with pity, the young man looked down into the beautiful, troubled face he loved so well. Those damnable Roman priests had little to do to bring all this distress on her!

"Darling," he said gently, "let me tell you, and don't worry any more. We're still permitted to take part in that sacred banquet. Jesus spoke of the bread and wine as a symbol of His love, and in partaking of this symbol in remembrance of Him and in appreciation of His love —"

"But He didn't say it was a symbol," broke in the girl, with a fleeting memory of Mary Anderson saying the same words.

[164]

"He said, 'This *is* My Body.' If He just meant it to be a figure of speech, why did He say—"

"My dear girl." Anthony was beginning to be exasperated, and he began his restless walk again. "Don't you remember the Articles of Faith? Article 28 says explicitly:

'Transubstantiation (or the change of the substance of bread and wine) in the Supper of the Lord, cannot be proved by Holy Writ but is repugnant to the plain words of Scripture—'

"Is it repugnant?" Val interrupted again. "It isn't to me, anyhow. In fact, I think that it is proved by Holy Writ. At least it says so in the Book of Common Prayer. Don't you remember how you say every Sunday: 'Take, eat, this is My Body'?"

"It doesn't mean that it actually *is* the Body of Christ, and you know it!" Frowning, he paused in front of her. "You know Jesus was always saying something like that: 'I am the door, I am the vine.' He didn't mean that He *was* a door, an actual door."

She thought this over. "Yes, that's true," she mused. "Let me see. I could say, for instance, 'I am a—a sieve.'"

Anthony smiled unwillingly, though hope began to stir in his heart again. If she could begin to joke about it—

"But I wouldn't say," Val went on slowly, "'This sieve is I, it's my body'—but Jesus did say, 'This is My Body,'" she finished triumphantly.

"He didn't mean it literally!" he responded angrily. What had come over the girl! "How could He have meant it literally? Val, that's bordering on the blasphemous!"

"Why is it blasphemous?" Val also began to bristle. "He said it over and over, and repeated it, and stuck to it. The Jews took it literally—I've been reading that chapter that Dr. Havern doesn't like—and they said, 'How can this man give us His flesh to eat?' And Jesus said, 'Except you eat the flesh of the Son of Man'—you know the rest of it. If He said it a half dozen times, and let them all believe it that way, and it wasn't blasphemous for Him, why is it for me?"

"I'm going to quote once more from Article 28." Anthony's tone was again patient.

'The Supper of the Lord is not only a sign of the love that Christians ought to have among themselves one to another: but rather it is a Sacrament of our Redemption by Christ's death: insomuch that to such as rightly, worthily, and with faith, receive the same, the Bread which we break is a partaking of the Body of Christ.' *That,* my dear, is the true meaning of the Eucharist." He might have been speaking to a sick child.

"I always did think it was a little foggy," replied Val, unimpressed. "I really never understood it. I thought maybe it was just that I didn't feel the mystical part, but I liked it though it always did seem to have something lacking."

"What is your Romanist definition, then? Do you find it any clearer?" The young man's irony was obvious, but she answered quite seriously.

"I'm not sure I have all the words, but it's something like this: 'The Holy Eucharist is the Body and Blood, Soul and Divinity of Jesus Christ, under the appearance of bread and wine.' That's it!" She was delighted with her good memory.

If she expected any commendation, Val was to be disappointed. It is not too much to say that he sneered.

"Wonderful! They've got you to believe that, have they? My dear girl, they've nothing to substantiate that claim. It's been proved. By no human test can any difference be found in that wafer *after* it is consecrated from what it was *before.* And yet you say it isn't blasphemy to call it God and to worship it!".

"How did you expect to find any difference?" she retorted, her eyes beginning to snap. "I never knew that anybody had thought he could isolate God in a test tube. What do you call *that,* if it isn't blasphemy?"

By this time tempers were running high, and all the softer emotions were forgotten. There is no surer way to break up the most loving friendship than by a hot religious argument. Anthony was beginning to remember that the first news he had about Val's apostasy had been through the despised Jasper; that this girl to whom he had given his love and complete confidence had been secretly negotiating with the enemy. She had admitted that it was years since she had first taken up the idea, and lately she had gone over to Rome completely, abusing his trust while outwardly professing constancy to himself and the Church he represented. In the bitterness of his hurt he lost control of a temper that had been too hardly tried in the past three months, and lashed out at her angrily.

"I doubt if we mean the same thing when we talk about blasphemy," he said harshly, "any more than we agree on the definitions of truth and honor and loyalty. At one time I thought we could; but that's not so any more, now that you take your moral standards from a degraded Roman clergy instead of from a priest of God!"

These words had hardly crossed his lips before Anthony realized their injustice. An innocent girl like Val could easily be deluded by an unscrupulous, Jesuitical clergy into this belief; and as a priest of God as well as a lover, it had been his duty to redeem her by kindness and sympathetic understanding instead of firing a lot of insults at her. After the instant of stunned silence which followed this brief tirade, he opened his mouth to apologize and explain that he hadn't meant a word of it, but by that time it was too late. Val also had reached the breaking point.

"You!" White with fury, she leaped to her feet. *"You're no priest!"*

That, of course, was the end, the final impiety. Anthony could have borne almost any other accusation personal to himself, than to have doubts cast upon his priesthood. Any girl who could so trick and betray him as Val had done, and then turn on him with a denial of the sacredness of his Orders, was not worthy of further consideration. He could not offer her any bodily violence such as he had lately given to her cousin under the mistaken idea that he was protecting her honor, but at least he need not exchange any further words with her. In icy silence he picked up his hat and left the house, closing the door after him with elaborate care.

CHAPTER IX

W ITH the feeling that only strenuous action could keep pace with his emotions after this stormy visit, Anthony tramped out into the rain. The day had been raw and wet, and now in the early afternoon it was at its worst. The air was choked with mist, the gutters running with a dark, unwholesome-looking fluid. The very walls of the houses looked sodden as he strode past; lawns and gardens that had been enchantingly gay only a few months ago were now bare and doleful, without even a merciful carpet of snow to hide their dank nakedness. Truly it was a fitting day for him and Val to come to the parting of their ways.

Their idyl had been all too brief. By way of turning the knife in his wound, Anthony counted the weeks back to that fair Sunday in October when he had first seen and loved Valerie Maddox, with her tawny gold hair, her rippling laugh. Ten weeks since he had taken her hand in his for the first time and looked into the depths of those limpid gray eyes. He would have sworn that only truth and honor were there. They were a sure index, so he had thought, to her clean mind and courageous heart.

She had acted the part admirably. In the bitterness of his disappointment over the way his job at St. Giles's had turned out, she had been his consolation. When, smarting under injustice, he had felt his control slipping, the thought of her mere existence had made him strong. Dr. Havern's conduct was nothing but a pin prick, momentarily irritating but soon forgotten when he remembered that she believed in him and sympathized with him and loved him. There never had been any need of discussion between them about the drawbacks of his position. From the beginning he had felt it due to the honor of the cloth, his own as well as the rector's, not to gossip, even to one whom he trusted as he did Val; and without a word being said she had understood and respected his silence. Never by look or word had she tempted him to lower his standards. For ten weeks he had been on the heights; for ten weeks he had been of all men the most fortunate.

Now, he thought dully, he was down to earth again. He had believed her to be the embodiment of truth, and she had been living a lie. If not entirely dominated by a venal popish clergy, at least she had been influenced by them as far back as her childhood, which just went to show how long and strong was the arm of Rome. Recently she had started to take instructions for the purpose of openly embracing that religion — just what those lessons covered one could only guess after her angry defense of the idolatrous theory of transubstantiation. Also her flat denial of his priesthood. His resentment began to boil up again. No doubt this last was something they had taught her very early, so that any possible influence from him could always be counteracted promptly. He could not but remember that she had always seemed afraid to have the engagement made public.

He turned into Tenth Street — might as well go back to the office and get to work. He only hoped Dr. Havern was still taking a nap, as the last thing he wanted to do was try to cope with the rector. He glanced idly up at a large apartment building just ahead, in the last stages of construction —

The next instant, in the lead of a hastily gathering crowd, Anthony was running toward the building. A tool had slipped from the hand of a workman on an upper floor and had fallen out of the window. The man clutched at it, lost his balance, and toppled through the opening onto the pavement below.

By the time Anthony reached the spot someone (he afterward learned it was the foreman) had already got there, and was kneeling by the inert figure. "Call an ambulance!" he was shouting. Then catching sight of the clerical collar under Anthony's raincoat as the young man dashed up, he said: "You'd better get busy, Father. He's not going to hold out long, I'm afraid."

Anthony gulped. This was his office as a priest, to give consolation to the dying. He was a priest, no matter what Val had said — perhaps not in the sense that this man meant, but a priest for all of that. Still —

[169]

"I'm not a priest," he heard himself saying, to his horror. "I'll get you one."

"Let me take you over in my car," volunteered a man who had just driven up and whose engine was still running.

The foreman bent to catch a whisper from the injured man.

"Yes, I will," he rumbled gently in reply; then called after Anthony who had just turned to go. "He's asking to have Holy Communion brought, will you tell the Father?"

Anthony nodded, then jumped into the car, which drove off at once. He was appalled at what he had just said of himself — he felt a traitor to his calling and his faith, but there was nothing else to do.

"That St. Columban's is the nearest church, isn't it?" observed the owner of the car, adding, "I'm not a Cath'lic m'self, but I got to hand it to your priests. They sure do come in handy in a case like this."

Anthony let it pass. There seemed no good reason to explain anything to this stranger whom, in all probability, he would never see again. The church was looming up directly ahead — in a minute more he would have given his message to the priest and could go away. He hoped he could as easily forget the lie he had given to his own convictions.

The maid at the rectory, also misled by his collar, admitted him without question when he asked for the pastor, and for the first time in his life Anthony entered a Roman Catholic parsonage.

The sturdy, middle-aged man sitting at the study desk lifted his head with its thick thatch of gray hair standing on end, and looked at the stranger with bright, keen, blue eyes.

"Good afternoon, Father," he said, rising with a cordial hand outstretched. His voice was deep and resonant, with the faintest touch of brogue. "Come and sit down and talk to me. I'm just trying to figure out why the Lord is so generous with His rain, when we already have plenty without bothering Him further."

In spite of himself Anthony smiled. Then remembering his errand, he sobered in the midst of the handshake.

"It's too bad to interrupt your sermon, sir," he said, glancing at the scattered sheets on the desk, and missing the sudden change of expression on the priest's face. "There's been an accident down the street—"

"Glory be to God!" The priest had his sick call kit in hand before Anthony could finish. "Is he conscious, do you know?"

"I think he is. He was moaning, and his eyes were open. And —and he asked for Holy Communion." Anthony winced, but went on steadily, "We have a car out here to take you over."

"Wait outside till I run over to the church for the Blessed Sacrament," ordered the priest, already through the door, catching his hat and raincoat from the hall rack as he ran.

Anthony returned to the waiting car with a word of explanation to the driver; and though his intention had been to go on immediately after telling the priest, curiosity or something else which he could not name held him.

In almost less time than it takes to tell it the priest was running down the church steps, and without a word he got into the rear seat which Anthony held open for him. Instinctively the others understood that his silence was not to be disturbed.

As they reached the scene of the accident an ambulance from the near-by hospital drew up, and the young surgeon gave the injured man the briefest possible examination, then stepped back.

"He's conscious," he said in answer to the priest's look. "I'll wait for you, Father."

The bystanders drew away and left the priest to kneel on the pavement by the injured man, who was lying where he had fallen, under a hastily rigged up shelter from the rain. There was a brief interval, the priest bending over the recumbent figure and seeming to listen to a faint whisper; then without turning he straightened up and gave a little jerk of the head which the young surgeon interpreted instantly.

He came forward at once, bareheaded, and dropping on his immaculate knees began in a low voice to say something which Anthony could not catch, evidently taking part in this last rite for the dying. The consecrated wafer was administered—Anthony could even see that the man had swallowed It—and

something else took place which he could not so well understand, as the priest with swift, sure motions gave the short form
of Extreme Unction. Then the priest stood up while the
stretcher was brought forward and the dying man was laid on
it gently.

No sooner had it been placed in the ambulance than the
surgeon bent over the man hastily, then turned his head toward
the priest who was following immediately after.

"All over," he said. "Poor guy!"

Presently, in response to the priest's question as to a surviv-
ing family, the foreman came up, looking very grave.

"Yes, Father," he said, his heavy voice subdued to a hoarse
murmur. "Name's Brophy. Fine old mother, too, the Lord
pity her!—and a couple of kids." He gave an address. "Would
you be wanting me to go over with you, Father?" There was no
question in the foreman's mind as to who was to break the news
to the stricken family. It was merely whether or not the priest
would want any company on the sad journey.

"It's not necessary," replied the priest, looking around for his
recent driver. "I'll take my own car if this gentleman will drive
me back to the rectory. You too, my son," he went on with a
kind smile at Anthony, who followed without a word.

"Tell the old lady I'll look after everything," called the foreman after them.

Anthony was irritated to realize how much he was stirred by
what he had just seen. In the short period of his own ministry
he had attended several of the sick and dying, and while this
rite was a little different from what he knew, in the main it
amounted to pretty much the same thing, he thought. The man
had been prayed over, had received the Sacrament, and had
died in the friendship of God. That was all that anybody could
have done, he or this priest or the Archbishop of Canterbury —
or the Pope of Rome, for that matter. Yet, explain it to himself
as he would, in some undefinable way he felt uncomfortable
about it.

"Do you mind coming along with me to see the old lady?"
asked the priest a few moments later as he and Anthony stood

on the sidewalk before the rectory, while their late conveyance drove away. "I'll probably need help. It's hard to tell a family that the good man's been killed. When I was your age I used to think I knew all about consoling the afflicted, but as my hair got grayer I've learned better. Did I tell you my name's Costello? Anthony Costello, at your service."

"And I'm Anthony Drew." Surprised out of his gravity by the small coincidence, Anthony gave that quick smile of his which the young ladies of St. Giles's liked to provoke. "If you really want me to go along, sir, I'll be glad to help in any way I can. I don't suppose I need tell you that I'm not of your faith, though."

"The car's right here in the garage. We'll have it out in a minute," was Father Costello's oblique response. "I'm glad to meet you, namesake. You must be the Mr. Drew that's been over at St. Giles's lately. I run into your Dr. Havern once in a while at the University Club, though the Lord knows I don't get time to see much of the place. You don't happen to be one of Livingston Drew's boys, do you?"

The surprised Anthony admitted he was, and again paid tribute to the long arm of Rome. Only ten minutes ago this Father Costello had never even seen him, yet here he had a very complete dossier worked out on him; while Dr. Havern, under whom he had served for nearly three months, still neither knew nor cared who he was. Anthony did not need to be too worldly minded to guess that if Dr. Havern had known, life would have been much sweeter and happier around St. Giles's.

The two clergymen talked of indifferent matters as they drove through the streets, but as they neared their destination the older man grew silent and seemed worried.

"God knows this is a hard thing to do," he said at last. "The old mother can probably take it. These women are given the grace of God or they'd never be able to go through life at all, and this is just one thing more for her to stand. But it's the children it comes hardest on, Lord pity the creatures! Well, we can but try. This is the house, I take it."

It was a neat, respectable if unpretentious little cottage on the edge of the fashionable West Side, and the white-haired old lady who opened the door was trimness personified in her print dress and snowy apron. She looked surprised at the quality of her callers, and made a quaint little reverence to them.

"Good afternoon, Fathers," she chirped. She was very like a sparrow with her bright, black eyes and quick birdlike motions. "Will you walk in? I'll have a cup of tea for you in a minute."

Anthony decided then that Father Costello's remark about needing help was just a polite fiction, unless he meant help from on high. So far as Anthony was concerned, from then on he was a lay figure in the scene enacted in the cottage sitting room.

Father Costello stopped the old lady as she was about to bustle away. "Let's talk for a little," he said gently, "and keep the tea for another time."

Mrs. Brophy glanced at him inquiringly; then something in his steadfast, pitying look gave her an inkling of what was to follow. Her eyes grew frightened, and she clutched her apron in both hands, as women do to give themselves support. "Is it Jim?" she asked, hardly above a whisper.

The priest nodded gravely. Then, instead of explaining what had happened, he said a strange thing.

"He had all of the Sacraments, Mother—all of them!"

The brave old face quivered, but all she said was, "Thank God! Oh, thank God!" as she dropped into the chair which Anthony placed for her. "Thank you, Father," she remembered to say to him, though her eyes still sought Father Costello's face, mutely asking for other and less important details.

Very quietly he told her everything. Jim's sufferings had been mercifully brief, he ended the recital, and the foreman was looking after all arrangements.

"I'll drop by and tell your pastor—Father Morgan at the Blessed Sacrament, is it? And don't you worry, Mrs. Brophy. God doesn't do anything without a reason, and He thinks more of Jim than even you do."

"Yes, Father," she replied, her eyes tearless, her voice as steady as ever, though she still twisted the apron in her gnarled old hands. "We just finished the nine Fridays last week, the boys and I. We were going to start another in January for — for Jim."

The priest nodded understandingly at this information which meant nothing at all to Anthony. Then as if she felt he needed an explanation of what the older clergyman had already grasped, she looked up at the young man who still stood beside her.

"Jim hadn't been to his duty in ten years, Father, not since Molly died. She was a fine girl, God rest her! and he took it very hard and very bitter when she left him. He wouldn't even try to understand how it could happen to him! But he was a good boy at heart, my Jim, in spite of the drink —" Her voice broke then, and Anthony patted her on the shoulder, wondering miserably how one could comfort this brave soul.

In their common religion she and this priest seemed to understand each other, but Anthony felt confused and irritated to note that practically all the solace Father Costello was giving her was just the assurance that he had arrived in time to administer the last rites. Of course, that was an important thing, but what did one say about the living? Shouldn't this man say something about her — pray for the consolation of this bereaved mother? Was he just trying to show how important he was, like Dr. Havern?

Presently she wiped her eyes and raised her head again.

"I didn't ask you to sit down, Fathers," she said with a composure which both men silently saluted. "Won't you please? It's very kind of you to come to see me."

"And how about the children?" Father Costello asked abruptly. "Should we send for them? I suppose you'd like me to tell them about — this?"

"Here they come now," she said with a faint smile as a back door burst open and sounds of strife were heard in the kitchen. Father Costello strode to the connecting door.

"Come in here, you two!" he ordered, and a moment later two boys entered, flushed and out of breath from the inevitable wrestling without which two normal boys cannot meet.

"Good afternoon, Father," they said with one voice, dividing the greeting between the two strangers, and seeming a little surprised though not overwhelmed by the presence of these unknown clergymen. Then noting the grandmother's evident emotion, the older, a boy of perhaps fourteen years, went toward her.

"What is it, Grandma?" he asked, glancing from the little old woman in her chair to the men who were still standing. "Anything about — Dad?"

She let go of her apron then, and held out both hands.

"Jimmy, dear — Larry," she quavered.

Father Costello took charge again.

"Jimmy, my man," he put a kind hand on the older boy's shoulder. "You're the head of the family now." ("God help you!" he added under his breath.)

The younger boy, who was perhaps eleven years old, began to cry, and buried his head in his grandmother's lap; but Jimmy stood motionless under the priest's hand.

"Accident?" he asked as steadily as his changing voice would allow.

"Your father had all the Sacraments," the priest repeated to Anthony's annoyance. "He's all right, lad." And not until this fact was established did he make any explanation about the accident, which he finally did in about twenty words. "And now I'll step along and see Father Morgan. Take care of Grandmother, Jimmy — and you, too, Larry. God bless you both. I'll see you again."

"You'll be wanting to get back to St. Giles's, I suppose?" asked Father Costello some ten minutes later after a brief but satisfactory call on Father Morgan, "or shall I drop you at home?"

"Look here," burst out Anthony. He had been seething inwardly for the past half hour, and could hold in no longer. "You didn't need any help going to that house. (St. Giles's, please.) There wasn't one thing you asked me to do. What was your object in taking me along?"

"It's nice to have some backing," the priest said, "even if it's just a silent partner. It's not easy to walk in on somebody you don't know, and tell her that her son's been killed. She packed his lunch box this morning, don't forget that."

"You know that wasn't why you took me," accused the other heatedly. "You just wanted to put on a show for me, so I could see how you do things!" He hated hypocrites, he told himself.

"Did I?" the priest considered. "Well, perhaps I did, partly, God forgive me! But mostly, I think, it was because you had started a work of mercy and it was fitting that you should get as much grace out of it as you could. And it doesn't hurt any of us to see a brave soul."

"She was brave, all right," went on Anthony recklessly. Having started this he might as well go on. "And her courage was all she had to fall back on. All you did was to say how well you'd managed in getting to the man before he died. That's important, I grant you. God knows I've thanked Him for letting me be on time to give some comfort to a departing soul. But the living have some rights. You'll say this is none of my business, and it isn't; but I must say I was shocked that you had no consolation to offer that poor old lady than just, 'I was there on time!'" Unconsciously he raised his voice to a falsetto on the last five words.

Father Costello tried to turn an appreciative chuckle into a cough. Then he said seriously enough, "And what better consolation could I have brought the poor woman?"

"Wasn't there anything to say to assuage her grief?" demanded Anthony. "Isn't anything required of your clergy but just the bare rites of your religion?" He turned in the seat to glare at his companion's grave profile.

"My son," said the priest, "our clergy are bound to do the corporal and spiritual works of mercy, just the same as any layman. Some of us, being humans with human faults, sometimes fall short of our duty, and then we're punished harder than the layman, because we're supposed to know what our job really is. Comforting the widowed and fatherless is part of it.

"But I put it to you, as one clergyman to another, what better assuaging could a woman have than to be told her son had been given a chance for heaven? I couldn't tell her to bear up, because she was bearing up. It wouldn't do any good to tell her that God would comfort her, because He already had done that, and she knew He'd keep right on. Her one idea since she'd borne her son, being the woman she is, was to get him into heaven. She knew he'd skidded off the track, the same as everybody else knew it. You can't fool that old lady — she doesn't need anybody to do her thinking for her. So, when you and I can come and tell her that, through the grace of God, the lad was given an opportunity to make his peace, what more could either of us add to that as a bit of consolation?"

Anthony had nothing to reply. He knew there must be some answer to this, but for the moment he couldn't think of it, his mind being occupied with another and more burning matter personal to himself which the priest's words had brought into prominence again. A good part of his world had collapsed this afternoon, but perhaps the worst thing of all had been his own betrayal. Not fifteen minutes after Val's taunt had sent him from her house, blazing with wrath, he had baldly stated that he was no priest at all — Judaslike, he had denied his high calling!

Just at this moment, when Anthony was scorching in the flame of his self-contempt, Father Costello was so ill advised as to break in with his gratitude for the young man's cooperation.

"'Twas a fine, generous thing you did, boy, and that poor soul we just sent on his way won't forget you when he comes before the Throne of Mercy," he said earnestly.

At a white heat, Anthony turned on him.

"Just what did you do for him that I couldn't?" he demanded roughly.

Grown wise in the ways of the human heart, the older man took no exception to this rudeness, realizing that it was wrung from an anguished soul. It must have been a bitter thing for the lad, sincere in all the intentions of him if his face spoke the truth, to stand by and realize his impotency at a moment like that. Maybe there was even more than that behind his little outburst. Professional courtesy, if nothing more, would keep his mouth shut, no matter what he might be thinking — a polite, well-brought-up youngster wouldn't forget his raising that way unless he'd got to a point where he couldn't stand whatever it was any longer.

"As man against man," he replied, "Anthony Costello could not do any more than you or any other well-intentioned but sinful human. But as a priest I could say with Christ Himself, 'Go in peace, thy sins are forgiven thee,' and I could put the living Body of Christ on his tongue. And that, my son, is what Anthony Drew couldn't."

"You have no right to say that!" flared Anthony. His quarrel with Val on this point was too recent for him to argue calmly. "I don't suppose that even you can really believe that what you put in that poor fellow's mouth was actually the Body of Christ! You know and I know it couldn't be anything but a symbol."

"A symbol wouldn't have done him much good at that stage," replied the priest mildly. "He'd have to take the real thing or there would be nothing more to it than giving him a drink of water in the Lord's name. And as to my basis for saying and believing it, go home and read John 6, my boy, and think it over."

"I've read John 6! I know as much about it as you do!" Who was this mountebank, anyway, that he thought he could instruct a regularly ordained minister on the Bible!

"I doubt that you've actually read it — you've only run through it," said the mountebank. "Sometime when you're feeling calmer, sit down and see what you can make of Christ's own words, 'He that eateth —'"

"My God, man! That wasn't to be taken literally!" Even as he said it, Anthony seemed to hear Dr. Havern making the same pronouncement, but he went on fiercely. "Jesus always spoke in parables!"

"Mostly," agreed Father Costello, "but that was one time He didn't. Everybody then took it literally, you remember. 'How can this man give us His flesh to eat?' they said, and six times Jesus declared Himself in the promise of eternal life after demanding faith from them. And four times did He repeat the simple words 'I am the Bread of Life.' If He wanted them to believe Him literally, how could He have made it plainer? If

[179]

He didn't want them to take it that way, why was He so insistent? Why didn't He just say He was only joking when the disciples got up and left Him? That was serious business; but it seems He was so much in earnest He'd rather lose His followers right then than take back any shade of meaning from His words. You remember He just let them go. Can't you imagine how the heart of Him was aching when He stood and watched them walk off, knowing what they'd be losing for all eternity? But He just turned to the apostles standing by, with their mouths open, belike; and He said, 'Will you also go away?'"

The car stopped, and with a start Anthony saw they had reached the gate before St. Giles's parish house.

"Here you are," said the priest, "and if it won't be stirring you up again I still thank you for your good offices. But I'd rather you didn't just remember me as somebody that was fighting with you the whole way, so let's start from here. Some time, if you feel like it, come over and see me, and we'll not talk religion at all." He held out his hand, and belatedly remembering his manners, the other grasped it warmly.

"Thank you, Father Costello. You've been very patient with me. I beg your pardon for jumping on you like that, but—I've had a funny kind of a jolt today." Poor Anthony stood beside the car for a minute, looking as if the bottom had dropped out of everything. "I can't agree with you, you understand that, but I hadn't any right to act like a boor. I'm sorry."

"Get along with you!" replied Father Costello, shifting his gears, "and don't be standing out here in the rain. God bless you, now." And he was gone.

Not two minutes later Dr. Havern came bustling into the office, red and indignant.

"Where were you?" he demanded of his subordinate who was morosely kicking off his rubbers. "I came in here half an hour ago and found practically three people waiting for me. Couldn't you get back from lunch before four o'clock?"

"Street accident," replied Anthony curtly, hanging up his raincoat.

"Oh!" After a pause the rector asked more mildly, "Anybody hurt?"

"Man killed." Sticking to monosyllables as much as possible. "Had to tell his family."

Mollified, the rector said, "Oh," again, and picked up the evening paper.

By preference Dr. Havern stayed as little as possible in the office, his own library being much more comfortable; but Mrs. Havern was entertaining at tea this afternoon, and the rector, after doing his smiling duty by the ladies, had felt fed up. Even the Spartan simplicities of the parish office were better than a lot of gabbling women, he thought.

"That was right, Drew," he said, settling himself in the visitors' chair. "Always be ready to console the unfortunate," he unfolded his paper, "and dying. Very, very good. Um! I see where the mayor has been at it again, the scoundrel! We'll have to get rid of him one of these days." In silence he skimmed through another column.

Anthony sat down at the desk and made a pretense of looking over the announcements for tomorrow, on which he had been working this morning before leaving for that interview with Val. His excuse of going out to lunch had been pure fiction, since he had taken no lunch; but he didn't even remember that now. Life seemed to hold nothing for him, food or jobs or anything; and these items about Sunday School Christmas trees and Ladies' Auxiliaries were too silly to think about. He was sore all over, inside and out. What was the use of making an honest effort at saving mankind from evil, if all the years of his preparation — work and study and prayer — were to go down in ruins at a breath? A self-willed, irresponsible girl had only to say a few empty-headed words, and all of his principles went to smash!

On top of this, as if he hadn't taken punishment enough, along had come this man Costello with his arrogance about his ministry, saying flatly that nobody but a Romish priest had any power or authority to administer to the dying! Did he think he was the only person, furthermore, who could interpret that confusing chapter 6 of John, over which the world's greatest minds found it impossible to agree? "You've only run through it" indeed!

A loud exclamation from Dr. Havern startled him.

"Did you see this, Drew? Did you see this? My God! It isn't possible!" The rector pointed a shaking forefinger at an item on the front page of the paper. "I can't believe it! Did you know anything about this—did he say anything to you?"

Anthony came to look at the paragraph over the rector's shoulder. It was a dispatch from New York, saying that the Most Reverend John Ranley, Bishop of a far western state, World War veteran, and writer of many devotional books, had just been received into the Roman Catholic Church. The bishop had been reticent in his interview with the press, stating merely that his plans were uncertain.

"No, sir, we didn't talk about anything like that." Anthony wondered dully why this seemed so important. If Val could apostatize and go over to Rome, what was there so strange about this step of Bishop Ranley who, as an Anglo Catholic, was already more than three quarters of the way?

"Why didn't he tell me!" lamented Dr. Havern, letting the paper fall to the floor, and actually wringing his hands in real distress. "He was always so hair trigger—always was when we were young men together. I was afraid that Oxford business would upset him when he went to England before the war, and I was right. It got him into the dangerous wing of the Church, but I never thought it would come to this!"

Anthony retrieved the paper from the floor, and the rector took it from him to read aloud the news about his friend. As he came to the part where it told that the bishop had once been a curate at stately old St. Udolph's, Dr. Havern interrupted himself to mourn again.

"How many times," he said unhappily, "in the old days down there, I stopped him when he wanted to do something rash! He always thanked me for it in the end, too, excepting that Oxford trip. He wouldn't take advice then— Do you know, Drew," he suddenly raised troubled eyes to his curate's, "I shouldn't wonder if he wanted to tell me about it and get my advice that Sunday he stopped here. He must have got cold feet and was afraid to tell me. Oh, I wish he had! I might have saved him!"

CHAPTER X

THE tide of life was at a low ebb at St. Giles's next morning. The rain continued, and Dr. Havern, really much cut up by the news of his old friend, hadn't even spirit to berate the congregation for being so sparse. Contenting himself with a long stare and a martyred sigh, he merely gave them an abridged summary of his famous talk on the Holy Land, and wearily left the pulpit.

He did pluck up heart enough to mutter a few caustic words into Drew's unresponsive ear about the choir which undoubtedly had not distinguished itself, due to colds in the head and the general depression that had settled on St. Giles's this morning, but that was a mistake. The rector had not intended his criticisms for Val's hearing; however, as she followed him over to the house immediately afterward and resigned, he naturally supposed that she knew all.

"My dear Miss Maddox, I was just kidding, as the boys say," he laughed waggishly, thereby making everything quite clear to his intelligent organist. "I have the highest regard for the choir, you know."

Val smiled and assured him she bore no malice.

"I really intended to come over last evening, only the rain was too bad," she went on. "I'll see you through Christmas, of course, but if you don't mind I think I'll get Miss Landis to substitute for me Sundays until you get somebody permanently. You remember she did very well that time my hand was hurt, and she won't have a bit of trouble."

"But why?" Much though he found fault with her behind her back, Dr. Havern knew that Val, in addition to being a conscientious worker, was a very promising young musician, far better than anybody he was likely to get for the salary paid her. "We simply can't do without you. I know you're over-worked (this job is killing around here; I'm ready to drop, myself), so suppose you take a vacation after Christmas and get a good rest. Go some place and stay as long as you like—a couple of weeks anyhow. Certainly, have Miss Landis. Charming girl, but nowhere near you! We'll just consider that settled."

She was firm, however, insisting that she was too busy just now to give St. Giles's the attention it deserved. She was so positive, and so steadfastly declined to consider even three weeks' vacation and a raise of salary, that he was forced to believe she meant it. A dark suspicion rose in his mind that the Brick Church, ever lurking in the background as a possible rival, had offered her more money and less work, and he resolved to do a little quiet scouting to find out what this meant.

"Well, if you must quit, you must," he finally agreed, though I hope you'll reconsider. Take a good rest and— You said you'd speak to Miss Landis? Be sure you impress upon her that it's only temporary. You might come back, you know, and then we'd have her on our hands. I mean, we hope you'll come back. But you will take care of Christmas, you said? That's fine!"

But it wasn't fine at all, he thought, muttering as he went on to the house that he didn't know why he was being so scourged. Everything had gone wrong this season, since Drew came. In the beginning, he told himself, he had tried to accept his cross. He had made every effort to instill some right principles into Drew who had been foisted on him, and tried to teach him industry and the value of earnest application. And now, after nearly three months of this fatherly guidance, he was pained to note that the fellow was proving himself a snake in the grass who bit the hand that fed him.

This, of course, was merely the way Dr. Havern, the poet, explained matters to Dr. Havern, the realist. In his less bitter moments the rector was more open with his other self about the inner meaning of this educational system, which at first seemed so hopeful. Now, strangely enough, it was backfiring. In spite of all the snubbings and fault findings, last-minute cancellations of evenings off, and other expedients for taking the heart out of him, Drew was getting on the map. He was becoming popular. The rector had not allowed him to do any preaching except to a virtually empty church on Sunday evenings, and lo! the viper was beginning to fill the pews. Not that there was any real congestion as yet, but some people were simply passing up the morning service and coming at night.

Next, Dr. Havern had turned over to Drew all the moribund committees and clubs which at that time were almost ready for a quiet burial, and now by Drew's underhand methods at least some of them were faintly stirring. That Child Welfare thing, for instance. Drew had even been asked to make a talk at some banquet about it, but luckily Dr. Havern had heard of it in time to stop that!

Also when the rector, as befitted a leading clergyman, had branched out into the Red Cross and other important national bodies, he felt a decent credit should be given him for patriotism and good citizenship. But to his dying day he'd never forget his sensations when Mrs. Wadleigh-Jones, the national chairman of one group, actually telephoned him — him, mind you! to let her talk to that charming young Mr. Drew. Needless to say, Drew didn't get that message. But in spite of all that, the fellow seemed as far as ever from handing in his resignation.

On top of that, here was John Ranley, practically lost in body and soul. The Sunday morning paper had a fuller account of him than last night's issue. It had given the rector quite a turn to see John's picture as a young man, looking at him from the front page, and to read about his former connection with St. Udolph's so many years ago.

And now, along came the Maddox girl to say she had a better job, or practically that, leaving her pastor in the lurch. He must speak to Davison right after dinner and have him find out where she was going; and if Savannah didn't have dinner on the table the minute he got in the house, he'd fire her!

Fortunately Savannah proved her mettle, having the right kind of a dinner smoking hot when he came in. After doing it full justice, followed by a restful nap, Dr. Havern felt better able to stand his misfortunes. It was too late to save the doomed John Ranley, but perhaps something might yet be done about the organist. Maybe Drew might be able to appeal to her better nature. He strode to the telephone to summon Drew, but remembering that the curate was spending the afternoon with his family, he decided to wait until just before Evensong when he could have a quiet word before Miss Maddox came in. He supposed she would have the decency to come tonight, at least.

As soon as he saw the lights go on he hurried over to the church, and found the curate in the vestry.

"Anybody come yet?" asked the rector in a conspiratorial whisper, jerking his thumb in the direction of the choir room. Anthony shook his head. "Then I want to ask you, what's all this about the Maddox girl resigning. Has she talked to you about it?"

Anthony's hand made a barely perceptible pause as he reached for his cassock.

"No, sir," he replied quietly. "This is the first I've heard of it."

"Well, I just wondered." The rector fidgeted nervously. "You seem to know her pretty well, and I thought you might have heard something. Do you suppose she took offense at what I said this morning? She acted as if she hadn't even heard me — said she'd expected to come over last night, but I don't know. It's going to be pretty serious if we have to start looking for another director for that bunch of girls. I'd even raise her salary — in fact, I said as much. Couldn't you just sound her out, Drew? Tell her I was only joking. I don't mean half the things I say."

But the curate declined.

"I'm sorry, sir," he said with a firmness the rector was obliged to recognize. "I'm afraid you'll have to ask somebody else. She wouldn't pay any attention to me if you couldn't get anywhere with her." After uttering this tactful speech, Anthony resisted an impulse to follow the girl's example and turn in his own resignation. It was such a simple way to get rid of trouble!

The rector sighed in discouragement.

"I shouldn't wonder but the Brick Church has something to do with it. They've always wanted her," he said plaintively.

"Did she say she was going to the Brick Church?" asked Anthony with interest, wondering if this was a sample of Romish deception. Then he regretted the impulse which had made him ask. Why should he care what excuse she made, so long as she relieved him from the embarrassment of meeting her?

"No, she didn't." The rector was trying to be fair. "She just said she had a lot of work to do, and couldn't spare the time for St. Giles's. Imagine! Couldn't spare time for her own church! I don't suppose you'd be willing to ask Dr. Keane at the Brick Church about it, eh? Oh, all right! I'll see if I can't get a little cooperation from somebody!"

Dr. Havern slammed the door behind him in an aggrieved way, then opened it again to put his head through the crack.

"Send Davison over to me the minute he comes," he ordered, and disappeared for the night.

Attendance at Evensong was excellent that night. The skies had cleared, and everybody who had missed the morning service on account of the bad weather came dutifully at night. The choir redeemed itself from the morning's poor showing, and Anthony preached a beautiful little sermon on the cleansing of the lepers. Everybody said it was a remarkably fine service, and a good many wondered why they hadn't thought before of going to church in the evening as a general thing instead of the morning. Mr. Drew was a far better preacher than Dr. Havern, and wasn't he good looking!

Anthony himself thought it had gone off pretty well, in spite of that uncomfortable tightness in his chest whenever he thought of Val sitting there at the organ. He had been tempted to use a text from the Lesson which seemed to apply to Val and her juggling with faith and doctrine:

Let a man so account of us, as of the ministers of Christ, and stewards of the mysteries of God. Moreover it is required in stewards, that a man be found faithful.

Of course, St. Paul had spoken only of the clergy in this

part of his epistle to the Corinthians, but it could be construed to fit anybody who had been so favored as that girl. The true faith had been given her to cherish for her whole life, and yet in only a couple of years she had deliberately thrown it away and had taken to herself the base coin of Rome. Well, let her, since she was so stubborn about it! His words of yesterday had meant nothing to her when with all his heart he had begged her to reconsider; so no doubt a sermon wouldn't reach her either. Instead, he talked about the loving kindness of the Saviour, and sent his flock away with a blessing, taking a cynical pleasure in calling down upon her head the benison of an outraged Deity. What did she know of the love of God!

But after all his gloom and lowness of spirits beforehand, Christmas came in quite joyfully for the rector of St. Giles's. The sun having once got out from behind the clouds, literally and figuratively, it stayed out. John Ranley disappeared from the headlines. The joint carol service proved a great success, St. Giles's choir holding its own with the best of them and leaving the Brick Church nowhere. The distribution of baskets to the poor on Christmas Eve was another soothing thing, as pleasant to the rector as to the poor themselves — or perhaps even a little more. It gave a man the real Christmas spirit, he said.

This spirit was amplified and strengthened by a dinner on the day itself, cooked in Savannah's most superlative style, to which the Haverns had bidden a few out-of-town guests, friends of long standing. Feeling more in charity with the world than at any time since the first Sunday in October, the rector bowed his thanks as the guests drank to his health in the first glass of port after dinner, sitting about the table at their ease. Mrs. Havern and the other two ladies had withdrawn, leaving the three men to enjoy a good masculine talk, while Savannah and her helper regaled themselves with drumsticks, chestnut stuffing, and plum pudding in the kitchen. "Peace on Earth" was written all over St. Giles's that evening.

"Good port, this," observed Mr. Butterfield after the health-drinking rite was finished, holding his glass to the light that he might enjoy its clear ruby color. "Do you mind telling us where you got it, Havern?"

"No, indeed!" Dr. Havern never minded a question like this. "Bill Ketteridge gave me a few bottles," his tone implying that this was an understatement, and that Butterfield was at liberty to imagine that Bill had really come across with a couple of dozen. "You remember Bill, don't you?" turning to his other guest. "Vice-president of the Federal-State Bank. You must know him."

Mr. Dodds, deeply impressed, gave a jerk of the head which might be interpreted either as meaning that he knew old Bill very well indeed or that he had never laid eyes on him. Mr. Dodds was essentially cautious, but saw no harm in giving the impression, if anybody wanted to take it, that he, too, moved in the higher Dun-and-Bradstreet circles. When he got home he would certainly tell the boys about this port.

"Didn't I hear that Bill was down in Florida this winter?" asked Mr. Butterfield, taking another sip with an air that showed he might have known nobody but old Bill would pick out a wine like that.

"Yes, Bill's there," replied Dr. Havern. "Some people have all the luck! What wouldn't I give to spend a couple of months down there, golfing!" He flexed his wrist.

"Why don't you go, then?" demanded Mr. Butterfield. "A man needs some relaxation. I can't get away, m'self — was just saying to m'wife this evening, this little trip's about all the vacation I'm likely to get this year, what with all that scrapping they're doing over in Europe; but I do think you ought to go if you can, Havern."

"Yes, you ought," chimed in Mr. Dodds earnestly. "You owe it to yourself, Havern."

"I don't see how I could," protested the rector, remembering Mrs. Wadleigh-Jones who had thought young Drew so charming. "I've got a big job here, Butterfield, with a lot of war work piling up, too, and most inadequate help."

"What's the matter with your young man?" Butterfield wanted to know. "Isn't he worth his salt? Let him do some of the work."

"Oh, the fellow means well enough," Dr. Havern was charitable, "but he's pretty green. I don't see how I could go away and leave the place in his hands."

He looked wistful, though, as he said it. Spending the winter in Florida had such a wealthy, comfortable sound—a bit daring, too, with war clouds looming and people beginning to talk about increased taxes and retrenchments. Bill Ketteridge apparently didn't mind letting the Federal-State muddle along for a few months—why couldn't that congregation do the same? They might appreciate him more when he came back, at that. This little dab of popularity that Drew had acquired was only a flash in the pan.

His friends, warmed and expansive in the afterglow of Savannah's cooking, and having nothing at stake in the problem one way or the other, continued to urge him to start thinking about himself for a change. A man's health should be his first object. They only wished they could go down and join old Bill. Mr. Butterfield was interested in the golfing possibilities, Mr. Dodds preferred the fishing. And while neither could see the faintest chance of shaking their own obligations, they both generously pressed Dr. Havern to build up his resistance against the hard times that were soon coming "to try men's souls, as the Bible says," finished Mr. Dodds piously.

Viewed in this light, it seemed flying in the face of Providence to neglect such a simple means for gaining spiritual strength; and after a decent show of reluctance Dr. Havern agreed to think it over. Rightly interpreting this as consent, and mellowed still further with more port, Mr. Butterfield took it upon himself to telephone down to San Sabastian and make reservations at the Don Bernardo Hotel for Dr. and Mrs. Wilbur Havern.

"Better go down on the plane, too." Mr. Dodds was also entering into the spirit of the thing. "Call the airport, Butterfield, and see what they can do for you. Why not go tomorrow, Havern?"

The airport had only two seats left for tomorrow night's plane, and couldn't undertake to hold them longer than another half hour from now. Reservations were coming in fast, they said. The three men hastily pooled all of their available cash, found they had just enough for the two tickets, and fled to the airport in Dr. Havern's car. In the stress of the moment it was decided best not to stop and ask Mrs. Havern what she thought about it. Time was precious, "and she'll be tickled to death," said her husband, who might be supposed to know.

To do the rector justice, he had been far more sparing of Bill's port than the other two men, and in no sense could he be considered as at all elevated; but it would not be overstating the case to say he was riding along on the wave of general enthusiasm. The trip to San Sabastian, therefore, grew more and more important as parish responsibilities faded. Devotion to duty is such dull work.

"And now," he said, putting the tickets into his breast pocket, "the next thing is to tell that fellow Drew."

This item, though disappointing as to immediate results, was gratifying in that it showed how much Drew needed some discipline, his apartment telephone being unanswered.

"Just as I thought," said the rector, retrieving his nickel, "he's out gadding. Well, I'll tell him in the morning."

"Don't be too easy on him," advised Mr. Butterfield. "Once give these fellows their heads and they get too big for their britches." To this Mr. Dobbs solemnly agreed.

The truant, as it happened, was at that moment blamelessly occupied in showing his young nephew how to wind up a mechanical jumping frog which Howard, Jr., had found on the Christmas tree, but, of course, the rector had no way of knowing that.

Feeling adventurous after buying those tickets, the three gentlemen then strolled around the airport station to inspect the building with a knowing air, and watched the planes as they came and went, with particular attention to the Florida ship. Mr. Dodds, who, due to an unfortunate phobia about heights, never went above the second floor of any building if he could help it, was very learned about aeronautical matters, and talked about taking the wind and three-point landings, while the others listened with respect tinged with envy. How did Dodds manage to pick up these technical terms!

Dr. Havern then said he would give that fellow Drew one more trial on the phone, and fortunately reached him at once.

"Oh, so you got back at last, did you?" was the rector's salutation. "Where were you?"

"At home, having dinner with my family," replied the curate cheerfully.

"Well, we'll not waste any time on that," went on the rector in a great hurry. "Be here tomorrow morning not later than eight. I've got to leave for Florida on the night plane."

The astonished Drew promised to come early, and Dr. Havern quickly hung up to forestall any questions.

The three men then drove back to the rectory, their pockets bulging with timetables and vacation literature, to be met by a plaintive hostess in a gray bathrobe, who told them that the other ladies had got so sleepy waiting for their lords that they couldn't hold out any longer. They had gone to bed, and Mrs. Havern implied that it was only a strong sense of duty that had kept her from doing likewise. She made no attempt to find out the reason for their absence, only bade them a faint good night and reminded Wilbur to put the cat out. She then faded away. Considerably dashed by this very tepid reception, the gentlemen followed suit and buried their enthusiasms under the blankets.

Anthony's day at home had been equally satisfactory, after its own fashion. For the past week there had been much anxiety about him in the home circle, his offhand announcement of the broken engagement having deceived nobody by its casualness; so it had been a great weight off everybody's mind when he appeared on Christmas Day, after finishing his duties at the church, staggering under the weight of such flowers, candy, cigars, and toys as could be bought on the way home. He'd had no time to go shopping beforehand, he said by way of apology for the lack of imagination in his purchases, but the relieved family declared they couldn't wish to have them bettered.

The party broke up fairly early, little children having to be put to bed after the joyful fatigues of the day, and everybody declared that the family had never spent a nicer Christmas.

Anthony remained behind for a chat with his father and mother, while Aunt Maude sat quietly by the fire. It was sweet and restful here in his father's house. He had felt that all day. They were his own people. They had all the same standards, the same traditions, the same high level of personal pride and self-respect. Their ideas were normal — no running around in search of the unattainable. He wished this day could last forever.

"Darling," his mother was saying as if she had read his thoughts, "couldn't you stay here tonight?"

He smiled at her in lazy content.

"I'll think about it," he said, reaching over to pat her hand. "I don't feel like stirring, but, of course, there is the job."

"Tell me, Anthony," said his father, "that is, if you don't mind talking shop, did Dr. Havern ever say anything about this Bishop Ranley who has just gone off the deep end? I seem to remember they were friends years ago, up here at the church. How did Havern take this business? You never saw the bishop, I suppose?"

"Once," replied his son, frowning as the vision rose before him of a man, weary and worn and old before his time, half fainting under the weight of secret anguish as he leaned on the edge of the altar he was never to use again. "About a month ago he dropped in on his way to New York, and I met him at the train and took him back again in the afternoon."

"How did Dr. Havern take it?" Mrs. Drew was also curious. "Do you suppose the bishop told him then?"

"No, he just came to say good-by, I imagine. Dr. Havern was surprised when he read about it in the paper later on." Anthony's face grew a shade more set as he remembered some of the other events of that never to be forgotten Saturday.

Aunt Maude gave a sudden titter.

"Anthony," she said, "you're so informative. He was practically weeping when I saw him the other day at that Chinese Relief tea. I tried to ask him about you, but he was so busy talking about himself I didn't get a chance."

"Did you really see him?" Mrs. Drew was diverted from the main theme for the moment. "My goodness, it's years since I've met Dr. Havern. I'm ashamed, Anthony, that I haven't got up to St. Giles's, but with all this Red Cross! And he did feel bad about poor Bishop Ranley, did he? I'm so sorry for him."

"Which of them do you feel sorry for, Caroline?" asked her husband, amused. "You'd be worried over the devil if you thought he'd been too near the fire and got scorched."

"Shhh, dear!" she reproached him mechanically. "Well, I feel sorry for both of them, then. Dr. Havern losing an old friend, and the poor bishop doing such a thing after all these years of good, saintly work. It's really shocking."

"He was awfully Anglican, wasn't he?" Aunt Maude gave a hitch to her sharp chin, and her black eyes glittered in the firelight.

"Oh, very! That's what makes it so particularly awful. Elaine Partridge was talking about him just this morning, and she's simply crushed! She used to go to his services all the time when she was west that summer, and she said he had the loveliest chapel in one wing of the cathedral, and wore such beautiful vestments. That's why Elaine decided to go to St. Timothy's when she came back. I honestly never liked that, myself. I sometimes feel that St. Timothy's imitates the Romanists too much, though that's not a very charitable thing to say. Anyway, Elaine was convinced it was right, so, of course, it was for her; and they do have lovely services at St. Timothy's." Mrs. Drew was broad-minded about it.

Aunt Maude gave her most parrotlike cackle.

"And now that Ranley's quit aping Rome and all that mumbo-jumbo, and has gone in for real Romanism, he's too *declassé* for Elaine any more. I'll bet she's singing right now: '*One step too much for me!*'" The cracked old tuneless voice rose in macabre parody.

"Oh-h-h, Aunt Maude!" Mrs. Drew was almost frightened at this sacrilege, and even her husband ventured a word.

"That's putting it pretty strong, Aunt Maude. You don't quite mean it, do you?"

"I do mean it—why shouldn't I mean it?" the old lady snapped. "I've always thought it was a mistake to allow all that stuff to get into the Church. It's dangerous. St. Timothy's is all very nice and aesthetic, and people like that Partridge think they've done something advanced and holy and cute when they go in for all those genuflections and incense and statues—you know yourself, Livingston, they've got confession boxes at St. Timothy's. I've seen them. Elaine and all of that crowd have been feeling terribly superior to us nobodies at St. Udolph's. But just suppose Elaine found herself falling flat on Rome's doorstep, like that poor fool Ranley. She wouldn't do much pious swanking around then, I can tell you!" She gave her favorite rap on the floor with her cane. "What do you think of it, young man?"

Anthony, who had been an absorbed listener, started at being thus sharply addressed, and colored a little as he felt the apprehensive eyes of his parents turned on him. Whether she really meant it, or was just feeling contradictory, the family terror had directed a new light on this question of the High, Low, and Middle divisions in the Church which had vaguely troubled him ever since he was old enough to notice it. It would bear thinking out; but right now he was in no position to act as umpire between the old lady and his parents.

"I think you belong to the Church Militant." He rose to give the old lady a snappy salute, then laughed and went over to kiss her. "You tell 'em, Aunt Maude! I've got to go."

"Oh, darling!" protested his mother, forgetting controversy. "Do you have to go tonight?"

"I think I'd better," he began, then broke off in surprise as the doorbell rang. "A little late for callers, isn't it?"

The newcomer proved to be none other than their own rector, who had dropped in on his way home from somewhere.

"I was just passing and saw you were still up. I didn't get a chance to wish you the season's greeting this morning, Mrs. Drew. Ah, Anthony, my boy. It's a pleasure to see you." Dr. Llewellyn had a priceless voice, rich and deep and mellow, and a smile that had been worth many cold hard dollars to St. Udolph's treasury. He now turned the smile on young Drew, real kindness in its every beam; and with the memory of all the scowls and black looks he had lately received from yet another rector, Anthony's heart grew warm under his clerical vest. "And how have you been?"

Anthony replied that they were keeping pretty busy, and wondered how this really capable shepherd of souls regarded his Brother in the Lord up at the North Side. An indication of Dr. Llewellyn's opinion might have been gathered from a faint ripple of surprise crossing his handsome face on hearing that St. Giles's even thought itself busy; but the look faded as breath from a mirror.

"Excellent, excellent!" commented the rector heartily. Anthony noticed with a fresh throb of pain that he did not ask for Val, with whom he had been much taken at their meeting that night not so long ago. Mother must have murmured a discreet word in his ear. "I'm sure you've been busy, because you haven't been in to see me. That musn't happen, my boy."

"How lovely the services were this morning," said Mrs. Drew, thrilled to see her darling boy so appreciated, and feeling that the rector was entitled to a kind word as well. "And your sermon was inspiring. I almost wept, it was so beautiful."

Dr. Llewellyn thanked her as he seated himself in the chair which Anthony drew up for him, while Mr. Drew poured him a glass of *Amontillado;* and the love feast would have continued had it not been for Aunt Maude, who wanted to finish her say.

"We were just talking about poor Bishop Ranley as you came in," she said, dropping the name into the placid pool of conversation as a small boy might throw a stone through a window. "What happened there, do you know?"

Dr. Llewellyn caught back a frown as he looked over at the tiny, witchlike figure, and he answered courteously though his smile had lost something of its spontaneity.

"Just the old difficulty about transubstantiation, I believe. That much-vexed question! Ranley was always an extremist, though a very earnest fellow when I knew him. Too bad this had to happen, but you and I will just have to pray for him."

"I doubt it," she snapped. "Once let Rome get him, and he's past praying for. Of course, we might try. And while we're at it, what do you say we start praying for the clergy and congregation at St. Timothy's? Or is it too late there, too?"

The rector laughed at this, privately wondering if the dear old soul wasn't in her dotage. Mr. and Mrs. Drew nervously joined in the laugh, hoping to convince the rector that it really was a joke, though Aunt Maude's beady eyes had nothing facetious in them.

"Dr. Llewellyn," Anthony broke in with the first thing he could think of to get the old lady off the subject, "did you ever know anybody at St. Udolph's by the name of Burnham, years ago?"

"Burnham?" the rector considered a moment, while Aunt Maude darted a sharp look at her grandnephew. "In the clergy, you mean? No, I can't think of anybody by that name."

"What do you want to know for?" demanded the old lady. "What do you know about Burnham?"

"Just a word or two that I heard you and Grandmother discussing once, when I was a little kid," replied Anthony, beginning to sense that for some reason his question hadn't been the life saver he had hoped, though he knew nothing except for that dim connection in his mind with Bishop Ranley. "Never mind. The name came up recently, and I thought you might know. Was it very cold when you came in, sir?"

"I can tell you about Burnham," said Aunt Maude before the rector could reply. "And you needn't go trying to change the subject, young man. This Burnham was in the choir here at the church forty-odd years ago, Dr. Llewellyn, so you wouldn't have any way of knowing him, unless his reputation stayed behind him when he left. He was a theological student then. Some mistaken person started him at it, I suppose. I doubt if he'd thought of it himself. He didn't belong in the pulpit — had too inquiring a mind."

"Don't say that, Aunt Maude!" begged her scandalized niece. Aunt Maude would have to say a thing like that!

The old lady waved her down.

"He could sing, I'll say that for him, a beautiful tenor voice. Ought to have been in opera instead of wailing out psalms and anthems. He thought so, too, after awhile, because one night he set fire to all of his theology books right in the middle of the cloister, and walked off. He did sing in opera some years later, under some funny name. He'd raised a beard, and nobody knew him but me. I'll think of that name presently — you'll remember it. He'd turned Theosophist or Buddhist or something, though I think that was mild compared to some of the things he did."

Aunt Maude couldn't have complained about not holding her audience, who were all hanging on her lips by this time.

"And now where do you think he is?" She was refreshed by all this attention. "He's a Roman Catholic priest at a perfectly awful church down in the slums, and right here in town. Near the bridge somewhere." She let this sink in, then turned on Anthony again. "How much of that did you hear me talking over with Emily?"

"Practically none," he replied feebly. This lurid tale was more than he had bargained for. "I just remember you and Grandmother muttering something about a man by that name who had been over at the church. Then you caught me listening and you both chased me, which I suppose is why I remember it at all."

"Mercy me!" ejaculated his mother.

"What do you think we ought to do about him?" demanded Aunt Maude of the rector. "Think praying will do him any good?"

"Who can say?" Dr. Llewellyn's poise was amazing under the circumstances. "The mercy of the Saviour is boundless." He looked at his watch, then rose. "I had no idea it was so late. Good night, Mr. Drew, Mrs. Drew — don't think of getting up, my dear madam. Most interesting story. Are you coming my way, Anthony?"

The two ministers left together, and Anthony drove Dr. Llewellyn the short distance between his father's house and the handsome stone rectory attached to St. Udolph's magnificent pile. Neither referred to Aunt Maude's story, though they both thought of it even while they talked of other things. Dr. Llewellyn disliked it fervently, as something discreditable to the Church which it were better not to air in public. At least the impossible fellow had got out long years ago, and was forgotten by everybody except an ancient gossip like that terrible little Aunt Maude.

As he left the car the rector held out a kind hand.

"I meant what I said, my dear boy. Come and see me — socially and otherwise. I like to keep my eye on my boys. And perhaps something may turn up." He nodded meaningly. "Good night!"

Anthony drove back to his apartment in a happier frame of mind than he would have believed possible. Dr. Llewellyn's parting words might be interpreted as a prospect of another and better job (the terms were practically synonymous in this case). St. Udolph's itself might be in need of a junior curate to run errands and do all the less desirable things which automatically fall to every rookie; but anything was better than St. Giles's.

And for another thing, he wouldn't always be in such danger of running into Val Maddox on every corner. They had been obliged to meet and even speak in the course of business since their breaking up. The carol service of last Sunday and the Christmas music this morning had needed a good deal of arrangement. Both he and Val had kept up a glassy calm on those meetings, and he could only hope that his self-control would continue to be as good as hers, so that nobody could get any hint of the stormy emotions raging inside him. As to what she was thinking, he could not make a guess. Beautifully groomed and perfectly poised as ever, she gave a maddening impression of complete indifference. It would be almost too much luck to get away from that neighborhood!

In this same hopeful mood he drove over to the rectory next morning, prompt to appointment, and found things in a state, the prospect around St. Giles's being far less rosy than it appeared last night.

The guests, due to various causes, not the least of which was old Bill's port, had been a little inclined to the morose in the dawn and appeared to be holding onto their manners by force. The holiday was over. They had a train to catch, entailing a lot of packing and hunting for mislaid articles and a lot of gabbling about what a wonderful time they'd had. After bolting their breakfast and getting ready to be rushed to the station, the collective private opinion was that it had been scarcely worth while to put up with all this inconvenience and sleeping in strange beds just to be able to tell the neighbors at home about spending Christmas in the city.

Their host was also suffering from a revulsion of spirits. This Florida trip was going to be frightfully expensive, as he had begun to realize when he signed checks to reimburse his friends for the money advanced last night for the tickets. Long distance calls, hotel bills, the new clothes Mrs. Havern would be sure to buy — he'd be swamped before he got through!

Again, why had he allowed himself to be rushed off his feet and persuaded to go tonight, if at all? There was no reason why he shouldn't have waited another day — another week, for that matter. Most of these considerations were so feelingly stated by his wife when he broke the news to her, as to make it sound as if she had thought them up by herself. Then branching out on an original line, Mrs. Havern gave it as her opinion that he was crazy. He disputed this hotly, though privately he was not so sure.

There was another strong objection to the scheme. He had seen it himself at the time, and had mentioned it. Young Drew wasn't to be trusted to carry on, singlehanded, the affairs of the parish. His friends had brushed this aside as of no moment, and under the candlelight and in the postprandial glow, their arguments had seemed sound. Now, in the cold bright sunlight of a new day, it didn't look so good.

When Drew arrived at eight, Dr. Havern was having car trouble, the engine refusing to cooperate. The guests, in a ferment over this last-minute delay, were expressing themselves according to their nature. Dodds alternated between advice to the rector to cut her wide open and offers to try *his* luck in getting her started. Butterfield kept snapping his watch open and shut every ten seconds, though Mrs. Butterfield only sighed patiently. Mrs. Dodds feared she had taken cold during the night, and was sniffing experimentally. Between all of this and the recollection of what Mrs. Havern had said to him in the privacy of their room about this ill-advised Florida jaunt, the rector's blood pressure was hitting a new high as the curate drove up.

Having just flooded the carburetor, Dr. Havern was at leisure for the moment to pay some attention to his assistant.

"This is a fine time for you to be coming in!" he began in a choked voice, his face turning a deep, rich crimson. "Wouldn't it be possible, just for once—"

Anthony broke in hastily.

"My engine's hot," he said, opening the doors nearest him. "I can get you to the train right away. We've plenty of time."

Butterfields and Doddses poured out on the sidewalk, bags and rugs flew through the air. Dr. Havern's car was left alone to drip itself dry at its leisure, while Anthony's cut the first traffic light and sped on, reaching the station in time for the guests to dart through the gates with minutes to spare.

"Well, at least that's done!" breathed the rector, smiling his sweetest and waving a hand in farewell as his visitors disappeared amid a babel of thanks for a heavenly time and the last-minute rescue, mixed with urgings to come on and not hold up the party. "Why I ever invited those people—! Good thing you got here when you did. I never was so nervous in my life." This was all the thanks Drew was likely to get for his help, and at that it was more than he expected.

"What's this about your going to Florida, sir?" he asked as they got into the car. Mrs. Havern, luckily, had decided to stay at home even before the engine trouble started, and the two men now drove back by themselves.

Dr. Havern hesitated. His misgivings were as strong as ever; but on the other hand there was something to be said for the peace and quiet of San Sabastian. After the excitements of a morning such as this the rector was feeling in need of a change.

Then there was the concrete fact that he had the tickets in his pocket right now. It seemed cowardly to turn them back after the agent had been so obliging about holding them for him, to say nothing of the heartbreak it would be to know that great silver bird would fly off without him (and Etta, of course) under its wings. And the reservations at the Don Bernardo — what excuse could he make to Butterfield and Dodds if he canceled everything and stayed tamely right here? He made up his mind.

"Yes, I'm going tonight, and probably shan't be back for a month or so. You'll have to do the best you can. Davison will probably help you out, but for heaven's sake don't let him or any of the vestrymen have too many fingers in it, or there'll be a lot of trouble later on. They've done enough damage now!" forgetting for the moment that the outrage of last October was now beginning to pay dividends in his having somebody to take over for the next couple of months while he basked under the southern sun.

It was now Anthony's turn to hesitate. One half of him yearned to tell the rector just where he could go. But the other half peered curiously into the future. The rector undoubtedly had nerve to go off and leave the parish in what he considered doubtful hands, but there was something of a challenge in it, whether or not he meant it that way. How would it be to have a free hand with the parish to see what could be done with it? It was worth trying. Dr. Llewellyn and St. Udolph's were forgotten on the instant.

"Mrs. Havern is going with you?" was Anthony's only acknowledgment that he accepted his new charge.

"Yes, Drew — yes, she is!" Dr. Havern's brow was creased with worry. "She's really not well, you know. She needs a good long rest."

In fairness to the rector, be it said, he was not trying to throw on his wife's shoulders the whole responsibility for the trip, his only object in thus making an invalid of her being to account for the opposition she was making. Etta had done a lot of fussing this morning, though she mercifully shut up when the guests were present; but he doubted if she would be so reticent when only the curate was there. Her protests, therefore, might be discounted as just a symptom of a nervous collapse. Dr. Havern saw more clearly than ever that he was entitled to this vacation, or at least would have earned the right by the time he got started on it.

CHAPTER XI

V AL had protested against including Jasper in the usual family Christmas party, saying she'd had about all of that boy's society she could stand, and she knew the rest of the relatives shared her opinion. They would take no pleasure in seeing him even on a day dedicated to peace and brotherly love. She had never told the family of his connection with the row between herself and Anthony, the memory of that unhappy half hour being too painful; but her lifelong dislike for him was now turned to positive loathing.

Her parents agreed that the party would go off much better without him; but later on Mrs. Maddox weakened. It was only Christian charity, she said, considering that his mother had died so recently, that they be as nice to him as was humanly possible. Val had replied to this that she didn't believe Jasper came under the heading of Christian — in fact, she doubted if he was even human. However, she was overruled in the name of charity.

Jasper surprised everybody, however. He looked wilted and harassed; and though he did pluck up spirit enough to comment on Aunt Josie's retouched hair, and asked if Tommy had yet worked off his condition in math, for the rest he was oddly silent.

"What's bothering you, Jasper?" inquired Cousin Hilary Fortune, marveling at this strange behavior.

Jasper had few reticences, and was only too willing to pour out the tale of the perfidious Larkin family who were still in control out at the New Sanctity, and who had lately injured him afresh.

"You know, I hold all those ninety-day notes, and when they fell due yesterday, I was just going to give that outfit a little scare. Not that I wouldn't really renew, you understand, but I'd just act like I wouldn't, and teach 'em a lesson. Don't you think that was a good idea?" He waited for the applause.

"Machiavellian, my dear boy!" replied Cousin Hilary. "Then, of course, they had to let you take over the pulpit."

"That's where the trouble was!" Jasper's face clouded again. "Every darned one of 'em came in and took up his note!"

"You don't say!" Uncle Billy had joined the group. "Why, Jasper, that was inhuman."

"That congregation must be a thrifty bunch to be able to pay up in full on the first go," said Hilary enviously, with a rueful memory of his own outstanding paper.

"No, they couldn't," contradicted Jasper. "Maybe a couple of them could have scratched it up, but most of them not. Oh, I found out what happened, and what do you suppose it was?"

"Don't tell me," begged Uncle Billy. "Let me guess. Old man Larkin lent them the money."

"Check!" added Cousin Hilary. "Only I'm betting it was the old lady. Let me know the next time she does the preaching, Jasper, because I'd like to go and hear her."

"Where did you find out?" demanded Jasper. "Somebody been talking to you?" and his eye turned toward Valerie at the other end of the room, greeting a fresh bunch of arrivals. Maybe she'd been snooping and tattling, just to get even with what he'd told her boy friend!

"Elementary, my dear Jasper, elementary!" replied the two gentlemen in unison, then solemnly crooked little fingers.

"It's nothing to laugh at," retorted Jasper angrily. "It was a pretty lousy trick, if you ask me."

"From your point of view, I guess it was," said Cousin Hilary, beginning to think he'd had about enough of Jasper's woes. "What did Santa Claus bring you, Billy, aside from a lot of slippers and neckties? Handkerchiefs?"

"Mostly," replied his cousin, and the two men laughed as they walked away.

Jasper glared after them. Being one of those sensitive souls who emerge from practically any situation with a grievance between their teeth, the youth had now received another insult. He didn't like being laughed at, and something must be done about it. He had met his Waterloo at the hands of the Larkin family, but at least that needn't happen with Hilary Fortune and Billy Maddox.

But on the whole the affair did him good. Jasper thrived on resentment. Revived and freshened by this new wrong, he waited in very good humor until the company was seated about the dinner table, when he came to life by boldly demanding of Cousin Hilary how he liked dropping all that money at Saratoga on the races.

"Makes you feel kind of wealthy, doesn't it?" he grinned, "so long as you can afford it." Everybody knew, of course, that Cousin Hilary's finances were not too sound at any time.

"That's enough of that, Jasper!" broke in George Maddox sharply, pausing in the act of carving to frown at the youth. Then, "What did you think of the President's talk, Hilary?"

Jasper subsided, well pleased with the progress made thus far, though Cousin Billy was still to be touched up. Then he cast a furtive look at his host which Val noted uneasily.

She, like the others, had been agreeably surprised at Jasper's mildness earlier in the day; but knowing him as she did, she didn't trust him too far. Now after this attack on poor Cousin Hilary it was all too plain that the temperate mood had passed, and no doubt Dad would be the next victim. She wondered if there weren't something in Jasper's own life that he didn't want known — something that wouldn't bear the light. She lost herself in meditation, while Jasper continued to eat steadily.

Presently the war talk lulled for a moment, and Jasper again found opportunity to break in.

"Cousin George," he piped, "how's the Pope today?"

Mr. Maddox leveled a stare at him.

"I don't know, Jasper," he said mildly. "Were your dispatches from the Vatican any different from mine?"

"Well, I thought you might know something," began Jasper.

"The Pope's pretty well, thank you," cut in Val clearly, fixing her grinning cousin with a dangerously glittering eye. "And how is the draft board today, Jasper?"

Jasper's pinkish complexion grew fiery red as he sent a look of hate at her, then it faded to a dull oyster white.

"W-what are you t-talking about?" he stammered, wiping a sudden dew from his forehead. "I don't know what you mean."

"Why, my boy," Hilary leaned forward solicitously, "you don't mean to say you didn't register?"

For the moment Jasper was of two minds, whether or not to pitch his plateful of turkey with cornbread stuffing, candied yams, and spiced cranberries straight into the informer's face.

"Well, anyhow, I'm not twenty-one yet," he mumbled.

"Oh, yes you are!" Aunt Josie was very emphatic. "You were born on September 19, 1919. It's an easy number to remember, and I remember it."

"I think it's our patriotic duty to turn him in," declared Cousin Hilary virtuously.

"What difference does it make if I didn't register?" Jasper's face wore a pale green tint, while his hands grew damp and cold. "There isn't going to be any war — for us, that is."

"Don't fool yourself," said Mr. Maddox. "I'll bet you anything that this time next year we'll be in it up to our necks. What do you say, Hilary?"

Hilary held exactly opposite views about this, but for the good of Jasper's soul he now intoned mournfully, "It's going to be tough on you, kid!"

From then on Jasper had little to say beyond short sentences beginning with "please pass —," and shortly after the mince pie course he took his leave, to everybody's relief, and the party waxed merry.

Nobody gave more than a passing thought to the absent youth, and they would have been greatly surprised had they known that he was spending an evening behind cautiously drawn blinds at his home, frenziedly packing. At the same time he was trying to think up something quick and effective to get even with the girl who had tattled on him. He had disliked her all his life, and now he hated her. He did not know how she had found out about his affairs, but the important thing was how to get her, good! At least he had already planted some seeds in Drew's mind about her, he thought, viciously snapping down the lock of his hand trunk.

After a few hours of broken and troubled sleep in which he was pursued by dreams of draft boards with slavering jaws, he arose with the slow dawn to finish his preparations for flight. By the faint light of a shaded lamp he cooked an unappetizing breakfast and finished his packing. His plans were made. He would buy a ticket to the farthest point he could think of (the money from the New Sanctity crowd, not yet deposited, came in well at this crisis), and disappear on that early train. Jasper was taking his Cousin's Hilary's patriotic scruples very seriously indeed.

But there was still Val Maddox to be told off. A pleasant thought here occurred to him: why not telephone Dr. Havern and let him know what his organist was up to? That would at least lose her job for her, particularly if old Havern were dragged out of bed to answer the phone. He'd be plenty mad after that!

This proved not such a good idea when he tried it around eight o'clock. The travelers had left for the train, and an irate Savannah, her disposition thoroughly curdled by the doings of the morning, answered his ring. "Ain' in!" was her sole response, unless one counted the slam of the receiver which nearly wrecked Jasper's eardrum.

Nothing was left, therefore, but to pull his hat low over his eyes and steal out into the sharp winter morning. He glanced around for any of the FBI who might be lurking in the vicinity, but apparently they hadn't yet been tipped off; so he locked his door, signaled to a taxi cruising about in search of trade, and piled into it with his luggage.

On the following Monday morning as he went through the mail, Anthony found a letter addressed to Dr. Havern in pencil, mailed in Chicago at the railroad post office, and apparently having lain in the local office over Sunday. In addition to his other duties, Anthony had been left the delicate task of deciding which letters were strictly personal and to be forwarded to San Sabastian unopened, and which were to be kept for his own attention. The handwriting on this particular letter was unknown to him, but something about it made him decide that it was parish business — a copy of a baptismal or wedding record might be needed in a hurry by some traveler. It had that look. He slit the envelope and read the following:

'I always knew your church was only half-baked Protestant, but I didn't know you kept a papist on your pay roll. Ask Val Maddox why she goes down so often to the Bridge Street Romish church.'

There was neither date, salutation, nor signature, but if Jasper had written his name in four-inch letters it would not have made the authorship clearer. Anthony's first angry impulse was to destroy the malicious thing, but before he had torn the page through he took another thought. If Val's cousin was going around scattering anonymous letters about her, it was high time she found it out, and, of course, Anthony would help her do something about it, as any man of decency would. He hadn't seen her since Christmas morning, but he had no doubt they would meet sometime.

The letter also threw light on another point. Val had not said where she was taking her lessons in Catholic doctrine, or from whom; but, considering the nearness of St. Columban's, he had naturally fixed on Father Costello as the instructor. Jasper's reference to Bridge Street brought up Aunt Maude's story of the madman Burnham, and Anthony's blood grew icy as he realized the sort of person who now had charge of the deluded girl's fate.

A few hours later when he left the office he did come face to face with Val, who was just crossing Tenth Street with her music case in hand. Having foreseen this, and in fact planned for it, he wanted to be calm and undisturbed and dignified. Instead, he was annoyed at the constriction in his chest and the humming in his ears, while his heart and lungs both seemed to have stopped functioning. He accosted her with a half ration of breath.

"Here's something you might like to see. Came this morning. I started to tear it up, but thought I'd better show it to you."

She thanked him formally, and seeing that he wanted her to read it at once, she opened Jasper's parting stab in the back.

"I might have known he would," she commented. "Little brute! He couldn't resist giving poor Dr. Havern a dig when he was really only after me. Did Dr. Havern see it?"

Anthony briefly explained the rector's absence, adding:

"It's mailed from Chicago. Do you suppose Jasper gave it to somebody to mail from there?"

"Sure enough, he did!" She looked at the envelope, and this time her smile was amused. "Then Uncle Billy and Dad were right. He did leave town. Won't they laugh when I tell them! He had some little misunderstanding about the draft board," she explained, seeing his blank look. "I don't suppose they'd really do anything to him, but we thought he needed a little scaring up. He just didn't register."

Anthony laughed, to his own surprise.

"Best piece of news I've heard in a long time!" he exclaimed, looking more like himself than at any time since the interview began. "I used to think I'd have to chase him off to parts unknown; but if he figured that out for himself, then the war isn't in vain." He laughed again. It seemed so natural and comfortable and good to be talking with Val in this way; and he added cheerfully, "It might not be so funny if they did catch up with him."

"Well, that's his lookout." Val also felt this quick reversion to their friendly state was delightful — too delightful. On a sudden their differences seemed of small account. She momentarily expected to hear him, or herself, asking what all the fuss had been about and suggesting that they go on as before the quarrel. All this past fortnight she had missed him with an ache of longing she sometimes felt she couldn't bear. It was pain just to see him, either in the sanctuary in his priestly robes, or on the street in raincoat and galoshes. It hurt her to hear his voice, even if he was only telling the janitor to sweep the mud off the church steps.

[209]

Knowing him as she did, she guessed that under his impassive exterior he was feeling every bit as wretched as herself, but with the added anguish on his part of total disbelief in the need for it all. Well, for that matter, what was the necessity? It would mean so much to the poor fellow, with his other worries, if she could just tell him she'd give it all up — that nothing was important but that they loved each other. She really didn't know much about the practical workings of Catholicity, had no idea how she would like it after her formal acceptance into the Church. There was a sort of glamour about it now, but on closer acquaintance she might find it no better than the faith which she was now about to abjure. She had been pretty enthusiastic, she remembered, when she had first joined St. Giles's.

All this flashed through her mind in an instant, but it was long enough for Anthony to sense that the girl was wavering. For himself, he was willing to call it off then and there. All the anger and resentment which had tortured him since their quarrel now suddenly disappeared. What was it all about, anyway. Were they going to let a foolish misunderstanding spoil their lives? If she would just give up this crazy, hysterical notion — it was not of her own making, he was sure — he would concede anything he possibly could. They loved each other! What in the world had made them fight that way? Just some of Jasper's malicious meddling, the little — A clerical vocabulary couldn't do justice to Jasper!

"Val," he said gently, "do we have to go on like this? Can't we just forget it and start all over again? I've been so miserable this last couple of weeks. Couldn't we wipe the slate, now that Jasper's gone where he can't make any more trouble?"

The girl laughed shakily. Not daring to look at him just then, lest she break down completely, she glanced instead at the letter in her hand. There in Jasper's spidery handwriting the words leered up at her: "Ask Val Maddox why she goes down so often to the Bridge Street Romish church."

The Bridge Street church, old St. Stan's, as she had learned to call it. Instantly she saw it, shabby and poor and forlorn to the eye of the uninitiated, yet to one who knew, rich with the prayers offered there every hour of the day. Prayers of light-hearted youth, of careworn middle years, of destitute, terrified old age. There they all were, offered up before the altar which housed the transcendent miracle of the Body of Christ. She, too, had been there many times, offering up her own petitions about this trouble between Anthony and herself, begging help for courage and strength to go on. She had even asked that this poor, hopeful boy, now looking at her with eager dark eyes, might be given the light to see the truth as she did —

"Oh, don't let me give in!" she prayed silently, frantically. "I've got more sense than to stand here and talk to him like this. At least I ought to have. Don't let me even hear him!"

Aloud she said, with a steadiness which she marveled at, considering the row her heart was making, "Anthony, I love you as much as I ever did, and just for that reason I'm saying: no! Please, dear —" as he stiffened with resentment at the calmness of her voice, which he considered pure callousness, "won't you try to understand? It isn't just a question of what we think of each other. In your job, what would you do with a Catholic wife?"

He was silent for a moment, then he asked quietly, "So you're going on with it?"

She nodded miserably.

"All right, then." He drew a long breath. "I hope you'll be very happy." With which polite untruth they parted.

Val got home somehow. Enough strength had been given her to stand by her guns, but the ache in her heart told her she was paying dearly for her victory.

"Dear Lord," she thought piteously, looking up into the empty blue of the sky, "this is getting almost too hard for a poor idiot like me to stand."

Fortunately her mother was away at a luncheon, and Val had a quiet afternoon in which to get hold of herself. This she did by memorizing another Bach fugue. What she needed was work, she thought, and systematically went at it to get the fugue to exchange places in her mind with the memories of the morning. By evening she was tranquil enough, except for this ceaseless nagging in the depths of her soul, ignore it though she would.

Her mother had called for her father at the office and drove him home around five, at which time Val was able to read aloud to them the note from Jasper. She giggled reassuringly.

"He did leave town then." Mr. Maddox inspected the postmark. "Good riddance! Did you tell Billy about this?"

"No, I thought I'd show it to you and Mother first." Very thoughtfully neither parent had made any comment when she told how she happened to see the letter, but she knew they would be immeasurably relieved if she could tell them it had been the means of healing the breach between her and Anthony. Perhaps it would be best to cure any false hopes in that direction before they got too strong, and let the dears get over their disappointment as soon as they could. She drew on her courage once more.

"Just so you'll know," she said lightly, "Anthony and I didn't make it up. He was awfully sweet about it, but it wouldn't do, as you can guess. A Catholic wife wouldn't get him anywhere, and I told him I couldn't backtrack."

Her father nodded silently, but her mother could endure it no longer. Reading the pain in Val's eyes, Mrs. Maddox burst out:

"My darling child, why do you keep this up? Is anything in the world worth making two people so unhappy? You're losing the most precious thing in life, just because of an idea. I know there are a lot of nice things about the Catholic religion, and I'll always be glad that I've learned something about it; but is it worth breaking your heart over, and making Anthony wretched, too? If you think you made a mistake in joining St. Giles's, well, you need not subscribe to everything Dr. Havern says. Can't you just believe in the Lord and keep His law, and let it go at that? Then you can marry that poor disappointed boy, just as you had planned, and have a happy life together doing good. You don't have to bother about all those indulgences and things that have come between you and a loving, good young man!" As she made this plea she put tender arms about the tall girl, as if to shield her from her own foolish mistakes.

Val looked down into the loving face raised to hers. Poor little Mother! She had just stated her own creed: to believe in God and do His Will so far as possible, and then for the rest to give herself up to her family. Her life with Dad had been founded on that principle, and she was now going on with her daughter. She had been so good in Val's religious wanderings, taking part in the services she didn't care about or understand, even at St. Giles's; and lately she had been reading up on a doctrine which she disbelieved and abhorred, simply because the child of her heart had taken the notion her destiny lay there. It was going to be cruel to wound this selfless, devoted little creature by telling her she didn't know what she was talking about.

Or did she, the wise woman, know there was nothing more to it than just a selfish wish on Val's part to quiet her own restless conscience at the expense of Anthony's peace of mind? If she married Anthony, there would be love and understanding between them. She could help him in his work even more than she had since he came to St. Giles's. He was expecting to look for another place soon, she knew. Possibly it would be at St. Udolph's itself, since Dr. Llewellyn seemed to be taking an interest in him. Not unmindful of the social implications attached to being Mrs. Anthony Drew, Val realized she would be in a position to do a lot, both among the poor and needy and in the higher circles. As his wife she would have the right to go along with him anywhere.

Her mother's thoughts ran parallel to her own.

"Darling," she was saying, "think how much good you could do, taking care of the poor people, and helping the young girls and boys to find themselves in life. You could have so much influence among the better class of young people, too — that may sound snobbish, but I don't mean it that way. You know, so many of the young married people of the wealthier set have so little feeling of responsibility toward their husbands and wives and — well, you know! You and Anthony, being what you are, could set such an example to them in the way of right living. You could do anything!"

"Yes," replied her daughter slowly, "I could do everything, Mother, except—I could never take communion."

"Oh!" Mrs. Maddox halted in her eager flight of fancy, and looked at the girl doubtingly. "I know, dear, you feel pretty seriously about that, and it is important—I guess." She paused again and considered. "But would anybody notice if you didn't? Or you might, just once in awhile—you'd have the right feeling about it (Father Burnham is always talking about the intention to do right), so would it hurt any if you did? Anthony would like it."

"Mother, dearest!" Val put her hands over her ears. The temptation was getting almost too strong when Mother set the picture before her in this practical way. "You've got to believe me when I tell you I can't do it. I just must go on, no matter how much it's going to cost me!"

"But, darling—"

"But, Mother! Don't try to persuade me against what I know I ought to do. You're making it awfully hard. I never could trust myself again if I took that communion, knowing as I do what the real communion is!" She was fighting herself now, trying to believe what she said. Mother had almost broken down her resistance—a little more, and it would be too much. Was she going to lose all she had been struggling to get? If He wanted her to stick, couldn't God give her any help?

"Alice, hold on a minute." Help came, as Dad laid a large, firm hand on the girl's shoulder. "Our daughter never sells out. Valerie, I take off my hat to you. Anybody who puts up that much of a scrap for what he believes is a man. Let her alone, Alice. She knows what she's doing."

His wife turned very pale as she looked up into his determined face and saw that he meant it. She shivered. But courage ran in that family, and she was soon able to smile a little.

"All right, dear," she said bravely, "if you both feel convinced she should, then it's all right. God bless you, Val, darling."

CHAPTER XII

LENT not only opened gloomily in 1941, but continued the same way throughout. The weather was stormy and cold practically the whole time, and Anthony won a bet he had made with himself that Dr. Havern would stay where he was until after Easter.

The rector took time out occasionally from his golfing and sea bathing to send a card to interested friends, letting them know that he and Etta were having a wonderful time. The Don Bernardo had extended itself a bit and given the rector a modest little room at a fairly modest rate, and life at St. Giles's seemed very remote from these blue summery skies with Bill Ketteridge positively in the same hotel.

He did send one real letter, which arrived on an icy morning in February, notifying his curate that he'd have to carry on awhile longer. Mrs. Havern was doing so well in the milder climate, and Bill Ketteridge and the rest of the gang had been so importunate, and what with one thing and another the rector believed it for the best interests of practically everybody that he stay on a few weeks more.

"Just do the best you can," he wrote kindly, "and we'll see what happens in the spring," adding with belated caution, "don't undertake anything new."

So Anthony won his bet, but beyond the satisfaction of a good guess there was no nourishment in it, as Anthony was chafing to get rid of the job. The parish itself was well enough, but another worry had come up, because this was the year when war began to close in toward the United States, in spite of all the wishful thinking about our two-ocean protection. The situation was growing tenser every day. Bulgaria had signed up with the Axis, the blitz over England continued, and who could tell what might follow? Anthony's brother and brother-in-law and most of his friends were already in uniform, and he was getting tired of the way everybody wound up their bragging about themselves with a patronizing:

"Of course, I can see why you can't be spared. I always say the home front has to be kept up, too."

The troops needed spiritual help right now, a lot more than they did in normal times, and if only old Havern would get home, Anthony could join up as chaplain in some branch of the service. He'd registered for the draft, of course, but though the clergy wasn't being drafted in the year-of-training program, he felt he ought to get into the game.

"They needed chaplains," he could still hear Bishop Ranley's quiet voice telling of the days back in the last war when he hadn't waited for the United States to come in before offering his services. It couldn't have been any worse than it was right now!

Another thing he didn't like was a brief chat he had with Father Costello, meeting him on the street along about the end of March. The two men were pretty good friends by this time, though Anthony had never made that call on his namesake which he had promised; so it was natural enough that they should stop and talk when they met. The priest was on his way to the chancery office "to try to dig up some help for Holy Week," he said.

"I lost two of my young men this week, one to the army and one to the navy; and while I don't begrudge them to Uncle Sam, I could wish they'd left their twin brothers behind them. But everybody's singing that tune now, so I'm no worse off than the next man."

Again cursing the necessity for explaining his own position these days, Anthony remarked that only for Dr. Havern's absence he, too, would be in uniform by this time.

"Otherwise I might drop by your place and lend a hand," he added with a friendly grin.

"I believe you would at that. And I don't know anybody I'd like better as an assistant, if you'd had the water poured on you."

"What makes you think you can pour it on so much better than anybody else?" Anthony flared up at once. "Do you mean you're questioning the validity of our orders?"

Father Costello scratched his chin thoughtfully.

"That would bear discussion. But as it happens, I didn't have that in mind just now. I was thinking of you more as a layman, a stalwart right arm of the Church. Somebody who wouldn't crack under the strain, no matter what happened."

Anthony glared at him, but said nothing.

"We need your kind badly right now," went on the priest seriously. "The whole Christian world needs good laymen as well as a good clergy, the Catholics as well as anybody. This war isn't just coming out of nowhere, as we both know; and the hand of God is getting heavy with wrath. I'll be frank to say I'd just as soon have you in the fold; but in or out of it, I'd feel better to know you were feeling friendly." He began to get under way again on his errand to the chancery. "Good-by, my son. Come and see me."

After this short talk Anthony got into his car and drove off indignantly, just missing a dog of mixed ancestry sunning itself in the middle of the street, and which now fled yelping. So everybody felt free to take a crack at Anthony's priesthood — first Val Maddox, and now this old fellow! For half a year he had been a duly-ordained clergyman, authorized to preach the gospel and administer the sacraments. For three months of that time he had been holding down a parish singlehanded and alone. A layman indeed!

Happily in the days that followed his wrath cooled. After all, Costello might have meant it kindly when he talked about Anthony's value as a Roman Catholic layman. The compliment had a dubious flavor to one not of that way of thinking; still he meant well.

Some evenings later Anthony showed he held no grudge by stopping on his way back from dinner to speak to Father Costello, whom he found walking up and down before the church steps. A reluctant spring was slowly arriving, and the priest was enjoying the mild April air as he waited for his choir to assemble.

"The lads won't be here a minute before eight o'clock, though they're supposed to come at seven-thirty," he complained. "They'll just stay a little longer at the latter end, however, so that's all the good it does 'em. Tenebrae, you know," he added.

Anthony didn't know, but thought it better not to ask. He nodded and observed that it would soon be Easter.

"I shall be glad to have it over," he said. "This is my first experience with Holy Week services, I mean, from the pastor's end of it. It's not at all the same as just being one of the congregation, is it?"

"And it wouldn't hurt some of them to take on a bit of responsibility, either, and find out what's to be done before the crowd arrives. 'Twould be an eye opener to most of them." Father Costello looked tired tonight, as well he might after the long ceremonies of Palm Sunday yesterday.

Anthony gazed at him sympathetically. "This is a busy week for you, too," he said kindly.

"So so," replied the priest without a smile.

"Did you have any luck in getting some help the other day?" Anthony was finding a peculiar interest, pleasant if guilty, in being this close to the workings of Rome.

"Yes, I got a couple of good men — just lent to me for the occasion, I'm sorry to say. But anyhow they'll lend a hand with the confessions before Holy Thursday."

"And you have the Lord's Supper, of course, on Thursday?" Anthony's flesh crept at this casual mention of confession.

"One of the heaviest Communion days in the year, God be thanked," replied the priest. "I only wish I could say we did as well every day. It's no war we'd be having at all if the people received Communion daily."

"Do you think that would be wise?" Anthony looked doubtful. "I don't mean to say one shouldn't take the Sacrament very often," he hurried on as the other glanced at him sharply. "But do you think we can get out of this war with honor if we don't fight? I hadn't understood that you Catholics are pacifists — isolationists, perhaps?"

"Personally I'm neither a pacifist nor an isolationist," replied Father Costello warmly, "though some Catholics might have different opinions. When things get to a point where nothing but a war can settle them, then I'm for the war. My point is that there'd be a lot less trouble if our people mixed up a little of the law of God with their dealings. And so long as we Catholics have the Blessed Sacrament with us," he smiled to lighten the speech, "there's no excuse for us not behaving ourselves."

"Why do you keep saying that the Sacrament is your exclusive property?" Anthony demanded with a frown. "You always talk as if nobody else had any rights."

The priest raised a quizzical eyebrow.

"What's the objection, now, to letting us poor Catholics have the Blessed Sacrament as our own particular property?" he asked genially. "We're the only ones who believe the Lord meant what He said when He founded it, so aren't we entitled to reap the reward of our faith? Of course, there's your St. Timothy's church on the hill yonder, with some of the same ideas as ours, but I don't know how the good people up there square their beliefs with your Thirty-nine Articles that make such short work of transubstantiation. What do you think about them? Or isn't it good manners to ask?" He smiled sweetly at Anthony, who winced and grew red.

Fortunately for Anthony, at this point three or four very young men came up, giving a curious glance at their pastor's companion, who they recognized as belonging elsewhere. These Father Costello introduced as members of his Tenebrae choir.

"And late enough they are," he said severely. "Run along inside and start getting the books ready. I see Ralph Sanchez and the Burns boys coming. Hurry up, there!" He raised his voice and an admonishing hand to the trio just rounding the corner. The boys disappeared into the church, and the relieved Anthony began to put himself in motion.

"I'll be getting along," he said. "I just stopped to say hello, and as usual started arguing," with a rueful smile.

"Come any time you want. There's nothing I like better than an argument. And if you're not doing anything special on Wednesday night, you might drop in at Tenebrae and hear these kids sing. Not that they'll be anything to brag about — hurry up, young Hastings, they're waiting for you! — but they've been working hard and they won't shame us, I doubt me. Eight o'clock is the time, and I don't insist upon it, you understand, but we'd be glad to see you. Ah, here come the rest of them!"

He herded the laggards into the church, while Anthony walked on toward his own domain, chilled with horror at the thought of going to a Roman service, and burning with curiosity to know what it was all about. The name had a sinister sound. Darkness, if he remembered his Latin, held dread possibilities. He also recalled that St. Columban's was the church where Val had first met disaster, pathetically young as she was at the time, and unfit to cope with the enemy. His own character he felt was now jelled sufficiently to make him proof against evil influences, and the service would probably be interesting. Still, it would be taking a long chance to go to it, particularly if anybody recognized him. He was beginning to be too well known in this neighborhood to be a free agent.

He went to bed in a very bad humor that night. He had laid himself wide open to the priest's counterattack, and only that the Tenebrae rehearsal had rung the gong at the right moment, he feared he might have come out a poor second. There wasn't much he could have said, either. There had been many times when he privately felt that aesthetic St. Timothy's was going too far in its Romanistic tendencies, though he could hardly admit this to an outsider. As a matter of fact, did Elaine Partridge honestly believe in the Real Presence when she bowed to the altar as the Romanists did? Anthony hoped he was fair enough to give everybody a right to his own opinion; still, as he had pointed out to Val in their hot argument, the Articles of Faith stated definitely that transubstantiation could not be proved.

As a sincere member in the lower and broader church, he had never held with any of what Aunt Maude called "mumbo jumbo," though he hoped that a right intention on the part of the ritualists would save them from actual error. But it was the dangerous wing of the Church, which poor Bishop Ranley had demonstrated to his ruin. If he had his way about it, thought Anthony, he'd abolish this aping of Rome and bring the whole crowd back to pure old Protestantism where they belonged. Somebody ought to start a reform, and once they got the rubbish cleared away, there should be a central head established to see that it was kept clean. No, that wouldn't do either. Smacked too much of Rome and its Pope.

Undoubtedly, though, Rome had a system that really worked. Highhanded, of course, but it did make for discipline. He toyed with the idea of Canterbury interdicting St. Timothy's, but gave it up. Canterbury would have no authority, in the first place; and anyway it had plenty of the same kind under its own jurisdiction which it was unable to suppress even if it wanted. Also would St. Timothy's quietly submit to anybody's orders, chop its confessionals into firewood, and put out its seven sanctuary lamps? Or would it tell the presumptuous High Command (supposing there were one) to mind its own business? Picturing Elaine Partridge bowing her neck to Rome, he fell asleep at last.

For the next two days, whenever he had time to think about it, Anthony was in a state of miserable indecision about going to that Romish service. On reaching home Monday night he had looked up the definition of Tenebrae in his Britannica, and had been faintly disappointed to note that the editors hadn't a word to say against it. However, it did sound as if it would be theatrical, and he felt good judgment would say that the less he had to do with that kind of thing the better. The invitation had been preposterous, and he'd do well to forget all about it.

Immediately after this he began to think differently. Wouldn't it be his duty to go and find out what was happening? In spite of Britannica's good opinion, he might discover something very wrong with the affair — something he could take to Val to show her the kind of an outfit she had joined. If he could bring her back to her senses, however little she deserved it, he felt it would be worth juggling with his own soul's salvation. She might even thank him for it sometime. In spite of his many pastoral duties, life had seemed very empty to poor Anthony these past months.

This consideration was uppermost on Wednesday night after forty-eight hours of seesawing between the two opinions, and he went, feeling reckless and abandoned, but hoping to slide in unseen. To his dismay, he was taken firmly in hand by an usher and marched up the main aisle to the last vacant seat in the church, which, following scriptural dictum, was in the very front row. Blushing all over and perspiring freely, he slunk into the pew and tried to make himself invisible. His only hope was that none of his parishioners were present to see what their acting pastor was up to. He was thankful that the rainy night had given him an excuse to wear his trench coat which looked like anybody else's, and that he had taken the last-minute precaution of wearing a muffler over his clerical collar, though that wasn't much of a disguise if anybody really knew him.

As his embarrassment subsided and he could give some attention to his surroundings, he glanced covertly at as much of the church as he could see, finding it large and substantial, even handsome. Instead of the darkness and gloom he had been led to expect, it was brilliantly lighted as for a festal event, though the altar decorations were of the simplest, being confined to six tall candles of a deep rust color. His curiosity was excited by an unusual arrangement of some other candles, set in a triangular frame on a single tall standard, and placed at some distance from the altar. These fifteen candles were also rust color with the exception of the one at the apex, which was white. He wondered at this.

In the body of the church it was very quiet. As the minutes went by, he gradually became conscious of a sense of expectation in the air which he tried to think was just his own heated imagination. But for some reason he felt as if that huge crowd was waiting for some great event above and beyond any ordinary religious ceremony.

Presently, and all together, the congregation rose to their feet, while, without any prelude of organ or voice, a double line of perhaps fifty men in cassock and surplice issued from the sacristy. In complete silence they genuflected in pairs before the altar, turned and bowed to each other, then took their places on opposite sides of the sanctuary. In some of these he recognized the boys he had met the other night, now looking wonderfully adult in their robes, though he decided that several at the end of the line must be priests, since they wore birettas; and, of course, Father Costello finished the procession.

Suddenly a voice seemed to flow out of the silence, intoning the antiphon which was immediately taken up by the others.

"Zelus domus tuae comedit me, et opprobria exprobrantium tibi ceciderunt super me."

Mindful of the limitations of a hastily-assembled amateur choir, Father Costello had made no attempt to teach his young men the melody of the psalms, but had turned his efforts into getting a smooth monotone and perfect timing. The rest could come later, he had decided, and the result was excellent in spite of the jaundiced eyes watching from the front pew. Anthony had come with the intention of finding fault with everything.

"Salvum me fac, Deus—" Back and forth the psalm proceeded, the two groups alternating the verses in steady recital. Their diction was excellent, but the pronunciation of the Latin was strange to Anthony's ears. He got an occasional word, *Deus —* something about God, he couldn't tell exactly what, and he found it disconcerting and irritating. It ought not be allowed here in the United States that a bunch of men should conduct a service in what was practically an unknown tongue, and nobody knew what they were saying. It seemed impossible that Father Costello, for whom he had some respect and confidence, should be leading these boys into anything forbidden and wrong; but still, Rome was Rome. He strained his ears to catch the meaning of their chant.

As if she sensed his need, the fat woman sitting next to him thrust her open prayer book into his hand, whispering in a friendly hiss: "This is it. Me glasses is broke." And with the Latin text and the English translation before him, he found he had the key to the mystery. Strangely enough, it seemed quite orthodox after he had caught up with the chanters.

"I am become a stranger to my brethren and an alien to the sons of my mother.

"For the zeal of thy house hath eaten me up: and the reproaches of them that reproached thee, are fallen upon me."

Anthony took time out to carp at the translation as being

different from what he was used to, though forced to admit that in the main it was an authentic psalm. Then the stark, desolate beauty of the lines gripped him.

"And I looked for one that would grieve together with me, but there was none: and for one that would comfort me, and I found none."

Psalm followed psalm — back and forth across the sanctuary beat the tremendous words.

"Cast me not off in time of old age: when my strength shall fail, do not thou forsake me.

"For my enemies have spoken against me: and they that watched my soul have consulted together.

"Saying: God hath forsaken him, pursue him and take him: for there is none to deliver him."

Right here Anthony began dimly to be aware that this was no mere sacred concert to which he was listening, not even an impressive ceremony. In that cry of penitence, that note of peril amid pressing foes, there came to him a sense of the reality of David, the Shepherd King, with his few faithful followers on the hillside of that eastern land — of that greater and even more desolate King in the Garden of Gethsemane. In fact, this could hardly be called a ceremony at all — it was something being done by this group of men in the sanctuary on behalf of the row upon row of men and women in the pews silently joining in this service of love and pity for the crucified One, in the Passion that was here being commemorated.

The voices died away, and in the stillness succeeding a tall young priest rose from his place at the left of the altar, went to the lectern in the middle, and began the first Lamentation.

"Quomodo sedet sola civitas plena populo —"

There was no need of the English text for this, and Anthony easily followed the well-remembered cry of the prophet, so appealing a prayer in the hour of penitence. The young priest's voice was sweet and full, the music had a strange haunting beauty; but if the singer had any consciousness of listeners behind him, there was no sign of it. His voice had a ring as if he were taking the Lamentation seriously—he was praying, not just singing.

As he watched the grave young face, which he could just see in profile, Anthony could not but think of John the Evangelist. So might the beloved Disciple have stood with his Lord and joined in His sorrow over the fate of Jerusalem. Then the Lament sank into silence. The singer walked quietly back to his seat, while the choir took up the Responsory, the prayer of the Redeemer in the Garden.

"Father, if it be possible, let this cup pass away from Me. . . . Watch and pray—"

Another of the priests advanced to the lectern and began the second Lamentation. It was at once apparent that he was less of a vocalist than the other man, but by this time Anthony had forgotten all about being critical. What difference if accident give a man a good or a poor voice in which to sing the liturgy? Only one thing is essential, the liturgy itself. The second singer had the same reverence and devotion as the first. He was giving his all, as much as the Lord had allowed him, as he sang:

"Jerusalem hath remembered the days of her affliction—"

After this was finished, the choir to the right of the altar (perhaps they were picked singers this time) rose and stood in their places to give the third Lamentation. This was harmonized, and very beautifully done, its every golden cadence the result of much patient work, the sacrifice of many hours of pleasure by Father Costello's boys. Subdued, yet full, their voices rose:

"O all ye that pass by the way, attend, and see if there be any sorrow like to my sorrow."

For an instant Anthony was standing in the Garden of Gethsemane, watching that lonely Figure bowed to the dust—

Then the curtain of time swung to again, and he was back at St. Columban's shivering as with cold. It had been too real. "If this doesn't stop pretty soon," he thought desperately, "I can't stand it!"

A return to the recitation of the psalms was a distinct relief, the heavy male voices booming out as deep calling unto deep.

Anthony surreptitiously brushed the cold drops from his forehead and breathed deeply.

It was not until Lauds had succeeded Matins that he began to pay atttention to the candles. Hitherto he had hardly noticed when the acolyte extinguished them, one at a time, after each psalm; but now a gradual dimming of the lights in the church, barely perceptible at first, brought out the importance of the candles. Those at the base of the triangle were still quite long, he saw, having been put out early; but those on the upper part burned shorter and shorter, wavering in the draft.

Steadily the recital of the psalms went on, one by one the candles were put out, and as steadily the lights grew dim in the church. A vagrant current of air swept through the sanctuary, making the few remaining flames bend before it. Anthony began to have a subconscious fear lest they all flicker out, and was relieved out of all proportion when they recovered and bravely glowed on until put out. It was almost with a sense of dread that Anthony watched the lone white candle on the top of the triangle still burning with its fitful, questioning flame.

By this time the church was practically dark. There was a heightened suspense when the *Benedictus* began with the full choir, and the acolyte left the solitary candle and turned to the altar. It was then that Anthony noted for the first time that the six tall candles were burning there, and he gave a little gasp of relief that there were still some left. So might he think of Jesus, abandoned by so many followers, but holding His chosen ones.

Relentlessly, as the *Benedictus* proceeded, the six were put out. All of the disciples, then, had left Him. As the final antiphon was sung, the words of the traitor were repeated, and the last candle—the white one—was borne away. Then out of the utter darkness came the voice of Father Costello as he recited the *Miserere* in the first spoken words of the service: "*Have mercy on me, O God, according to Thy great mercy—*" the final act of contrition given forth by David, the great model of penitence.

There was a brief pause while the last prayer was said in

silence; then came the thunder of the rocks, as imitated by the men in the sanctuary beating upon their books. The candle was replaced, as the symbol of hope, pardon, and resurrection; and as the light slowly returned to the church, the men arose and departed as they had come, in complete silence.

Anthony returned the Holy Week book to his neighbor, then waited in his place while the crowd surged out into the aisles. He didn't want to speak to anyone, and was vaguely conscious that the rest of the congregation seemed to feel the same way as they slowly and quietly left the church. He had no idea of how much time had gone by since that double file of men made their silent entrance and began the first Nocturn. It might have been an eternity for all he knew, and he was afterward astonished to learn that it had taken less than forty-five minutes. He badly needed a little time to think it out and brace himself to meet the commonplace again, but he also wanted to get away before anybody started gabbling about how lovely it all was. It had been a beautiful, touching service, and he would see Father Costello, of course, and congratulate him — but not just now!

At that moment Father Costello, divested of his surplice, came through the sacristy door. His eye fell on the young man as he turned, and even from a distance Anthony noted that he seemed surprised. Then he came over at once, though oddly enough said nothing at all nor seemed to expect any comment from his guest. In companionable silence they walked down the aisle until they reached the rear of the church.

As they shook hands at parting, Father Costello muttered, "My work's cut out for me this night!" and with a friendly nod made his way through the long lines of penitents waiting their turn at the confessionals. He disappeared into the box with his name up over it, while Anthony suppressed a start as he realized from sounds and motions behind the curtain in one of the confessionals near him that the dread institution was already in operation there.

He lingered a moment in the vestibule, strangely unwilling to tear himself away from this fascinating closeup of the workings of Rome, though his conscience urged him to get along as fast as he could. No good could come of his being here tonight, it told him, and he had to admit it was probably right. He'd just see what was written on this sheet of paper tacked to the wall, and then he'd go. He looked, and his nervous system, already heavily taxed by the evening's experiences, simply blew up. With gooseflesh prickling all over him, he read:

'Men wishing to take part in the nocturnal adoration Thursday night will please sign their names here.'

So this was the way Rome did things! he thought frantically. All that beautiful service of prayer and song had been camouflage for strangers to see — perhaps even for some of the well-meaning Catholics who didn't know any better. And afterward, in the silence of the night — !

All his life Anthony had carried a dislike and distrust of Rome considerably greater than that felt by the average man in his situation. His reading had always taken a bias against the feared Church — there had always been available to him plenty of that sort of literature; otherwise he had tried to ignore the church, for which reasons he actually knew very little about it. Tonight was the climax. Call it hysteria, perhaps; but this shock, coming as it did after the strange emotions of the past hour, and mixed with that ever gnawing resentment against the hated clergy who had poisoned Val's mind and torn her from him, Anthony's common sense left him without ceremony.

A thousand weird pictures flashed through his head, of idols, sacrifices, bloody oaths. The old sinister legend of guns cached under the church. Might it be possible that tomorrow would be the night?

Quickly he got away, his head throbbing with plans for exposing this Jesuitical plot. Something would have to be done to meet craft with craft. Maybe there had been some providential reason for his unhappy sojourn in this neighborhood. God had made him an instrument for unmasking Rome in all its hideousness!

CHAPTER XIII

TO THE end of his life Anthony would never forget that tenth of April which dawned so fresh and new washed after last night's rain, as innocent looking as if no horrible excesses were to sully its close. His determination to go to that nocturnal affair at St. Columban's was as strong as it had been last night. Apparently Dr. Havern had let this thing go on under his nose all this time, while he fooled along with petty squabbles with the Brick Church over community concerts and Christmas trees, but Anthony wasn't going to follow his lead. Whether or not this business was something that recurred regularly, only time could tell; but at least the papists had grown so strong in this district that they could now come out openly with a public announcement pinned up where anybody, friend or foe, could see it.

With anger he recalled Father Costello's equivocal compliment of a few days ago about his fitness to help in some religious crisis that was coming on. The priest had talked piously, but he had been very definite about the need for another strong arm for the Church, which might mean something more than just averting the wrath of God and all that. Anthony had almost believed the man, too. He had come to have a real liking for the priest and was inclined to trust him. Clearly the crafty old bird had been working for just that. Humiliating though it was to admit it, Anthony believed the priest now thought he had the victim where he was ripe for plucking. Anthony's plans, perforce, were limited to getting into that church tonight, but he had no doubt that once in, the rest would come.

From time to time, as the day wore on, he drove past the church on more or less legitimate errands, to keep an eye on the situation. People came and went in swarms all day, many of them children dressed in white and accompanied by proud and anxious mothers. Surely nothing very dreadful would happen with all those little kids present, he thought. There was an outward look of piety to it, with all that sudden burst of bells ringing in the morning, and the little girls' fluttering white veils and flower baskets; but it made the coming of night seem more sinister.

In all this distraction of mind, tormented by that impious affair down the street, haunted by memories of Tenebrae last night, he had his own duties at St. Giles's in commemoration of the day, with a sermon on the Last Supper; and it was a job to keep his brain clear and functioning. He managed it somehow.

His church was well filled that night, he was thankful to see, jealously remembering the crowds passing in and out of St. Columban's. St. Giles's had only a small congregation, but they were responding nobly to the call of the holy season without any of the devious methods used by Romish hirelings. He gave his best to his people, and was touched to see how reverently they reacted to his plea for a devotional reception of the sacrament.

He did not guess that possibly his sermon might have had less effect had there not been some emotional appeal in his own manner, of which he was entirely unconscious, when he stood before them looking very boyish as well as very handsome in his priestly robes, also faintly unhappy. The congregation, older people for the most part, saw something moving in that troubled young face as he read the Epistle of the day.

"'Whosoever shall eat this bread and drink this cup of the Lord unworthily, shall be guilty of the body and blood of the Lord,'" read Anthony, his heart very sore as he remembered how he had trifled with his own conscience in going to that place last night. "'But let a man examine himself, and so let him eat of that bread—'" And he would be there again tonight. He was doing it in defense of the right, but he knew how dangerous it was. In saving others, he might himself go down in deep waters.

Deliberately he picked his text from John 6, an act of defiance directed at both Dr. Havern, who had scouted the miracle of the loaves and fishes, and Father Costello, who had insulted him by telling him to go home and read the chapter. He exhorted his people to come to the table of the Lord and eat of that miraculous food " 'which endureth unto everlasting life,' as we are told in that Gospel which is so hard to understand," he concluded with a little quiver in his voice.

At last it was over, the people gone, the church locked up for the night, and Anthony was free to start his investigations whenever he judged the time to be ripe. People still surged about St. Columban's in an apparently endless stream, very chatty with each other and quite as if nothing sinister were abroad tonight. Many of the visitors were women. Anthony suspected that so long as these were around, the real exercises would not begin; and that being the case, he was sure the ladies would take their own time about leaving. He walked past the church on the other side of the street, then went back to his apartment to wait as patiently as he could until the females were cleared out. Being very weary after his day's work and the long emotional strain (he had hardly slept at all last night), he decided to rest a bit on his sofa.

Something woke him — it might have been the clock in St. Giles's tower striking midnight, and he started up in fear lest he had missed his chance to get into that meeting. The women surely must be gone by now. Also, and he cursed his own stupidity, the doors might be locked against him, in case those unholy rites were to be carried on secretly. Well, if he was too late, something else would be done — nothing to be gained by giving up and just staying here! He grabbed his hat and coat and started for the door.

He had no intention of wearing even so slight a disguise as he had on last night. He would fire under his own colors, he thought with the fierce joy of a crusader. If he were recognized and refused admission, so much the better. It would be proof, in a way, that the business was illicit and unrighteous. Carrying his head high, with his clerical collar in full view of anybody who wanted to see it, he strode out into the bright moonlight.

The collar was seen instantly by several men, strangers to him, who came down the steps of St. Columban's just as he started up; but so far from doing anything untoward, they

[231]

merely touched their hats, saying, "Good evening, Father," and walked away. The surprised Anthony, who had braced himself for something different, muttered a reply; then exulted. If they took him for one of themselves, that was their lookout, and it made his own job easier. He might still need a password, but would have to chance that.

The door opened to his hand without difficulty, nobody challenged him, and he softly crept into a quiet and apparently empty church.

He was too late, then. For a moment he stood uncertainly at the entrance, feeling let down and disgusted with himself. That unlucky nap had made him miss the whole show, and those men he had just met outside, after finishing their unhallowed rites, were on their way home. The lights were still burning, but probably somebody would be around in a minute to turn them out and clear away whatever paraphernalia had been used. His trip had been for nothing.

Then, far down one of the side aisles, he saw a particularly brilliant glow of light, seeming to come from behind one of the great pillars; and at the same time he was conscious that people still lingered in the front pews on that same side down near the front. So far as he could see there were only a few, and they weren't doing anything except kneeling quietly. It had struck him, judging from the small number of departing worshipers he had met, that the affair hadn't been very successful and had been cut short on account of the poor attendance. It was only ten minutes after twelve right now. Perhaps these fellows here had just not made up their minds to go home yet, or maybe there might be another demonstration later. He believed that having made the effort to come, he would stay and see what happened, if anything.

Sure enough, after he had tiptoed a little way down the aisle to an inconspicuous seat, he saw that this blaze of light came from a small altar decorated with flowers and candles. This, no doubt, would be the place for the ceremonies, as he could see nothing else to indicate the grand mysteries, either in preparation or in process of being cleared away. The large center altar where Tenebrae was held last night had now been stripped of its fittings. This could have a sinister meaning, though perhaps it was just because the big altar was being cleaned. It seemed desecration to have anything unholy going on among those spotless calla lillies on the little side altar, but one could never tell what these warped natures might think was fitting.

Presently he noticed a little stir among the watchers, the sound of a throat being cleared, and then a voice rose as if beginning the ritual. With his heart beating fast, Anthony leaned forward to catch every word.

"*In the Name of the Father and of the Son and of the Holy Ghost,*" said the voice surprisingly, and the rest of the assembly added a hoarse "*Amen.*"

What kind of nerve was this? Anthony wanted to throttle the reader for using that sacred preface. He recognized the man as someone whom he had met on welfare boards, and who was said to be a very promising young lawyer. Probably he had been selected as the leader of this business on account of his clear, powerful voice, which now rang out boldly.

"*Most sweet Jesus,*" the young lawyer read on, "*Redeemer of the human race, look down upon us, humbly prostrate before Thy altar.*"

Completely mystified, Anthony listened closely as the Act of Consecration continued to the end, followed by the litany. There was something wrong here, he thought confusedly. This outfit must be abandoned indeed if they began idolatrous rites by saying, "*Heart of Jesus, Son of the Eternal Father, have mercy on us!*" It didn't make sense.

After the litany the reading went on to other prayers in honor of the Blessed Sacrament, very devout sounding and even beautiful. Then there came a slight pause, during which the listener heard a faint rattling or clicking, as of beads being pulled out of pockets, after which the men went through the Apostles' Creed in due form, and followed it by reciting the rosary. The young lawyer continued to lead, and the rest answered him loudly.

Slowly Anthony's astonished incredulity changed to acute

embarrassment. Was it possible he had been making a fool of himself, crashing into this quiet little laymen's service? Unless he completely misunderstood the signs, these people were spending a midnight hour in real prayer. After all, it was Holy Thursday, the same night in which Jesus had reproached the drowsy apostles — *"Could ye not watch with Me one hour?"* Maybe these Romanists, for all their peculiar beliefs and customs, had a sincere piety somewhere in their composition, and were in truth watching with Him. With a wordless apology, both to the men and to the Lord, Anthony slid to his knees.

The hour went by, partly in praying aloud, partly in devout silence. In the stillness of the night Anthony heard the far-away sound of his own church clock striking one, just as the noise of an opening door and shuffling feet indicated that another contingent had arrived to take over this nocturnal adoration. Down the aisle trooped these newcomers, fifteen or twenty of them, dropping on both knees to make a profound obeisance in front of the altar before they went into the pews. Anthony's friends rose up then, made the same reverence, and walked out silently. In a moment or two another group hurried in as if late to the tryst; and after a short wait another leader opened the proceedings with another prayer.

On and on through the night this continued. Sometimes the worshipers were few, sometimes they came in surprising numbers. The prayers varied to some extent, though always the rosary was included, no matter what else was said. After a little uncertainty about this, Anthony surprised himself by giving the rosary his approval. Everybody knew it, for one thing, and could say it with heartiness. Nothing better than the Lord's Prayer could be found, of course; and as for the Hail Mary, he decided that was quite appropriate. Mary the Mother of Jesus had been with Him during His crucifixion, and it was fitting that her earthly children should include her in their vigil during this night watch. After hearing the prayer endlessly repeated, Anthony learned it quite well, and was able to answer up as fluently as anybody.

In time he began to notice that all the decorations on the

altar were grouped around and directed toward the gilded tabernacle; and connecting this with the double genuflection which
the men made coming and going, more light began to dawn.
A swift glance at the main altar showed him that the tabernacle
there was standing open and empty, indicating that the Blessed
Sacrament had been taken away — brought over to this repository, where It rested among the lilies. With quickened percep-
tions he felt that the stark bareness of the high altar meant
more than just preparation for a good scouring. It might be
that, the Sacrament having gone out from it, there was nothing
left worthy of adornment. Some other explanation might be
the right one, he thought, but this seemed reasonable.

At least these people were consistent. Not only were they
keeping their vigil in honor of the Lord, but they believed they
were keeping it before Him physically present on the altar. In
their sincere, if misguided, faith in the Sacrament, that difficult chapter of St. John held no puzzle for them.

Feeling charitable and broad minded, Anthony conceded that
there was some faint reason for the Catholic belief. In the
Epistle he had read tonight St. Paul had said something which
could be turned that way — in fact, it came in the Prayer of
Consecration which Anthony had also said tonight, *"take, eat,
this is My Body . . . do this in remembrance of Me."* That might
be construed —

Like a startled mustang, Anthony shied away from this trend
of thought. His quarrel with Val had been on just that. On no
account could he admit there was any sense or truth in that
wild idea. It was all right for these Catholics, because they
didn't know any better; but it wouldn't do for him! He hastily
thought of something else.

These people really were living up to their faith at some
inconvenience to themselves. Probably every man here would
have to go to work in the morning, but they seemed to be sacri-
ficing their rest very cheerfully. Take that truck driver, for instance, who was being head man at this watch. He belonged to
the music house where Anthony had bought his piano, and had
a voice as powerful as his good right arm. Among those answer-

ing his lead were a couple of interns from the hospital, white uniforms showing below their overcoats; and old Professor Ridley, principal of the high school. Jimmy Carter, no doubt, didn't mind the lateness of the hour, three in the morning being nothing to the leading man in Sam Dupree's Repertory Company. The same could be said for Tommy Hilliard of *The Morning Sun.* But the great majority present were plainly not night owls, and needed their sleep.

The guard changed again. They were just settling into their places when the sacristy door opened, and Father Costello came in quietly, wearing his cassock with his cape thrown over his shoulders, and looking tired but serene. He gave a casual glance at the thirty-five or forty laymen in the pews, then made his own deep reverence to the Blessed Sacrament and knelt at the *prie dieu* a little to one side of the repository. Opening his breviary, he began his own private devotions without any further reference to the rest of the watchers. And just as if the clergy were not present, after the usual brief pause to let the laggards get settled, Judge Crozier began in his deep voice:

"How lovely are Thy tabernacles, O Lord of hosts: my soul longeth and fainteth for the courts of the Lord."

The first dim light of morning was beginning to show grayly above the housetops as Anthony, stiff and cramped from his long vigil, left the church. The rosary was in full swing just then. It was a good time to leave unnoticed, and get home before the town awoke. He had no desire to have people looking at him and wondering what he had been up to, spending the night in a Roman Catholic church. As a matter of fact, he didn't know himself. Too fatigued to think, all he wanted was to get to bed and bury his interior turmoil in complete oblivion. Tomorrow — today — after he was rested and got back some of his sanity, he would think it all out. He'd find out then what it had meant and what he really did believe; but now he was too tired.

He slept deeply and woke a little before noon, but found no spiritual stimulus in even the coldest bath or the hottest cup of coffee. Outwardly he seemed quite normal, and was able to get through his duties for the rest of the day without attracting attention, but so far from being able to make any decisions about his internal life, his brain was just as numb as it had been at five this morning, and refused to function. He was conscious of a heavy depression in his soul, a sensation as of troubled groping in the dark after something formless and unknown; but beyond that vague nightmarish feeling he was unable to fix on anything. He tried to ask divine help in this state of miserable emptiness, but the words didn't mean anything to him as he said them, and he doubted if God were interested. In fact, God seemed so entirely remote and withdrawn that his feeble prayers couldn't even reach the Throne.

Some of the denominations in the neighborhood were conducting a joint Three Hours' service that afternoon, and, of course, Anthony was late. He might have slept much longer had he not been roused by a telephone call from Miss Landis, who now had Val's job, the distracted organist wanting to know what about the *Sevenfold Amen* which had been overlooked in the rehearsals. She also asked if she should wait for him before going over to the Brick Church.

As best he could he set her right concerning the *Amen*, and begged her to go along to the church when she was ready, adding that he would follow shortly. He made no explanation as to why he was late, either then or in response to some annoyed glances from his brother clergymen, when he got there during the Lutheran minister's sermon. Fortunately his own half hour came midway in the service, so the delay was not fatal.

In all his life he had never felt less like doing anything than his portion of the service, his only comfort being that his material had been prepared early in the week, leaving nothing to chance. Also he had a break in that the massed choirs of the churches, having worked up an elaborate musical program, obliged with a very long number in his period. This cut down his time considerably, for which he blessed them silently. His audience found him a bit lifeless as to delivery, though his subject matter was pleasantly devotional; and the ladies agreed that he was far and away handsomer than any of the other five clergymen on the platform.

He sat down after that, with an outward appearance of joining in the rest of the service, though very little of it made any impression on his tired brain. What interest he had was in wondering what St. Columban's was doing now. Last night he had noticed something on the bulletin board about the Mass of the Presanctified being celebrated at noon today. It might have been worth seeing, if he hadn't this other obligation on hand.

In the evening, according to custom, the Holy Communion was again given at St. Giles's to those of the parishioners who preferred their own quiet service to the elaborate program of preaching and music held at the Brick Church this afternoon. This time Mr. Drew made no effort to preach, and this seemed reasonable to his people, who thought he showed in his face and voice the strain of the Three Hours. They also noticed that he seemed particularly reverent in his administration of the Sacrament. At its close he dismissed them with a blessing, commending them to the care of "the Crucified One who died that men might know the Truth," a departure from the ritual which in ordinary would have meant only a suitable reference to Good Friday. Tonight, though, some of them found it strange. He certainly turned a little paler as he said it, and his voice had a queer drop at the end which sent them home feeling awed and uncomfortable, though they didn't know why. What was the Truth, then? he thought in the dreary emptiness of his soul.

Saying that he would himself look after the locking up, Anthony dismissed the sexton for the night; and turning out all the lights except those in the chancel, he began to clear off the altar. As he picked up the communion set he noticed that a little of the bread had been left on the paten and a sip or two of the wine in the chalice. As this frequently happened, there was nothing odd in it; but he looked at them curiously as he stood by the altar. They were the type and figure of the Lord's Supper, instituted two thousand years ago, and still partaken of with reverence as he and his people had done this night for the good of their souls.

But the service was over now and the use for the symbols was done. He would now take them over and burn them in the study fire, in the usual way, though he suspected that the sexton often just threw them out for the birds to eat, if he was in a hurry. He wondered what Father Costello did with the residue of the Lord's Supper after a communion service; but by the blood which suddenly ran colder in his veins, he found he needed no answer. He had spent a long night before the Sacrament of the Romanists, and he knew what they did.

Mechanically he moved about, tidying up and seeing that everything was secure, no lights left burning, the leaky tap over the wash basin forcibly shut off. Then, before he finally left, he knelt before the altar and tried to pray for guidance, but the old dullness had again taken possession of him, and nothing came of it.

In this state of suspended animation he went to bed to fall into an exhausted slumber, waking next morning with the resolution of minding his own affairs and not meddling with what could only get him into trouble. There was plenty of work to be done on his own legitimate job without running after the Romanists.

About midmorning he heard St. Columban's bells burst out in a joyful peal, and all his curiosity awoke once more. For a time he fought it off, but after a little, yielded and went to see what was happening, telling himself that having gone rather far into the hidden things he might as well go to the end.

The short Mass of Holy Saturday, after its tremendous preliminaries, was come to the Communion by the time he slipped into the back of the church, and he looked on with astonishment. Two long lines of communicants extended well down the center aisle while others knelt at the railing in a solid wall. Father Costello, assisted by another priest, was giving the Host to these people, while yet another priest, with a boy at his elbow, followed in his wake and continued the distribution to the ever-changing line at the railing.

At the close of the ceremony Anthony had a demonstration as to what was done with the remainder of the Lord's Supper, as the ciboria were put back into the tabernacle and the door locked securely. He smiled wryly, then for the first time looked around the church while the final prayers were being said.

Something in the atmosphere of the place told him that the ritual of mourning was over. A sense of joyful anticipation went through the church like a morning breeze blowing away the mists of night. The dark hangings had been stripped from pictures and statues, the priests' vestments were white and gold. Tall vases of lilies stood at the high altar — the Lord had come back to His own! It wouldn't be official until tomorrow, but even now the word was come to those who had watched and prayed at the tomb. It was the end of the Sabbath, as it began to dawn toward the first day of the week —

Before the brief vespers were finished, Anthony left as quietly as he had come, and went back to his own concerns. The Ladies' Guild had already arrived at the church and, deep in palms and lilies, needed his approval of certain plans they had worked out for the adorning of the altar. The sexton was on a stepladder, tacking up vines under their direction, but the ladies would change the whole scheme, so they said, if Mr. Drew had any other wishes. And on the heels of this in came Miss Landis for a final checkup on tomorrow's music and to receive compliments on yesterday's.

Mr. Drew admired everything, music, lilies, vines, and palms; said he wouldn't change anything for the world, and then shut himself up in his office for a tussle with the Easter sermon.

The sermon was a long time getting into shape, and he was doubtful of its value when it did come through; but it seemed not to matter. He was just putting away the finished pages when his mother called up to remind him that he was expected home for dinner tomorrow, and gently upbraided him for his neglect during the past week. He answered affectionately, promising to be as prompt as possible, and hung up in entire unconsciousness that there was something in his voice that brought alarm to her mother heart. It was nothing she could put her hand on, she thought in vague disquiet; but she determined to get to the bottom of it tomorrow when he came home.

Easter morning broke clear and beautiful, gay with spring flowers and spring millinery, and mocking Anthony with its every sparkle. He felt old and dried up as he went over to the church for the early service. The night had done nothing but bring him troubled dreams, nor did the bright morning have any message for him. It was just another day to be got through.

He was still tired and foggy of brain, he dreaded preaching that inane sermon, and he didn't see how he could sit through the long musical program (Miss Landis was very lavish in her use of the pedals, and went in heavily for trumpet effects). And more than anything else did he wish there were some way of dispensing with the communion service which he would have to go through twice today. He tried to argue with himself about this. Easter Sunday was the day of days for the reception of the Eucharist. The congregation expected it — love as well as custom prescribed it. Hitherto, of all the services he conducted, Anthony had approached Holy Communion with the greatest enthusiasm as being that which justified everything else. Why, then, on this first Easter Day of his ministry, was he so reluctant?

After that affair of Thursday night he should have taken time out to shake himself loose from this morass — of doubt, maybe, though it wasn't that he really did doubt his own tenets. It was just that he was not sure any more if they were worth believing. He'd felt almost normal yesterday morning, after a night's rest and before he let his curiosity run away with him again to go back to the church. After that he had gone flat again.

The early communion was well attended by the good people of St. Giles's, as might be expected on the great feast day. Touched by their piety and envious of their fervor, Anthony went through the service with a prayer in his heart that in time he might again come to equal them in faith. Meanwhile he would try not to show how much of an effort it was this morning even to read the words that heretofore had meant so much to him. It was fortunate that the first part was all pretty much routine.

As it fell out, things went far better than he had dared to hope, the congregation carrying their part fervently in the recitation of the Commandments and the Creed. Greatly cheered, the young minister began the prayers, and all ran smoothly until he knelt to say the Communion Prayer.

"Grant us therefore, gracious Lord," he read the familiar words, *"so to eat the Flesh of Thy dear Son Jesus Christ and to drink His Blood —"*

An icy finger seemed to touch his spine. He caught his breath and stopped dead. What was this he was saying? He was calling it the Body and Blood of Christ — that which he had said it could not be! Did he mean it, or didn't he?

With an effort he pulled himself together. He had just enough presence of mind to cough a couple of times, before the people could begin to wonder at the pause; and over the humming in his ears he heard himself finish the prayer. Then rising to stand before the altar he began the Prayer of Consecration which he had always loved, holding his voice as steady as he could while his heart beat so fast it nearly choked him. He thought the congregation must surely hear it through the silence.

"'For in the night in which He was betrayed . . . this is My Body. . . . Do this in remembrance of Me.'"

From the depths of his tortured soul he cried out:

"What is it I am to do in remembrance of You? What do I take — what do I eat?"

And the answer shook him with its mighty impact:

"My Body!"

Somehow he finished. Wiping the cold beads from his forehead, he stood for a moment looking at those tiny cubes of bread on the plate before him. If the intention of Jesus had been for Anthony to change it into the divine Flesh, he had not the power to fulfill the wish. It was still just bread.

Desperately he read on, and presently his people were kneeling at the railing, looking to him to administer to their spiritual need. And just as he always did, Anthony laid the bread in their hands and gave them the cup to drink. They remembered afterward how gentle he had been with them that morning.

The eleven o'clock service was lovely indeed. The church was packed with worshipers, everybody in that warm glow induced by piety and a becoming new hat. The altar and chancel were a bower of beauty, thanks to the Ladies' Guild. Miss Landis quite let herself go on the organ, to the great admiration of her audience; and the choir, what could be heard over that melodious uproar, was in excellent voice. Even the dubious sermon went over well, as Anthony noted in a detached way, letting his eyes wander over the sea of bright faces upturned to him as he stood in the pulpit. Everybody probably was so uplifted in that wave of good feeling which swept through the church that even a mediocre talk would be judged charitably. Anyhow, it was short.

A goodly number remained for the Holy Communion after Morning Prayer, and for the second time Anthony went through the service, though every word hurt him inexpressibly. It was right, though, that he should do what he could. These people, always kind to him and friendly, truly believed in their sacrament, and were entitled to receive it. It was the least he could do for them.

Looking very tall and distinguished in his cassock, he stood at the church door to shake hands warmly with his people as they left. He never missed a name as he wished each one the blessings of the season, in addition to which his tone had a ring of genuine affection which his spiritual family found flattering if a bit puzzling. Also, if anybody had been observant, he would have noticed that Mr. Drew was saying "good-by" a lot, instead of just "good morning," something that might have suggested a clue to what followed. But nobody thought of the small circumstance, though they all felt he had been unusually charming.

After everybody had left, Anthony wandered around the church, looking it over carefully as a man will who sees a place for the first time — or the last. He ran a caressing hand over the brass eagle holding the Bible on its wings, he looked long and wistfully up at the pulpit he was never to fill again. Then slowly and painfully he mounted the step leading to the altar.

This was where he had stood, only six months ago, to begin his ministry, with the right to preach and to pray and to offer sacrifice. He remembered the first time he had held the communion service, how awed he had felt, how privileged to bless the bread and wine and administer them to the people. He had been absolutely exalted, and at the same time very humble that such an ordinary person should be allowed powers like that. Six months, and where was his ministry now?

With a sense of shock, dulled somewhat by the ache in his chest, he realized that at the moment he was standing, literally, just where Bishop Ranley had been that rainy morning last November when he read the same service for the last time. Wondering at his own shortsightedness, Anthony recalled the interpretation he had put on the older man's soul-shaken emotion at the time of the consecration. Then he had thought it arose merely from distress at the insult offered to the bishop's real, if preposterous, belief in the Sacrament. Now he understood only too well; and even in his own pain (or because of it) he pitied John Ranley from the bottom of his sore heart. Ranley's world had been destroyed. In the Truth of God there could be no compromise.

Well, there was nothing to be gained by staying here. With gentle hands Anthony put away everything he had used in the service just past, closed and locked the cupboards. It was the sexton's duty, but Anthony thought he'd like to do it himself. Then he took off the cassock that had been so dear to him, looking at it sorrowfully. So might John Ranley have gazed on his priestly vestments when he, too, gave up the ministry he could in conscience no longer exercise. With a sigh Anthony folded the robe over his arm. He would never wear it again, but he couldn't part with it.

On the back of an envelope he carefully composed a telegram to Dr. Havern, then went over to the rectory to leave the keys with Savannah. She greeted him with a wide smile.

"Yessuh, Ah'll tek care of um," she assured him. Then, noting how tired and white he looked, her own face grew grave. "Y'all don' feel none too good, Misto' Drew," she said, giving him an anxious frown. "Ain' been none too peart all week, neither. Nemmine, Ah'll shake yo' up a aig with some fixin' — won' tek a minute!" She started to bustle away.

He thanked her, but refused, grateful for the sympathy and wishing that anything simple like an egg, with or without fixings, could cure what ailed him. He added that he was going home to dinner, whereupon her face expanded in relieved smiles.

"Ah lay yo' mama mek a difference in what you been eatin'," she predicted. "She ain' stan' no foolishness — *she* know how! Yeh, yeh!" laughing full-throatedly.

"As a matter of fact," he said, trying to laugh with her, "I am pretty tired, and I think I'll go away for — for a rest. I'm just sending a telegram to Dr. Havern. You won't say anything about it just yet, will you? Of course, I'll be around for a couple of days to straighten out my things, and probably I'll see you again; but I want to tell you, Savannah, that you've been very kind to me, and I'll never forget it."

"Lawsy!" she exclaimed, round eyed. Then with a sudden foxy look she smiled again, and nodded fatly. "Nawsuh, Ah ain' tellin' nobody. An', honey, Ah ain' blamin' you. Send y'all's telegram, an' then git outn here as fas' as yo' foots kin tek you, befo' nobody comes back!" And she stood at the door, waving her apron in farewell as he went down the walk.

Anthony carefully put away his cassock in his closet and sent the wire over his own telephone. After this was done he wearily started to get out his car to go home. He'd have to make explanations there, he knew, and dreaded it. Mother would be grieved, while Aunt Maude would think (and probably say) "I told you so!"

And then he did something which he could never explain afterward, though at the time it seemed inevitable; for instead of going home he followed a strange inward compulsion, and drove straight to St. Columban's rectory.

Father Costello was none too pleased when the maid announced a caller just as the priest was sitting down to his long deferred breakfast after the solemn high Mass at which, as pastor, he had been the celebrant.

"Can't they pick out the worst times!" lamented the hungry man, pouring out his first cup of coffee. "Ask him if he can't come back this afternoon — who is it, anyway?"

The maid, who was new and nervous, stammered that it was some priest. "He's young," she added by way of explanation.

"Tell him to come in and have some breakfast, then," ordered Father Costello.

The elderly housekeeper, who had taken a discreet peek through the office door, here fluttered in agitatedly.

"It's the young lad from St. Giles's," she said in a strident whisper. "And he's that nervous he's walking a hole in the office floor."

Father Costello bolted his coffee, then left the room in one stride. His namesake had been on his mind considerably these past three days, even in the midst of the many and wearing duties of Holy Week. In fact, he had given the boy a special intention in the Mass he had just finished. Drew had looked rather shaken the other night after Tenebrae — he wished he'd had time to talk to the lad then, but the penitents were knee deep around his confessional.

Though expecting to learn that something of a religious nature was worrying the young man, and being in readiness to offer such counsel as seemed best, he was not at all prepared for the white face Anthony turned to him as he came in, or to hear the words with which the young fellow greeted him.

"Father Costello," said Anthony in a perfectly strange voice, full of such despair as the priest hoped he'd never hear again, "I've come to tell you I'm licked!"

CHAPTER XIV

IN A contented frame of mind Dr. Havern returned to his hotel that same bright Easter Day after the services at San Sabastian's most fashionable church. The rector of St. Simon-by-the-Sea (splendid man, really) had come down with a bad case of tonsilitis just the day before, leaving a terrified young curate in sole charge; and Dr. Havern, always the Good Samaritan, gallantly went to the rescue. Out of consideration for the vacationing public the time of services was put back an hour today, twelve o'clock; and the congregation showed its appreciation by filling St. Simon's to overflowing.

Under the inspiration of talking to an audience who could afford long winter vacations in large and costly suites at the Don Bernardo, he quite surpassed himself in his sermon. He felt like one of them, even though he and Etta often complained that their dinky little room wasn't big enough to swing a cat. And after the service he remained at the church chatting with some of the permanent congregation, who seemed to appreciate having a metropolitan preacher in their midst. Mrs. Havern said she believed she'd go back to the hotel and see if there was any mail; and this was all right, too. Etta hampered his style a little sometimes.

When he did get back to the hotel he was met by a contingent of the male guests, whose number approached mob dimensions, in their golfing clothes. For once these gentlemen had chosen the better part and had gone to church this morning instead of worshiping the Lord from the golf links; and now, feeling very virtuous and a little smothered, were on their way to the great open spaces as fast as they could make it. Some of them greeted the rector boisterously.

"Come on, Doc," urged a ruddy, fattish gentleman named Burchard, who carried under his arm a package that gave off a cool, gurgling sound. "Just time to get in a round before lunch. Do you good after all that preaching."

"Whale of a sermon, too," added another and even fatter man, signaling a bellboy to hurry up with those bags. "Can't imagine how you thought it all up—here, boy!"

Dr. Havern laughed self-consciously and a little wistfully. It would be nice to have a workout on a day like this, and in such good company. Burchard, here, must be worth a couple of million at the lowest estimate. Preaching certainly was a great tax on his vitality—still, it being Sunday and he having actually conducted the services, perhaps it would be more fitting to postpone his game until tomorrow. It looked better.

"Thank you, thank you both!" he replied genially, rubbing his hands together as if he washed them of all earthly pleasures, "some other time, not today, my dear boys. But you have a good round, and think of me — yes, indeed!" He laughed again and clapped Burchard on the back, to show how broad-minded he was.

"Woop — look out!" Burchard held his precious package out of harm's way. "Well, see you later. That telegram for me, boy?"

It was for Dr. Havern, whose blood curdled as he took it, though he smiled fixedly. He believed he'd never get used to telegrams — they always scared him to the soul. He thought he might if he received as many as Bill Ketteridge did. When Bill was here he got slathers of wires, but he acted as if they didn't amount to anything — shoved them in his pocket if he happened to be talking or was interested in something else. Bill hadn't been at the Don Bernardo since early February, but his influence lingered. Dr. Havern negligently dropped the envelope into his coat pocket while he continued to urge the players to have a good time. He rather liked the way he carried it off, at that.

Chatting gaily with a couple of elderly ladies who got off the elevator on the same floor, he maintained his air of peace and good fellowship until he got into his own room. Then he snatched forth the telegram.

Mrs. Havern, already comfortably lying on the bed in their small room, and reading the home newspaper, glanced up in surprised displeasure as a roar of anguish broke from her lord.

"Wilbur! don't shout like that — it's Sunday!"

"I don't care if it is Sunday!" he retorted, though in hoarse, muffled tones. "What do you suppose that hound Drew has done?"

"Well, what?" she answered. "Sit down and don't fuss, or you'll have a stroke. I've just been reading in the paper —"

"Etta, for heaven's sake! What do I care about that infernal newspaper? Just listen to this: 'Can you return at once? Am leaving for the army immediately.' Can you beat that!" He cast himself into the easy chair by way of emphasis.

[248]

"Is Mr. Drew going into the army?" His wife looked almost animated. "I think it's very nice of him. (Wilbur, don't yell like that!) Every young man ought to do that. I was reading—"

"Nice!" he tried to howl in a whisper. "Nice that we have to pack up and go home, just because that—that—"

"I shouldn't mind," she returned tranquilly. "I'm getting tired of it here. I'd rather do more than just sit— Look, Wilbur, did you ever see this young man? They say he used to live in town, back home, but I don't remember him. His name sounds like that girl who plays the organ in church."

He took the paper from her gloomily. There was never any use in trying to sidetrack Etta if she wanted to say something. Disgustedly he regarded the picture of a young man with wide ears and close-set eyes, being taken into custody by somebody, the FBI most probably, since the caption was "Draft Dodger." The story, featured a little because of its local interest, was about a youth named Jasper Maddox, who was being picked up somewhere in the Middle West on account of his failure to register for the draft. In his attempt to avoid military service, young Maddox had roamed over the country rather extensively; but the authorities having been tipped off by somebody, not specified, he was at last discovered being very busy in anti-Catholic circles, and was now held pending further investigation, the article concluded.

"Do you suppose he's any relation of the Maddox girl?" Mrs. Havern wanted to know. "And will they do anything to him?"

The rector replied that he didn't know and didn't care. The FBI could hang him up by his big ears if they wanted. What was burning Dr. Havern up right now was this peremptory message from that fellow Drew.

"That's what I get for taking him on in the first place!" he said bitterly. "Just as soon as he gets to be of some use, off he goes and leaves me in the lurch."

"Well, I don't know, Wilbur. Maybe he thinks he ought to." Still deeply concerned in Jasper's fate, Mrs. Havern replied absently. "I don't suppose you thought to get any tickets— He *has* funny ears. I always say people like that aren't normal. I'd rather not go by plane, though. Made me sick coming down, you remember. They say here they had to track him all the way to the west coast, and then back. Queer, wasn't it? I'll start packing right after lunch. Aren't you beginning to feel hungry?"

After this speech the rector gave up in despair.

"I suppose that means," he said icily, "you're getting hungry, so it doesn't matter about me! Come on." Thinking sadly of those happy golfers, he led the way to the coffee room.

There was some satisfaction in pausing at the desk and telling the attentive clerk to see what he could do about reservations — "you're sure you don't want to go on the plane, my dear?" — as he had received an urgent summons, and must leave tonight. After all, it was creditable to have important affairs waiting his return which nobody else could handle. But it still didn't excuse that fellow Drew!

Meanwhile that fellow Drew had lost no time in getting his affairs in order. Though he did not take Savannah's advice too literally about getting away before the rector's return, he did burn his bridges so that there was no going back.

Coming home after that exhausting morning, he had been dismayed to see the whole family assembled, with Howard and Jeffrey, home on leave, very spruce in their uniforms. They'd all have to be told now, and wouldn't there be a lot of commotion! Well, perhaps it was best to get it all over at once, and then maybe he could rest a little. Though far calmer in spirit after his brief talk with Father Costello, Anthony was bone tired.

"My dear, how late you are!" Mrs. Drew exclaimed reproachfully, then quickly added, "what's the matter, darling? Are you ill?"

He assured her that he was only tired. "I never put in such a week in my life," he said quite truthfully.

"Well, we'll have dinner, and then you'll feel more like yourself," said his father, though he took a keen look at his youngest. The boy must have lost ten pounds since last Sunday.

"What do you do up there?" demanded Muriel, scarcely waiting for the grace Anthony pronounced almost inaudibly. "I can't imagine what there would be to do in a little place like that."

"Dearest, let him alone," begged her mother. "If he's that tired he won't want to talk about it." And she then dismissed the subject by saying, "I'm afraid the roast has got rather dry, but think of what the poor people in Europe and China have to suffer!"

"This suits me all right," replied Howard. "Think of what we poor soldiers have to put up with."

"It hasn't hurt you, old dear," said Peggy callously. "Since you went to camp you've put on all the weight that your little brother has lost."

"I'll catch up with him," predicted the little brother, taking advantage of his sister-in-law's lead. "As soon as I get to camp I'll start eating, if I have to do KP duty to get at it."

"Oh, are you going?" chorused the family, immediately interested, beginning to pepper him with questions.

To all inquiries as to when, how, and where, he replied that he didn't know. He'd wired Dr. Havern today, and supposed he would be back at once.

In the discussion which followed, he took little part beyond a general assent to the proposition that the war was likely to last a good while, and that everybody would have to pitch in and do what they could. Fortunately the rest of them had plenty to say in support of this, and agreed violently among themselves.

As he looked from one eager face to another Anthony's heart almost failed him. Would he have the nerve to go through with it? They'd never get his point of view if he tried to explain those first soul-rending doubts, or the despair that had come with horrible certainty. They wouldn't know what he was talking about. Only Val might have understood—Val! His heart gave a great leap.

When they were out of the dining room at last, he went and stood by the fireplace in the library, looking around at the circle grouped about. The memory of Val's troubled eyes rose before him as she had looked that rainy afternoon when she, too, had a confession to make and dreaded to hurt him.

"I've got a little speech I want to give you," he said abruptly, his throat suddenly constricting as six pairs of eyes turned upon him instantly. "You'd be sorry for me if you knew how much I hate to do it, too."

"Oh, darling!" exclaimed his mother, her usually placid face lined with distress. His lack of appetite had not escaped her. "Don't you feel well? Are you going to have an operation?"

"You might call it that," he replied dryly. "You all thought just now that I was going as a chaplain, but I'm not. I'm giving up the ministry. I found out it just — didn't work."

Surprised though they were, the family took this announcement without too much strain. Privately most of them had wondered at his choice of a profession in this day and age, though nobody but Aunt Maude had questioned his right to do what he pleased. Apparently he'd had enough of it by this time, as they had thought he would. Still, they did feel sorry for him — it must be a disappointment, also humiliating, to have to come and say he'd made a mistake. A murmur of commiseration went around the circle; then Muriel voiced their common thought.

"Lucky thing you can go into the army now," she said, nodding her dark head wisely. "After the war nobody will think anything about your changing over to something else. Though I know how rotten you feel over it, honey."

"That's right," Howard backed her up. "There's bound to be a period of readjustment, and lots of us will be starting on a new line. Don't you worry, kid."

"You can always come in with me, son, you know," added his father.

Anthony smiled mirthlessly. They were taking it very calmly, this thing that had shattered his world for him.

Aunt Maude cleared her throat with a rasp, and gave an emphatic tap on the floor with her cane.

"Is that all you've got to tell us, young man?" she demanded, her beady eyes snapping. "It seems to me your mountain has brought forth a very insignificant mouse. I never did think you'd stick to all that nonsense, or at least I hoped you'd have sense enough to quit when you got it out of your system. Funny kind of wild oats for a young man to sow, I must say, but I suppose it wasn't any worse than the usual kind."

"Leave the boy alone, Aunt Maude, can't you? He's not enjoying this!" Mr. Drew, usually a little in awe of his ancient relative, was moved to speak sharply. "It's not easy for a man to admit he was wrong. I admire you for that, Anthony."

"Thank you, Dad, and I hope you'll feel like that when I tell you the rest, which I hate to do like the very devil!" He swallowed an obstruction in his throat. "Aunt Maude is right. I haven't told you everything. I'm afraid I'm giving up the Church, too."

This second bomb proved less of a dud than the first. Mother's cry had real anguish in it, while the others gazed at him astounded. This really was a blow!

"There were some things I just couldn't reconcile," he went on hurriedly. "It always puzzled me that the different branches of the Church held such contrary views, yet were still in communion. It was the communion itself, as a matter of fact, that got me going — er — it didn't make sense —" He ran down at this point, seeing total incomprehension in their eyes, and feeling oddly powerless to explain himself.

They tried to understand him. After they got their breath, the family made a real effort to discuss it sensibly. They let him state his case; then affectionately told him that nothing in the world was worth all this unhappiness that had worn him down to the bone this past week. They sympathized with him, though he very soon saw they had but the faintest glimmer of why it had been such a heartbreak to him. His mother was tearful, but only suggested plaintively that he might get a transfer to St. Timothy's if he felt he must have it that way. Mr. Drew summed up the collective opinion.

"I'd say you ought to follow your own conscience," he said, looking at his tall son with a generous pride in his spiritual courage. "I suppose most men go through a stage like this, and then later on they come to realize that with all its faults the church gives them a certain stability, if you get what I mean. Then they settle down and take it as it comes."

"I'm glad you said that, Dad." Howard had a relieved look on his handsome face as he made his own confession. "I'll admit that right now I don't see a lot of use in some of these creeds and things, though in the main I think the church is a good influence in the community. Of course, Peggy and I will see that the youngsters go to Sunday School, and get a good start, principles and all; and later on they can think for themselves. What do you say, Jeff?"

Jeffrey looked thoughtful.

"Well, I don't know," he said slowly. "I'm not much of a churchgoer myself. It's all right, of course." He hesitated a moment. "I never thought much about it, but hearing you mention your children I got to thinking about my own kid. I'd want him to act for himself, but how would he know?"

This abstract speculation was too tame for Aunt Maude, who rose from her chair and stumped rapidly over to the youngest member of the party as he stood by the fireplace, listening intently to the masculine opinion being expressed. Looking up a long distance into his face, she transfixed him with her eye.

"All this fiddle-faddle is getting nowhere," she said sharply. "What's you're trying to say is that you're going over to Rome." She shook a compelling, bony finger at him. "Aren't you?"

With the sudden feeling that he had not a care in the world, Anthony smiled down at her.

"Probably," he said cheerfully.

For a moment even Aunt Maude was shocked into silence by this frank admission; then the color surged into her withered cheeks and she shrilly berated him like a fishwife.

"That's why you were so interested in hearing about that renegade Burnham!" she concluded, with the menacing finger stabbing at him through the air. "I wondered at the time if you weren't getting mixed up with him!"

He denied this, gently and with an impersonal sympathy for the angry old woman whose fury seemed the expression of some deep disappointment.

"I assure you he was just a name to me, out of nowhere, when I asked about him last Christmas. At that time I didn't know there was any connection with—with Val. It was after that I found out she was taking instructions from him."

The feminine babble that broke out here gave him a pretty clear idea of the burning suspense of his womenfolk during all these months of silence.

"Val? Has Val joined the Roman Church? You never told us!"

"I suppose she's joined by this time, though I don't know how long it takes. She was just studying then when we broke up. That was the cause of it all."

"I think that was very strange," commented his mother indignantly. "What in the world made her do that?"

Not clear as to whether she thought the outrage had been Val's Romanism, or her rejection of himself, Anthony made the shortest explanation he could to cover both points.

"She had practically the same trouble as I've had about the Sacrament; and when she realized she was going to become a Roman Catholic, she said she couldn't do that and be the wife of a minister."

Curiously, this seemed to make a difference. A reflective pause followed, during which Aunt Maude gave an audible snort and marched back to her chair, in which she sat glowering.

"Well, I always did say that a married couple ought to have the same religion," said Mother wisely, "though as a general thing I think the wife ought to follow her husband in that."

"But, Caroline," protested Mr. Drew, with a glance of humorous apology at his son, "you're going on the assumption that diplomatic relations are to be resumed. Is Mother getting a little ahead of her ticket, Anthony?"

"So far as I'm concerned, she's quite correct." Embarrassed but greatly relieved at the turn their minds were taking, Anthony marveled that they could feel that way about this great change in his life. "Val doesn't know about this yet, but I have hopes."

"Everything is going to be all right." Muriel came over to kiss him soundly. "Val would be perfectly crazy if she went on fussing now! Then you can have a military wedding, and I'm to be bridesmaid." She turned to address the family. "Isn't it lucky he's going into the army!"

And on that happy note the family conclave adjourned.

Though still panting for more details, Muriel and Peggy considerately bore their husbands off, leaving Anthony to put in the call they knew he was dying to make. They only hoped Val knew how fortunate she was in getting a boy with principles like that, and such a swell conscience. She'd be a fool if she made any further trouble.

As he neared the Maddox home, Anthony hoped that, too. Val had answered the telephone pleasantly enough, and said she would be glad to see him, but that didn't necessarily mean she would be particularly receptive to what he was about to tell her. The big obstacle to their marriage, of course, had been the difference in religion, which was now about to be set right when he joined her in the ancient Church; but still, almost anything could have happened since that memorable Saturday afternoon four months ago.

Very nervous and anxious only to get the painful explanations over at once, he broke the news to her almost the minute he got into the house, and with even more abruptness than he had used with his family.

"Val," he said in a voice he didn't recognize, "I just want to tell you that you were right and I was wrong. I'm going over to Rome." Unable to go on, he paused and waited for her outcry.

To his stunned amazement, she made no response whatever, unless he could count her slow nod, while her face expressed nothing more than acceptance of the news.

"Aren't you even surprised," he asked after a moment.

"No, not really," she said, looking up at him thoughtfully. He had declined a chair, feeling that he could do this better if he were on his feet. "I knew you would, though, of course, I couldn't say just when."

"You knew more than I did, then!" his exasperation was pardonable. This was no way to take the news of his spiritual earthquake. "How could you know?"

"I offered my First Communion for you on Holy Thursday," she answered simply. This seemed to be a full explanation so far as she was concerned.

A prickling sensation ran down Anthony's spine.

"Holy Thursday?" he whispered, while the memory of that terrible day flashed before him. "My God!" He sat down limply.

She was startled then, and came to kneel beside him.

"What is it, darling?" she begged anxiously, with her arms about him, her amazing calm broken by the sight of his perturbation. "Did something go wrong?"

He told his story, and long before it was finished Val was weeping tears of pity.

"Oh, you poor boy!" she sobbed, "you poor boy! And I wasn't there to help you!"

"That's a thing a man has to fight out alone," he replied, with a long painful breath at the recollection of that horrible moment when he realized his impotence to offer the Sacrifice. "Nobody can help him. He's got to make his own decision." Then he glanced down at the fair head buried on his shoulder, and thought of how he had resented her piteous explanation last November, that she wanted to fight it out by herself before worrying him with it. He gave a wry smile of self-reproach. "At least I didn't have anybody to fight me and put obstacles in my way while I was doing it, as you did."

By and by her parents were called in to share the good news. Mr. Maddox shook hands heartily, saying, "Well, well!" over and over, as if it were something entirely original each time, while Mrs. Maddox broke down and cried.

"Have you made up your mind what you will do next?" asked Mr. Maddox after the first excitement cooled and they were able to go into the practical. "If you need a job, Anthony, I can always find a place for you in my joint. Unless you would like to go with your father, of course."

Anthony thanked him, and admitted that his father had spoken of taking him into the bank.

"But first I'm going into the army," he went on. "Beyond that I haven't any plans — did all this happen just in one day? It seems like a thousand years!"

Val patted him on the back understandingly. She ached with sympathy for the pain and bewilderment he had gone through. Did anybody know about that any better than she?

"The army will be enough job for anybody," she said reassuringly. Then as a sudden thought struck her, "By the way, did you know that our Jasper is likely to be in there, too? Unless they put him in jail. What is it they do to draft dodgers?"

"I suppose we can trust them to give him what's coming to him," responded her father grimly. "I'd like to see a good, hardboiled Irish drill sergeant working him over!"

"I wonder who did report him," mused Val. "By the way, has he written any more of those 'J'accuse' letters lately?"

Anthony shook his head.

"He got tired, I suppose," said Mr. Maddox, "when nobody took the trouble to answer him, or else he got so interested in all of that Ku Klux stuff he hadn't time for anything else. I know I didn't turn him in, though I often thought I'd like to."

Mrs. Maddox only folded her lips a little tighter, and said nothing.

The week was nearly over before Dr. Havern arrived — on Friday night, in fact. The hotel clerk had gone to some trouble to get reservations for the eight o'clock train that Easter Sunday night, but as the day wore on Dr. Havern had grown more and more reluctant to leave. He felt it in his bones that he was not likely to come this way again in a hurry. Also, since he had foregone his golf game today through the strictness of his principles, it was only fair that he should wait over until Monday to taste the joys of the open once more before going back to those Mothers' Meetings and Girls' Friendly tea parties.

So after dinner he balked. To Etta's outcry that she was all packed hours ago, he responded firmly. They could just as well go Monday night as tonight, he said. Therefore, the tickets were exchanged, the bags unpacked, and on Monday Dr. Havern had a rousing game with his friend Burchard. He lost rather spectacularly, which had not been in the program; but his feelings were soothed by the tender of a farewell banquet by Mr. Burchard, who was good natured when all was said and done, though a trifle beefy, and who had been rendered still more mellow by having made a hole-in-one during the game.

Tickets were again exchanged, bags unpacked, Etta went to

bed at nine o'clock in a great huff, the party being strictly stag. The rector ate heartily of *lobster thermidor* and other favorite dishes, and next day he complained of fatigue, refused food, and begged to be left alone to die quietly. Consequently the tickets had to be turned in again.

He recovered eventually, and came home with his wife, his bags, and his souvenirs, in a train that was hours late. There were various causes for the delay, but Dr. Havern chose to blame it all on the army. A ridiculous business, he said, that respectable, law-abiding citizens should be held up indefinitely to let troop trains go by, when everybody knew the country wasn't going to war! Completely used up by the trip, he crawled into his bed vowing to have a heart-to-heart talk with Drew early tomorrow. The fact that the latter had already resigned robbed him of the pleasure of doing some spectacular firing, but at least he could tell the fellow what he thought of him.

As it happened, Anthony did come in fairly early on Saturday, wearing a buttoned-up raincoat, so the rector did not even see that his one-time curate wasn't wearing clerical clothes. He was in a great hurry, wanting only to explain a few loose ends of parish work, and thereafter to deliver some choice remarks on his own account about the wrongs he had suffered during the past six months. Being courteous by nature, however, he first asked for Mrs. Havern, and made the right number of inquiries about the trip.

This was an opportunity not to be resisted, and the rector instantly plunged into an account of the scores he had made, and the sermons he had preached, illustrating as he went along with anecdotes in which the names of Bill Ketteridge and Sam Burchard loomed large.

"And how have things been going with you?" he went on, adding hurriedly lest Drew should start in and tell him, "what is all this I hear about your going into the army? Don't you think this is pretty short notice to give me? I must say I think it very inconsiderate. Very. And I shall insist that you take both services tomorrow, as I don't feel up to it myself — terrible journey yesterday, with all those troop trains blocking the way.

There's your army for you! Somebody ought to complain to the government. It's nonsense, anyway, this war talk! So you'll have to take both services tomorrow."

From his superior height his ex-curate looked down at him appraisingly during this harangue. The old boy never changed — hadn't even expanded enough to find a new way to cuss him out. Well, what did Anthony care, anyway? He smiled with such a sunny beam that the rector blinked.

"I couldn't possibly," said the emancipated youth almost affectionately as he edged toward the door. "I left a long letter for you in the office, to bring you up to date about the parish. Good-by, sir. Glad you had a nice time. Remember me to Mrs. Havern, won't you?"

Speechless, the rector gazed after the tall figure striding down the walk. This must be a bad dream — it wasn't possible that the ingrate had simply walked out on him! He sighed piteously and went back to his study for a brief rest before tackling the day's work. He'd have to take both of those services tomorrow, after all, and he was a sick man right now. All right, then, he would read the services; but Davison and those meddling vestrymen were going to have to provide him with another curate before next Sunday, somebody who could be made to understand his place!

The hot weather came with a rush that year, and very early. The month of May was hardly half gone before Dr. Havern's thoughts were turning wistfully toward Lakeside, where the Butterfield and Dodds families had taken cottages for the summer; and by Decoration Day the rector had about made up his mind to write these onetime guests and give them a hint. After all, they'd had a pretty good time last Christmas!

"What a day this has been!" he sighed late in the afternoon of Memorial Day, dropping into a chair on the shaded side porch where the breeze, if any, could fan his brow.

His wife, deep in the society page of the evening paper, muttered an absent "Um," and went on reading absorbedly.

"Thank heaven," he continued, mopping his head and neck, "the day after tomorrow will be Whitsunday, and then we can

[260]

close down for the summer. I don't know what I'd do if we had to run any longer. Savannah!" raising his voice, "what's happened to the lemonade?"

"Yessuh," responded the handmaid, appearing on the instant with a coolly tinkling pitcher. Silently she placed it on the little table at his elbow, and poured brimming glasses. After serving the rector she carried one over to Mrs. Havern, giving a covert glance at that lady, who had suddenly become rigid.

"Ah-h-h!" sighed the rector, after a long, refreshing drink, and handing the glass to Savannah for a refill. At the same time he cast a severe eye on her. "What was the matter this morning?" he asked accusingly. "You were late."

"Ah was at a—a weddin'," she replied with something like defiance; but before he could go into the matter further his wife gave an exclamation.

"Wilbur! Do you know what it says here in the paper?"

"How should I know what it says in the paper?" he said in the monotone which takes care of a silly question like that.

"It's about your Mr. Drew and that Maddox girl," said Mrs. Havern, her eyes still on the item. "They were married today."

Dr. Havern winced violently and raised a forbidding hand.

"Etta, how dare you! I will not have that fellow's name mentioned in my presence. After what he did to me last month!" He gave an indignant flounce in his chair, and drank some more lemonade. Then, curiosity getting the better of dudgeon: "Who married them?"

"And it's the strangest thing!" went on Etta, precisely as if there had been no interruption. "It was over at St. Columban's at a Romish Mass. It says here that he and the Maddox girl have both turned Romanist, and it must have been quite a wedding. They had two priests—that Father Costello, you know, and somebody by the name of Burnham. Can you imagine!"

"What could you expect of a fellow like that?" Dr. Havern's sneer was perhaps the most successful he'd ever accomplished. "And all the little people from down the valley were there, I suppose, with their chickens and eggs and market baskets. How I ever managed to tolerate him all these months—"

"But, Wilbur!" Etta dropped the paper in a crushed mass on her lap while she gave him that look which warns a man he is about to be put in the wrong. "This isn't that Mr. Drew. Mrs. Otway told me all about him after we got back from Florida."

"Why should I care who he is?" The second sneer was even better than the first one—loftier and more godlike. "I don't want to hear anything about him, now or ever!"

With a faraway look in his eyes, Dr. Havern sipped his lemonade in an elegantly abstracted manner, as if he had put by all things mundane and thought only on the higher good; but after a moment he smiled indulgently and came back to earth.

"Well, my dear," he said, turning to his wife with a gently humoring air, "I suppose you want to tell me, so I'll bite. And who is he, then?"

Etta gave him a withering look, and silently handed him the paper. Savannah went about softly, gathering up magazines and straightening cushions with great exactness, now and again turning a glistening eye on her employers.

Still playful, the rector hummed a stave from "Here Comes the Bride" as he skimmed through the account of white satin and point lace, rose tulle and delphiniums, until his shocked eye fell on these appalling words:

Mr. Drew is the youngest son of Mr. and Mrs. Livingston Drew of Cyrus Avenue. . . .

The Bridal Chorus faded into silence as Dr. Havern slowly turned to ice. This couldn't be! Livingston Drew's son—

"Why wasn't I told about this?" he croaked at last, as he leveled an accusing eye at the wife of his bosom.

"I'd have told you long ago," she defended herself, "only you wouldn't let me talk about him. You always get perfectly wild if anybody even mentions him, you know you do, Wilbur Havern! And so, of course, they didn't invite us to the wedding, and it must have been awfully interesting with everybody in uniform like that," she wound up regretfully, taking the paper from his nerveless hand to read the article through again.

A faint moan escaped the rector as he, like *Lord Jim,* pondered the might-have-beens. That new organ, for instance. Livingston Drew was known to be very generous with the church when he was interested in anything — And, of course, there were some boys in that family, but for some reason Dr. Havern had never heard that any of them had gone into the ministry. It seemed like a conspiracy of silence!

"If I'd just known yesterday!" he mourned aloud. "And it was only this morning —"

At this instant they both remembered Savannah, and simultaneously they turned upon her to demand just what wedding she had attended today. But the handmaid had vanished.

THE END